For one timeless instant the car continued as though nothing was wrong, and then it seemed to bunch itself like a wild animal crouching for the attack. It swerved wildly to the left, then fishtailed back to the right, and in the middle of its rightward spin collided with the outside wall. It rebounded and launched itself into the air, bounding end over end like a skier doing stunts off a ramp. The Lola disintegrated just as it was designed to, but in the direction it was heading, it was going to hit the low retaining wall in front of the pits nose-first at around a hundred miles per hour. And it was going to do it a mere twenty yards from sixty-plus school kids. . . .

Mac could only watch numbly. His puny magics were useless here. *Now the whole tank goes,* he thought. *We have to get the kids out of here —*

There was no way; in a second shrapnel would be filling the air. "Get them down beneath the seats," he shouted. He, Lianne, and the chaperons started pushing the kids down.

He became aware of a tingling at the base of his skull. The hair on his arms was standing up — and he realized that he had been feeling this sensation since the moment the car started to go out of control. His mind gave the sensation a name.

Psi. TK.

D.D., the Healer, the Empath, Mindspoke with quiet amazement. *:The car hasn't exploded yet. The power is coming from near you, Mac — :*

Somebody nearby was keeping the car from blowing.

Mac Looked around him. One fragile-looking little girl sat, transfixed, watching the disaster. Motionless, silent, unblinking, she could have been a statue of a fifth grader, except for the breeze that blew her wispy blonde hair around her face and caused her plaid skirt to ripple around the tops of her white kneesocks.

And from her poured incredible power.

WHEN THE BOUGH BREAKS

A NOVEL OF THE SERRATED EDGE

MERCEDES LACKEY

HOLLY LISLE

BAEN

WHEN THE BOUGH BREAKS

This is a work of fiction. All the characters and events portrayed in this book are fictional, and any resemblance to real people or incidents is purely coincidental.

A Baen Books Original

Baen Publishing Enterprises
P.O. Box 1403
Riverdale, NY 10471

ISBN: 0-671-72154-2

Cover art by Larry Elmore

First Printing, February 1993

Distributed by Simon & Schuster
1230 Avenue of the Americas
New York, NY 10020

Printed in the United States of America

This book is dedicated to the kids who came through the hospitals where I've worked, in desperate need of help, and to the many, many more, equally desperate, who never got that far.
— **Holly Lisle**

And to those who haven't given up — because help is out there.
— **Mercedes Lackey**

● Chapter One

Maclyn, Knight of the High Court of Elfhame Outremer, leaned forward over the steering wheel of his classic '57 Chevy and flicked on the radio. Q-103 FM was playing two-fer-Tuesdays and had just finished up a set by Fleetwood Mac. The DJ cut into the fadeout, chattering, "Coming up for all you April Fools — two-fers by Phil Collins, The Beatles, and Grim Reaper. But first . . . a Guns N' Roses two-fer. . . ."

"Aw Gawd, not Guns N' Roses. If I want to listen to a garage band, I'll find a good one. . . ." The engine growled and downshifted as his convertible pulled out of the secluded dirt road into traffic. The driver of a late-model Ford Taurus glanced over at them and did a classic double-take, jerking her head around to stare. Mac flashed a grin in her direction, and she waved before driving on.

His elvensteed, currently taking the form of a Palomino-gold '57 Chevy convertible with cream trim, was a traffic stopper. Rhellen didn't cause quite the disruption to traffic he would have in his regular form, Mac reflected, but he was still impressive. And women loved him.

With any luck, he would impress the socks off of Lianne McCormick.

Mac pushed his troubles with the Seleighe Court out of his mind. There would be time to deal with Felouen and her demands. The present, as far as he was concerned, wasn't the time.

"Okay, Rhellen, let's make some time," he told the car. "Tonight — we *party!*"

The elvensteed growled affirmation and accelerated past two Fayetteville city policemen and one North Carolina Highway Patrol trooper, hitting seventy-five without causing so much as a chirp on their radar.

With Rhellen in full charge, Mac made it to Lianne's apartment complex running seemingly just under Mach One. *She,* the current human lady of his interest, if not his dreams, was sitting on the deck of her apartment grading papers, a tiny frown of concentration on her face. He pulled up silently and vaulted out of the car in equal silence, which gave him a chance to admire her before she spotted him. She was slender, with short, soft chestnut hair, deep blue eyes and pale, flawless skin — she had the fragile, ethereal look frequently attributed to one of his own people. She had, too, the blazing energy of a human — she was, he thought, one of the delicate mayflies of the sentient world.

Like all humans.

Here today and gone tomorrow. He felt a moment of poignant loss and suppressed it. *But today will be a lot of fun, anyway.*

He intentionally crunched some gravel on the walk to let her know he was there.

She looked up, and her face lit with an amazingly sweet smile. "Hey!" she said. "Glad you made it. I was beginning to think you'd changed your mind. Or come to your senses or something." She grinned when she said that, but Mac felt the pain of old rejection masked in her voice.

"Stand up a gorgeous gal like you?" he asked. "Not in this lifetime."

She chuckled and arched an eyebrow. "Yeah, yeah — sure, sure. So are we going to go someplace, or am I going to spend the rest of the evening checking math tests?"

He smirked. "You won't even remember what math tests are."

"I could live with that." She shoved her papers inside the front door of her apartment and locked it. "Let's go."

He showed her to the Chevy, and waited for her eyes to light up. Which they did, as predicted.

"Wow!" she whispered, and ran her hand slowly along one gleaming fender. "What a beauty. I've never seen one this color — or in such perfect condition."

Mac felt Rhellen's pleasure and grinned. "Custom job. I'm pretty proud of him."

"I'll bet." A puzzled expression crossed her face. "Him?"

she asked. "I've never heard anyone refer to a car as *him* before."

"In this case, it's appropriate," Mac assured her.

Lianne stood back and crossed her arms over her chest. She tipped her head to one side and studied the car. She went down on one knee and carefully examined the undercarriage. Finally she nodded. "You're right. Definitely a him."

He'll love you for that, Mac thought. *I think, lady, that you've just won yourself a friend.*

Rhellen preened under all the attention.

"By the way," she said, as she climbed into the passenger's side, "you haven't forgotten the field trip tomorrow, have you? I hope you're ready for it; you're going to need all the help you can get."

He laughed. "Forgotten, no. Worried? Also no. What's to worry about a herd of kids who're probably car-crazy to begin with? It'll be a snap."

She didn't reply; just smiled, the kind of enigmatic smile found on the Mona Lisa. The smile that said — "I know something you don't know, but you're going to have to find out for yourself."

The kind of smile his mother Dierdre would give him —

For a moment, he was taken aback by it, enough for a nagging little worry to intrude.

Then he dismissed it. What could this mere human know that he, with all his centuries, didn't? Ridiculous. He'd enthrall her little flock, dazzle her with his cleverness, and it would all be a pleasant day for everyone concerned.

Right now, he would concern himself with *tonight.* Tomorrow was not worth even thinking about. . . .

Looks like the troops have arrived. "Hey, beautiful!" Mac shouted across the parking lot at Lianne as she jumped out of the first of the two bright yellow school buses to arrive at Fayetteville International Speedway. "What's a babe like you doing in a place like this? Sweetheart, where have you been all my life? Come, let me take you to the Casbah, where we will make beautiful music together. We will make lo—"

She made a shushing motion at Mac and blushed. "Like tigers," he finished. Neither the gesture nor the blush escaped the noisy herd of children who followed her out of the bus.

"O-o-o-ooh!" yelled one boy. "Miss McCormick has a boyfriend!"

"Miss McCormick has a boyfriend," someone else repeated.

A chant started. "Miss McCormick has a boyfriend — Miss McCormick has a boyfriend . . . "

Maclyn regretted his impulsive teasing. He had obviously just made things difficult for her, and he suspected she didn't appreciate the attention she was getting.

A teacher from one of the other buses, a good-looking woman in her mid-thirties, stared at him curiously, then walked over and whispered something to the beleaguered Lianne. Lianne nodded slowly, and the other woman raised an eyebrow. She gave Mac an appreciative once-over as she returned to her own flock of children.

He was used to getting those calculating looks from women. Usually, he enjoyed them. This time, for some reason, he felt embarrassed.

Lianne got her class lined up and led them across the pavement toward him. She sent him a killing glare as she and the rowdy fifth-graders advanced.

"Lianne, I'm sorry. I didn't realize that they would do that," he said.

"I'll bet." The kids behind her had taken up a whispered refrain of "Miss McCormick sitting in a tree, K-I-S-S-I-N-G," and Lianne did not look mollified in the least by his apology. "The only way you wouldn't have known they would do that is if you'd never been a kid in the fifth grade before."

And there, he thought, *you have it. I haven't* ever *been in the fifth grade. So how was I supposed to know? It's not my fault your class is a mob of little barbarians. I'm innocent — this time. Unfortunately, there is no way in the world that I could convince you of that without blowing my cover.*

He smiled at her, shrugged helplessly, and tried to look

boyishly ingenuous. "What can I say?" he asked. And then, in a louder voice that carried to the last kid in the back of the last line, Mac introduced himself to the class. "Hi. I'm Mac Lynn, and I drive racecars."

:Och, and he drives the maidens wild, he does, too!: came an impish, entirely uninvited thread of Mindspeech. *:You have only to ask him, and he'll tell ye so!:*

:Mother!: he snapped, trying to regain his aplomb.

:So gallant, so regal, so handsome. And so modest he is — his hat sometimes even fits him these days! Why, he drives race cars, does he? Sure and what a fine man he must be!:

:MOTHER!:

Despite Deirdre's teasing, it was a good opening line. The kids calmed down and studied him, checking, he suspected, to see if they recognized him from television.

Mac didn't mind. It wasn't likely that they would, but the moment of their uncertainty would buy him their attention. He could take it from there. He drew on his years of racing experience, and with purely elvish fervor, translated his enthusiasm into terms that drew the sixty-plus fifth-graders in front of him wholeheartedly into the world he loved.

"What do you watch on television?"

Mac was answered by a barrage of titles — almost all of them cop shows or adventure cartoons. "See, now, on all of those shows, you get to watch car-chases, or the heroes drive hot cars. Think of Don Johnson without the Daytona, or Magnum without the red Ferrari — it just doesn't work, right? Hey, your folks drive cars, you see ads on TV, there are roads practically everywhere — people are in love with cars. Some of us love 'em so much we want to drive 'em for a living. Think any of you would like to do that?"

A chorus of "Yeah!" and "Sure!" came back at him.

They were in his pocket. It was time to get them moving — show them the sights. He asked them, "So . . . do you want to go look at some racecars, or what?"

They cheered.

Nice kids, he thought. *I'm glad I decided to do this.*

* * *

Gruesome bunch of larvae, Mac thought. He'd spent the better part of two hours showing the kids garages and pits, the medevac helicopter, the infield and starter's tower, and introducing them to mechanics and crew chiefs and various race drivers. Including his mother.

They'd enjoyed his mother, who just happened to be his crew chief. D.D. Reed (not as close to Dierdre as Mac Lynn was to Maclyn, but it would do) was ninety-five pounds of lightning and thunder, all wrapped up in one coveralled, pony-tailed, hellcat package. She took no guff from anyone and handed out twice the grief he ever gave *her.* She also looked half his age.

She gave him lip mental *and* audible, the mental over Lianne and his ego, the audible over everything else — much to the entertainment of the rest of the pit crews: his, and everyone else's within hearing. His crew knew the secret, of course, and thought it hilarious. Of the rest, there were a few more SERRA mages nearby that had a notion — and to those left, it was *still* funny to hear a "girl" giving hotshot Mac Lynn a hard time. Those who couldn't "hear" the telepathic comments were very nearly as amused as those who could.

The kids — *little sadists* — had loved it.

He'd also spent the better part of two hours watching them stick chewing gum on walls and under ledges when they thought no one was looking, kick each other in the shins, poke and prod each other and then stare off innocently into space when someone screeched. When he'd joked that some cars were held together with bubble-gum, one kid actually, sincerely, offered him his. Freshly chewed. Mac couldn't believe it.

He had no idea how many lug-nuts would be missing by day's end. He'd listened to their gross jokes. He'd answered their weird questions. He'd had more than enough. Finally, it was time to sit down on the small stands and watch the drivers speeding alone around the track in the time trials.

Mac was ready for the break. As kids wiggled and squealed and squirmed and passed notes and stuffed paper down each other's shirts, he knew a moment of sheer gratitude that he had been spared the indignity of fifth grade.

:*They'd not have had you. You were worse than any of them.*:

He sighed. :*Thank you, Mother.*:

His mother might have been right, he reflected. Nevertheless, he felt admiration for the guts of the teacher who had to put up with this sort of nonsense on a regular basis. He rolled his eyes and grinned over the kids' heads at Lianne.

She raised her eyebrows in a mime of disbelief at her class's behavior and grinned back.

Cars roared around the track, and from their front-row seats in the pits, the smell of oil, gasoline, exhaust, and hot rubber numbed the nose while the howling of engines numbed the mind. The few fans in the stands screamed and cheered at their favorites, as if by sheer volume they could push the drivers to better times. The palpable electricity in the atmosphere always got to Mac — that excitement was what had originally pulled him out of the timeless magic of Underhill and into the very human world of auto racing.

In between runs, the kids asked *more* questions.

One stub-nosed kid with bright brown eyes waved his hand in the air at Mac and bounced up and down on his bleacher seat until Mac was sure it was going to have a permanent bow in it. "Yes?" he asked warily. He'd already had more than a taste of what fifth grade boys considered reasonable to ask.

"I want to drive a racecar when I get out of school, but Mom and Dad say I have to go to college. Did you have to go to college?"

That question seemed pretty harmless.

Lianne, however, gave Mac a warning look.

Oh, yeah. College. That great babysitter of the post-adolescent masses. Naturally Lianne is going to want me to be strongly in favor of it.

Mac shrugged helplessly. "No. I didn't go to college, but I wish I had." It was an easy lie. With luck it would mollify Lianne. "A college education is a good idea. If nothing else, it will give you something to fall back on if racing doesn't work out."

The look in her eyes when he said that, though, made him think he should have quit with a simple no.

And just then, D.D. popped up. "Mac doesn't need college," she said, with a sly look and a toss of her blond ponytail that told him she was going to zing him again. "He doesn't even need a brain; he never uses the itty-bitty one he's got. He has the rest of us to think for him. We don't believe in overstressing anything that weak. Now *me*, I needed every mechanical engineering and physics course I could cram."

The kid looked confused. "Why?" he asked. "You're just a mechanic."

D.D. cast her bright green eyes up to the sky. "Gloriosky. *Just* a mechanic? Sweetie-pie, I not only have to know *how* every part in that car works, I have to know *why*. This is leading-edge technology here; what we've got on our cars your daddy won't be able to buy for ten, maybe twenty years. There's no manual for what we're doing; we're working real automotive magic out there."

"I'll say," one of the crew called out. "And D.D.'s the great high wizard of Ah's. She can tell you what's wrong with an engine just by *listening* to it."

"And you don't get *that* kind of expertise working on a dune buggy in your back yard — right, Mac?" she finished triumphantly, and vanished back behind a stack of tires.

:There. Saved you again.:

With the sinking feeling that he was getting deeply mired in something he was never going to escape from, he sought a graceful out. A flash of deep blue on the track caught his eye and promised sudden salvation.

"Much as I hate to admit it, my crew chief's half right. Here's the other half. There's more to racing than driving fast —" he told them " — more even than winning races. Racing is a business. And it's a tough one. If you can't make that business pay off, you won't be racing." He waved over to the starting line. "Look at Number Fifty-eight, the car getting ready to start now. That's Keith Brightman. He's driving a '93 Lola Wombat right now. He owns it himself. He has an efficient crew and a talented mechanic, and he's a very good driver — but if he didn't know how to run a business, he wouldn't be able to race his own cars."

D.D. appeared from somewhere else. "And if he didn't know his engineering, he wouldn't be able to trouble-shoot his vehicle while he's driving it. Half the time he tells his crew what's wrong, which is a heckuva help, let me tell you, and more than Tom Cruise here can do."

She vanished again. Mac chose to ignore her.

"Keith is a good example of somebody who is doing what he wants to do because he has the smarts and the guts, and because he isn't afraid to work hard. If you want to be a driver, use him as your example."

"Does *he* have a college education?" the school-hater asked with a hopeful glance towards the deep-blue Wombat.

"You bet," Mac said. He'd picked Keith as his shining example of racetrack virtue for precisely that reason. It was going to pay off, too, he could tell. Lianne sent an appreciative glance in his direction. "College was where Keith learned about mechanical engineering, and probably learned how to run a business," he added. "And had fun doing it."

"Brightman, K. Mech-E, Rose-Hulman Polytech, class of 1987, cum laude!" screeched a voice that was getting tiresomely familiar, from just behind Mac.

The Wombat took off with a roar, and the questions stopped. The kids watched the car intently. Maclyn could tell they were impressed. Hell, he was impressed. More than it ever had before, the Wombat *moved*; Keith was putting on a real show. Mac could hear a difference in the engine, a rich, deep throb of power that grabbed deep in his gut and twisted; the rookie's mechanic had made an exotic modification somewhere. That damned Wombat was flying like it thought it was a fighter plane and had forgotten the ground.

What has Brightman done to that engine? Wonderful stuff, Mac mused. *Magic with gears and cylinders — and maybe something Mom can duplicate. I hope she's listening.*

*:I am — what do you think I am, tone-deaf? I also happen to be
Watching it. Teach your grandmam to suck eggs, why don't you.:*

Maclyn had to give the Wombat's crew credit. On a shoe-
string budget and what amounted to little more than
native genius, they were putting themselves in a position to
give the big boys a run for their money.

Mac's ears followed the car even after it was out of sight.
:He's taking seconds off of the best time we've had so far.: Mac
commented to his crew chief.

:I'm paying attention, Mac.: D.D. retorted. *:Unless someone
else comes up with a miracle, he's just gotten the pole.*

The car did a flawless lap and dove into the final curve as
if it owned it — and there was a sudden hollow, popping
sound. It wasn't much of a noise really, but Mac's throat
tightened, and his mouth went dry. The sudden hush of
the crowd in the stand across from the pits was the first
indication of the seriousness of the problem — then the car
became visible from the right side of the pits, and Mac saw a
tiny trail of smoke and sparks that streamed out from
beneath the front wheels.

D.D.'s voice was in his head, all humor gone. *:Sweet Daana
— Mac, a control arm just sheared! The lad's going to lose her any
second —:*

For one timeless instant, the car continued as though nothing was wrong, and then it seemed to bunch itself like a wild
animal crouching for the attack. It swerved wildly to the left,
then fishtailed back to the right, and in the middle of its
rightward spin, collided with the outside wall. It rebounded
and launched itself into the air, bounding end over end like a
skier doing stunts off a ramp. The Lola disintegrated just as it
was designed to, but in the direction it was heading, it was
going to hit the low retaining wall in front of the pits nose-first
at around a hundred miles per hour. And it was going to do it a
mere twenty yards from sixty-plus school kids.

"No!" Mac heard someone bellow, and realized the voice
was his own. *Gods and demons,* he thought. *Oh gods above —
Keith isn't going to make it out of there, and we aren't going to make
it out of here!*

A deep bass *whump* marked the car's impact. Bits of car

ricocheted back towards the crowd, and others came over the retaining wall; flames spurted from the engine pinwheeling across the asphalt. Screaming fans saw impending disaster and panicked. They jumped off the sides of the stands and tumbled to the ground, packing and running like frightened cattle in a slaughterhouse pen.

The roll-caged cockpit skidded upside-down in the middle of the track, trailing sparks. It followed the flaming engine unit as though they were strung together, its trajectory matching the engine's — one of the worst possible scenarios Mac could imagine.

They're built to come apart to save the driver, dammit! Mac thought in anguish, as he watched the cockpit collide with the engine right in front of the stands. Fuel spurted from the ruptured fuel-cell, torn open lengthwise, next to the limp driver. The spreading puddle of fuel inched nearer the shooting flames. *I can see the flames. Gods, I can see the flames — alcohol fuel should burn almost invisibly — this is even worse than it looks. Keith's gotta be dead by now.*

Mac could only watch numbly. His puny magics were useless here. From the paddock, vehicles were gunning to intercept the wreck before it had even stopped moving. He heard a metallic whine, building in pitch, as the track medevac helicopter started its engines. *Now the whole tank goes,* he thought. *We have to get the kids out of here —*

There was no way. Shrapnel would be filling the air in a second, and it would fall everywhere, even in the paddock. "Get them down beneath the seats," he shouted; he, Lianne, and the chaperons started pushing kids down.

He became aware of a tingling at the base of his skull. The hair on his arms was standing up — and he realized that he had first felt this sensation right after the car started to go out of control. His mind gave the sensation a name.

Psi. TK.

D.D., the Healer, the Empath, Mindspoke with quiet amazement. *:No one has been hurt yet by the flying debris. The car hasn't exploded yet. It's coming from near you, Mac — but who's responsible? There isn't a SERRA Psi out here, and no elves but us, and none of the mages have the right spells. . . . :*

Somebody nearby was keeping the car from blowing.

Mac Looked around him. One fragile-looking little girl sat, transfixed, watching the disaster. Motionless, silent, unblinking, she could have been a statue of a fifth grader, except for the breeze that blew her wispy blonde hair around her face and caused her plaid skirt to ripple around the tops of her white kneesocks.

And from her poured incredible power.

In the crowd across the track from the paddock, one woman ignored the people milling around her — seemed even to ignore the accident. She read the face of a meter whose needle was in the far right-hand side of the red zone; she wore a cool, satisfied smile. Then she locked long, perfectly manicured fingers around a voice-activated mini-recorder and whispered into it.

"The accident went off flawlessly — shouldn't be enough left of the car to prove sabotage. Rumors were right — definitely telekinetic activity here. Localized it to the pits across from where I'm standing, but too many people around to get a definite fix. TK is preventing the explosion of the car, though — bet anything on that — think one of the racing people must be our target. This explains why the Fayetteville track has such a good record, maybe. I'll try to move in for a closer read."

She stuffed the meter and the tape recorder, still on and ready, into her bag, and worked her way out of the crowd.

The fire crew sprayed foam on the blazing engine block and the spreading puddles of fuel; Heavy Rescue cut away bits of twisted metal. Mac stood transfixed, watching the kid who stared at the wreck.

:Catch her before she leaves — I want to talk to her!: D.D. ordered.

He agreed absently — then his attention was drawn to the racetrack, where one of the rescuers gave a triumphant shout.

They pulled Keith Brightman out of the car — and he stood on his own.

A number of things then happened at once. From their hiding place beside the stands, the crowd went wild. The rescuers and the young driver sprinted for the pits and the little cover they provided. Lianne noticed that one of her students was still in the path of potential danger, and Mac saw her pull the girl down behind the bleacher.

And that was when the fuel cell blew.

Shrapnel flew across the infield and into the pits. Mac winced at the sound of metal-on-metal as pieces of car went into the mesh that protected the stands. The crowd's cheers became terrified screams.

:Dammit!: Mac thought as he huddled for cover behind a stack of tires. *:The kid's got to be a line-of-sight TK. Lianne broke the contact when she moved the kid.:*

There was a pause. Then D.D. told him, *:I can still feel the child, Mac. She's controlling the shrapnel. And no one's been badly hurt yet.:*

Mac looked through the huddle of scared fifth-graders for the girl. Sure enough, she was peeking over the bleachers, still intent on the wreck.

The air cleared, and the crowd started climbing back into their seats. Several young soldiers on leave from Fort Bragg organized the mob of fans, then moved quickly through the crowd, looking for wounded. They escorted the three folks with small lacerations down to the infield medic.

There were no other injuries.

Down in the pit, Lianne McCormick and the other fifth-grade teachers efficiently rounded up their own crowd, herded them into a raggedy line, and marched them toward the exit.

"Lianne!" Mac bellowed. "Wait a minute!"

Lianne came back — the rest of the field trip contingent kept going. "We have to leave, Mac. This is the sort of thing parents have heart attacks over — we want to have the kids safely back to school before any footage shows up on a local newsbreak."

"But I really wanted to talk to — "

"Gotta go, Mac," Lianne interrupted. "See you soon?"

He forced a smile. "As soon as possible."

She hurried after her students.

Mac's watched his little TK trooping away, way to the back of the line — when, as if she felt his stare, she turned and looked directly at him — and the look in her eyes became one of startled recognition.

"Elf —" he read on her lips. "You're an elf —"

He nodded, staring past her young face into her old, old eyes.

:My name is Maclyn of Elfhame Outremer. My mother Dierdre Brighthair and I need to talk with you.:

She didn't respond to his Mindspoken request. She did, however, start to walk toward him —

And her face changed. Mac would have sworn that her eyes had been dark brown — but they weren't. They were light green. The appearance of age and wisdom, the look of recognition that had been in them, were gone. Instead, her face reflected pure terror. She wrapped her skinny arms around herself and stared at him in wide-eyed dismay. Then she fled. She disappeared into the crowd of kids, leaving Mac standing open-mouthed and bewildered.

:Mother: he noted, *:That was, I believe, the strangest encounter I have ever had with a human being.:*

D.D. had witnessed the last part of the odd exchange, and for once she had no sharp comeback. She only nodded, and replied, *:Something is very wrong there, Mac. I don't know what it is, but there is something seriously wrong with that child.:*

● Chapter Two

Although he was attuned to his crew well enough that he would have *known* if any of them were hurt, Mac checked on them anyway. Everyone was fine, though one of the boys had sustained bloody knees from a slide across cement. D.D. was on the ground beside him, hands full of gauze, with a roll of adhesive tape in her mouth.

:If you don't hurry up, you're going to lose our TK:, D.D. said acidly, as he slouched against a tire-wall to watch her.

What was the rush? He knew where the child was. She wasn't going to escape them. *:She's in Lianne's class. I'll find her later, it's no big deal.:*

He felt his mother's impatience at that assumption, and if she'd been acidic before, her reply could have etched glass. *:I want to talk to her now, Maclyn. That makes it a "big deal.":*

The times Dierdre had taken that tone with him could be counted on both hands, with fingers left over. It instantly became a big deal for Mac. He hurried after the vanished fifth-graders, determined to hold up the buses long enough to borrow Lianne's TK student for a few minutes. Instead, he careened into a woman who'd been reaching to open the door Mac burst out of. She fell off her four-inch spike heels and landed on her rump on the cement.

"Why don't you watch where you're going, idiot!" she snapped.

She was gorgeous, in her early thirties, with porcelain-white skin and a flawless figure. She glared up a him through a tangle of waist-length red hair and snarled, "You could kill somebody that way."

Real red hair, too, he thought, distracted. *Not bottled.*

"I'm sorry," he said, and offered his hand. "I was trying to catch someone."

The woman was fidgeting with something in her purse — some sort of little black box. Suddenly she looked up, and seemed to actually *see* him — and her glare melted.

Eh?

"She isn't too bright if she didn't let you catch her," the redhead drawled. She gave him a slow, sensuous smile and extended her hand, allowing him to help her up, taking her time about it, too. She was slow to let go of his hand, holding onto it while she tested her ankles to make sure they still worked. Mac suspected that the little wiggles were also so that she could make sure he took a good look at her legs — which, painted into brown leather jeans, were admittedly worth looking at. She flipped her hair — he found himself thinking of it as The Hair — out of her face, and giggled.

"I suppose I'll survive." She looked up at him through her eyelashes. "You're one of the drivers, aren't you?"

Mac was wearing his Nomex suit. It was a bright red one. He might have had "RACECAR DRIVER" carved on his chest, and been a little more obvious, but he doubted it. He sighed and nodded. *Takes a real genius to figure that out,* he thought. *Lovely package, but I don't think there's anybody home inside the wrapper.*

He had lost interest in empty-headed humans a few hundred years before this one had been born. There was one advantage to the Folk; the rare cases with nothing between the ears but air tended to fall prey to Dreaming, which took them effectively out of circulation. "I'm glad you weren't hurt," he told her, doing his best to exude polite, *distant* sincerity. "I've got to run, though. I've got to catch a kid."

She pouted. She actually *pouted.* "If you wanted any of the ones on those school buses, you're too late. They just pulled out."

"Damn!" Mac muttered aloud, without thinking.

She used his immobility as an excuse to come closer, and laid her hand on his arm. "What's wrong? They steal something?"

"No," he said shortly. "Hell — probably . . . " He shook

his head, then looked down at her hand as if he was unpleasantly surprised to find it there.

She was observant enough to take the hint and removed it.

I know where to find the girl. And D.D. knows I can't outrun a bus. She should be reasonable. "It doesn't matter, really," he told the woman. "Sorry I ran over you."

"You're the best-looking thing to run over me all week." She flirted with her eyes shamelessly and giggled again, though she didn't make a second attempt to touch him.

The giggle grated on Mac's nerves. It sounded false — and anything that false made Mac very wary. It felt like — bait. And bait meant a trap.

And a trap meant that there was a lot more under The Hair than she was letting on.

"I'll let you get back to whatever you were doing," he said, taking a cautious step backwards.

"Oh, you don't need to leave. I was lookin' for you anyway . . . Mr. Lynn." She looked at him with those big blue eyes, and leaned towards him, exuding a sweet sexuality.

That's bait, all right. Wonder how many poor fools took it?

He took another step backwards; she was oblivious to his sensitive nerves. "I . . . write — free-lance, y'know. And I just had to interview someone who knew about racing after that accident. It was just like *magic* the way nobody got hurt, don't you think? I mean, that looked like a *terrible* accident."

What is she getting at? What's she after? "It looked worse than it was," he murmured, looking for a way to get past her without knocking her over again.

She ignored his remark as if she hadn't heard it. "And the way the driver walked out of there — I've never seen anything more *unbelievable* in my life. And all that metal flying everywhere, and not hitting anyone — well, I simply have to know how often a thing like that happens. You'd have to have *nerves* of *steel* to have a job like yours and run the risks you do every day. And I just knew you were the person to help me, Mr. Lynn. I mean, I've always been a big fan of yours."

"I'm sure you have." *Big fan of mine, eh? So why have I never seen you at the track before? And why didn't you recognize me? And what were you looking for in here, if it wasn't me?*

She finally paused long enough to take a breath. "So will you let me interview you? I can't promise national publication, but I'll do my best. And the publicity would be wonderful for you, I'm sure."

She was lying, and he knew it. It wasn't just her tone, or his shrilling nerves. He'd seen her eyes flickering to the name tag on his suit just before she called him Mr. Lynn; he'd caught the awkward pause in her speech when she told him what she did. And he didn't believe for one minute the Sweet-Southern-Honey Vapor-Brained-Belle routine she was laying on him. She was no more from the Deep South than he was. That accent was as assumed as the one Dierdre used among mortals. The odds that she was a writer were slim — the odds she was a free lance were even slimmer. She was working for someone. And that look in her eyes — no, she wasn't anywhere near as dumb as she was playing. But now Mac was . . . curious.

:Curious? Curious, are you! Is that what you're calling it now? Were you curious with Lianne last night, hmm? An' would ye be carin' what was between this one's ears if ye had her between the sheets, then?: His mother Sent him a wicked laugh. *:I think not. Och, my laddie! He's a curious one for sure. Always mighty curious with the ladies.:*

:Mother, you will *die young if you keep that up.:*

:Too late for that, child. Besides, I'm only trying to teach you something—the next trap might be baited so attractively that you forget it's a trap.: But then his mother's tone became serious. *:I saw you couldn't catch the child. Another time for that, then. If you really want to know about this little fishie, though, reel her in. I'll have a look at her.:*

:Right.: And suddenly Mac was all warmth and admiration. "Call me Mac," he told the redhead, and held out his hand. "Come on back and I'll introduce you round."

She shook his hand and turned up the wattage on her smile. "And you can call me . . . Jewelene. Jewelene Carter."

:Yeah, sure,: D.D. snickered. *:And you can call me Dolly Parton.:*

*   *   *

Gawd, what a day.

Lianne unplugged the hot-air popper and carried her buttered popcorn into the living room. She sprawled on the couch and stared out the sliding glass door at the dappled sunlight on the grass of the apartment quad. *I ought to go outside and sit in the sun on the deck and grade papers and listen to the birds,* she thought guiltily. *It's a gorgeous April day, and they're singing like mad, and love is in the air, and tomorrow it might be too cold or too wet to sit outside.*

I need to unwind. Fresh air will do me good. I'll regret it if I waste this weather. Platitudes exhausted, she sighed, but she didn't move. She was too wrung out to move.

She couldn't concentrate on grading papers. She couldn't concentrate on averaging out grades. She was still mentally at the racetrack, with Mac shouting for everyone to take cover, a car about to blow up in their faces, fire, smoke, people screaming — and Amanda Kendrick sitting up on the bleacher staring at the disaster and trying to commit suicide. The entire business ground one more time through the seemingly endless loop it had worn in her memory.

It had been close. Amanda was no more than behind the bleachers when the motor blew — and there had been hot metal flying *everywhere*.

Except where there were people, Lianne mused. *But that was luck. Amanda isn't stupid — not really. She had to know she was in danger. So why did she just sit there like a — what?*

It was a bizarre accident. Everything had been stacked against them. It was a wonder somebody wasn't dead. She'd heard later that only three people had been injured, and those had been fixable with a stitch or two. It seemed impossible. There had been no dead kids whose parents had to be phoned, no trips to the emergency room in the back of a wailing ambulance holding some bloody little hand, no six-o'clock news rehashes with plenty of gory film. There could have been. In fact, she didn't see how any of those nightmares had been avoided. Lianne decided she was about ready to believe in miracles.

So, really, it had ended very well.

I'll never go on a field trip again, though. Anybody who takes fifth-graders on one of those things should automatically get a prescription for Valium from the Board of Education.

Lianne sighed again and snuggled further into the plush cushioning of the couch. Her mind flicked back to Amanda Kendrick.

Something is wrong with this picture, kiddo. Amanda wasn't frozen in shock at the sight of the accident. She was watching — fascinated — eating it up. She was furious when I pulled her down from her seat. And after the explosion, she was watching again.

Lianne munched popcorn and pondered. It wasn't the first time she'd caught Amanda doing something odd, only it was the first time it had been anything so ghoulish.

She needed to talk to Amanda's family. Again. Her nose automatically wrinkled at the thought. The Kendricks were one of Fayetteville's *good* families. Daddy was a corporate lawyer, Mama was Vassar, Junior League, Arts Council — and raised champion Arabian horses. They were both Old Money, and both times Lianne had talked with them, she walked away from the conference feeling undereducated, poorly dressed, that her hair was messy, her makeup was smudged, and she had runs in her hose.

That's not being fair to them, though. They're also concerned, attentive, and determined that their kids won't get a hothouse view of the world from education in Fayetteville's exclusive — and sheltered — private school. They want both of their girls to get a real-world education.

The Kendricks were always frustrated and somewhat at a loss when they discussed Amanda. Lianne could understand that. Amanda's IQ and achievement tests said she ought to be the hottest thing in school since the hand-held calculator — and her grades were erratic, to put it kindly. She was slipping through the cracks of the educational system in spite of her family's concern, in spite of her teachers' attention — in spite of everything.

As she thought about the family, something finally clicked.

Mama was actually Step-Mama, wasn't she? Doing

yeoman work, as far as Lianne could tell — but not even Super-Step-Mom could work miracles if Amanda was getting twisted ideas from somewhere else. Lianne wondered if the problem might stem from the real mother or the step-father.

It would be worth discussing with the Kendricks at their next conference. She decided she would set that up in the morning.

Better yet — I have the number here somewhere. Why don't I call now? Then I'll be able to work.

The phone rang only twice.

"Kendricks'." The voice was female, cultured, and clipped.

Ah, joy, Lianne thought. *None other than Amanda's step-mother.*

"Yes, Mrs. Kendrick. This is Amanda's homeroom teacher, Lianne McCormick. I've called to see if I could set up an appointment to meet with you and Amanda's father."

"*Again,* Miss McCormick? I'm beginning to wonder where the problems *are.* Andrew and I have visited with you more this year than we have with all of Amanda's other teachers put together. I think there is something significant about that."

Great. Obviously the assumption now was that Amanda's problems were her teacher's fault. Lianne took a deep breath, prayed for patience, and sternly stepped on the nasty little thought whispering that they might be right. "I regret having to call you. However, I'm noticing some odd behavior from Amanda, and I'd like to discuss it with you."

"I'm not sure I have the time to get away," the voice on the other end of the line said. "There's been some trouble with the horses, and we don't like to leave the stable unwatched."

Lianne saw an opening to get a closer look at Amanda's home life. She leapt at it. "I do understand that you've both been in a great many times this year, and I appreciate the difficulty that causes you. I'd be happy to come out to your home after school and talk with you. In fact, I think that might reassure Amanda that I do care about her progress."

There was a long pause. "Well, that's kind of you, Miss McCormick — "

Lianne heard an evasion coming and headed it off. "I don't mind. In fact, why don't I stop by tomorrow — say, six o'clock?"

There was another pause. "I do have plans tomorrow — I've scheduled an afternoon with the trainer to look at my two-year-olds — we're getting ready for some of the national shows." Then, perhaps realizing that she'd just put her horses' show status in front of her child's welfare, she immediately added, "But the day after tomorrow, I'm free, and I'll see if Andrew can wrap up with his clients in time to be home by six. Does that sound suitable?"

Lianne smiled. "That will be fine, Mrs. Kendrick. I'll see you at six on Friday."

She hung up the phone and pressed her back against the wall. *Feels like I just won the first round of the International Chess Championship.*

The room was enormous, beautifully decorated, absolutely immaculate — a sweet, perfect, peach-and-white little girl's bedroom as envisioned by a top designer. Stranger was unimpressed. Stranger knew the cost of the perfect bedroom. Downstairs the battle raged, and soon it would be time to pay the price.

Gods, they're fightin' again. That bodes no good for her. Stranger bit the bottom lip, tried to figure out a strategy that one of the others would be able to carry out.

Strategy was what Stranger was best at; even before — hundreds of years before — Stranger had been able to plan, to devise — to win. But a winning strategy required a willing army. The three-year-old, even if she could be lured out of hiding, would be no help — but if the three twelve-year-olds could be introduced to each other and enlisted, Stranger might be able to work something out. Stranger thought the elf would help — if the others could be made to go to him. They wouldn't trust *anybody*, but then, they didn't believe in elves. Maybe they would trust someone they thought didn't exist.

Her name wasn't really Stranger. It was Cethlenn. But she was a newcomer, and at first, the others refused to acknowledge her existence. Then she'd done them some favors. They'd reacted by giving her a name. To them she was Stranger. It was her badge of honor, and she wore it proudly.

Stranger's eyes watched twelve-year-old hands form numbers on the paper, carefully shaping out a long division problem. Stranger didn't know a thing about long division, and didn't care. The math could wait. Someone else would come along later and do it. Stranger was more interested in the fighting downstairs.

The Father was raising bloody hell, the Step-Mother was cold and hateful.

The Father's voice carried clearly up the long, curving stairwell and through the carved wood door. "You don't do a goddamn thing with her. That's the reason her teacher keeps calling, wanting conferences!"

"She's yours — not mine. I didn't marry you so I could be caretaker for that psychotic little rodent, Andrew. You deal with her." The Stepmother didn't like Amanda, but that was nothing new.

"She needs discipline from you, too, Merryl!" The Father's voice dropped an octave. A bad sign.

The Stepmother sneered; she had wealth enough on her own that the Father couldn't cow her. "I'm sure she gets more than enough *discipline* just from you — and I have Sharon to look after. I can handle normal children."

"Sharon is getting big enough that she could stand a bit of discipline. You coddle her too much." The Father's voice turned threatening. Stranger had heard that tone of voice before.

The Stepmother's voice could have frozen boiling water — and was just as threatening. "You keep your hands off of Sharon. I won't have you turning her into another Amanda."

"Worthless, useless, frigid bitch! If you were any kind of

a woman, we wouldn't be having this problem with Amanda!" the Father yelled, losing control, thus losing the argument. The Father wouldn't like that.

The kitchen door slammed. Then Stranger heard the tread of heavy footsteps on the stairs.

"Amanda," the Father's voice shouted from the other side of the door, "Your pony is standing in filth. Get down to the barn and clean out his stable. Now."

Stranger tried to hang on, tried to control what happened next, but the others were panicked. They pushed to get in. Stranger tried to tell them what to do, but they wouldn't listen. They were too scared. They hid in the closet, wrapping their arms around themselves, and ignored Stranger.

"No, no," they whispered. "No, Daddy, no." The little voices crying inside Stranger's head made the hair stand up on the skinny little-girl arms. Stranger shivered and screamed at the others to listen, to run, to get away — to find the elf. She was so preoccupied with trying to rouse them that she ignored the real enemy standing outside the door.

But finally, when the Father got tired of yelling outside the door and came in to get Amanda, Stranger went away instead.

"Mel, I've got a winner on this end."

Melvin Tanbridge rocked back in the soft glove-leather chair and watched the sun set over the ocean through the tinted glass wall in his office. "Secure line?" he asked.

"Scrambled," the other voice affirmed.

"Then tell me more, baby."

"Our target, I'm almost certain, is a racecar driver named Mac Lynn. I had too big a crowd to eliminate all the noise, but he's the best possibility. I got a chance to talk to him later, and even latent, he flicked the needle on the meter. I don't think he's too bright — all glands and no brains — but he has plenty of talent. And, my Gawd, Mel, the film I have of this accident — you'll have to see to believe. There's no chance that this one's just a fluke.

Besides, the readings on your little monitor were all red-zone. I'm FedEx'ing the film, some taped notes, and an 'interview' I got with the driver to you — it will be on your desk tomorrow."

"Fine." Mel tapped one manicured nail on the ebony desktop and smiled. "Nobody said we needed a nuclear physicist anyway. If he's stupid, he'll be easier to control. So — get a little background on him so we know what we're dealing with — then bring him in."

His agent chuckled. "On it already. I'm running a couple of goons that I brought with me today on the off chance I'd get lucky — maybe I'll be able to FedEx *him* to you tomorrow."

Mel laughed. "Sounds good. Who are you running?"

"Stevens and Peterkin." The voice sounded pleased.

Mel nodded and shifted the phone to his other ear. He picked up a pencil, started writing on a yellow legal pad. "They'll do. At least for pulling in a dumb jock."

"I'm going to need an alibi, and my clearance."

"First make sure he's the one. I don't want to have to feed any more mistakes to the sharks." Mel made another note under the first on his paper. "You set for money?"

"For the time being. If things get expensive, I'll let you know. But the cost of living here is nothing compared to California."

Mel's attention drifted from the phone to the scene outside his window. A girl in a wetsuit rode her board in on the crest of a breaker.

"Mel? You still there?"

He dragged his attention back. "Yeah. I'm here. Report in tomorrow, let me know what happens." He hung up the phone, and pulled a dull black box identical to the one the woman at the racetrack had from the top drawer of his desk. He aimed it at the girl on the surfboard and depressed the switch. The needle on the meter didn't twitch.

He shrugged and put the box back in his drawer.

Mac sat on a folding chair beside the Victor III while

D.D. and her current human boyfriend, a twenty-six-year-old engineer-turner-biker, tinkered on it. They lay underneath the car, only visible from the knees down. An occasional *thunk* issued from under the car, but the three were otherwise, to all appearances, companionably silent. The human boyfriend — Redmond something-or-other — was concentrating on the car. And probably, Mac thought, sneaking an occasional grope of D.D.

None of it interrupted D.D.'s inaudible conversation, but then she had a lot of — skill. Mac wondered if the boyfriend knew how old she was. . . .

Probably. D.D. didn't believe in keeping that kind of secret from someone she let into her bed. Chances were he was one of the changelings from another Elfhame. Maybe Fairgrove, birthplace of the Victor III; they grew a lot of mechanics down there.

:Your little fish is no fish at all,: D.D. remarked.

No surprise there. *:I knew that. But what is she up to?:*

:My impression, laddiebuck, is that she's out a-hunting — and with you her quarry. Nathless, you needna think 'tis your handsome body she's lusting for. Nor your mind, though I doubt that occurred even to you. I'd say from the smell of her, 'tis magic she's hunting.:

He tightened his jaw; that was unwelcome news. *:Dangerous?:*

Mac heard an audible snort from under the Victor. *:Not to such as you and me. Merely amusing. But to another human, now — aye, there's danger there. And I'm not for certain that she knows her target. There was, after all, the child today. Not a shield on her, and projecting like a woman full-grown. Sure, I'd wager you were nothing but a convenient bit of misdirection.:*

:So much for my masculine charms, *hey, Mother?:*

The snort this time was derisive. *:I always thought you sold yourself too dear.:*

D.D. rolled out from under the car and stared intently into her son's eyes. "Go make yourself useful somewhere," she told him out loud, and added in Mindspeech, *:Lead your little not-fish a merry swim. No doubt she's waiting for you. Be sure she thinks you're her quarry for true. While she's chasing you — who are old enough surely to take care of yourself — you'll be* *keeping her away from that child — who cannot protect herself.*

:A good point.: The woman had looked expensive, from the clothing to the perfume. Someone was paying her well, if she was a hunter. A child would have no chance against her.

:And no forgettin' now!: she reminded him. *:About that child; you may deceive the woman all you like, but we need to find her.:*

He headed through the parking lot with the late afternoon sun baking his back and the glare of reflection angling inconveniently into his eyes from the few cars that were left there.

And as D.D. had anticipated, the woman *was* waiting, Hair and all.

Mac suppressed a smile. The self-named "Jewelene" lurked in the shadows of a closed concession stand near where Rhellen was parked. He couldn't actually see her — but her anticipation was palpable. She wasn't going to be a problem —

A tingle at the base of his neck slowed him down.

No, she wasn't going to be a problem. The two men who were sneaking up on him from slightly behind and to either side could have been, however, if he hadn't been expecting something.

How to play it?

A vision of the Three Stooges, chased by villains, succeeding by sheer ineptitude, came to him from his last hotel room cable-TV binge. He smiled slyly.

Rhellen, old friend, you and I are going to have some fun.

His step became jaunty. He whistled a cheery rendition of "Laddies, There's Trouble, Oh, Trouble A-Comin'." The tune was one he and Rhellen had used as a signal when tavern-hopping back in his days as a colonial rakehell. It had always been useful for assuring a backup or, if need be, a quick getaway.

He took in the slight change in attitude in the elvensteed, and felt his partner signal that he was ready.

Mac grinned and, without warning, bolted for the

concession stand. "Jewelene!" he yelled. "Hey, baby! You waited around for me! Fabulous — and, gorgeous, it's your lucky day. I've got the whole afternoon free."

The two gorillas who'd been casually working their way through the parking lot, following him, changed direction. "Jewelene" looked wildly for some place to hide, and realized there wasn't one. She looked straight at him, made an "Oh-what-a-surprise!" face, and smiled.

He caught her lightly by one wrist.

"Mr. Lynn," she said, and forced a bright smile, "I didn't expect to run into you again."

He leaned against the concession stand and gave her his best come-hither look. "Baby," he purred, "we both know that's not true. Why else would you be waiting around by my car after everyone else has gone home? And it's Mac — remember?"

"Right — Mac."

He slid an arm around her waist and moved her towards Rhellen. "You don't have to pretend with me. The first time I saw you, I knew we were meant for each other. And I could tell that you knew it, too." He gave her a quick little one-armed hug that threw her off balance. She fell against him.

Out of the corner of his eye, he caught the panicked glance she threw at her two goons.

"Uh, Mac . . . " She tugged ineffectually at his arm, then gave up. "I'm glad to see you. Really. But I was waiting to talk to some of the other drivers — for my interviews. I think I can sell this story to *Playboy*, but I need more, ah, input."

"Honey — Jewelene — why didn't you say so? None of the drivers are here right now," Mac lied fluently. "But I can take you to a bar where most of us hang out. I'm sure we can round up some other drivers for you to interview. And the atmosphere of our hangout will be great for your story. And I can give you any kind of 'input' you want." He tugged her toward the Chevy.

"Well, hey, that's — ah, really nice of you. Go ahead, and I'll follow you in my car."

Mac laughed. "I'm a professional driver, babe. You couldn't keep up with me if you wanted to."

Her goons were finally in position behind Rhellen, crouched down against his rear fender. "Jewelene" relaxed. "Okay then, Mac. Thanks. Very much."

Mac had a hard time keeping himself from laughing aloud. He wrapped his arms around her tightly and pulled her into an extended kiss. "Wonderful. And after you get your interviews, we'll go home and interview each other."

She smiled back, and he noted a vindictive gleam in her eye. "Yes," she agreed. "We'll do that."

He escorted her to the passenger side of the car and opened the door for her. She climbed in, completely confident. He walked around the front of the car, and noted the movement of one of the men around to Rhellen's driver's side. The other, of course, would be sneaking around behind him. He patted the hood.

Everybody ought to have an elvensteed, he thought —

Rhellen radiated satisfaction and chuckled in agreement.

:Ready?: he asked the elvensteed. He waited long enough to catch Rhellen's assent, and then made the single step forward that changed him from target to missile.

As he rounded the front of the car, both men lunged for him. The driver's door swung open and flung the first one back, and Rhellen edged forward just enough to knock the second one down. Mac slipped into the seat to find "Jewelene" trying with all her strength to open her door and get back out. He grinned. His door closed, the car started itself up, and "Jewelene's" head jerked around.

"The weirdest things have been happening around here lately," he told her, as he drove Rhellen away from the two bewildered goons, who were scrambling for their own car. She stared at him, wild-eyed and open-mouthed. "I've found out it never pays to let your guard down." He laughed. "So, beautiful, are you ready to get your interviews?"

She was staring behind them at the dwindling parking lot. Mac glanced into the rearview mirror; there, two hairy guys in jeans, tee-shirts, and ball caps were jumping into an incongruously clean, expensive navy-blue sedan. They came tearing out of the parking lot like they'd been bitten by denizens of the Unseleighe Court.

She nodded slowly. "Yeah. Yeah, let's go."

"Okay, Rhellen," Mac drawled. "You heard the lady. Let's go."

Rhellen accelerated to his top speed. They launched into Raeford Road's six-lane roller derby, shouldering aside a steroidal poser-mobile and causing the owner of a brand-new Mercedes to jam on brakes to keep from marring its expensive paint job.

Mac rested his hands lightly on the steering wheel but let the car do the actual work. "Jewelene" yelled, "Jesus, slow down!" and started fumbling around the seat and the doorframe.

"What are you doing?" Mac asked.

"Looking for the seatbelts. Slow down! Where are the damned seatbelts?"

"Honey, this is a mint-condition fifty-seven Chev-ro-let," he drawled. "There ain't no seatbelts. They were an *option* back then."

Rhellen dodged a Porsche, weaved on two wheels past a semi, darted into a hole exactly two inches longer than he was, then bolted in front of a cop car and accelerated. Mac casually took one hand off the wheel and flicked on the radio.

"Come on, Baby, come on! You've just got to release me — " Wilson Phillips sang cheerfully.

His passenger was white beneath the painted blush, and looked as if she agreed wholeheartedly with the trio. "Jesus God! Mac, slow down or let me out of here!"

He chuckled, exuding machismo. "Relax, baby. I'm a professional. I do this all the time."

She turned to him, pupils wide with real fear. "Not with me in the car!"

He gave her his best impression of a man whose masculinity has been called into question. "Look, baby, if you don't like my driving, you can walk."

She grabbed his arm and shook it. "Dammit, that's what I already said! Let me walk!"

Rhellen whipped out of traffic into a Kwik Stop parking lot and hit the brakes so hard he almost stood on his grille. "Jewelene" was flung against the dash, then back into her seat. The contents of her purse erupted into the interior of the car and bounced everywhere.

Mac hid his delight. Under the auspices of throwing things back into the bag to get her out of his car, he managed to pocket her driver's license and also got a look at some very esoteric toys she was carrying.

Voice-activated tape recorder, stun gun, brass knuckles, Mace, thumbcuffs, little packet of fake ID's . . . all sorts of neat stuff — plus the mysterious little black box. Interesting. I'd love to get a look in her closet sometime.

Then he shoved her toward her door — which opened smoothly.

He sneered at her. "Have a nice walk. It's too bad about your attitude, baby. You would have had a terrific time — but it's your loss." He slammed the door on her heels. "Have a nice day, bitch," he called after her.

"Arrogant pig!" she screeched. Or at least, that was part of what she screeched. The rest was incoherent, and probably not Webster's English. She spun away as he laughed at her, then flounced toward the road.

Several G.I.'s leaned out of the windows of a passing car and yelled. She shot them the bird, and they retorted with a jeering obscenity. Another car full of G.I.'s right behind them slowed and tried to offer her a ride. He saw her take out her can of Mace. The driver of the car shrugged and grinned, and he and his friends drove on.

Her goons would probably find her soon enough. And if they didn't, Mac figured she would enjoy her little hike in the nice April weather. Especially in *this* neighborhood, and with sunset coming on — and looking the way she did. That wouldn't be the last offer of "temporary employment" she'd get before she found a cab. This was a G.I. town, and G.I.'s have two things on their mind when they get off base. . . .

And "Jewelene" was certainly dressed for the part. Between The Hair and the Spandex, she'd be lucky if the cops didn't pick her up and run her in just on general principles.

Mac looked at the driver's license he'd stolen. "Rhellen," he told the elvensteed, "I think Ms. Belinda Ciucci of Berkeley, California, is going to *love* Fayetteville — what'cha think?"

The '57 Chevy rumbled a deep chuckle of affirmation and cruised on.

● Chapter Three

Thank heavens it's only an hour till lunch.

Lianne eyed her students with weariness that bordered on desperation. *And I'll have several minutes of blessed silence while we do the spelling test. Of course, I could have a lot more silence if I just shot them. Nice idea. I like it a lot.*

The three-minute pencil-sharpening break was over. It was time to get everyone back in order.

"Sit down *in your seats, facing forward.* Be quiet, get out your pencil, get out your *paper. Use* your pencil to write on the paper — write the following things. Your name — yes, Keith, when I say your name, I *do* mean the name your parents gave you, not any name you think is really cool today. The date. Today's date. It's on the board. Look at the board. Copy the date. Get it right. Your life depends on it."

Lianne tapped the blackboard with a piece of chalk for emphasis and counted mentally to ten. The fifth grade Mafia had apparently declared that today was Silly Day — every simple chore required detailed instructions. Even usually wellbehaved kids like Latisha McKoy and Marilee Blackewell were misbehaving. The first time she told the class to sit down, almost all of them sat on the floor. It was a bad moment — for the continued existence of the kids, as well as for her.

She hadn't done anything to them — yet — that would lose her this job. Her guardian angels were probably taking bets on how much longer that could last, though.

"Fold the paper neatly in half, *longwise.* Write the numbers one through twenty-five, down the left side of the paper — Arabic numerals, William, not Roman numerals — no, Snyder, you may not go to the bathroom during a test — I don't care if your big brother *did* tell you it's your Constitutional right. He lied. Write the numbers twenty-six through fifty down the fold in the center of the paper."

*Because we have learned never to say the words "center fold" —
in any context — in a room that holds fifth-grade boys, haven't we,
Lianne?*

"Jennifer, Latisha, you do *not* talk at any time during
a test. Not even if you dropped your pencil, Jennifer —
getting it back does not require conversation. Maurice,
close the book!"

Ten minutes of orders. Now, finally, she could give the
test.

"Number one — concentration. CON-cen-TRA-tion.
School work requires *concentration.*"

Not murdering you little monsters requires CON-cen-TRA-tion.
Lianne felt her teeth grinding and tried to relax her jaw
before she splintered something. Crowns were expensive,
and they didn't come under the heading of "injuries in the
line of duty."

She studied her charges. Twenty-six heads bent over
their papers. Twenty-six hands wrote out creative versions
of the spelling words, some that would bear no relationship
to any word ever written in the English language. The
Death Row Five snuck surreptitious glances in her
direction to see if it was safe yet to use their microscopically
handwritten cheat sheets. If they spent half the time
studying that they did in cheating, they'd be straight-A
students. Beth Hambly sat primly in the front row, carefully guarding her (surely perfect) answers from the prying
eyes of less perfect classmates. William Ginser, foiled in his
plan to number his paper with Roman numerals, was
misspelling his words in some ornate style that bore a
striking resemblance to German Blackletter.

*If he'd just put that kind of energy into learning to spell the
damn words in the first place —* She sighed. *Then he wouldn't be
William.*

Amanda Kendrick, sitting in the back corner of the classroom, stared out the window.

"Eight. Contradiction. CON-tra-DIC-tion. If you say
something that means the opposite of what I have said, that
is a *contradiction.*"

Amanda didn't move. Lianne had noticed, on and off

during the morning, that Amanda was quieter than usual — but *usual* was awfully quiet. Now, though, she looked closer.

The total absence of expression on Amanda's face made Lianne shiver. *Is she breathing? Yes, she is — a little. Good God, she looks dead. She is breathing — but she sure as hell isn't here. And I don't think I'd want to be wherever she is right now. She hasn't done a single spelling word — no, screw the spelling test. I don't want to call her down in front of the rest of the class. Not right now. She doesn't look like she feels too well.*

Lianne cruised through the words on the test, making up sentences on autopilot. She couldn't stop looking at Amanda.

The dead look is in her eyes. They're glazed — could she be having some sort of a seizure? Maybe I need to call a doctor. But she doesn't look physically sick. And the few times I've called on her, I have been able to get an answer out of her — she just drifts away right afterward.

Lianne bit her lip.

We're going to take a break after this test, and I'm going to talk to her.

"Thirty-nine — " Decision made, her attention snapped back to the rest of the class. Her loss of vigilance had not passed unnoticed. "Snyder, Maurice — I'll take those papers, gentlemen, and you may sit out the rest of the test. You've just earned yourselves F's. Anybody else like to try? No? Thirty-nine. Interception. In-ter-CEP-tion. What you have just seen, folks, was the *interception* of two cheat sheets."

The rest of the test went without incident.

Lianne got everyone started reading Thomas Rockwell's *How to Eat Fried Worms,* a book she had fought long and hard to get on the fifth grade required reading list. It proved to her students that reading really was fun — she'd converted more book-haters with that — plus *A Light in the Attic,* and the *Alvin Fernald* books — than with anything else she used. They wallowed in the gross-out joys and Machiavellian plotting of a kid who got dared into eating a worm a day and the friends who'd bet him he couldn't.

With their attention fixed on their books, she was free to take care of Amanda.

She walked to the back of the room, squatted down beside Amanda's desk, and waited. Amanda kept staring out the window. There was no sign that the child knew she was there.

"Amanda," Lianne whispered. "I need to talk with you." She got no response.

Lianne rested her hand lightly on Amanda's shoulder, and said, "Amanda, is something wrong?"

The girl's whole body shuddered, and her face turned toward Lianne — and Lianne pulled her hand away, horrified. Pale, pale jade green eyes stared back at her, stared *through* her, lips pulled back from teeth in an animal expression of fear, or rage — or both. The face was not Amanda's face, not a child's face — if it was human at all. The expression was fleeting — there, and gone so fast Lianne wondered if she'd really seen it — then one of the girls behind her and towards the front of the class started shrieking. Others yelled, desks squeaked, and something hard hit Lianne on the back of the neck. She spun towards the front of the class, started to yell at the kids to stop fighting, and froze.

Impossible.

Loose chalk flew from the chalkboard as if thrown by an angry child. Closed chalk boxes opened themselves, spewed their contents into the air — the liberated chalk rained against walls and ceiling and floor and kids. Bulky blackboard erasers pelted students and furniture, fell to the floor, and leapt up to attack again.

The neatly stacked spelling tests on her desk launched themselves into the air, to join with piles of loose construction paper from the bulletin board corner and reports on *The Planets of Our Solar System* that had suddenly come to life.

Books fell off of desks to the floor. Pens and pencils leapt from desks to smack against the windows. The classroom door opened, then slammed shut, then opened again to allow a stream of paperwork to escape out into the hall.

The children's screams didn't cover the sound of paper snapping in the nonexistent wind.

Lianne had just enough time to realize that what she saw was *real;* it actually was happening. Then it stopped.

Projectiles in mid-course slammed into some invisible wall and dropped to the floor. Papers swirled downward like rainbow-colored autumn leaves. The door shut with a soft click.

There was silence.

Everyone waited. Scared, big-eyed kids looked at her for direction.

She didn't know what to do. So she cleared her throat, bent down, tentatively picked up a piece of chalk, then another. They didn't attack. She picked up a handful of paper.

"Okay, folks — everyone all right?" There were tentative nods from the kids as they looked themselves over and made sure they were still intact. "Good. Then let's . . . let's get this mess cleaned up." She tried to sound brave. God knew, she didn't feel it. "Whatever happened, it's over now. When we've finished, you can all read until the lunch bell rings."

Lianne's knees felt weak. She made her way to the front of the class, put all the chalk and loose erasers around her desk back on the blackboard, then sagged into her seat and rested her head in her hands.

Two days in a row. Right now, I could be convinced to give up teaching forever. The racing accident, the Attack of the School Supplies, Amanda's weird behavior —

Amanda! I forgot about her!

Lianne looked up, expecting to see Amanda frozen at her desk. Instead, she saw the girl chatting with Brynne Lassiter as the two of them cleaned up one corner of the mess.

Amanda glanced in her direction, saw Lianne watching her, and smiled brightly. She bounced up to the desk, and handed the young teacher her gold Cross pen.

"Your pen fell beside my desk."

Lianne tried to smile. "Thank you, Amanda," she said.

"That was really strange, wasn't it, Ms. McCormick?"

"Strange doesn't begin to describe it." Lianne looked closer at the girl, then closed her eyes and rested her forehead against the back of her hand.

"Are you okay, Ms. McCormick?" Amanda asked. She sounded so normal!

"I'll be fine, thank you. Just—just go back to your desk now, please." Lianne felt herself struggling to breathe, felt the room starting to reel, but her skin felt cool to her touch. *No fever.*

She was light-headed — certainly sick. She had to be. *Amanda's eyes are blue.*

Mac woke up with sunlight streaming through the sheers in the window of his hotel suite.

Dammit. Forgot to pull the drapes again. What time is it?

He looked at his clock on the tacky vinyl-veneer almost-Scandinavian dresser that sat in a puddle of sunshine. Green digital numbers, muted to pastel by the light, glowed reassuringly back at him. He stretched with feline grace. *Eleven-fifteen. No hurry. I've got plenty of time for room service.*

He rolled over to the phone that rested on the equally cheap nightstand and dialed. A bouncy-sounding girl at the other end took his order for French toast and bacon and orange juice and the fruit plate. It would be up shortly, she assured him.

Mac smiled and rolled over on his back. *A nice hot shower, I think, while breakfast is getting here — then maybe a little TV. Out in time for the maid to straighten the place up, take Rhellen for some exercise down Bragg Boulevard, drive over to the school to see where Lianne works. Then a stop by the track so Mother doesn't think I've vanished into the ozone. I'll tell her about the outcome of the Belinda Affair. She'll enjoy that.*

It felt like the start of a wonderful day.

Of course, any day that started out with room service and a maid couldn't go too far wrong. Maclyn approved of room service.

He lolled in bed, not quite ready to plunge into the pounding spray of a shower, when he noticed a flash of blue and a dull gleam of gold on the other side of the open door that led to his usually-dull-beige suite living room. Curious, he crawled out of the bed and went to take a look.

:Not a very early riser, are you?: The Mindspeech was female, frosty — condescending, too.

Felouen — beautiful, irritating Felouen — lounged on his couch. She wore a cobalt blue silk Court jerkin heavily embroidered with gold over a soft, pale-blue silk blouse. Gold-and-sapphire chains draped around her neck and wove through her pale amber hair. Her long legs — in matching blue trews — were thrown indecorously over one of the couch's overstuffed arms. She hadn't bothered to take off her knee-high blue leather boots. She lay her head back on a cushion and stretched, sending a languorous, sexy smile in his direction.

"A little overdressed for the area, aren't you?" Mac remarked.

:And you're a little underdressed.:

It was a legitimate comment. Mac was stark naked. "You didn't make an appointment. You don't let me know you're coming, you take your chances."

She smiled. *:And this time I won.:*

Mac refused to be amused or flattered. "I have plans for the day, Felouen. Go home."

:I have plans for the day, too, Mac. I want you to come Home with me.:

He glared at her. "What is this? You can't get me to play warrior for the Court by guilt, so you fake lust? I don't believe you, dear."

She laughed out loud, delighted. *:Fake lust! You'd suspect that, with every other elvish maiden sighing after your broad retreating back? My bonny lad, I needn't fake lust.:*

She sat up. *:But the Unseleighe Court —:*

He blanked out her Mindspeech and turned his back on her. "I won't play defender of the lands with you, Felouen. The lands don't need a defender."

Unable to continue her conversation in the more compelling Mindspeech, she shifted with bad grace to physical speech. "It isn't play," she snapped. "The minions of the Unseleighe Court surround you, even now."

"Ooooh, *minions,*" he mimicked. "I'm terrified." He crossed his arms over his chest. "They don't bother me, I don't bother them."

If anything, her voice grew colder. She sounded like his old sword-instructor, Siobhan: deadly, deathly serious. "You know evil doesn't work that way, Maclyn. The

Unseleighe Court grows stronger with every back that's turned to it. The darkness has spread to our corner of Underhill — the filth is leaking through even there. Soon enough, it will be able to conquer even the strongest and best of those who could have defended against it. If you don't face it now, you will face it later — on its terms."

There was a knock at the door. "Room service," someone called.

"Yeah — just a minute." Mac pointed into the bedroom. *:Get in there — then vanish:*, he told the elven warrior. He pulled his bathrobe off of its hook on the coatrack, put it on, and opened the door.

A smiling busboy pushed the cart into the room. "Mornin', Mr. Lynn," he said. "All ready for the race Saturday?"

"You bet, Sam. You gonna be there?"

"Nah." The young man shook his head, disgusted. "Cain't. I'm scheduled to work. I'm pulling for you, though."

"Thanks." He signed for the food — on the Fairgrove account, of course — and grinned as the busboy left. But the grin vanished with the closing of the door. Mac turned and stalked into his bedroom, expecting to find Felouen waiting for him.

She was gone. *Good,* he thought. *The day is looking up.*

But the feeling of Presence hadn't abated —

On his bed, gold gleamed. He could feel it. He didn't need a closer look. He knew exactly what she'd left.

Shit. The day is looking down.

Mac felt pretty much the way someone who'd just found a leaking radioactive canister in his house would feel. He stared at the lovely gold circle and swore creatively.

Finally, he picked it up. *Uh-huh. I should have known she'd pull something like this. One of the Rings.* He pulled a scrap of silk out of a drawer, and carefully wrapped the bit of jewelry in its insulating folds. Then he shoved it into the leather pouch he kept with him. *Well . . . maybe D.D. will take it off my hands.*

*   *   *

In spite of Mr. Race-Driver's machismo, he doesn't drive so damn-all fast. That stupid shit yesterday must have been to impress me. Ooooh, ooooh, I was so impressed. Gonad-brained jerk-off!

Mac Lynn's '57 Chevy with its custom colors was about as easy to keep track of in traffic as if it sported strobe-lights. She'd always been good at tailing — this was so simple it was dull.

My commission is the same whether I have it hard or easy. I guess I shouldn't knock it.

Belinda downshifted and slipped in behind a pickup as her target slowed and turned into the elementary school parking lot. She chose an unobtrusive spot about a hundred yards down the road, U-turned, and parked. Then she settled back with a bottle of mineral water and a packet of fresh sliced vegetables to wait Mac out.

Her old partner in the Berkeley P.D. had given her endless grief on her choice of stake-out munchies. Ed had hated rabbit food. His idea of stake-out rations was a cold Philly steak sandwich, a stack of Domino's pizzas, and a carton of Mountain Dews. Of course, Ed had given her good-natured hell about almost everything. Sometimes she even missed him.

She missed him at that moment. He would have loved trailing a race-driver with a classic car. He would have known Mac's racing stats and would have tried endlessly to get her to be interested in them. They could have had a wonderful argument about racing, and what it did to the environment. That argument would have segued into solar versus fossil fuel, and Middle Eastern politics, and even — she grinned thinking about it — psychic phenomena. Ed wouldn't have believed the accident yesterday was anything but an accident. He would have argued until his last breath — in spite of her neat gizmo, in spite of the lack of casualties, in spite of everything. Ed had loved to argue.

Debate, he'd called it.

She bit her lip, and glared out the window.

In the end, he had died arguing — debating. He'd had a lot of practice, and he was very convincing, too. She'd wanted to believe him. But he hadn't had as much practice lying as he had at arguing. He'd caught her with the dead mark in the alley, taking her cut to look the other way, and no matter what he said, old Honest Ed could not have meant it when he said he wouldn't turn her in.

She'd hated killing him.

The job wasn't the same after that — it was ruined for her.

She bit viciously at the carrot stick.

Damn Ed, anyway!

She could have been happy in the police department for years.

It was Moonchange, tide change, sea ebb at Fayetteville's Loyd E. Auman Elementary, where the thundering out-rush of the pounding surf of children battered against the lone swimmer-to-shore, who was Mac Lynn, Mighty Racecar Driver—

Or maybe it's more like the charge of the lemmings, Mac thought, as he watched small children trample all over each other in their race to leave.

Fascinated, he stopped to watch.

Teachers bellowed and directed and commanded in voices that would have done a drill sergeant proud — Mac wondered how many of them joined the Marines following a few years of teaching so they could get a vacation. Parents leaned out car windows and screamed for their youngsters to hurry up. Kids shrieked and yelled insults and questions and promises to call each other, fighting to be heard over the general uproar. The school bus engines rumbled bass counterpoint.

The odors of asphalt and bus fumes and new-mown rye grass mingled with the smells of books and stale baloney sandwiches and sweaty gym clothes. Noise, commotion, odors: all were overpowering. For a moment, he wished he was Underhill.

But if I went there right after all of this, it would feel like some-one had plugged my ears and my nose, muffled my brain in silk, and put dark glasses on me. It would be too subtle, like that awful French food.

There was rarely anything subtle about the world of humans.

The buses filled slowly, then, abruptly pulled away — little pockets of traveling riot. Parents drove off with their young, the few walkers vanished into the distance — and quiet returned suddenly, like the descent of the theater curtain. Mac watched as teachers sagged with relief against the building or their cars, or turned with slow and tired steps to head back inside.

He went inside after them.

Lianne's head rested on her desk. Her eyes were closed and her hands were locked over the back of her neck. To Mac, she looked pale.

"Bad day, huh?"

The teacher looked up at him, blearily, too exhausted to register surprise at his appearance. "Hell day."

Mac grimaced by way of showing sympathy. "I'm sorry. You want a back rub? Or maybe you'd prefer that I drive you home?"

Lianne buried her head in her hands again. "I want to crawl into my bed and die."

Mac shook his head. "The first part of that idea doesn't sound too bad. Tell you what. We'll go over to your place and crawl into bed, and I'll bet I can get you to change your mind about dying."

"I doubt it," Lianne groaned. She sounded sincere. She sounded *frightened*.

Mac leaned his palms on her desk and waited until she looked up, then stared intently into her eyes. "It can't be that bad. What's wrong?"

Lianne pushed away from her desk and started gathering up her things. She turned her back to him. There was a long pause, filled mostly with the sounds of her stacking papers and breathing rapidly. Finally, she said, in a small, hesitant voice, "Mostly, it seems that my classroom is haunted."

Mac started to laugh, but stopped himself when he noted the tension in her shoulders. "You aren't kidding."

"God, Mac, I wish I were." She sighed and turned, and he could see the brightness of impending tears in her eyes. "You're — you're going to think I'm crazy, but it happened! All the kids were so scared — "

And so were you — "Tell me," he urged. "Lianne, I've seen plenty of things that seemed crazy at the time." He grinned at her, the lopsided, *very* Celtic grin that always won women's trust. "I may not hang crystals in my car like Bill Gatlin, but I'll go along with Will Shakespeare."

" 'There are more things in heaven and earth, Horatio, than are dreamt of in your philosophy'?" She managed a tremulous smile. "You know, I think I believe you. . . . "

Mac said nothing, only continued to smile encouragingly.

She took a deep breath and relaxed, just a little. "Partway through reading today, papers and chalk came to life and started flying around the room on their own, attacking people. The door opened and slammed shut — it was a madhouse in here. Then it just stopped. I was terrified."

"I'll bet." He put warmth into it, so much that Lianne smiled at him. Mac felt a twinge of excitement. Something was up — it seemed a bit of a coincidence that he should be hunting a telekinetic kid when inanimate objects suddenly came to life in that kid's homeroom teacher's class. Mac was willing to bet that something about the visit to the track had triggered the girl. Maybe the accident.

Time to do a little fishing, he decided.

"What were you doing when it started, baby?" he asked, urging her to keep talking. "Do you remember?"

She nodded. "Oh, yeah. It was weird. One of the kids in my class had been lost in space all morning — I'd assigned everyone to read, and I went back to her seat to talk to her. I didn't get the chance to, though. I hadn't any more than gotten Amanda's attention when the classroom just — blew up."

That name sounded familiar. "Amanda . . . is the name of the kid?"

Lianne didn't notice his increased interest. "Yeah. You might remember her from our little disaster yesterday. She was the skinny blond girl who wouldn't get down behind the bleachers. She's an odd kid."

Mac felt a surge of triumph. *There are no coincidences. I knew it. Same child — and the accident was the trigger.*

He nodded casually. "I remember her — she always act like that?"

Lianne picked up jacket, bag, and papers and headed out the door. Mac followed.

"Yes, no, and maybe," she told him. "Nothing about her makes sense. Her aptitude tests indicate that she should be one of the smartest kids I've ever taught. . . . "

"And?" he prompted, taking her elbow.

Lianne sighed. "And sometimes she is. One minute she's sweet and chatty and willing to discuss the lesson, and the next she doesn't even seem to realize there is a lesson. Her spelling tests are a trip. She'll either slaughter the words entirely, or she'll get them all perfect — and sometimes she'll kill the first half of the test and ace the second half. As far as I can tell, she has no attention span. And sometimes she really likes me, and sometimes she really hates me — and I don't have any warning before she goes from one attitude to the other."

Mac frowned; there was something about those symptoms. . . . "That is strange."

"She has parents that care — they have lots of money, she has all the advantages — " Lianne shrugged. She waved to another teacher who was coming down the long hall toward the stairs from the other direction. "I'm not the only one she's this way around. Her health teacher says she went into a rage during sex ed the other day. Said that she started screaming that anyone who could do something that disgusting was a whore or a slut or worse — I guess Amanda used a few words Nancy had never heard before. What's funny was, they were talking about where babies come from. Really low key, really mild — and all of a sudden, there goes Amanda, right off the deep end."

A sick feeling had started in the pit of Mac's stomach when Lianne began describing Amanda's behavior. It grew worse with every detail. By the time she'd finished, he was sure something was horribly wrong with the child. He just didn't have any idea what.

They walked out of the hot hallways, redolent with chalk

dust, ink, schoolgirl perfume, and sneakers, into baked-asphalt parking lot heat.

Mac held onto her elbow as she started towards her own car. "Let me drive you home," he urged. *I have to find out more about this child — or better yet, get Lianne to take me to her.*

But Lianne shook her head with a stubborn determination he was beginning to know well. "Mac, I appreciate it — but I'll be fine. I have to get some groceries, and I want to go home and just soak in the tub and think for a while." A bit of breeze touched the little tendrils of hair that had escaped from her French braid. Not enough breeze to cool, just enough to be annoying.

Azaleas, dogwoods, and a goddamned heat wave, all blooming at the same time. Welcome to April in North Carolina, he thought.

He persisted, in the forlorn hope that she had been worn down enough to give in to him. "Are you sure?"

This time her nod was quite determined. "I'm sure."

Mac shrugged. "Okay. I really guess I ought to stop by the track before D.D. sends out search teams, anyway." *Try a different tactic.* "May I see you tonight?"

She finally gave in to his persistence, yielding with a willing heart, if the smile that answered his was any indication. "I'd like that. But — how about just an evening in? I'm too tired for anything that involves going out in public."

He pretended to consider it. "Hmm. Never tried one of those before. . . . "

She lifted a skeptical eyebrow, and he laughed. "It's a date," he said, and gave Lianne a tight hug and a kiss. She returned the kiss with startling enthusiasm, and Mac caught his breath.

They are so warm, so bright . . . so enchanting —

And so fleeting —

He pulled away quickly and forced a grin. "Gotta run, babe. See you tonight," he told her, and turned away. He didn't want her to see the pain in his eyes.

— And they die so soon, he thought. *So soon . . . and anyone who loves them dies a little bit with them. Not again. I won't ever let myself hurt that way again.*

*   *   *

Redmond Something-or-other was pawing Mac's mother again, back in the corner behind the tire stacks. Mac heard D.D. giggling and whispering, and her young lover's erratic breathing. It was, he reflected, a hard life that gave a man a mother who looked ten years younger than he did — when she was nearly two hundred years older.

"Hey, D.D.," he yelled. "You're never going to get my car ready doing that. Chase your stud-muffin off with a nice big tire iron and get out here."

"There's more to life than cars," she yelled brightly, but she and the stud-muffin appeared. Redmond, looking flushed and flustered, was struggling with his buttons. Mac suspected he'd gotten the zipper back in place before he came out of hiding.

D.D., of course, was unfazed. "I didn't think you were going to join us poor peons today," she said, flaunting her pony-tail. "And Redmond and I didn't see any reason to waste a perfectly good day if you weren't even going to show up."

"Mmmm-hmmm." Mac looked over at the dark corner of the garage. "Fooling around on the cement behind the tires has got to be one of the more romantic ways I could think of to spend a day."

She laughed at him. "We pump grease our own way, we do. You're too stuffy, Mac. You wouldn't know a good time if it bit you on the ass."

Mac smiled agreeably and made a tsk-ing noise. "That's the difference between you and me, D.D. If it bit me on the ass, *I* wouldn't call it a good time."

D.D. laughed and flipped him the finger. "You'll never know what you're missing."

He cast his eyes up to heaven, as if asking for help. "Gods, I hope not. You're one short step above delinquent, and if you weren't such a good mechanic — "

"But I *am*," she replied impudently. "So you indulge me."

"So I do. Hey, D.D. — I just remembered. A friend of yours stopped over at my place this morning — she had a present for you, but she couldn't find you, so she left it with me." Mac fished the scrap of green silk out of the bag in his pocket, and started to hand it to D.D. . . .

But D.D. kept her hands shoved firmly into her pockets. *:Bullshit, Maclyn, my love.:* "What friend was that?" she asked out loud.

"Felouen," Mac said. He saw no point in lying. *:I'd appreciate your help here, Mother.:*

:No doubt — but I'm not going to interfere in your relationship with the Court. You have some responsibilities that you're evading — I won't force you to live up to them. I also won't help you get out of them.: Out loud, D.D. lied for Redmond's benefit. "Felouen and I can't stand each other. I wonder what she's up to."

:She stuck me with a Ring, Mother. Won't you please take it off my hands? Before it calls too much attention to me?: Mac proffered the silk again. "She wants to be friends, D.D. Why don't you just take her present? You can always give it back to her later if you don't change your mind about her."

:You deal with it, kiddo.: "If she wants to be friends, she can find me herself. If you see her again, give her present back to her. And tell her what I said. I'm sure she'll be seeing you again."

Mac muttered, "I'm sure she will."

He held the Ring in his fingers and wished that it would go away. It radiated warmth, power, assurance — and a broadcast beam that would tell every Unseleighe thing in the area that a Seleighe warrior was among them.

Just exactly what I needed for Christmas.

● Chapter Four

Elementary school. The racetrack. Penney's at the mall. Barnes' Motor and Parts. Three — count 'em, three — fast food joints. No — she thought, watching with disbelief as Mac pulled into a Kentucky Fried Chicken, *Make that four fast food joints.*

"You sure know how to show a girl a good time, fella," Belinda muttered. "If this is how hot-dog race-drivers spend their days, I'll pass."

She'd never tailed anyone duller in her life. She'd spent her entire afternoon driving in circles around Fayetteville, watching Mac gorge on junk food and run apparently pointless errands. It was getting dark, she'd put monster miles on her little silver Sunbird, she had to go to the bathroom, and she was, for the second time, almost out of gas. Mac hadn't taken a potty break or fueled up his accursed Chevy once. Belinda would have given anything to know how he'd accomplished that second trick. Those beasts were supposed to guzzle gas, everyone knew that. His gas tank couldn't be *that* big.

He hadn't spotted her. She knew he hadn't spotted her. Except a suspicion kept nagging that nobody, absolutely nobody, could or would spend a day in such a boring manner unless he was trying to mislead a tail.

But finally, at about seven-thirty, Mac's aimless wandering ceased, replaced by apparent commitment to a single direction and increased speed. *Now we're getting somewhere,* Belinda rejoiced.

She had to fall further and further back as they left the center of Fayetteville and traffic thinned. For twenty minutes, they sped along roads that became increasingly deserted. Suddenly, on a narrow country lane, Mac left the pavement entirely, bounced along a sand two-rut through a fallow field, and screeched to a halt in front of a stand of stunted hardwoods along the field's back perimeter. There were no buildings anywhere around. There were no cars passing by.

This is going to be good, Belinda gloated. *If he has something going on back there, I'll make sure he finds a nice little surprise waiting for him the next time he drops by.*

Belinda saw him creep out of the Chevy and sneak into the woods. She turned off her headlights, drove in as close as she dared, then rolled down her window. She left the keys hanging from the ignition in case she needed to get out fast, crawled out of the window to keep from making any unnecessary noise, then trailed him on foot.

Bless him for wearing light colors, she thought. His white windbreaker nearly glowed in the dark. She edged past the Chevy — *cautiously* — she still couldn't explain the incident with Stevens and Peterkin — and slipped into the trees. She moved quietly. She'd had plenty of woods experience. Mac apparently hadn't. He sounded like a buffalo dancing on potato chips — she'd never heard such a racket from one person. She could have followed him blindfolded.

He worked his way up a rise and into a clearing. She saw him plainly. He stopped, illuminated by the light of the half-moon riding almost overhead. Then he turned. Fifteen yards behind him, she froze.

With preternatural clearness, she saw him look right at her. She saw him grin. His eyes fixed on hers, he mouthed the words "Hi, babe," and he waved at her —

Then he vanished. Poof. He didn't hide, he didn't move, he just — plain — vanished.

For one stunned moment, she couldn't think at all.

Then her mind started working again, beginning with a long list of things she'd like to call the sonuvabitch.

The boss, Belinda thought with some bitterness, *ought to be thrilled by this.*

From back where she'd parked, she heard a whinny and the sound of horse's hooves on dirt. She heard the "ding, ding" sound that could only be caused by someone opening her car door with the keys in the ignition. Still in a state of shock, she listened as a motor — her motor — kicked over.

What?

Mac had vanished and now someone was stealing her car!

Released from her trance, she turned and broke into a full-out gallop, screaming, "Get the hell away from my car, you thief!" as she ran. Branches slapped her face and tore at her clothes. Thorns ripped at her hands and tangled in her braid. Full-sized trees seemed to jump in front of her. She arrived in the field in time to see her car, headlights on, back out into the highway. The driver flipped the interior light on for a moment, just so she would be sure to recognize him. It was Mac. He waved, and tooted her horn, and drove off.

There was a light-colored horse running behind him. Pacing him, she'd have said.

"Give my car back, you bastard!" she shrieked. She pulled her gun out of her shoulder holster and fired one shot in sheer frustration. She heard the crack of shattering glass, and a laugh. Red tail lights disappeared in the distance.

Now her nice little rental car had a bullet hole in it. And a broken window. For which, no doubt, she'd be charged the worth of the entire car.

Shit! But, no — it doesn't matter. He stole my car, he didn't have anyone with him — therefore, he had to leave his. The Chevy. He'll have taken the keys — but I learned a lot from the P.D. I'll just hot-wire his damned Chevy.

She turned to walk back to Mac's car — and found hoof-prints and emptiness.

There was no car.

Mel Tanbridge grinned and fished out a pen and a yellow legal pad from his desk. He'd just mined a new sure-thing cash-crop angle out of his latest issue of *Science News*, and he wanted to get it down on paper while the idea was still fresh. The members of Nostradamus Project's auxiliary organization, Nostradamus Foundation International, paid well to get their pseudo-science delivered to their doorstep, and he worked hard to make sure it arrived full of juicy tidbits that would keep the money rolling in.

He looked over the *SN* article, which, in very careful terms noted a variance in the ability of rhesus monkeys to pick symbols shown on a computer screen when the symbols were chosen by a human researcher compared to random assignment of the symbols by the computer. The article, "High-Level Pattern Recognition in Rhesus Monkeys," noted that the monkeys picked the correct symbol from a random stream about 13 to 17 percent more often when the human researcher was choosing the symbols. The article noted that this happened even when the monkey was not able to see the researcher, eliminating the chance of visual cues from the human. The article suggested that the human researchers' attempts at randomness displayed a subconscious choice pattern picked up by the monkeys, and noted that the rhesus monkeys had a strong affinity for pattern recognition.

Mel snorted.

"Telepathic Contact Between Humans and Monkeys Confirmed In Independent Studies," he scratched down on the legal pad. "Rhesus monkeys are the first non-human species to demonstrate telepathic abilities — reading the minds of researchers in carefully controlled double-blind experiments conducted by — " He paused. One wanted to be very careful about naming names in these things. Some of his pet flakes, he suspected, also read *Science News.* " — by an independent simian research facility in Florida." He carefully copied in the statistics and a few, slanted quotes, referred to *Science News* as a "professional journal for scientists," and hit his pitch.

"Nostradamus Foundation International must raise — " He thought about it. How much did he want to raise this time? A couple million dollars would be nice. A couple million dollars would permit him to put out glossy four-color fliers and advertise in all his favorite magazines and expand his carefully cultivated list of fools who could be parted from their money. It would also permit him some breathing room to continue with his covert and highly illegal, but real, search to acquire a stable of TK's and other psi talents. " — two point four million dollars to continue its exciting research into projects like this." "Like" was an important word in Mel's vocabulary. He used it a lot. With that one little word, he could infer, without actually stating, that his foundation was involved in simian psychic research. *My ass! Simian psychic research. What an angle. God, I love it.*

"Finally, paranormal phenomena have become a legitimate domain of scientific exploration, and NFI is spearheading that exploration. Your participation has been essential to NFI's research in the past. We need your help now."

He drafted out a series of boxes, starting with twenty dollars and ending with a thousand, and noted that he wanted a place at the bottom of the fund sheet for "participants" to check "current areas of research" they would particularly like to see expanded, with a write-in line for "other." Those little mini-surveys were great. He'd been on the lookout for an animal project ever since some lady had written requesting that NFI expand into "telepathic research with other life forms." She'd added a long, handwritten letter (on pink cat stationery), with her check for twenty dollars, stating that she firmly believed her cats could read minds. Mel made sure she got a nice note back stating that NFI thought psychic cats were a good subject for research. He'd added "non-human psychic research" to his list immediately.

Mel loved New Agers.

He spun the soft leather executive chair to face out the window, leaned back, and laced his fingers behind his head. The taste of success was sweet. The last letter, scavenged from a *National Geographic* article on eskimo shamans, had netted him about a million-five. This one, his instincts told him, was good for easily that much.

"Fran!" he yelled.

His secretary leaned in the door. "Yes?"

He indicated the legal pad. "Get Janny to set that up in bulletin format — yellow paper and black ink, a line drawing of a telepathic monkey — tell her to keep it understated and scientific-looking. Make sure the drawing is of a rhesus monkey," he added. He closed his eyes and sighed. "Some of these people might notice."

"Okay. Mel, do you want to look at your mail? You have a FedEx package, some bills, some junk, and a few responses from the last mailer."

"Bring 'em in." The bills would wait, the responses he loved to open personally — money in the mail was a wonderful thing. And the FedEx package ought to be Belinda's TK film. He felt a rush of adrenalin. There might be nothing to what she had — but Belinda wasn't one of the true believers. She thought the whole Nostradamus Project was a dodge. If she was convinced she had something real —

He suppressed that line of thought. No sense setting himself up for a disappointment. "Bring in the VCR from the conference room while you're at it."

Lianne opened the door, wearing an oversized pink tee-shirt with Garfield on it and a pair of tight blue jeans, minus knees. Her deafeningly pink socks bagged around her ankles, and her hair was tucked behind her ears and held in place by barrettes. She looked about twelve. Mac had really been hoping she'd be wearing something from Victoria's Secret — or maybe nothing — but he hid his disappointment bravely.

"Hey'ya!" She looked him over and grinned. "You look like a man who expected to be greeted by a woman wearing Saran Wrap." She winked. "I don't go to the door that way, you know. If I did, my mom would be on the other side."

Mac squeezed her to his chest and kissed her passionately. "That wasn't what I was thinking at all," he lied. "I was just thinking you were the prettiest bag lady I'd ever seen."

He followed her into her apartment, admiring the way she walked, and kept close as she led him to her television set.

"I went for comfort, I'll have you know. I had a very bad day." Lianne gave him a wan little smile and a tight hug.

"I'm glad you're here. I rented a couple of movies, got a huge bag of popcorn, and I've got all the makings for daiquiris — unless you'd rather have diet soft drinks — ?"

"Decaffeinated?" he asked cautiously.

"Nah — I like my caffeine." She made a face. "Why have a cola without caffeine? You might as well not bother."

He answered her face with one of his own. "Whereas I like to sleep at night. No, really, I'm allergic to caffeine. Daiquiris will be fine."

She pointed out the bag on the TV cabinet. "So. Pick the movie you want to see and get it ready — I'll do the daiquiris."

She vanished into the little apartment kitchen. Mac pulled three clear plastic boxes out of the paper bag she'd indicated and studied the titles. He grinned as he peered at the first label. *The Man With One Red Shoe*.

He'd seen that one at least a dozen times. He closed his eyes, replayed the opening credits, recalled the slinking, skullduggerous beat of the score, and chuckled softly. *Tom Hanks, Lori Singer, Carrie Fisher, Dabney Coleman, Charles Durning and Jim Belushi. A casting miracle,* and *a great script,* and *hilarious, too; elvish nominee for an all-time Oscar.* He put the movie on top of Lianne's VCR. *Probably that one,* he decided.

Violent machinery sounds ground out from the kitchen. Mac's smile took on a bemused air. What was she *doing* in there? Was that making daiquiris? It sounded more like chainsawing down a Buick. He shrugged. The ways of humans were inscrutable.

He glanced at the next title she'd rented. He liked Bette Midler a lot, and Danny DeVito — *nasty little man, in this one at least* — was well cast. *Ruthless People* wasn't quite in the same league as her first choice, but on the whole, he approved.

When he saw what her third pick was, though, he dropped the other two movies back in the bag without another thought. He put that cassette into the VCR's slot, checked to make sure it was rewound — gloating all the while at his competence with human machinery — and flashed a Cheshire grin at Lianne when she came out of the kitchen with a mammoth bowl of popcorn balanced in the crook of her elbow and a bright pink daiquiri in either hand.

"Strawberry," she said. "Fresh strawberries my mom picked and dropped off yesterday."

"Sounds tasty." It did — and it smelled tasty, as well. The fresh strawberry-smell was mouthwatering.

She smiled at his expression. "I already tried mine. It's pretty good. I can't think of a better combination than strawberries and popcorn. So — what are we watching?"

He set the bowl of popcorn and one of the frothy pink drinks on her coffee table, and hit the on button of the remote. "Just wait and see." He favored her with a sly smile.

"I rented them, you doofus. I already know what the choices are." When he still wouldn't tell her, she rolled her eyes and snorted. "Mysterious men just give me goosebumps."

Belinda sat on the berm of the dark, lonely road, reloading the chamber of her handgun and wishing Mac were standing in front of her so she would have a target. Reloading was mostly an excuse to sit down for a minute. After all, she'd only used the one bullet. But she'd been hiking along the road for nearly an hour and a half. Her feet hurt, she was tired, she was pissed off, and she really would have liked to have taken time for a good long scream, but that wasn't practical.

Besides, police training had left an indelible mark on her subconscious when it came to firearms. She firmly believed that one empty chamber would be the one she needed — so it would never, never stay empty.

I hate him, she thought, rage coloring everything she did. *If he wasn't worth a ruddy fortune to me alive, I'd kill that two-bit jock just for the fun of it.*

But he'd proven to her that he was exactly the person she was looking for. His psychic tricks verged on the magical — that vanishing act, even more than the business he'd pulled with his car doors — had guaranteed his fate in

Belinda's book. That slimy little shit Tanbridge would be
willing to pay through the nose for Mac Lynn. And soon.
Real soon — because her patience wasn't going to hold out
much longer.

She sighed and got up. She was spending a lot of time
walking on this job — something she would pay Mac Lynn
back for. At least *this* time when he stranded her, she hadn't
been wearing high heels and tight leather pants.

Ten minutes further down the road, after a wide detour
past an abandoned house that would have to be repaired
before it would even be suitable for ghosts, she spotted a
gleam of silver off to her right, reflected in the moonlight.
As she drew nearer, the gleam resolved into the shape of a
Sunbird.

My car! she thought. *I don't believe it!*

Suspecting a ruse, she dropped into the woods and
edged up to the vehicle from the passenger side, working
her way through grass and weeds that reached to the
Sunbird's door handles. He hadn't locked the car. She
checked for booby traps, held her breath as she opened the
passenger door, and — heart racing — eased herself onto
the passenger seat and across to the driver's side.

My God, the keys are in it. And the tank still shows half full. She
smiled, bemused. *I'll be damned. Maybe I won't have to skin the
soles of his feet with a rusty knife after all.*

She turned the key in the ignition, and the motor kicked
right over. She put the car in gear and gave it some gas. It
moved — sluggishly — onto the pavement.

Flop-flop-flop-flop, flop-flop-flop-flop.

She hit the brake, turned the motor off, and leapt out.

She stared for a full minute at the car's tires, tires that
had been completely hidden by the tall grass. Her anger
grew to monumental proportions. In a blind fury, she
kicked the door, and screamed "You *son-of-a-bitch*!" into the
empty night.

"I'll kill you," she ranted. "I'll kill you, I'll kill you, I'll kill
you! I don't need the money this bad — I don't need anything this bad. You bastard! You rotten, stinking, stupid,
sneaking *bastard*!"

She stared at her car again, and hot tears of pure rage rolled down her cheeks. The tires — all four of them — were flatter than soggy pancakes.

After the ordeals of the day, Stranger watched the children with apprehension. They huddled, separate and isolated, in the darkness of the beautiful little-girl room and wept in silent, tearless rage. Her heart went out to them.

Och, if there was but a way to show them each that they are not alone — she thought.

She knew all of them — Anne, battered and abused, always angry, who lived only to deal with the Father in all his giant horror; Abbey, the sheltered, the brilliant, charming scholar who loved learning; Alice, the repressive puritan who hated everything that failed to meet her impossible standards of righteousness — and the silent, frozen, tortured husk that was all that remained of the original Amanda. Each of the first three would acknowledge *her* presence — none would admit that their "sisters" existed. The three-year-old Amanda was unreachable, hiding forever inside her frozen shell of fear. Amanda would never come out, without a miracle.

But they need each other sa' badly — if they could only come t'gether, they'd be whole again. And then — Stranger stared up at the milky reflection of moonlight on the wall — *then they could fight back, couldn't they? For all that they're only children.*

Well, then, it's up to me to introduce them, isn't it? A bloody nightmare that's likely to be, but best begun is soonest done.

Abbey was the easiest to reach. She stayed in the frilly pink bedroom, and did not ring her world with guards and traps. Alone of all the girls, she still retained the childish wish to please. She would listen to the ancient voice of Stranger.

:Abbey, can you hear me?:

Abbey, blue-eyed and blond, sniffled and nodded. *:Yes, Stranger. Wh-what do you w-w-want?:*

Cethlenn made her thoughts as gentle and persuasive as she could. *:I have a surprise for you.:*

Abbey perked up a little. *:Is it good?:* she asked hopefully. She alone of all of them retained the ability to hope.

Stranger reflected on the answer to that and sighed. Was it good that there were four little girls and one ancient Celtic witch living in the body of one child? Probably not — but it felt necessary. Stranger had come late to this little drama. She had her own ideas about what had shaped the weirdling child in whom she found her own spirit suddenly awakened. She had ideas, too, of what cures there might be.

:Och, it's good enough, I suppose. I've a giftie for you, little Abbey. Secret sisters, hidden from all the world save you. Would you like to be meeting them, then?:

The child pondered. *:Are they little kids like Sharon?:*

:Not at all,: Stranger assured her. *:They are like you — almost magical.:*

That was the key word. Abbey's eyes widened. *:Oh, yes, Stranger. When can I meet them?:*

Cethlenn, the Stranger, smiled grimly. *:Come with me, child. I think now would be a good time.:* She enveloped Abbey's spirit in her own, and with some difficulty slipped both of them through tiny cracks in the barrier that grew between the children. On the other side, Anne curled in a ball, silent, rocking back and forth, staring at nothing. Anne's world was unremitting gray, with all the shifting featurelessness of unformed nightmare — except for the walls. Everywhere in Anne's world, walls crawled up and up and up until the eye couldn't see any further. They were brick or stone or shiny black glass, but they were everywhere.

When Stranger and Abbey appeared, Anne looked up and shrieked with fear. Her eyes dilated, and she jammed herself up against one of her omnipresent walls.

:Anne, I've brought a friend for you,: Stranger said, her voice soothing. *:You don't have to be alone anymore.:*

Anne cowered and stared. *:A-lone,:* she crooned. *:A-lone, a-lone, a-lone . . .:* Objects materialized in the hazy space that surrounded the three of them and began to spin through the air. Lit cigarettes and burning matches, ropes and riding crops — all took up a stately waltz around Abbey's thin body, then darted in one by one, charging closer and closer to the other child's face. Abbey winced away.

:Stop it, Anne,: Stranger demanded, and moved next to the child under attack. *:This is Abbey, your sister.:*

:Sis-ter, sis-ter, sis-ter,: the green-eyed child chanted. *:I — don't — want — a — sis-ter.:*

The flames grew bigger, the coals at the ends of the cigarettes brighter and more menacing. The riding crops became bullwhips that cracked like thunder. The ropes coiled and struck out, serpents of hemp. All of them wove around Stranger and Abbey in a tighter and more lethal dance, faster and faster, until Abbey began to scream.

:Out!: Cethlenn commanded, and with the flick of her fingers, she and Abbey were through the barrier, back in Abbey's safe haven.

Abbey sat on her bed and sobbed, while Cethlenn sat next to her and stroked her hair. *:I don't want any more surprises, Stranger,:* the child told her gravely.

:No,: Stranger replied softly, *:I rather imagine you don't.:*

Cethlenn sat, the tearful child cradled in her arms, and stared off into space. *Well then, lassie,* she thought to herself, *will ye be havin' any more bright ideas this evenin'? Let's hope not.*

"I love *The Princess Bride*. I could watch the sword fight scene all by itself a million times." Lianne snuggled deeper into Mac's shoulder and munched popcorn. On the screen, the fight raged. Inigo made a remark about Bonetti's defense. The Man In Black laughed. The swordsmen battled across the rocks, near the cliff — Inigo switched the sword from his left hand to his right, and the tide of battle turned.

"Probably reminds you of your job," Mac drawled.

Lianne's left eyebrow flickered upward, and she snorted. "I should have it so easy. Even the Fire Swamp and the Rodents of Unusual Size would be a piece of cake compared to fifth grade at Loyd E. Auman."

Mac punched a button on the remote and the TV went off.

"Hey," Lianne yelped. "You can't turn off *The Princess Bride*!"

He turned to her wearing the most serious expression

he could muster. "We've already watched the whole movie once and the sword fight three times. Lianne, I want to hear about what happened in your class today. This is important."

Lianne sighed. "I know, but . . ."

He shook his head. "No 'buts'."

She considered his expression, then stiffened her shoulders. "Okay. It just sounds ridiculous, but it was real. Stuff was flying around the room, Mac — books, chalk, pens and pencils, paper — it couldn't have been a draft or a breeze. I don't know what it could have been. I have no logical explanation for what happened."

"Life doesn't require a logical explanation, Lianne," he replied as persuasively as he could.

But she shook her head, violently. "Yes, it does. I refuse to sink to the level of the Shirley MacLaines of the world. I don't flitter after every goofball anti-intellectual guru who promises the keys to the universe — no math required. I don't approve of all this New Age mumbo-jumbo. The real world doesn't need it. The real world needs mathematicians, scientists, artists, builders, writers, teachers, nurses — the real world doesn't need any more flakes." She drew a deep breath. "There are already enough of those."

Mac grinned wryly and hugged her closer. "Oh, I don't know, baby. I think the real world could use a bit of magic. You know, a few elves and fairies, some bogans to play the bad guys, some ghosties and ghoulies. . . ."

"Life's too short to waste on fantasy," she said, but he could tell she was weakening.

This, from a woman who watches The Princess Bride? "Life's too short to waste on math. Anyone who tells you otherwise is selling something." He grinned.

She frowned. "You'd make a great fifth-grader."

"The world will never know." Mac kissed her cheerfully on her nose, then took a more serious tone. "This morning you were as upset by your student, Amanda, as you were by the stuff flying around in your room. Why?"

Lianne rolled over and looked directly into Mac's eyes.

"I want to understand what's the matter with her. As a matter of fact, I'm going out to her house on Friday to talk with her folks. You'd know the place, I'll bet. Kendrick's Bal-A-Shar Arabian Stables. I know it is going to sound silly—but you know what bothered me most today? I just had the craziest feeling, with that *poltergeist* business going on in my classroom, that *Amanda* was really the one responsible." She stopped and pursed her lips. She was watching him for a reaction. "Now I really sound nuts, huh?"

Mac brushed his finger along the line of her eyebrows and slowly shook his head. "Nope — you sound like you have good instincts."

"You think Amanda *might* have had something to do with — oh. Stupid me. You're humoring me." She turned her back to him, grabbed the remote control, and turned the TV back on. The Man In Black leapt from the cliff, did one great swing from a vine, followed up with a back-flip, and landed next to the sword he'd tossed point-down into the sand.

"Who *are* you?" Inigo pleaded.

The Man In Black smiled. "No one of im — "

— Click.

"Don't turn the TV off, Mac," Lianne snapped. "I want to watch this."

He snapped back. "Don't pout. I can't talk to you with the TV on, and I want to discuss this."

She rounded on him, fury in her eyes. "Well, I don't! I don't want to be patronized, I don't want to be humored — I don't want to be remembered as that amusing little schoolteacher you dated once upon a time who had a problem with poltergeists in her classroom and bats in her belfry! I'm going to watch the movie. If you don't want to do that, you can just leave."

I don't want to leave. I had a lot of other plans for this evening, Mac thought, and sighed, mentally. *Give up on the child for a moment. Now that I know who and where she is, there are other ways of reaching her.*

He slipped his hands under her giant tee-shirt and nibbled gently along one side of her neck. He felt her shiver, then start to pull away.

"I wasn't making fun of you. I *believe* in poltergeists and fairies and — " he dropped his voice to a low whisper " — even elves. I think that part of the universe is real, even if you don't. But you're tired, and you probably want to forget about work for a while. I'm sorry I brought it up. Let's find something else to talk about."

"Like what?" she asked, suspiciously.

He breathed into her ear. "Oh, you — and me — and maybe a little snuggling."

Lianne smiled and rolled over against him. "I have a better idea," she whispered. "Let's skip the talking entirely."

It was painfully early. Mac stared at the dull green glow of the alarm clock, then rolled over to look at the woman asleep by his side. She slept on her stomach, the sheet tangled around her knees, her face buried in the crook of her left arm. Her breathing was soft and regular, almost inaudible. Even asleep, she glowed with vitality.

Fascinated, Mac stroked the soft skin of her back and lightly caressed the smooth curves of her buttocks.

She wriggled against his touch, moved closer — and her breathing told him she was awake.

"Hi, there," he chuckled.

She squinched one eye open, smiled at him, and sighed. "Hi, yourself," she said softly. "It isn't time to get up yet, surely?"

"Not really. And don't call me Shirley."

"Oh gawd. It's too early for Zucker jokes."

He softened his smile and caressed her cheek. "I was just watching you sleep."

"And so you decided to wake me up." Lianne giggled. She had a charming giggle. "Mac, you are such a fink. But, boy-oh-boy-oh-boy, I don't want to get up yet — "

An idea occurred to Mac. "Tell you what. I'm completely awake, and I won't get back to sleep again. Why don't you go back to sleep, and I'll put together a terrific breakfast for you — you can eat in bed, and then the two of us will take a nice long shower together, and then we'll go off to work. Okay?"

Her muffled response reached Mac through the baffling of her pillow, under which she had buried her face. "How could I refuse an offer like that?"

He laughed. "You can't, so don't try."

Mac rolled out of the bed and started to walk to the kitchen.

Lianne's voice stopped him.

"You didn't really mean it about the elves, did you?"

He looked back at her. She was propped up on her elbows, studying him intently.

"Mean what about the elves?" he asked carefully.

Her eyes were wary. "That you believed in them."

Mac grinned at her and winked. "Of course I meant it."

She snorted and buried her head back under the pillow. Mac laughed and went on into the kitchen.

Bacon, an omelet, hot croissants, some waffles — or maybe crepes covered with powdered sugar and fresh whipped cream — fresh-squeezed orange juice . . . mmmmm. Sausage. Link sausage. What else? Mac's imagination reviewed the possibilities. *I think I'll do this one without magic. No point in wasting the power when there is a kitchen full of human food to use.* He flipped on the light in her kitchen, wandered over to the fridge, and opened it. *Wonder where she keeps the croissants.*

None were evident. In fact, he didn't see any bacon or link sausages either. No waffles. No crepes. The orange juice was plainly marked, but when he tasted it, it most definitely wasn't fresh-squeezed. He found eggs, but the steps necessary to change them from raw egg to tasty omelet eluded him.

He did see a Betty Crocker cookbook. *I've seen June Lockhart making breakfast for Timmy and his dad on* Lassie. *How hard can it be?*

He picked up a cookbook at random, opened it, and paged through the index.

Eggs And Cheese — page 101. He thumbed through the pages until he found comprehensive descriptions on how to buy and store eggs, how to measure and use egg equivalents, and a mass of information on cheeses. There were pictures of a woman's hand over a big, flat pan, and instructions that described the making of poached eggs, shirred eggs, fried eggs, scrambled eggs, souffles, egg foo yong, and dozens of varieties of omelets.

Good enough. He rummaged through the kitchen until he found a pan that resembled the one in the picture. He put together as many of the listed ingredients as he could locate. He couldn't find any fresh green peppers, but he did find a jar labeled "Hot Red Chili Pepper — Ground." In the tradition of the cookbook, he substituted a cup of red peppers for the suggested cup of green peppers. Lianne had an eight-ounce can of tomato sauce in her cupboard, but it didn't have a pop-top on it, and Mac couldn't figure out how to open it, so, with the competent smile of a man who can adapt, he added eight ounces of tabasco sauce — which, he reasoned, was bright red and should be the same thing. He broke the three required eggs with enthusiasm, and very carefully picked out most of the pieces of shell. There didn't seem to be enough omelet for two people though, so he added another three eggs.

Satisfied, he stirred his ingredients around in the little flat pan, and following instructions, located the knob on the stove that said "oven," and checked the instructions. It was supposed to take forty minutes to cook an omelet, but he really didn't want to spend that much time on it. He thought for a moment. The instructions called for 350 degrees. If he doubled the temperature, he should be able to halve the time. But the oven wouldn't go any higher than 550. Well, actually, it did go to BROIL. *That must be about 600–700 degrees.* He turned the knob to broil. Carrying his embryonic omelet carefully by the pan's plastic handle, he placed it into the oven.

Nothing to that. I might as well see what else I can whip up.

He paged through the cookbook. Pictures of delicious roasts and beautifully prepared fowl caught his eyes. He read down the instructions for some of the dishes. *I could do that,* he thought, fascinated. The world of humans was amazingly accessible, if one simply knew where to look. Page after page of substantial human dishes — that anyone could make.

He became absorbed in pictures of London Broil and Sweet-and-Sour Meatballs, Broccoli-Tomato Salad and Swedish Tea Rings. The time slipped past.

The sudden shriek of the smoke alarm brought him out of his reverie. The kitchen was redolent with the stench of burning plastic. Smoke roiled from the front of the oven.

"Shit," Mac muttered, admiring the succinctness of human vernacular. With a glance, he silenced the smoke alarm. With another, he formed the smoke into a compact ribbon and sent it trailing out the entryway in a neat, steady stream. He pulled open the oven door, surveyed the melted ruins of the skillet handle and his prodigiously grown and dreadfully blackened omelet with dismay. He made a gesture of dismissal, and skillet, omelet, and mess vanished.

Lianne called from the bedroom, "Was that the smoke alarm?"

So much, he thought, *for doing a fabulous breakfast the human way.*

"That was your imagination."

"I suppose it's my imagination that I smell smoke, too."

"Absolutely. I'm bringing breakfast in now." *To blazes with it. I'll do it my way.* Mac visualized his own breakfasts from the hotel, and out of thin air and elven magic, recreated an exact duplicate of the best one he'd ever had, down to the little rose in the cut crystal bud vase. Then he doubled it. He lifted up the heavy silvered serving tray he'd materialized, and trotted into the bedroom with it.

Lianne rolled over and sat up, and her eyes grew round. "Wow! When you talk about breakfast in bed, you aren't kidding." She looked over the steaming croissants, the huge, cheese-filled omelet, the two steaks — broiled, medium rare, the big crystal glasses full to brimming with fresh-squeezed juice, and the bowls of fresh fruit. "And where did you get fresh cherries this time of year?" she asked.

Mac shrugged and grinned. "You like?"

"I like." She took one of the cherries and bit into it, and closed her eyes with ecstasy. "God, that's good." She looked at Mac with eyes that seemed to see right through him. "I'm beginning to realize why you believe in magic, though. The fancy trays and the cut crystal aren't a bad trick, considering I've never owned anything like them in my life, but these — " She indicated the little bowls of rich red fruit. "There won't be any cherries available around her till the middle of June. I know, because I haunt the grocery stores for 'em every year. If you found these — that's magic."

"You bet it is." Mac dug into his omelet and steak. "Stick with me, kid. You ain't seen nothing yet." He grinned at her. The wincing he saved for inside.

Carelessness like that, he thought ruefully, eyeing the out-of-season cherries, *will blow your cover all the way to Elfhame Outremer. And beyond.*

● Chapter Five

D.D. had MIX 96 turned way up. She was sprawled under the engine of the disassembled Victor, tinkering with something, singing along at the top of her lungs with a Creedence Clearwater Revival cover of "I Heard It Through The Grapevine" that Tank Sherman had dug out of the Golden Oldies box. Mac grinned. He wouldn't admit it to her, but D.D. didn't sound too bad on backup vocals.

He waited until the song was over and something odious by Madonna started to play — then he turned the radio off.

"Hey!" D.D. yelled without looking up. "Turn that back on. I'm listening to it."

:Mother, Mother, what would they be sayin' back home if they could see you right now? The shame — och, the shame of me own fair mother disgracin' herself so.:

:Can it, kiddo.: Dierdre was unfazed. She stood, wiped her hands on her overalls, and turned to face her offspring. "I'm not believin' me own eyes," she said for the benefit of everyone. "Mac Lynn, the perennially late, is in here at eight o'clock in the morning. Ye gods, man, fetch me water before I faint."

"Ha-ha." *:Stopping in to let you know — I found the homebase of our little TK. I'm going by there later today to see if I can talk to her.:*

D.D. turned back to her engine block and returned to her tinkering. Mac sat down on a stack of tires to watch her.

:Good,: the pony-tailed terror remarked as she loosened bolts. *:'Bout damn time. I may graduate you to nearly-competent.:*

Mac grinned. *:Actually, there is something you can do that would be a lot more help.:*

:If you're still hoping I'll talk to Felouen for you —:

Mac snarled out loud, and realized a comment was necessary for the benefit of the non-elven who were present. "While you're working on the steering, D.D., tighten it up. It felt like you had it patched together with rubber bands and wishful thinking on Wednesday." Inwardly, he added another snort. *:Not even close, Mother. I think I know how to take care of Felouen. This is something else entirely. I suspect Belinda Ciucci will be back. And after last night, she's going to be looking for my hide nailed to a board. Unfortunately, that might put an edge on her. Entertain her and her two goons for me, if you would. I don't want her getting close to the kid.:*

Dierdre chuckled. *:She still haunting your backtrail, is she? That I'll be happy to help you with.:*

Maclyn was out on the track when Belinda showed up. D.D. spotted her making nice to Brad Fennerman from the SpelCo team, batting her lashes and leaning forward just enough to give him a really clear view of her cleavage.

D.D. wrinkled her nose with disdain. The woman was a menace — and an embarrassment to both her species and her gender. She decided to watch, though, to see what Belinda's angle of attack would be.

It was only when she caught the girl's gaze skim past a point in her own pit area that she noticed a pale, hulking shape hovering in the shadows over Mac's thermos holding a little baggy full of something white and powdery. *Interesting. No doubt Mac's young admirer has a Borgia event planned here. Probably not true poison — I suspect they want darlin' Mac alive.* D.D. grinned and made sure the intruder thought she was far too involved in her work to notice him.

White powder went into the Gatorade. She saw a steady stream of it pour in — saw the man carefully twist the cap back on the thermos, then slink out along the row of stacked tires — saw him signal Belinda. The girl didn't acknowledge the signal, but she abruptly looked at her watch, gave a dramatic sigh, and wriggled away on her high, high heels.

She'll be around a while yet, D.D. figured. *She's got to have some plan for draggin' him out of here under everyone's noses. Och, this ought to be delightful.*

Mac did three more laps before he roared in.

:*She's been by,*: D.D. informed him without preamble. :*Such a sweet, innocent lass she is, too, I canna imagine why you're suspectin' her at-all. Be sure to drink all your Gatorade — your friends went to such trouble to drug it for you.*:

Mac smiled slyly. :*Did they now? Well, then —*: He went straight to his thermos, groaned, "God, it's so hot out there today, I could drink almost anything," and drained the contents in two long gulps.

:*Now, Mother, do I pretend that it affected me and bug the hell out of them when I disappear from their car — or do I just go about my business and drive them really nuts?*:

D.D. shrugged and grinned. :*Your call.*:

Tucked into a dark corner of the pits, Belinda waited. Mac had swallowed every blessed drop in his drugged drink — she tried to keep her glee in check, and failed — and Peterkin had dumped a whole twelve hundred milligrams of Seconal into the stuff just to make sure the jackass got enough to knock him out even if he only drank half. In fifteen to thirty minutes, according to Belinda's drug reference, Mac should start getting sleepy. In an hour or two, if they didn't get him to a doctor, he'd end up in a coma. In between that time, she needed to get him out of town.

She had her story worked out to perfection. The line would be that she and the boys were one off-duty EMT and two friends who just happened to be racing fans — they could take good care of their hero, the big racecar driver, and get him to the E.R. faster than an ambulance could hope to arrive. They would claim expertise and supplies on hand. There would not be anyone who would doubt that Mac Lynn was on his way to the hospital. There would be no interference from the airhead mechanic or any of the other crew. The first of several switch-cars was waiting outside. The plan was perfect. She didn't doubt that Mel had a doctor on his payroll somewhere — she wondered, however, how long she could leave Mac in a coma without Mel considering the package he received "damaged goods."

She entertained herself with images of what she was

going to do to Mac when he was helpless and in her care. She wondered briefly about the mechanics of castration. The idea appealed to her, and it wouldn't damage his TK ability any — would it? *With my luck, it would finish his talent off for good. After all, that's where men's brains are.* Maybe she should leave his balls alone and just cut off his head.

Feeling more cheerful, she glanced at her watch. With a shock, she realized that almost an hour had passed. Mac was still working — and there was no visible sign that the drugs were affecting him. She looked over at Peterkin and Stevens in their hiding place across the pits. Both shrugged.

She bit her lip and stared at the wide-awake driver. *He drank it, dammit! I know he did. I saw him with my own eyes.*

Could Peterkin or Stevens have double-crossed her? Yes, obviously — but why would they?

Unknown. However, the easy way to tell would be to try an equal dose of Seconal on them and see how it worked. If there was something wrong with the prescription she'd finagled out of the doc-in-a-box in LaJolla, Peterkin and Stevens would be fine. If they had double-crossed her, they would get what they deserved. Either way, she didn't lose anything.

She made a curt signal and slipped away from the pits. Her two stooges followed her out to the parking lot.

Felouen, in a cream silk blouse and tailored cashmere skirt and blazer, her hair pulled back in a classic chignon, appeared behind Maclyn and D.D., smiling wryly. "What charming friends you have. No wonder you'd rather spend your time here than in Underhill."

D.D., her face and overalls dirt-smudged, torque wrench in one gloved hand, smiled politely. "We all have our little hobbies, dear." Her smile widened as she watched Felouen wince away from the Cold Iron wrench. Mac wished he dared smile.

Instead he sighed. "Still overdressed, hey, Felouen? Why don't you go home and change into something more appropriate?"

She frowned. "I'm here on business. Dierdre, you've served your time on Council — I really do not need to speak with you. But I must speak with Maclyn for a moment."

D.D. nodded, and lost the smug smile. "I'll leave you two, then." Whistling a Killderry reel, the delicate mechanic moved back to her prized auto, leaving her son to fend for himself.

:*Thanks, Mother.*:

:*You know where I stand on this.*:

Mac shrugged and turned to glare at Felouen.

The elegant warrior gifted him with a frosty smile. "I need your company for a few moments, Maclyn. Please come Home with me; I'll show you what you need to see, and then, if you still feel that I am imposing needlessly on you, I will take back the Ring and the Council will decide on your standing within the Court."

Maclyn didn't quite grimace. "More signs and portents?"

Felouen didn't change her expression by so much as a twitch of her eyelid. "Please — just come with me. If you choose to scoff *after* you have seen what I have to show you, so be it."

Maclyn sighed. "You are so damned irritating — you and your bogeys and doom-crying." But he followed Felouen into the office, and through the temporary Gate she'd formed there.

They appeared at the border of Elfhame Outremer, where the edges of order collided with the infinite black Unformed, next to the Oracular Pool. The border, usually firmly fixed and still, billowed unsettlingly while Maclyn watched, pushing dark tentacles into the shield that walled the Ordered Land. The effect looked enough like something big trying to break through that Maclyn cringed when one tentacle brushed within a few inches of his thigh. More tentacles pressed suddenly from the same spot, as if they had become aware of his presence.

"What's doing that?" Mac asked, more disturbed than he cared to admit.

"There's nothing out there that I or anyone else can find," Felouen said. "That's all just unformed energy — and a feeling of fear and rage and hatred. It's been getting worse."

"I see where you might be worried," he admitted.

She shook her head. "Not yet, you don't. I'm afraid there's more. Look into the Oracular Pool."

Mac turned and studied the flat, deep blue sheet of water nestled in its shallow concave of mossy rock. After a moment, his reflection disappeared, replaced by darkness. For a long moment, nothing was visible in the Pool; then, with jerky, shambling movements, blood-spattered horrors streamed out of the Unformed — misbegotten nightmares with gape-jawed lopsided heads jammed neckless onto narrow shoulders, stick-like arms and legs terminated by terrible claws, sketchily formed bodies that bore no resemblance to anything Maclyn had ever seen, or ever heard of. They bared monstrous fangs and ran screaming after tall, blond, graceful runners that fell before them, bleeding from jagged, terrible wounds — and the Pool dimmed, and once again Maclyn looked at his own reflection.

He stood, speechless, staring into his own eyes.

"It's time to let go of the memories, Maclyn," Felouen whispered. "It's time to stop pretending that you'll find her again, and come back to your own kind. We need you here and now. *I* need you. Those humans do not, nor do you need anything of theirs."

"I still love her," Maclyn said, still staring stiffly into the Pool. *That isn't the only reason I stay, but it's a reason. I know you wouldn't understand the others.*

"She's dust these last two hundred years, Maclyn," Felouen said, reasonably, calling up a despair he'd begun to forget. "Sure and she loved you — 'twas your own folly you loved her, too. You were both young, but she grew old and died, and you're still young — and still searching for her among mortals who are destined to leave you just as she did."

Despair turned to anger, and he turned on the source of that anger. "Have you ever loved anyone, Felouen?" he snapped, restraining his wish to strike that impassive face. "Has anyone ever really gotten through to you?"

For a time, Maclyn got no answer. Finally the slender warrior responded, turning a face full of a loss that matched his own, speaking in a dull, lifeless whisper. "Yes. I've loved without hope for more than two hundred years — " Her voice cracked, and she fell silent.

Maclyn turned and studied her. She had her back to him; her shoulders were stiff and her spine was rigid and erect. His hands clenched and unclenched. "I'll hold on to the Ring, Felouen. I have something else I need to take care of now — and it may be important; I don't know yet, and I'm not taking on anything else until I do know. The fact is, I'm not sure what this thing I'm involved with means, or how much trouble it's going to entail for all of us. There *is* a child involved, and you know I can't turn my back on a child. I'm not promising to get involved in this problem here. But I won't say that I won't, either."

Felouen nodded but said nothing, and kept her back to him.

Maclyn Gated back to the garage, and the Gate closed off behind him.

In the office, he stared at the plain round wall clock that ticked off the seconds and minutes and hours that formed the limits of humans' lives, and he bit his lip. He could not keep himself from remembering that one of the elves that fell to the shambling things in the Oracular Pool's vision had been Felouen.

Amanda-Anne slipped off the bus and hurried down the lane, between the long lines of neatly painted fence, the gentle green, clovered swells of pastures, black and bay and glossy chestnut Arabs who stood head to tail, grazing peacefully and swatting flies from each other's faces. She detoured around the stables, moving carefully along a route that not only hid her presence from anyone working in the barns, but also from anyone who might be in the house or the yard. Sharon was still in primary and got home from school half an hour before she did; it was essential to keep close watch for her. Sharon would tell the Father and the Step-Mother where she went. Sharon was a big tattle-tale, but she couldn't help it. The Step-Mother made her that way.

The grass grew taller back of the stables. It edged a woodland dark and cool and quiet even in summer, with stands of pines marching in long, neat rows, bordered and filled in by scrub oak. Amanda-Anne moved across the beds of pine needles in near-silence, being sure she went a different way than the times before, consciously leaving no path. The pines merged with swamp on the right, full of snakes and cypress, with older hardwoods on the left — not first growth, but large, sturdy trees nonetheless: oak and magnolia and sycamore, ash and gum. Amanda-Anne went to the left, up a gentle incline.

At the top of the little hill sat an immense, ancient holly. Patches of pale green moss spotted its dappled silver-white bark, a few red berries still hung on in defiance of the season. The old tree's branches bent so low they touched the ground, and spiny evergreen leaves formed a screen so that the base of the tree became a fortress, well protected, with only one narrow entrance. That entrance, invisible except from a difficult approach through a stand of scrub oaks and blackberry canes, was formed from a branch that arched higher than the others and left a narrow gap that could be crawled through by a small, determined child.

Amanda-Anne, experienced in the delicate negotiation of thorn and thicket, got inside without snagging her school clothes or getting dirty. Once inside, she breathed deep and stood up straight. Amanda-Anne retreated to the background and Amanda-Abbey came out.

Things sparkled under the tree — decorations hung on bits of thread and string that decorated Amanda-Abbey's magpie nest. Tiny glass beads scavenged from an outgrown pair of Sharon's moccasins and a green carved glass bead saved from a broken necklace that was the only token she had of her real mother hung next to little round mirrors glued back-to-back, rescued from a favorite sweater that Daddy had ripped apart when he was mad

once. Bluejay feathers, bits of fragile shell brought back
from trips to the beach house at Ocean Isle, a broken, but
still pretty, stained glass suncatcher of a hummingbird, the
cut glass baubles from a pair of discarded earrings, one
rhinestone pin — all swayed and glittered and turned with
every scant breeze. There were comic books wrapped carefully in plastic and hidden in the tree's only reachable
knothole. A worn saddle blanket served as a rug.

Amanda-Abbey leaned against the tree trunk in her
secret home and watched her collection catch the light.
Amanda-Anne's fingers stroked the cool, almost smooth
bark, her ears drank in the hushed murmurs of safe, isolated, protected woods. No one would find her; no one
would hurt her — not while the tree guarded her.

The child closed her eyes and felt the warmth of the sun
on her face and studied the cozy speckled yellow glow of
the inside of her eyelids. A few birds chirped and fluttered;
squirrels raced along aerial throughways and chattered
pointed squirrel insults at each other.

The light that flickered through her closed lids grew
brighter — much, much brighter.

She opened her eyes.

Something was happening in front of her. Her green
carved bead was glowing with warm, glorious inner light. A
swirling mist began to curl out of it, emerald-green shot
through with flecks of gold bright as tiny suns. The mist
stretched and grew, and within it a form took shape — a
form wrapped in rich green-and-gold tapestries, taller
than anyone Amanda knew and handsome and smiling,
with eyes bright as new leaves, long blond hair held back by
a gold, jewel-studded circlet, and the neatest pointed ears
Amanda had ever imagined.

"Wow," Amanda-Abbey whispered. "That's really cool."

Amanda-Alice sensed something that required her
attention. From her white, pure castle, she stretched out
feelers, then, finding what she sought, withdrew them
again in shocked disgust. *It's magic. Magic is evil.*

*   *   *

The green man produced a shimmering wand and waved it in a circle in front of her. Sparkles of light scattered and danced in front of the child, weaving patterns in the warm spring air.

"Magic," the child whispered. Then, *There's no such thing as magic*, she thought. Amanda-Abbey was sure of this. *So this isn't a real elf. It's just imagination.*

Amanda-Anne kept quiet, watching, paying close attention, taking notes. Appearing out of thin air was a good trick. If she could learn it, she could hide from the Father. The magic lights were pretty, but they didn't look useful. Even so, Anne could sense power in them. Power was something she wanted.

The amazing man seemed to look right through the scrawny child in the tartan plaid skirt who stared at him — and then, silently as he had come, he folded into the scintillating fog from which he had emerged and was drawn back into the glowing bead. The light in the bead gleamed an instant longer, and then flickered and died.

"Gone," Amanda-Abbey said, wistfully. "I want him to come back." She thought. *If I can figure out why he came here, maybe I can bring him back.*

She inched over to where the bead hung. She blew on it once. Nothing happened. She walked around it, staring. It remained just a bead on a string. She pushed it once with a single index finger, and watched it swing in a few short arcs, then stop. Still, nothing happened. She closed her eyes and wished the magic back into the bead again, without luck. Tentatively, she reached out and broke off the fine strand of thread at the branch, then tied the makeshift bracelet around her wrist. Almost immediately, the single bead on its weathered thread sprang back into glowing life, and the mist spiraled forth once more.

The green-garbed man reappeared right in front of her and winked at her, then laughed soundlessly and hid behind the holly's trunk.

She walked around the tree, stooping under low

branches and her dangling decorations. He was gone.

A flash of green light from behind her alerted her, and she turned to see him again, this time on the outside of her tree-fortress. He waved, and she waved back and watched him, but she did not follow him beyond the protective circle of the tree's branches.

Stranger's voice broke into her thoughts, making herself known. *:Don't fear him, lass — 'tis good luck to meet one of the Fey folk.:*

:He isn't real, Stranger.:

There was gentle laughter in her head. *:Of course not, child. 'Tis still good luck.:*

Amanda-Abbey giggled at the apparent nonsense in that, and when the green-garbed elf vanished again, she rubbed the bead on her wrist, like a waif summoning a genie from a bottle.

The bead glowed again, and the elf reappeared in his gorgeous robes and glowing green cloud, but this time he settled cross-legged in front of the girl, floating an inch off the ground.

He smiled shyly.

Amanda-Abbey smiled back. "Can you talk?" she asked.

"Of course," he answered. "Can you?"

She giggled. "What a silly question. I just did."

"And so did I," he retorted, and winked.

"But you aren't real," she pointed out. "So I thought maybe you couldn't talk. Do you have a name?"

The elf pulled back his shoulders and in solemn tones, announced, "I am Prince Maclyn Arrydwyn, son of the fair Lady Dierdre Sherdeleth and of the Prince of Elfhame Outremer. I am rider of great metal steeds and horses of air and magic, guardian of the Twilight Lands, immortal walker among mortals." Maclyn bowed slightly from the waist. "And who are you?"

"Everyone calls me Amanda — but my name is really Abbey." Amanda-Abbey returned the bow gracefully.

The elf — Maclyn — nodded seriously. "I see. So then, shall I call you Amanda, as everyone else does, or shall I call you by your true name?"

The child grinned. "Call me by my true name. Nobody else but Stranger knows it."

"Very well." Once again he bowed, gracefully. "And who, by the way, is Stranger?"

Amanda-Abbey giggled. "If I knew that, she wouldn't be Stranger, now would she? Do you grant wishes, like in fairy tales?"

He considered her request. "Hmm. I do magic. Would that be good enough?"

"Magic isn't real," she insisted.

:Magic is wicked, wicked, wicked!: A voice screamed in Amanda-Abbey's head, but Amanda-Abbey refused to listen to it. Magic was just silliness and tricks with mirrors. Everyone knew that.

"Isn't it, now? Let me show you, and you be the judge." Maclyn touched the string that held the bead to Amanda's thin wrist, and it glowed softly. When he pulled his hand away, the bead was strung on a beautiful, intricate gold chain.

Yes-s-s! Amanda-Anne watched closely and whispered to herself. The elf pulled energy from somewhere, made it do things. *I can . . . almost . . . see how — but . . . whe-e-e-re?*

"Oh," Amanda-Abbey gasped. "How beautiful, and how wonderful. Do something else."

But Maclyn smiled and vanished.

"Wait!" Amanda-Abbey cried.

The elf reappeared in the woods a little way off. He beckoned, and the girl hurried out of her hiding place, heedless of the thorns and the briars. Her blouse snagged, and she got some pulls in her sweater, but the elf had vanished again and reappeared still farther off, and she couldn't take time to be worried about mere clothes.

She darted through the woods with the elf always appearing and disappearing in the dimming light just ahead of her. Suddenly Amanda-Abbey noticed that she was moving through fog that got thicker with every step she took, and that she didn't recognize anything about the part of the woods she was in. The trees were farther apart, and taller than any trees that she had ever seen, and incredibly beautiful. Leaves of silver and gold brushed against her and rang gently with every touch or puff of the faint breeze. Lights in soft greens and muted blues, gentle reds and bright yellows, flittered and danced through the branches high overhead, and the sound of a tiny waterfall somewhere nearby tinkled merrily in her ears. Voices whispered from above her, and at a distance, there were sounds of laughter, and dancing, and a jig played inhumanly fast by virtuoso performers.

:I know where this is,: Stranger told Amanda-Abbey with a satisfied voice.

Amanda-Abbey whispered, "Really? Where are we?" Suddenly she was no longer so certain that elves and magic were impossible. She was no longer certain of anything.

From right beside her, Maclyn said, "Welcome to Elfhame Outremer, Abbey. This is my home."

"It's beautiful," the child whispered, in a voice full of wonder.

Evil, evil, evil, thought Amanda-Alice. *Only the devil does magic; that's what the Sunday-school teacher said. This green man is the devil, and this place must be hell. I'm telling Father about this. He will know how to punish the devil — I know he will.*

Amanda-Abbey felt a vague sensation of disquiet. It seemed as if part of her mind wanted to rebel, to run away from the lovely haven in which she found herself.

"Yes, it is beautiful," Maclyn answered. "I thought a special girl like you would be able to appreciate such a magical place."

Amanda-Abbey raised her eyebrows. "Why me?"

He spread his hands wide. "Because of the magic you do," he said, and his words had a ring of sincerity about them.

She stared at him, puzzled. "I don't do magic. Magic isn't real."

He shook his head. "Wasn't it magic that kept the racecar

from hurting anyone at the track the other day? Wasn't it
magic that sent all the erasers and papers in your classroom
flying?"

Amanda-Abbey giggled; where had he gotten these
stories? Racecars? Erasers? What was he talking about? She
didn't remember anything like that. "I don't know what
you mean."

Amanda-Anne, satisfied that she had figured out the
elf's magic tricks, looked up and noticed the darkened,
twilight sky. Fear gripped her. The Father would be furious
— the Step-Mother would tell him that she was late. She
shoved her way to the front, grabbed control of the body,
and stood, rigid and trembling. Her eyes met those of the
elf, and she shivered. "Home!" she wailed, suddenly terrified. *Late! I'm . . . late! Home!* She used the information
she'd garnered from watching the elf to draw in the earth-
energy that pulsed through Elfhame Outremer, and
promptly removed herself to the safety of the holly tree
hide-out.

Amanda-Abbey was back in control and back in familiar
surroundings. She didn't even flinch. "Wow!" she
whispered, crawling out of her nest in the muted sunlight
of early afternoon, still impelled by a powerful urge to get
home, "What a neat dream." She studiously avoided noticing the green bead on the gold filigreed chain that hugged
her wrist, or the dirt and snagged threads on her school
clothes.

Amanda-Anne took over control as Amanda walked
through the woods. She trotted home by a different route,
alert for watchers of any kind.

Cethlenn had been aware of the elf's presence, but she
had been unable to wrest control of the body away from the
children long enough to beg for help. Now, hurrying back
to the child's terrible home, she swore softly and wondered
what she could do to save her child host.

*   *   *

Lianne drove up the long, winding lane past carefully tended fences and manicured pastures, well-maintained, picturesque old barns, and a riding ring set up for trail training, with jumps and bridges and barrels. Over to her right, a young man put one lean gray filly through her paces on a lunge line, while two hawk-faced men in tweed jackets and caps watched and commented.

She noted the exquisitely kept ornamental gardens, the flawless landscaping, the elegant half-timbered home that bespoke good breeding and old money — and she shook her head in bewilderment. This Eden was more than she could ever hope to aspire to. In her whole life, she could never hope to live so well, to have so much. Where was the worm that gnawed away at Amanda? And how could it survive in such a place?

She parked her little yellow VW bug to one side of the house, clambered out of the car, and smoothed her skirt nervously. She felt suddenly shabby and plain — and on very shaky ground.

Stomach in knots, she strode up the walk and rang the bell. After a long wait, she heard the click of heels in the hall. The door swung open noiselessly, and Lianne pasted a confident smile on her face.

Merryl Kendrick gave her a cool, polite nod and said, "Won't you come in, Miss McCormick? Amanda is upstairs doing her homework — I can call her if you would like."

"Not just yet, please," Lianne answered, and found herself following Merryl through a long, perfectly kept maze of glossy mahogany halls and decorator-perfect rooms. She studied Mrs. Kendrick's back and winced. Merryl Kendrick would have been a good six inches taller than Lianne in flats. In heels, the other woman towered over her. Amanda's step-mother was casually dressed, the elegance understated — but every article of clothing spoke of more money than Lianne could put into her wardrobe in an entire year. She shouldn't let all that money have a psychological effect on her, Lianne knew, and knew at the same time that *should* was a meaningless word. All that money, all that power, did have an effect on her. It weakened her position, it weakened her credibility. As much as she would like to pretend otherwise, she was not an equal among peers in this world. And she would have to act as if she were, for Amanda's sake. Because whatever was wrong with Amanda was wrong in spite of all these evident advantages.

"Tea?" Merryl asked.

"Thank you." Lianne took the seat the other woman indicated and glanced around the sun-room. It seemed to her that she had seen it in a *Better Homes and Gardens* spread. With its Mexican tile floor, hand-adzed timber-framed beams, and walls of glass looking out over a scenic view of the estate and a lovely, wild patch of woods, it was breathtaking.

And sterile.

There were no family pictures, no knickknacks, no personal touches whatsoever to mar the carefully conceived vision of the designer. As she ran her memory back over what she had seen of the rest of the house, she realized it was all the same. The house was lovely, but it looked as if no one lived there, or ever had.

That's a middle-class prejudice, she told herself. *Only the middle class insists that a bit of disorder is healthy.*

Merryl returned and placed a heavy pottery teapot and a matching cup in front of Lianne.

"Thank you." The young teacher poured herself a cup of tea and sipped at it gratefully.

"Of course." Merryl Kendrick nodded gracefully. "Andrew will be home any time. In the meantime, we can drink our tea, or you can fill me in on what you perceive to be the problem."

What I perceive *to be the problem. That's nicely put. The problem is no doubt going to be my* perception, *and not the problem. Ah, well, face it right out.*

She decided on a frontal assault. "To the best of your knowledge, Mrs. Kendrick, is there any history of mental illness in Amanda's family?"

The other woman's lips curled in a faint smile over her own cup of tea, and one eyebrow raised slightly. She leaned back in the peach-and-mint wing-backed chair and crossed her legs. After a moment, she chuckled. "Well, that's certainly getting to the point." Merryl Kendrick sipped slowly at her tea. "Actually, yes — there is. Funny you should ask. Andrew's first wife had a long history of psychological problems — paranoia, delusions, depression, psychoses. She was hospitalized — Andrew obtained a divorce, but made sure she was well taken care of until her death."

At Lianne's startled expression, Amanda's step-mother nodded slowly.

"You see, she died about two years ago. Suicide. I understand these problems are sometimes . . . " Merryl picked delicately around the word " . . . hereditary."

Lianne held her breath, closed her eyes, and let it out again, slowly. "Sometimes," she agreed.

"Dana's parents — Amanda's natural grandparents — aren't quite normal, either. We've done the best we could for Amanda — limited her contacts with them ever since her mother's death. . . . " Merryl Kendrick seemed to be actually relishing this. "It doesn't seem to be helping, does it, Miss McCormick?"

Lianne blinked, choosing her words with care. "Amanda is having serious problems in school this year, behavioral as well as academic. I'm not the only teacher that has noticed this. It's in her records, if you'd care to see them." *There. So much for "my perception."* "I can't say that her problems stem from her mother, or her mother's death, or heredity, or anything else. All I can say is that she needs help, and I don't know that I am able to give her the help she needs."

There were thundering feet on a stairway, and Amanda burst into the room. Her sweet, blue-eyed face lit up when she saw her teacher, and she ran over and hugged her vigorously. "I didn't know you were coming over tonight, Miss McCormick. Don't you like my house?" The child turned to face her step-mother, still smiling. "I got all of my homework finished, Mother. May I go outside for a while?"

"Not now, Amanda," Merryl said. "I'm expecting your father home any minute."

"As well you should, darling," Andrew Kendrick said from the doorway, slipping a cigarette pack into his crisp breast-pocket. "I'm sorry I'm late — one of my clients was quite distraught and needed a bit of extra time."

Lianne had been watching Amanda, bemused by the girl's cheerful countenance and normal manner — so she didn't miss the change. Amanda's face turned from her step-mother to her father, and a series of unreadable expressions flashed across her features. Her mouth fell slightly open, giving her a dull, witless look.

And her pale, pale green eyes stared at the man in the doorway with a cross between canny hatred and stupefied terror.

The flesh stood up on Lianne's arms, and chills raced up and down her spine.

There was a crash from another room. Andrew and Merryl looked at each other, and Merryl cleared her throat. "You evidently let one of the cats in with you again, Andrew."

His eyes focused on his child. "No doubt," he agreed. "Amanda, I see you've been playing in your school clothes again. You've soiled them and ruined the fabric. Please go upstairs and change into your stable clothes, then go clean your pony's stall. I'll be out to check on your work when your mother and I have finished speaking with your teacher."

"Yes-s-s . . . Father," the child said. Her voice grated; low, animal-like. She was as much a different child as if Amanda had been picked up and physically replaced.

Lianne felt her pulse begin to race. *Wrong,* her mind screamed at her. *This is wrong! It's weird! It's awful!* It took every bit of control for her to keep her seat, to keep smiling while Andrew Kendrick crossed the room, took a seat next to his wife, and smiled at her and said, "Well, ladies, what solutions have you reached?"

His voice was cheerful, his eyes bright and kind and concerned — so why did every nerve in Lianne's body insist that some invisible force was dragging monstrous talons across a giant blackboard?

"Miss McCormick deduced Dana's problem from Amanda's classroom behavior." Merryl looked into her husband's face. Her body posture and gestures indicated sincere concern. "She *says* she isn't the only teacher to have seen problems with Amanda."

Her husband dropped his eyes. "Dana," he said, and Lianne would have sworn she could hear real anguish in those two labored syllables. Her instincts told her that, no matter what she saw, or thought she saw, Andrew Kendrick was a phony. Merryl was the perfect foil for him, and the two of them had snowed her from the beginning — would have kept her convinced that the problem was in other directions. But Lianne knew kids. She'd been well acquainted with thousands of them in her eight years of teaching, and she'd seen that unguarded expression of Amanda's before. The look in her eyes, the little girl's actions, the abrupt change in her attitude — those things had given Lianne a name for the sick feeling that weighted her down and dragged on her every breath.

Child abuse.

She needed to get out of the house, get help — but first, she needed one more tiny reassurance that she'd really seen what she thought she'd seen.

"I think Mrs. Kendrick and I have stumbled across the problem. And I think I may have thought of a solution." She had to have parental permission for this first step. Unless the child revealed something on her own, or there were physical evidences, there wasn't anything that could be done that Andrew Kendrick with his money and influences couldn't counter. "I can't promise anything, but I'd like your permission anyway. I'd like for Amanda to be seen by one of our counselors. I think there are a great many things troubling her, probably related to her mother's death, and I think that having some time with the counselor, starting on Monday, would give her a chance to talk those problems out. It would at least give us an idea of what we're dealing with."

Lianne waited. She watched concern crawl across Merryl's features like a spider, watched Andrew's eyes harden, watched them glance at each other — *we have to keep our secret* expressions that gave the teacher her answer.

"I don't think so, Miss McCormick," Andrew said, still smiling — but with the smile artfully condescending. "I think you may be right, that psychological help would be in order for Amanda — but I don't think that a school counselor who works for peanuts and sees his, ah, *clients* in the sardine-can atmosphere of public education would be of much use. While we want Amanda to be mainstreamed in a public school, and not sequestered away in a private and privileged academy, I don't think my open-mindedness runs to welfare-quality counselors. I'm sure we can find someone much more suitable through our contacts."

Bingo, Lianne thought. *And dollars to donuts she'll never go to see anyone, because they can't take a chance of Amanda talking to anyone.* Outwardly, though, Lianne kept her expression neutral. "Of course, Mr. Kendrick. I wasn't suggesting that our counselor could provide therapy — only that she might be able to give us a direction in which to look for the problem. However, I'm sure that *your* choice of counselor will be even better. Just let me know when you come up with someone."

The teacher stood. "I've taken enough of your time. Thank you for talking with me. I think we've come up with some positive avenues to explore, and I'm sure Amanda will benefit."

Merryl and Andrew walked her back through the maze to the front door and showed her out, making small talk all the while.

And when I get home, you creeps, I'm calling Social Services. And we'll see if you get away with blaming your kid's behavior on your ex-wife to them.

● Chapter Six

"You didn't ask to be excused," her step-mother called from the dining room.

"Amanda Jannine Kendrick, get back to this table at once!" yelled Daddy.

Amanda-Abbey, halfway up the steps to her room and running headlong, reluctantly turned and plodded back to the dining room.

"Where were you going in such a hurry, young lady?" her daddy asked her.

He glared at her from the head of the table. Her step-mother, lingering over hot tea and a wafer-thin slice of pound cake, shook her head with annoyance. Sharon sat next to her real mother, looking secretly pleased that Amanda was in trouble again.

Amanda-Abbey looked from one adult to the other, and her fingers twisted against each other. She took a deep breath.

"May-I-please-be-excused-I-have-to-go-clean-the-pony 's-stall," she said in a rush.

Her step-mother nodded curtly. "Wear your coveralls. I don't want those clothes ruined any more than they are."

Her daddy just smiled, playing with his lighter, tumbling it end-over-end between two fingers.

"I won't get them dirty. Promise."

Amanda-Anne took over, hurling the child's scrawny body out of the dining room and up the stairs two at a time and into her room at breakneck speed. She grabbed worn coveralls from their spot behind the hamper and darted into the closet, closing the door behind her. Trembling and breathing hard, she flung on the coveralls in the darkness, then crept to the door. She listened, soft ear pressed against the cool, white wood. On the other side, there was nothing but silence.

Silence, Amanda-Anne knew, was very bad.

There were two sets of steps, one on either end of the hall. Both had landings halfway, and closets at the top and the bottom —

Amanda-Anne closed her eyes and *thought*. No answers came to her, no pictures. And every minute she wasted gave the Father one more minute —

She bolted out her door and to the left, heading for the front stairs, which were farthest from the dining room, praying that she had guessed right.

Past the top closet and down the stairs — safe.

Around the landing — still no sign of Him.

Down the rest of the stairs — only a little further to go.

Past the partly-open door of the closet at the bottom of the stairs — and an arm shot out and grabbed her and dragged her into the closet.

"Boo," the Father whispered. He laughed softly in the darkness of the closet, and his hands pinned her against the smothering piles of coats. "You're lucky I'm not a monster."

Amanda-Anne struggled to get away from him. The Father tightened his grip until her arms hurt. "Monsters wait in the dark for bad girls, Amanda. Getchells and mor-rowaries, slinketts and fulges. Big, drooly monsters with bloody red teeth and sharp claws and white eyes that glow. Slimy, slippery shapeless things that slither and drip burn-ing goo and won't even leave your bones behind for anyone to find you, *Amanda*. And it's almost dark outside, *Amanda*. They'll be there any minute. Hungry monsters. When you go outside to clean your pony's stable, be sure the monsters don't get you."

Someone picked up after the seventh ring. A masculine voice said, "Hello?"

Lianne closed her eyes and leaned her head against the wall next to her phone. Getting through to the govern-ment agency after-hours had been a morass of answering machines, people who were home but not on call, and people who were on call but not at home. The hospital emergency department's Cumberland County Social

Services' after-hours emergency phone numbers were one week out of date. The person she'd finally reached, after an hour of trying, had given her four numbers that *might* put her in touch with the person she needed. She had tried three of the numbers, and they hadn't. This was her last hope, and she clenched the receiver in her hand until her knuckles went white. The real live voice on the other end of the line wasn't getting out of this until Amanda's rescue was guaranteed.

"Hello," she said. "This is Lianne McCormick — I'm a teacher at Loyd E. Auman Middle School."

"Don Kroczwski. What can I do for you?"

Lianne took a deep breath. "I suspect that one of my students is being abused. I want her family checked out."

"What kind of evidence do you have of the suspected abuse?" The man on the other end of the line sounded tired; bone-tired and heartsick.

Lianne's voice went tense on her. "Evidence?"

"Do you have reason to expect imminent danger to life or limb?" he asked — or rather, recited.

This wasn't what she had expected. "For example — ?"

Kroczwski sighed deeply. "For example, does the kid say either of his or her parents said they were going to kill him or her? She or he have any old cigarette burn scars, rope burns, broken bones, bruises on the face or body, brothers or sisters who have died or been hospitalized in the last few weeks — anything like that?"

Lianne's stomach contracted at his list of horrors. "*She*. Her name is Amanda Kendrick. And no. Nothing like that."

The voice on the other end of the line sighed. "You got any reason to think the kid will be dead tomorrow if I don't go over there tonight?"

The teacher bit her lip. "No," she said softly. "She shows psychological damage — personality problems — but nothing that makes me think her parents will murder her."

"Okay. That's a problem, Ms. McCormick. I know that you know your students. I understand that you probably can tell when something is wrong, and I trust your judgment and your instincts, but I have to have something tangible. Bruises, something the kid told you, something I can show a judge. I can't walk up to her parents' house and tell them they are being investigated for child abuse because their kid's teacher has a bad feeling."

"But I know something is wrong."

"Ms. McCormick, I believe you, but let me give you an idea of how wrong things can be. I have a neighborhood outbreak of syphilis among three- to nine-year-olds that I'm investigating; I just got a call from the Cape Fear Emergency Room about a little girl whose mother dumped hot oil on her because she wouldn't be quiet. I have a five-month-old baby with broken arms and broken legs that the mother's boyfriend threw across the room and whose four brothers and sisters have to be gotten out of that situation. I have a dead kid who showed up in the morgue whose body hasn't been claimed. I have a list of call-in's from concerned neighbors and teachers and relatives as long as my arm with complaints that may or may not end up with a bunch of little bodies in little body-bags if I don't take care of them yesterday — and it's already almost tomorrow. Child abuse is the year's biggest growth industry. I understand *wrong* — I really do. You give me something to go on, and I'll be out there to check on your kid in a heartbeat. Okay?"

Lianne's throat tightened. "Okay," she whispered. "If I can find anything, I'll call you back."

The voice sounded even wearier. "Day or night."

Tears started down Lianne's cheeks. "Okay. Thanks." She hung up the phone. Images of infants with arms and legs in plaster casts, little children with burns given to them by the people they wanted to love, with bruises and cuts and old scars and new wounds — kids who'd been shaken, beaten, screamed at, starved, tortured, raped, neglected — those images swirled around in front of her eyes, blurred by tears. And all those children began to have Amanda's face.

Amanda's pony was not kept in the main barn with the pedigreed Arabians Merryl Kendrick raised. It had its own quarters — a neat little doll-house version of the bigger barns, one Andrew Kendrick had ordered to be built for Amanda when she was five. It sat next to the main stables but did not connect with it in any way. Its cheerful, red-painted sides and white trim gleamed in the twilight; warm, yellow light spilled out of the opened top half of the front Dutch door. The neat, cedar-chip path crunched under Amanda-Alice's feet as she scurried down to finish cleaning the pony's stall.

"Lazy slut," Amanda-Alice muttered under her breath. "You should have cleaned the barn when you got home from school. Then he wouldn't have made you come down here now. Stupid, wicked, worthless tramp — out chasing evil elves when you should have been working. You deserve to be punished. You deserve it."

Amanda-Anne didn't have time for guilt. In the near-darkness, things moved. Shambling phantasms pressed close, deformed grotesqueries chittered in her ear, and — "Come to us, Amanda — we're hungry," unseen things whispered from the shadows, while their awful stomachs growled.

No! Amanda-Anne thought, and lurched into a gallop.

Out of the corner of her eye, she saw that the darkness gained. The horrors were almost upon her — she could feel their breath on the back of her neck —

"No!" she shrieked, and heard them laugh.

And then somehow she was through the barn door, intact and uneaten, and the door was closed behind her. The heavy wooden bolt dropped into its brackets, and Amanda-Anne was safe from the monsters.

In the stall, she picked up the pitchfork and began loading manure and straw into the little wheelbarrow. Her pony, Fudge, poked his head into the barn from the pasture entrance and whickered.

"Vile, filthy beast," Amanda-Alice snarled. "You leave these messes to get us in trouble, don't you? You don't deserve supper."

She ignored the bin of sweet feed in the corner, avoided looking at the little Shetland, and continued mucking the stall with short, sharp, angry jabs.

*   *   *

Andrew Kendrick paced the living room floor. Merryl curled in one of the overstuffed chairs, contracts spread on the floor around her.

The man punched one closed fist into the palm of his other hand. "That child is a disgrace. When I was a child, my behavior was excellent. I never had a visit from one of my teachers. And for that woman to suggest school psychiatrists — "

"Counselors," Merryl corrected. "Only counselors. Public schools don't keep psychiatrists on staff."

"It doesn't matter. How dare that child cause me this sort of humiliation? How dare she?" A scowl carved itself deeper into Andrew's face, and his complexion flushed a hotter, uglier red. "She obviously hasn't had enough discipline," he growled.

"Jesus," Merryl muttered. "Leave the kid alone for once."

Andrew turned his anger on her. "Stay out of it, you bitch! She's my child, my responsibility. As you keep reminding me. It's up to me to make sure that she grows up to be a useful adult. She won't if you ruin her with your lax attitude. Look at Sharon. She's getting old enough that she needs firm discipline, and you let her run wild. She'll be worthless when she grows up."

Merryl's voice went flat and dangerous. "Leave Sharon alone."

Andrew stiffened and glared at his wife. "We'll see," he told her. He walked heavily toward the outside door. "I'm going to make sure Amanda does a good job on that stall. She's going to clean it until it's done right, even if she's out there all night — she's going to learn that I'm in charge around here. And she's going to learn that she has to do what I expect." He stopped and stared at his wife with cold, ugly rage. "That's something you could stand to remember, too, Merryl."

He stalked out, slamming the door behind him.

Belinda sat cross-legged on the bed in Peterkin's shoddy

hotel room, two decks of cards spread in front of her on the cheap polyester bedspread. "Black three on the red four . . . okay, and that opens up the red jack to the black queen . . . hah! Moves that to *there* — yes!" She briskly restacked, completed, and removed piles of cards.

A rustle from the foot of the bed distracted her. She looked over from her game of Napoleon's solitaire to the floor, where Stevens and Peterkin were turning blue. "Oh — hi, guys." Her voice was bright and cheerful. "I thought you were dead already. Would you mind hurrying it up a little? I have plans for the evening." She grinned — perky, sexy, and charming, obviously a woman having a good time — and turned back to her cards.

She played a few more moments and sighed with minor annoyance. "Dammit! I almost won that one." She riffled the cards together, staring at her two thugs.

"Seems my prescription was okay, huh? At least it's working pretty well on you two. Well, fellas, I don't know why you wanted to double-cross me, but I guess we've proven that wasn't a good idea." She smiled at the dying men and began laying out the cards again. "Jerks."

She spread out a deck of poker cards and began another game of solitaire, latex-gloved hands shuffling with some difficulty.

Peterkin made strangling noises, then quit breathing. Froth foamed out of his mouth. Belinda smiled and flipped her hair back out of her face.

"That's good — that's very good. You did that nicely, Joe. One down, one to go, Fred-ol'-buddy. Let's see if you die well, too."

Fred Stevens lay on the dingy green carpet, sucking air like a beached fish for over half an hour after his partner threw in the towel. When his breathing ceased, Belinda folded up her cards, took both men's wallets, changed the ID's and other important papers, and dumped the wallets back on the dresser. Then she walked down to her car. When she came back, she carried a large shopping bag. She emptied the bag onto the bed and strewed her purchases around the room: a small packet of crack cocaine and the attendant drug paraphernalia, a white feather boa and a large, skimpy leopard-spotted negligee, a queen-sized pair of fishnet hose and patent leather shoes with six-inch spike heels — sized 12EE — a black leather men's bikini, battered handcuffs, and a well-worn bullwhip.

Then she cut the clothing off of both men with a pair of heavy-duty bandage scissors, the kind EMT's and paramedics used, rolled the clothes into a ball and stuffed them into her now-empty bag. She rolled Stevens onto Peterkin in the best "compromising position" she could manage, considering he was the smaller of the two corpses and weighed more than twice what she did. But police training came in handy. When she had them more or less posed, she put the shoes on Peterkin's feet and the handcuffs around his wrists, and draped the feather boa once around Steven's neck. Then she stood, breathing hard, and chuckled softly.

"That ought to amuse the investigators for a while," she whispered, and grinned cheerfully. She looked at her watch. *Time to see what my race-driver is doing. I need to be able to collect him tomorrow.*

The front doors of Amanda's barn rattled. The child was busy shoveling manure into the wheelbarrow and didn't notice the noise the first time. The second time, however, she stopped and cocked her head to one side, listening. The noise did not recur a third time, and after waiting a moment, she nodded with satisfaction and resumed her cleaning.

She didn't realize the Father had come into the barn through the pasture door until she heard the top Dutch doors click, and the heavy thud as he carefully dropped the door-bar into the brackets.

Inside the pony's stall, all the Amandas stiffened. Cethlenn noticed the change in their attitudes and froze, listening.

A series of light clicks followed — the sound of a key in a lock, the sound of light furniture being moved, the clink of metal.

Suddenly, Cethlenn realized that Amanda-Alice and Amanda-Abbey were gone. The only one who remained with her was Amanda-Anne.

Thud, thud, thud — the Father's heavy steps left the storage room, walked slowly closer —

Then the Father was right there, standing in the doorway of the stall, completely filling it. Cethlenn watched with Amanda-Anne, staring up and up and up at the huge form of the man.

"The stall looks very dirty, Amanda," the Father said. "What a very lazy, nasty, dirty little girl you have been." He smiled, his lips pulled back across his teeth so that they gleamed in the light of the naked, dangling light bulb.

Inside their head, Amanda-Anne made a mewling sound that died before it reached their lips. Cethlenn shuddered.

"I ought to make you lick the floor clean," the Father said. "Would you like that?"

Knives and whips and ropes and sharp, hot things danced in Amanda-Anne's head, and dull red rage blurred the child's vision. Cethlenn was forced back by the spreading fury, and fear clutched at her.

The Father's smile got bigger, and he took a step toward them. "I said," he whispered, *"would you like that?"*

Oh, gods, just answer him, child, Cethlenn thought.

"No," Amanda-Anne said.

"No," the Father mimicked, his voice a chilling falsetto. "Oh, no. You wouldn't like that. But you're a dirty little girl, aren't you, Amanda?"

The child stared at him, silent.

"I said, you're a dirty little girl, *aren't you?*"

"Yes," Amanda-Anne said.

"And we know what dirty little girls really like, don't we, Amanda?"

Amanda-Anne wrapped her frail arms around herself and stared up at the Father in silent terror. Cethlenn felt sick.

"Don't we, Amanda?"

"Yes," Amanda-Anne whispered.

"I can't hear you."

"Yes," Amanda-Anne said.

"Dirty little girls like to make their Daddy happy, don't they?"

Amanda-Anne's throat tightened, and she nodded.

"Good," said the Father. "Then come here. I know what you like, don't I, you dirty little girl? Tell me you like it."

Amanda-Anne walked forward, moving like a creature drugged.

"Say, 'I like it, Daddy.'"

The child was silent.

The Father grabbed her and shook her. "Say, 'I like it, Daddy.'"

"I like it . . . D-D-Daddy," Amanda-Anne croaked.

"I know you do, you little whore." He picked the limp child up and carried her into the storage room.

Oh, gods, Amanda, I'm sorry — I can't stay here — I can't watch this! Cethlenn shrieked, and vanished.

Lianne sat at her little kitchen table and dried her eyes. She had done what she could for Amanda for the time being. It was Friday night — she couldn't do anything else about the child until the next morning at the earliest — so she needed to get herself under control.

I've been under an awful lot of stress lately, she thought. *It isn't like me to cry like this. There have just been too many unexplained things happening in the last few days.*

She leaned back in her chair. *I've taken care of this now, though. Things will get back to normal. I know they will.*

Her eye strayed to the kitchen sink — to a rainbow sparkle and a flash of white metal.

And the feeling of otherworldness returned. She got up and walked over to the sink, and picked up the crystal carafe that Mac had produced — seemingly out of thin air — for their delightful breakfast in bed. She hefted it in both hands, studying the flawless faceting of the crystal and the incredible quality. One eye closed, she gnawed on her lip as she appraised it, and a whole number followed by a surprising quantity of zeros ticked off in her brain. She fingered the silver serving tray, and then picked it up and studied it. It was *real* silver, and solid, too, not plate — and Lianne pondered the odds of finding such exquisitely crafted silver with nary a maker's mark on it. She picked up a cherry pit and studied it as if it were something likely to burn her fingers. She tilted her head, and her eyebrows furrowed, and then, with a thoughtful expression on her face, she turned out the kitchen light, went into the living room and plopped down on her couch and stared off into nothingness.

"When you have eliminated the impossible, whatever is left — no matter how improbable — is the truth," she said softly to no one.

Amanda-Anne lay in the bathtub, staring up at the ceiling. Steam swirled around her, and a thick layer of sweet-scented bubbles pressed against her skin like fat kittens. Amanda was oblivious to the warmth and the sweetness and the light. Her mouth still tasted of oily cotton, her wrists and ankles still stung and chafed, and she *hurt*.

And in her mind's eye, nothing existed but the storage room, with its little cot and its dim light, and its supply of ropes and rags, and its awful locking door.

She rubbed absently at her wrists — and her fingers brushed across her real mother's bead, still strung on the lovely gold chain.

And the image of the elf pouring himself out of the bead in a stream of green mist came to her. She sat up in the tub and stared at the bead. Let Abbey pretend that the elf wasn't real. Let Alice complain that he was evil. And let that goody-two-shoes Stranger think that the elf would help them. They didn't know about Anne, but Anne knew about them. And she knew better than to believe their silliness. Amanda-Anne knew that Alice was stupid, that Abbey was wrong, and that Stranger meant well but was looking for help in the wrong direction; the sweet-faced elf was too soft and too gentle to do what was needed. But he had shown her the trick of his magic without meaning to. Without even knowing that he had done so. Her eyes narrowed as she considered the possibilities of the scene that played itself out in her mind, and softly, the child began to laugh.

Don't want . . . the elf, she thought. *Just . . . the smoke. And the wind.*

She stared at the bead, forcing unfamiliar patterns into the rhythm of her will, and slowly her green eyes glowed.

For a moment, nothing changed.

Then a flicker of light came to life in the heart of the bead — not the pure green light of earlier in the day, but a throbbing, pulsing, angry red light. Without words, Amanda-Anne spoke to the red light and carefully explained to it exactly what she wanted. Then she waited.

The bead grew brighter, and the bathroom was suffused with the ugly, bloody red glow. Then heavy smoke poured out of the bead and hung over the bathtub. It swirled around the child, threatening, menacing.

Amanda-Anne's eyes grew lighter, her pupils constricted to pencil-points of darkness in the centers of the white-green, and as if it had suddenly seen something to fear, the red cloud recoiled. With a kind of reluctance, it crawled in a thin line up the wall and out of the bathroom through a slight gap in the window high overhead.

Amanda-Anne held her breath as the last traces vanished from the bathroom. She listened, every muscle tense and straining to catch the slightest sound in the still night air.

Then, from the direction of her barn, there came a very satisfying crash, followed by thunderous clattering and the scream of a full-sized hurricane compressed into a tiny box. The noise and the destruction raged for as long as Amanda-Anne could maintain her concentration.

When she reached the point of exhaustion, she released the storm she had summoned, sending it back to wherever it had come from. Then, a diamond-hard smile on her tiny face, Amanda-Anne settled back into the bath-water and relinquished her place to Amanda-Abbey, who actually liked stupid, childish bubble-baths.

*   *   *

Mac left the track late and with too much on his mind. There was Felouen, with her strange and completely unexpected intimation of unrequited love, and the Oracular Pool, with its images of terror and disaster. There was the sensation of intangible evil at the border of the Unformed World, and the turbulence of the shield. There were his problems with the Seleighe High Court, and with that low and vile woman who had tried to poison him. There was beautiful, ephemeral Lianne, whom he suspected was falling in love with him. And last, but certainly not least, there was the child, Amanda, who had followed him into Underhill without flinching, and who had then promptly returned to her own world on her own power and of her own accord — in spite of the fact that there was no way she should have been able to do that. Maclyn was tense, and unsettled, and somewhat scattered.

And so, for the first time, he failed to notice a sleek brown Ford Thunderbird that maintained its position four cars behind him all the way from the street beside the racetrack parking lot to Lianne's apartment.

Lianne answered the door with an unnervingly perceptive expression in her eyes. "Hi," she said, gave him a brusque kiss, and immediately asked, "Where's the movie?"

"The movie?"

"The *movie*. C'mon, Mac — just this morning you said, and I quote, 'I'll pick up the movie tonight. I think I'll get *The Man With One Red Shoe*, since we didn't watch it last night.' After breakfast, and before we headed out the door. Remember?"

"Of course I remember," said Maclyn, who remembered no such thing.

"So where's the movie? You forgot it, didn't you?"

"I just forgot to bring it in with me. It's in the car. I didn't forget to rent it."

Like hell, I didn't forget, he thought while he trudged back to Rhellen. *What in Oberon's name was I thinking this morning? — I burned breakfast, I fixed something else, we rolled around on the bed awhile, we took a shower, we ran out the door — I still don't remember anything about a movie. At least,* he mused, *I promised one I've already seen. Be a bitch to pull it out of thin air if I hadn't.*

He opened Rhellen's door, concentrating hard, and a VCR cassette in a clear plastic cover appeared on the seat. He picked it up and returned to the apartment.

Lianne's expression as he handed her the tape was decidedly weird. He started to ask her what was wrong, then thought better of it.

She walked over to the VCR without a word, and pushed the eject button. A movie popped out. She opened the plastic case of the tape he'd provided for her, and turned her back to him.

She stood silently for a long moment, while Mac grew more and more tense. "Jesus, that's a neat trick," she said finally, and turned around. "Who are you — really?"

Maclyn hedged. "Why do you ask?"

She smiled. "You were very close with this. Your label is almost perfect, except you're missing the copyright date, and there's only a gray box where the small print would be — if I hadn't had an original here to compare, I bet I never would have noticed the difference."

He nodded, maintaining a calm exterior while his brain raced wildly. In her hands she held two copies of *The Man With One Red Shoe.* One of them had been obtained from a video rental store. The other — well, it *hadn't.* He felt the tempo of his pulse increase. "Maybe the copy I picked up was pirated."

"Oh, I'm sure of it," she said with a wry smile. "Out of thin-fucking-air. We never said anything about movies this morning, Mac. I only said that to see what you would do — because there is something very odd about things that have happened in my life since you showed up. It strikes me as uncanny, for example, that neither of us said a word about you picking up this movie, and yet, when I asked you about it, you happened to have it in your car. Wherever this came from, Mac Lynn, it wasn't a rental place."

He stalled for time, trying to think, but unable to make his mind work. This wasn't the way it was supposed to happen — it wasn't supposed to happen at all, actually. "I see.

So I was correct in thinking I hadn't said anything about movies in our rush this morning? How interesting. You see, I have an imperfect memory for minutae. It usually isn't a problem."

Her arms were crossed in front of her chest. "Perhaps more of a problem than you realize. There is, of course, the silver tray — real silver, of incredible quality, with no maker's mark. I don't buy it. There are the out-of-season cherries. And of course we can't forget your willingness to believe that papers were indeed flying around my classroom of their own accord." She took a step toward him. "You are very interesting, Mac Lynn. You are charming, you are handsome, and you are great in bed. But you are not what you seem to be. Now I want an answer on this, and I want it right now. Who — or what — are you?"

Finally, she was getting somewhere.

From her position behind the shrubs outside of the apartment window, Belinda stared through the slatted mini-blinds at Mac Lynn and his girlfriend. She recognized the girl — had seen her before, in connection with Mac Lynn. She frowned, determined to remember where she had seen that face, and suddenly she recalled the girl striding across a parking lot —

Bingo! She's one of the teachers at Loyd E. Auman. I followed him there that one time — and that explains why he was over there in the first place. That's where his piece of ass works.

Belinda's face lit up with a beatific smile. His girlfriend could give him to her. Just grab her and stash her someplace, then tell him his girlfriend was dead unless he did exactly what she said, and have him follow instructions that would deliver him voluntarily to Mel's doorstep.

Voila, she thought, *a nice paycheck for me and a well-earned vacation that doesn't involve chasing spookies — preferably someplace far away, with mountains and ocean and deferential waiters.*

Cozumel, she decided, *or maybe Greece.*

They appeared to be arguing. That was good from Belinda's point of view. *He might stomp out, leaving her alone tonight. In which case, I'll just knock on the door and grab her when she answers it, thinking he's come back to apologize. If he stays the night, of course, I'll just pick Little Miss Teacher sometime tomorrow — or after school Monday.*

That seemed like a good, sound, workable plan, and much less complicated than trying to drug him again. It also meant she didn't need to sit in the damp shrubbery catching a cold. Belinda stood up and headed back to her new rental car. Stake-outs were much more pleasant when accompanied by Perrier, Bach, and croissants.

She moved into the area of darker shadow that lay between the teacher's apartment and the parking lot, and noticed two disturbing things as she did. The first was that Mac's car wasn't in the parking lot anymore.

The second was that what had seemed, out of the corner of her eye, to be laundry hanging out between the apartments, wasn't. It was a big, light-colored horse.

And no sooner had she identified the horse for what it was than it had her jacket between its teeth, and she was flailing through the air to land on the beast's back. She reached for her gun, the creature bucked, she grabbed the beast's mane to keep from hitting the ground —

And things got a little hazy from there.

Belinda decided pretty promptly that she must have fallen off the horse anyway and knocked herself silly and wandered around a bit. It was the only explanation that made any sense. Otherwise, she would have had to admit that the horse had turned into a car that drove itself, and that it had driven her onto the street in front of the old abandoned Fox Drive-In, and dumped her by the side of the road before cruising off into the night. It would have implied that the car had *chosen* to abandon her where hookers plied their trade and G.I.'s and out-of-town businessmen and restless locals went looking for action.

It would have implied that the fight Belinda got into with the pimp and the big buxom blonde and the transvestite and the two horny guys in the red Camaro was the fault of a goddamned '57 Chevy.

And no matter how spooky things got, Belinda wasn't ready to admit that.

*   *   *

Mac faced Lianne, and swallowed hard. Humans weren't anywhere near as gullible as they'd once been — at least some of them weren't, he decided. The room felt uncomfortably warm.

"I'm a racecar driver," he said with an ingenuous smile.

Lianne nodded, her expression grave. "A racecar driver is the least of what you are, Mac Lynn. I've always made it a point to date within my species before this, but I think I've not even managed to live up to that one simple rule this time. Have I?"

Maclyn stood, studying her, thinking fast.

Lianne saw the evasion coming and headed it off. "Mac, I'm to the point where I won't believe anything but the truth. And please give me credit for being able to tell the truth from a lie — remember, I deal with ten-year-olds on a daily basis." She smiled wryly. "Besides, I doubt that the truth is going to be anywhere near as ludicrous as what I've suspected."

"Wanna bet?" Mac muttered.

Lianne heard him. "No," she said. "But lay out your cards anyway and let me take a look."

"Okay." He took a deep breath and studied her. "You've heard of Faerie, of course."

"One of my best friends is one."

"Not that kind of fairy."

"I was being facetious. I've heard of Faerie. Up to this point I've found its purported existence likely to be the product of hallucination and overdoses of wheat-smut, but I'm a logical soul. Presented with sufficient proof, I'll believe just about anything. I suppose you're going to tell me you're the elf-king of Fairyland or something."

Mac's right eyebrow arched up. "I'm an elf. Not 'or something.' And I'm fairly high up in the line of succession, but I'm not the king, or even the prince."

Lianne sighed and said to whatever higher powers inhabited the ceiling, "I'm taking this rather well, aren't I?" She studied Mac for a long, silent moment, then said, "Granted I've already seen enough to convince me that you aren't normal — but would it be too much to ask for some proof that you are what you say you are? Seeing that we've been sleeping together and all?"

Maclyn gave her a very Gallic shrug — and his human seeming faded away. He presented himself to her in his full elvish glory, from the gold circlet on his head to the sweeping white folds of his ermine cloak, to the rich white-on-white textures of his silk-embroidered tunic and velvet leggings. He showed her himself, pointed ears, pale green slit-pupiled eyes, and inhuman smile.

"My lady," he said, inclining his head with courtly grace. "Is this sufficient proof?"

Lianne sat down sharply on the coffee table. Her eyes went round and she whistled softly. "I'll be damned," she whispered. "An elf. A damned sexy one."

She cocked her head to one side and studied him closely. "A question, then."

"I'll answer it if I can."

"What are you doing hanging around me?"

And isn't that just the question? Maclyn thought. *I wish to hell I knew the answer.*

• Chapter Seven

Andrew McCormick heard the first sounds from the barn just as he was locking up the house for the night. He ran to the window and stared out at the hellish red glow in the dark that held the stable area. It was clearly coming from the pony barn. At first his mind couldn't recognize the disaster for what it was — but then he shook himself out of his paralysis and reacted.

"Fire!" he shouted to Merryl. "There's a fire down in the pony barn! Call the fire department, *now!*"

He pulled on boots and sprinted out the back door. If anything, it looked and sounded worse now that he was outside. He could barely hear the terrified whinnies of the pony above the roar that came from within the shed.

He goaded himself into a run, heading down to the barn, wondering if he would be able to get into the secret storeroom and thinking of the money that was going up in smoke in there. Thinking of all the — special things — that were going to be destroyed, and that were going to be even more difficult to procure the second time than they had been when he'd first obtained them.

Merryl passed him on the path, flew to the right and to her own barn, full of pedigreed mares and foals, her prize stud, her champion filly — the objects of her real passion and her love. Andrew heard her throwing open her barn doors, chasing the horses out into the pasture and away from the impending disaster. He clenched his fingers into tight fists, outraged at her care for the animals and her indifference toward him.

He watched her working frantically, momentarily distracted from his goal. *She has a lot of nerve, ignoring me. Amanda's mother learned what happens to people who ignore me. I've been too easy on Merryl.* He fumed with smoldering rage as he raced towards the pony barn, wondering if he could save anything without Merryl seeing it. He wasn't really thinking about the barn, nor about the fire — not, at least, until was he nearly at the structure.

Realization that there was something very strange going on stopped him like a stone wall. *I don't smell any smoke,* he thought. It sounded like there was a war going on down there, and it certainly *looked* as if the place was being over-run by the fires of hell — wind that screamed like a damned and tortured thing, the crash and thud of heavy objects hitting against the walls, the screech of nails ripping loose from beams — and the terrible red light still gleamed through cracks, but there were no tongues of flame visible and no smoke to smell.

What the hell — ? he wondered.

A piece of board blew past him, and some unidentifiable bit of shrapnel grazed his cheek — and Andrew watched dumbfounded as gaps appeared, as if something or some-one from inside battered away at the barn. The night air was thick with a sense of rage, of hatred so dense and pal-pable he could feel it brushing against his chilled skin like damp, drowned hands. His heart pounded with fear that was not even his own, and his mouth went dry and his breath came fast in spite of his struggles to control his emo-tions. He found himself backing away from the barn, and found that he could not stop himself, could not make him-self walk back toward it.

From behind him, he heard the wail of sirens and the squeal of tires turning into the lane. The fire engines' flash-ing red lights joined the peculiar illumination that came from the barn — the night pulsed red. *Blood,* he thought, clutching his arms around himself. *The world is bleeding.*

The firemen were unrolling their hoses, shouting to each other, pointing out their target. Merryl was still loos-ing horses out into the field.

Andrew saw none of it; instead, he had been inadver-tently thrown back to his own childhood.

He saw the little beagle puppy he'd "bought" when he was eleven from the kid down the road — bought with marbles and a brand-new baseball glove and a brand-new football. The puppy he'd smuggled home and made a wonderful soft bed for and hidden under the house because his father had said, "No dogs," but he'd wanted it so bad —

His puppy, laid out on a board, belly up; its little muzzle wired shut, its eyes wide and staring, its paws nailed into place. And his dad, furious, shouting at him, "Now you'll know to listen to me, won't you, you little bastard! Next time you disobey me, this will be you!" And the knife, in his father's hand, slitting the little beagle's white belly open, and the pup's eyes rolling in terror and pain —

And the blood pulsing red and redder around his father's fine doctor hands, pulsing like the lights from the fire engines — and again he tasted the anguish and the fear —

And the red glow in the barn just — went away.

Thick, suffocating silence crowded in to fill the void and darkness. The firemen paused, and stared. The horrible noises that had been coming from inside had stopped, abruptly, almost as if a switch had been flipped. The terrible feeling of rage and fear made the same abrupt departure.

Then sounds rushed back and revived the night: the chirping of crickets and the whinnies and stompings of the horses out in pasture, the stamp and crunch of one fireman's boots as he walked, flashlight in hand, down to the barn, and pulled the battered and sagging door open.

And his voice, awestruck as he aimed his flashlight into the dark recesses of the structure — "Je-e-e-e-ZUS, Johnnie, get a load of this!"

The rippling motion of the border had lulled her into a near-trance. Felouen sat, her back pressed against the smooth rock base of the Oracular Pool, staring into the nothingness, and she worried. Maclyn might come around. He might help against whatever was coming. Then again, enchanted by his other interests, he might leave her to fight and die alone.

There had been more to the visions of the Oracular Pool than the one brief glimpse it had shown Maclyn. War was coming — a long and savage battle with the outnumbered elvish forces lined up against hordes of Unseleighe unlike anything the Kin had ever seen before. Her friends would fall, and she would fight on, uselessly, would herself be gravely wounded, would flee and be captured, would suffer at the hands of the unstoppable things from the Unformed. And only then would she die. She had seen her own death. It was not a good one.

She had seen another vision as well, an alternate future in the inscrutable reflections in the Pool. Maclyn would stand at her side, with the battle raging as before — but the enemy would be fewer and weaker, the tide of battle would turn in the Kin's favor, and she would live. So she sat and pondered, staring out into the non-place on the other side of the border with loathing.

Felouen sensed the change before she saw it.

A presence born of fear and rage and hatred swirled into being in the Void, reached out and clawed at her from that nothing-world. It sent her to her feet, recoiling from the tentacles that reached with sudden intent directly for her.

From the Nothing, flickers of blood-red light began to glow.

" . . . so you see, she was human, and I loved her, and when she died, I thought that everything about me that had mattered had died, too," Mac said. He sat on one side of Lianne's couch, again wearing his human seeming. "Everything about her was so brief and so painfully fleeting, and the harder I tried to stop time, to hold her life in my hands and keep her with me, the faster I saw the years tear her into shreds. She died nearly two hundred years ago, but there are still times when the thought crosses my mind that if I went back to Tellekirk, I'd find her there."

He locked his hands together, and he stared at his shoes. "In you, I see that same frightening beauty, that same — life — that burns so hot and so fast. I cannot stay away from you. And I find myself longing for your brief, blazing beauty, and wondering how you can burn your life so fast."

Lianne pursed her lips and blew a soft sigh through them. She got up and walked over to one of the bookcases that lined the walls of her bedroom, and perused the shelves. Finally, with a nod, she pulled down a deep green leather volume and flipped through the pages.

"We've done some thinking about that ourselves," she said, and looked down at the page she'd chosen. "Here —" she pointed, and read aloud.

"For a man cannot lose either the past or the future: for what a man has not, how can anyone take from him? These two things then thou must bear in mind: the one, that all things from eternity are of like forms and come round in a circle, and that it makes no difference whether a man shall see the same things during a hundred years or two hundred, or an infinite time; and the second, that the longest liver and he who die soonest lose just the same."

She paused to let the quote sink it. "Marcus Aurelius — a Roman philosopher and leader from way before *your* time — said that, and I suspect he's right. Even though I'll live — at most — a hundred years, and you'll live God-only-knows how long, we were both born, we will both live the span of our days, and we will both die. I mean, you *will* die *eventually*, won't you?"

"It's been rumored," Mac said, a faint hint of the beginning of a smile at the corner of his mouth.

She gave him a real smile. "Don't pity us humans, then. Time runs at a different pace for you and me, but my life will be as full as yours. It will just happen faster. It won't seem to me that I got cheated — I'm doing things with my life that matter to me and to other people. I'm teaching children, and to me, that is an important and meaningful job. I have friends who care about me, and a family that loves me, and I'm doing what I can to make the world a better place. And as for your long-gone love, I guarantee you that if she *lived* her life, and could see where her presence made a difference, she didn't feel cheated either."

Lianne sat back on the bed, put the book down beside her, and pulled her knees up to her chest so she could wrap her arms around them. Now was the time for a little noble self-sacrifice, and it made the smile she had given him fade away entirely. "I think you're doing yourself an injustice hanging around humans, though, Maclyn." She did her best to hide the tears that brimmed in her eyes; she didn't *want* to give him up. She really didn't. But it was for his own good. "Look for someone who exists in your own timeframe — who won't get old and die between two blinks of those gorgeous eyes of yours."

She did her best to look brave and happy — but all she could manage was a smile as transparent and empty as a soap bubble on the wind.

Maclyn listened to her words and tried to find some hope or comfort in them. She looked so beautiful. Mac's gaze roamed from the curve of her ankle to the full swell of her breast, to the plainly-written pain in her eyes, and words surged from his lips before he could stop them. "You don't have to get old so fast. I could take you into Elfhame Outremer, Lianne. There, you would live at the pace of *my* years." He faltered, and further brilliant suggestions died in his throat.

What in all the hells of the Unformed Planes had he said that for? Did he love her? Really, truly *love* her — as an equal and a companion with whom he could sustain interest for some significant span of his own long life? Was he infatuated with her humanness? Or was he — even less noble — burning with desire to fix the long-dead past?

An unbidden memory of Allison — fair, dainty, dark-eyed Allison, two hundred years dust — choked his throat and stopped his tongue. To Allison he had said those same words, had begged her to let him stop time for her. Allison had refused him, had told him about her God and her Church and her Bible, about God's demand that only he had the right to count the measure of a man's life. At first he had argued with her — fruitlessly, and then he had stayed at her side, using what time she let him have, while she grew old quickly. Allison had not lived her life fully. She had spent her days railing at an unjust Deity who gave life unequally. He had watched her turn bitter, as she wrinkled and fattened and her tongue went acid. Suffered, as she studied him secretly from beneath her lashes, hoping some sign of age would scar him. Mourned, as eventually she hated him because it never did. Yet, often enough, even in the old woman, the young girl who loved an elven prince could be found. And in those moments, Maclyn had felt his heart ripped to tatters.

He remembered Allison while he stared at Lianne, wondering at his motives, trying to guess what she hid inside her shielded thoughts.

"That's a hell of an offer," the young teacher finally breathed. "What's the catch?"

He shook his head. "I'm not certain. For Allison, it was her religion. She didn't think God would forgive her for thwarting death."

Lianne grinned, a devilish, teeth-bared grimace that was half humor and half wry self-deprecation. "Not my problem." The strange smile vanished, and the woman rested both hands on his thigh and stared into his eyes. "Let me think about ramifications — especially what this would mean to the two of us. And give me a while, okay? I've got a kid in school who's in trouble, and that's left me with a lot on my mind."

Mac heard only the first part of what she said and nodded. Then her last statement she'd made caught his attention. "What do you mean, 'a kid in trouble'? You haven't said anything about it to me before, have you?"

She frowned a moment. "Sort of. Do you remember Amanda — the little girl from the racetrack who wouldn't get out of the way of the explosion?" She looked at him, her eyes uncertain.

Only too well. "I remember her."

She grimaced. "Yeah. Probably you do. That was pretty bad. Well, I went to talk to her parents today. Something is very wrong there — I suspect abuse. I called Social Services and reported it, but the guy I talked to said that, since I don't have any hard evidence, he can't go out there to check on her."

Chills ran along Maclyn's spine. "Abuse?" he asked in a voice gone ominously flat.

Lianne must have heard the change in his tone and laughed without any humor. "That's how I feel, too. Every time I see something like this, I want to kill the people responsible. God, I wish I could *prove* she was being abused, to get that guy out there — but I'm on such thin ice. I've never seen any bruises, she's never *said* anything to me about it — although *that's* normal for abuse cases, actually — she doesn't miss a lot of school. It's just, her personality isn't right. Not right at all."

What would happen, Mac wondered, if he told Lianne everything he knew about Amanda? Would she be able to believe in Amanda's magic?

Why the hell not? he decided. *She believed I was an elf easily enough.*

"I'm willing to bet Amanda is the reason everything in your classroom came to life on you the other day," he told her. "I know for a fact she is the reason nobody got seriously hurt at the racetrack."

Lianne gave him a long, clinical look. "What — exactly — do you mean by that?"

He licked his lips. "She does magic — controls inanimate objects. Makes them move."

"Tele — um — telekinesis?" Lianne asked. "Moving things with her mind?"

He nodded. "I think that's the term."

Lianne's expression grew harried. "Aw, c'*mon*," she snarled. "I bought you as an elf. You don't want me to believe in that, too! Next you'll be insisting on the validity of Bigfoot, flying saucers, and the effectiveness of the two-party political system."

Mac snorted. "No, I won't. I'll just want you to believe in your student. She's special — but she *is* hiding something. She wouldn't admit she could do magic."

"Mac," Lianne replied as if she were talking to one of her students, " . . . maybe that's because she can't."

"Sensible, logical theory — except that I saw her," he persisted stubbornly. "I watched — and sensed — her work her magic."

"*Ergo sum ergo,* " Lianne muttered. "It is, therefore it is."

"Don't get grouchy. While she was looking at Keith's car, she kept it from exploding. As soon as you pulled her out of the way, it blew — but she was able to see it again at that point, and she controlled almost all of the shrapnel. *I saw her.* More than that, I sensed the flow of power."

Lianne still looked skeptical, but Mac sensed she was weakening. "So what you're saying is that if I had left her alone, the car wouldn't have blown up at all?"

Mac shrugged. "Who knows? I am saying that the SERRA drivers were lucky she was watching the race that day. Keith owes his life to her."

"Great. Fine. She's a helpful little brownie. So why did she send everything in my classroom flying?" Lianne set her jaw stubbornly.

Mac sighed. "I don't know. There are a lot of things about her that I don't know. But I think we can find some answers. Tomorrow — well, I'm racing tomorrow — why don't you come out and watch me? You can keep my mom company in the pits — "

Lianne forgot about the child entirely. "Your *mom?*" she said, her jaw dropping.

"Oh . . . " He smiled weakly. "I forgot to mention that, didn't I? Uh — D.D.'s my mother."

Silence for a moment, while Lianne absorbed the information. Then — "She looks five years younger than *me*," Lianne wailed.

Mac deemed it time to get the discussion back to more serious subjects — or, at least, subjects he could do something about. Getting D.D. to change her apparent age was not one of them. "Don't let it bother you. She looks at *least* that much younger than me. Anyway, after the race, we can all three go out to Amanda's house and poke around a little. We'll see if we can find out anything. D.D.'s been concerned, too, ever since the day of the accident."

Lianne flung herself backward and down onto the bed and slapped herself dramatically on the forehead. "Gosh, what a brilliant idea! It becomes obvious why elves rule the world. Why didn't *I* think of that? I mean, why would Andrew or Merryl Kendrick ever notice two racecar driving elves and their daughter's schoolteacher tromping around on their posted, private property, looking for magical mystery clues like something out of Scooby Doo — on a Saturday, no less, when they're probably home all day?" She scrunched her eyes closed in mock-agony.

Mac formed his will into a familiar shape and draped that shape around himself. "I don't see the problem," he said.

"You're kidding." Lianne opened her eyes to stare at him, then looked all around the room. She sat up, and her expression became more and more puzzled. "Mac?"

"I'm right here," he said from the spot he'd occupied since the moment they both sat down.

"I don't see you."

He took the little "I'm not here" spell — pirated from a human mage named Tannim — off of himself, and smiled at her as her eyes went round. "And I don't see the problem."

She sighed and flopped back again. "Maybe there isn't one."

Mel Tanbridge waited three hours beyond his absolute cut-off time, and still neither of the two calls he was expecting came. With growing disbelief, he acknowledged that they might never come.

He was more than willing to accept the fact that either Stevens or Peterkin could be bought off, if enough sweeteners were added. He was not willing to admit that Belinda could buy them *both* off — not on the money he was paying her, and certainly not at the same time. He knew they weren't the brightest guys in the world, but he couldn't imagine them making the sort of world-class bumble that would alert her that they were *both* reporting to him on her activities, even if she realized that one of them was.

And they didn't realize that he was paying each of them the same bonus to report on the other.

So why hadn't at least one of them called in?

The answer was fairly obvious.

The three of them had captured Belinda's race-driver TK, and he was even better than anyone had hoped for. Belinda had seen dollar signs and had convinced Stevens and Peterkin that they could make a lot more money if they joined forces with her and kept their catch to sell to the highest bidder, instead of handing him over to the man who rightfully owned him.

Mel considered that scenario from all angles. It was the only one that made sense. Considering the healthy mix of bribes, threats and terrorism he'd used on Belinda's two assistants, they should have stayed loyal under almost any circumstances. Therefore, Belinda must have convinced them she was coming into an unbelievable fortune to get them to double-cross him. For that matter, knowing what he had on her, she had to have convinced herself of the same thing, in order to forget how important it was for her to remain loyal.

None of them had stayed loyal. Therefore, Mac Lynn was the biggest telekinetic find ever — and Mel was more determined than ever to own him.

Belinda had only had two days to hide her trail and her booty. However, with both Peterkin and Stevens in her camp, all three of them knew how many bases he'd had covered, and how little he'd trusted any of them. They would be more than careful, they'd be paranoid.

He glared out his smoked glass window at the night and watched the ghost breakers run up the beach, the white of sea-foam all that was visible in the clouded dark. He planned for ten minutes, and when he was satisfied, he dialed a number from memory. Moments later came a drowsy hello.

"This is Tanbridge. Set things up to fly to North Carolina tonight. I'm going to Fayetteville. I'll meet you on the strip in two hours."

He hung up, then glanced around the office. Not much lying around that he'd need to take with him. As a matter of fact, there were only two things in the office that he was going to need. The TK meter.

And the gun.

*   *   *

Andrew forced himself to walk to the barn. He stood next to the fireman with the flashlight and stared in at the devastation. It was all-encompassing and complete — but his first feeling, on looking in at the destruction, was one of relief. Nothing inside of the barn was recognizable anymore — including his large collection of special items. The pony's stall was ripped to shreds, and the pony had evidently kicked through the back doors to escape; he was out at the far side of the pasture cropping grass. *Lucky for him*, Andrew reflected. *He wouldn't have survived whatever did that*.

Whatever it was, it hadn't been a fire. Vandals? Only if they had come equipped with a log chipper and managed to run every item in the barn, including tack, feed barrels and hardware, through it in a matter of minutes.

The presence of other people around him, talking to him, gradually seeped into his awareness. He turned and found that while he'd been lost in his shocked reverie, two sheriff's deputies and the sheriff himself had arrived.

"Can you think of anyone who would want to do this to you, Mr. Kendrick?" the sheriff asked.

Andrew thought for a moment. "Dozens of them," he said. "Merryl won't sell her horses to just anyone — maybe someone who didn't measure up to her standards wanted to see if he could force her to lower them. For that matter, I've helped my clients acquire a number of profitable enterprises through hostile takeovers in past years. I've made enemies on the way. However, I can't think of any of them who would be able to *do* . . . that." He nodded back toward the barn.

One of the deputies said, "We've seen it, sir. It's pretty unbelievable. I don't know how they could have been so destructive."

The other deputy said, "The firemen said they saw red light coming from inside the building, but that it went out suddenly."

Merryl spoke up. "We all saw it. Apparently, whoever did this wanted us to think it was a fire. It looked like one."

Andrew agreed. "It was a very convincing special effect. The whole setup was very realistic, and very frightening — I'm not ashamed to admit I was terrified. However," he yawned "it's over now, and it's late, and we all will have plenty of time in the morning to hash over the details of this. I don't think there is anything more we can do tonight. So if you don't mind, I'd rather deal with it tomorrow."

"That's reasonable, sir," the sheriff said, "It's a clear night. Any tire tracks or other evidence will still be available in the morning. We'll be out first thing. Until then, I'll be glad to leave someone here overnight to keep an eye on things."

"Not necessary," Andrew said dryly. "There's an old line about horses and unlocked barn doors that seems appropriate right now — "

The sheriff shrugged. "That's up to you. If you see or hear anything out of place, though, let us know right away."

Andrew nodded shortly. "I'll do that."

Watching them leave, Merryl said, "I think you should have let them post a guard."

He sneered. "Do me a favor and don't waste your time on thinking. It isn't what you're best at. I had reasons for not wanting them here."

The knowing look she turned on him made him suddenly uneasy. "I'll bet. What were you hiding in there?"

He reacted to his unease by issuing threats. "Don't push your luck, Merryl. Don't ever forget, you can be replaced."

From her bedroom window, Amanda-Anne watched the police cars leave, and watched the Father and the Step-Mother trudge slowly toward the house. She smiled. The Father's secret place was gone. Now he couldn't hurt her anymore. He would never hurt her again.

She felt the power of her own dark magic coursing through her and savored the sweet taste of revenge. No one, *no one*, would ever hurt her again.

Under the covers, Lianne tossed and turned. Mac's

warmth next to her was, at the moment, more disturbing than comforting. She almost wished that he hadn't spent the night. She would have liked to sit up, to drink hot tea and stare off into space knowing that she wouldn't have to try to explain to him why she wanted to. She would have liked to pace — but stalking around the apartment would wake him up. She listened to him breathe, slow and steady, deep in sleep, and tried not to resent his presence.

He's not human, she thought. *He's very wonderful, but he's not human. No matter how well we get along, there are things we can never see in the same way. His mother is hundreds of years old, he says. She's still young — he says she'll live until she gets tired of it. My mom and dad are nearing sixty, and might have another twenty.*

What about children? Could we have them? What would they be? She winced, rolled over and buried her head under her pillow. *That's unpleasant, thinking of your own possible children as "what," not "who." More than likely, from my understanding of genetics, there could be no children.*

He loved children — he said the elvenkind intervened in the lives of battered and abused human children because they rarely had children of their own, and they valued them so. He would want to have them someday, wouldn't he?

He said that time in Underhill was changeable, that a day there could be a minute here, or a day, or a year, or a hundred years. Lianne tried to imagine dropping into Elfhame Outremer for a quick visit with the in-laws, and returning to find everyone she'd ever known dead a hundred years ago. Like the old fairy tales. She shuddered and tried to think of something else.

When I divorced Jim, I thought I could save myself from stupid mistakes. I promised myself, "I'll never fall for someone who's wrong for me again — I'll never let myself get hurt like this again." I was so goddamned sure that I knew something finally, dammit! I thought I'd learned my lesson, that I was only going to go out with men who wouldn't lie to me, who could be trusted. Now look at me. I'm in love with the wrong person again.

That was the worst of it — never mind that he wasn't

human, never mind that he would live damn near forever
and she would be gone in no time, never mind all her
doubts and her confusion. The cold, bare fact that scared
her the most was that one: she really did love him.

She burrowed deeper into the covers and pressed her
back against his. It was going to be a very long night.

Mel Tanbridge surveyed his hotel room with distaste. At
four-thirty a.m., anything should have looked good, but
the fact was, he expected quality. No, dammit, he expected
the best. The best he could do on no notice wasn't good
enough — he hadn't been able to get the penthouse in
Fayetteville's Prince Charles hotel, just a suite — and while
it was a nice old hotel, it wasn't a nice old five-star hotel. He
hadn't stooped to anything below five-star accommoda-
tions in years. The service was good and the suite was clean
and spacious, with furniture of excellent taste, but the
room didn't have a private jacuzzi — and there wasn't a
sauna in the entire hotel. He hadn't had time to check out
the amenities in the gym — or even if there was a gym —
but he doubted that they would be of the technical level or
variety he was used to. After all, this was a military town.
He doubted that a military town would have accommoda-
tions anywhere that he would find acceptable. That was
just the way they were.

There would be a gym somewhere, he decided. And he
would find it in the next day or two. After all, he needed to
stay in shape. A healthy body equaled a healthy mind —
and he had the healthiest. It was his competitive edge.

That edge was important, especially in light of his
subordinates' betrayal. Their trail was probably a full two
days cold. All the more reason, he decided, not to start
down it without sufficient sleep. A healthy body, and all
that. . . . He left a wake-up call at the front desk for noon,
climbed into bed, and was instantly asleep.

Belinda checked herself out of the Cape Fear Emergency
Department and slipped into the waiting cab. She gave the
driver the address to the school teacher's apartment

complex, then sank into the back seat, thinking ugly thoughts. The stitches in her scalp throbbed, and knowledge of what the wound looked like hurt her just as much. She'd borrowed a mirror from one of the nurses to check out the damage to her hair, and had been appalled. A patch the size of a monk's tonsure had been shaved around the slash that guy in the mini-skirt and fishnet hose had made when he brained her with a handy beer bottle. She wore a huge bandage of white gauze and bulky pads that covered the shaved spot for the time being, but when it came off, she was going to be left with an awful mess. She'd been eight the last time she'd had short hair.

Mac Lynn and Mac Lynn's girlfriend, and Mac Lynn's car crew, and anyone else Belinda could think of were going to pay for her hair.

Soon.

However, the anesthetic was wearing off, and she felt dizzy and sick and tense. She needed to find a drugstore to get her pain medicine and her antibiotic prescriptions filled, and then, she had to admit, it would be really nice to take a day off. Maybe even two. The idea of lying in a soft bed taking drugs and not getting kidnapped by horse-cars, beaned by drag-queens, or scalped by bored young doctors was an idea she found appealing right now.

Maybe she could consider her time off the clock as workman's comp. Mel could basically go screw himself if he didn't agree. After all, he was taking it easy out in his beach complex in California. What was he going to do about it?

Her immediate future more or less settled, she closed her eyes and tried her best to ignore the breaking day. *The motel and bed,* she thought. *And no more stinking adventures, not for a while.*

A few drops of rain spattered on the cab's windshield, mixing the fine coating of dust into thoroughly opaque mud. Belinda looked at the sky, startled. It had been clear the last time she'd seen the sky. The clouds must have moved in really fast.

She smiled. Rain was a good omen for her. People didn't look around when it rained. They ran to their cars and got straight in. They didn't sightsee. She considered revising her morning plans. She'd take a free ally any day.

Mac's car was parked where she remembered it. The cabbie pulled up where she directed him, but suddenly Belinda found that she didn't want to get out of the cab. *I'm almost convinced that damned Chevy is watching for me. Which is ridiculous, except that I don't have any other way to explain what happened last night.*

I have to pick up my car, though. I need it.

The cabbie gave her an impatient look. "You're on the clock, ya' know," he drawled. "No big deal for me — but you're gonna find it right expensive. I ain't gonna sit here all mornin' for free."

"Yeah, right," she answered. The rain was no longer just a few splashes on the windshield. Now it slashed down in sheets, whipped across the front of the car by gusts of wind. "Drive closer to that brown Thunderbird." She prayed that nothing had happened to the latest of her rental cars. She couldn't afford to experience too much more of Mac Lynn's version of fun and excitement.

The cabbie rolled his eyes, but moved his vehicle so that it formed a screen in front of the T-Bird's driver-side door.

Belinda paid him off, then jumped out of the cab. Once in the T-Bird, she locked the doors. She ignored the cabbie's raised eyebrow. He hadn't had her night. He wouldn't understand.

Belinda sat in the dark safety of her car, watched the raindrops sheeting down her windshield, and listened to their soothing thrumming on the roof. Outside, the world lightened in tiny increments, gray on gray on black, revealing shrubs heavy with water and pines swaying in the driving rain.

The monotonous brick-box apartments were laid out in a grid, with parking lots with separate entries at each square. She moved to the last parking slot three rows away from the teacher's place, cut off the motor, and watched. She was comfortably hidden behind cars parked in the lines ahead of her, and scattered tall Carolina pines — trees that reminded her of the California palms with their trunks that soared thirty feet before the first limb sprouted. Her position gave her a clear view of anyone leaving the apartment.

It couldn't have been more than fifteen or twenty minutes before Mac and his little teacher came flying out of the apartment and dove into the Chevy.

A good, hard rain will never fail you. I knew it. Belinda smiled and, when they pulled out, followed them at a discreet distance.

At the Fayetteville International Speedway, the first fat drops of rain hissed onto the tarmac. More followed, faster and faster, and the patterns made by the first drops were obliterated by water that fell in steady streams, and then sheets, and then in waterfalls that whipped sideways in the steadily increasing wind.

Dierdre, already at the track and doing final pre-race work on the Victor, sighed with resignation at the roaring deluge outside of the garage. The weather station had hinted at this — but torrential rains weren't supposed to be part of the picture until Sunday. She closed her eyes and concentrated on feeling the shifts of air currents and pressure cells. After an extended time, she opened her eyes again, and surveyed the rich red Victor with dismay. *Surprise,* she thought. *We're going to have a whole weekend off, whilst the be-damned weather craps on our heads. Oh, joy. 'Tis not a natural rain, either. This has been pulled in by heavy magic somewhere nearby.*

Time to call her son, the slug, and tell him he wasn't going to have to get out of bed.

She headed to the phone, then stopped. She could have sworn that she'd just heard Rhellen's familiar rumble from the parking lot — even over the rain. She queried her own elvensteed, who was leaning against the back wall keeping dry.

Afallonn rumbled her surprised affirmation.

D.D. looked up at the wall clock, just to make sure time hadn't slipped past without her noticing. It was six-oh-four in the morning, a good three hours before Mac's earliest voluntary wake-up hour. *Will miracles never cease?* she wondered.

Maclyn swung into the garage, a sheepish grin on his face. Behind him was his schoolteacher girlfriend, and the expression on *her* face was patently unreadable.

"Well, Mac, shouldn't surprise me that the first day you show up early for a race is the day they're sure to cancel the whole show."

"Hi, Mom," he said.

:Mom?: D.D. was sure her jaw had hit the floor. *:What the bloody hell — ?:* she asked for his ears only.

He sighed. "Rule number one, Mom — never date a pragmatist. Slips of logic and technique convince them that the impossible isn't, whereas girls who operate on blind faith never will believe you're anything but what you appear to be. She figured the whole thing out."

Well. The cat was out of the bag — for now. It wouldn't take but a wee spell to put it back in, but she doubted Maclyn had told his girlfriend that. No harm in waiting to see if she might be a useful addition to the SERRA folk. "In other words, you dated somebody smarter than you for a change." D.D. snorted. "I keep telling you you've not the brains to keep company with any but the dim girls — but you won't listen to me, will you?" She grinned at Lianne. "Sons know everything, whether they're elven or human, I imagine."

"My mom made a few similar remarks concerning my brother," she said.

"All this came as a shock to you, no doubt," D.D. added.

"Oh," Lianne agreed. "Rest assured."

D.D. gave Lianne a wary look and braced herself for what she felt sure was the impending "big news." "Well, if you're here with my brilliant son, and you know our wee bit of a secret, I expect there's something the two of you will be wanting to tell me."

Surprise flashed in Lianne's eyes. "Uh — not really — ah, D.D. Nothing like *that*, in any case. Actually, Mac mentioned that you were interested in a student of mine. Amanda Kendrick. He said you wanted to find her because she was, um, telekinetic."

Dierdre tried not to make her relief too obvious. "Quite," she said. *I sense the need for a spell of forgetfulness, once we have the wee bairn.*

But Lianne's next words drove all that out of her head. "I have reason to believe her father is abusing her. Mac is going out with me today to her house. He thought you might like to come along."

D.D.'s face had flushed at the mention of abuse. She swore softly in Gaelic, then said slowly, "That explains a great deal, my dear. This — wouldna be the first time I've seen something like this. It breaks my heart, lass, that humans who do not appreciate children have them and hurt them because they don't want them, while we, who would give anything to be able to have more, cannot. Aye, I'll go with you. Do you plan to take the child, Maclyn?"

Maclyn frowned. *:Not now, Mother. She doesn't know about the changelings yet.:* "No. Lianne has the Social Service people taking care of that. She simply wants to get information that will hurry them out to Amanda's house faster. I showed her Tannim's spell-gift, so we can stay unseen."

:Well, we'll see,: Dierdre told him. *:If the situation's bad enough, we'll take the child and befuddle your light-of-love.:*

He winced.

"This rain won't stop today, nor tomorrow either, most likely," D.D. said. "There won't be a race. So we might as well leave."

Belinda pressed the button on her little black box as Mac hurried by, and the needle waggled to around nine-point-five and stopped. That was only what she expected. She couldn't get excited about Mac anymore. He was too-fucking-much trouble. She pressed it again at the teacher, and nothing happened. No surprises there, either. But when she tried a third time on Mac's little blond mechanic, the needle danced like a fish on a line and dove across to ten.

"I'll be damned," she muttered. It couldn't be any harder to get hold of the mechanic than it had been to abduct that son-of-a-bitch Lynn. Granted, she hadn't seen the mechanic *do* anything — but after the demonstrations she'd gotten from the driver, she was willing to trust the meter, skip the dog-and-pony show, and just collect the warm body and go home.

She waited as the three pulled out of the speedway's parking lot, then followed them again.

Visions of herself as Marlin Perkins on safari danced in her imagination, and she wondered momentarily if it would be possible to get Mel to send her one of those hypodermic dart guns and a big supply of knock-out dope. *Probably not. Mel was starting to get cranky about finances the last time I talked to him.*

She wasn't worried about that, either, though. The Fed-Ex people would be trotting in with her next cash payment, as well as Stevens' and Peterkin's money, on Monday. Since she didn't have to pay either Stevens or Peterkin this time — *and since I haven't mentioned their unfortunate demise to Mel yet* — she could just hang on to the whole thing. Their cash would make a nice addition to her finances.

That reminded her that she really needed to call Mel and assure him that things were progressing nicely. It would be a shame if she didn't keep this job long enough to collect her bonus — especially after all she'd suffered through to get it.

• Chapter Eight

Cethlenn "woke" with no memory of anything since her
escape from the Father in the barn. It was early morning,
she knew — light came through the bedroom windows in
the morning. Whether it was the next day, or a day in the
next week, or in the next month, she had no way of knowing. Time was a fluid thing to her in this body; hard to
catch, impossible to hold. She wondered if she would ever
get used to it.

Rain poured down outside of the little pink-and-white
bedroom, framed in the ruffled curtains like an illustration
from a child's book. The teddy bears sat on the windowsills,
just so — the Step-Mother insisted that they stay in the
windowsills because that was where the decorator had
placed them. The expensive handcrafted doll-house was
filled with porcelain dolls which smiled with sweet
insincerity. Everything in the room, in fact, was just so
except for Muggles, the terrycloth dog a child had traded
to Amanda-Abbey for a small, exquisite porcelain figurine.
Amanda-Abbey had smuggled the figurine out of her room
for show-and-tell when she was in first grade, and made the
deal in the school cafeteria. Muggles looked like the last
remaining survivor of a battle between Cethlenn's own folk
and the Roman invaders, but he had three advantages
none of the other toys in the room had. One, he was
eminently huggable. Two, he could be smooshed down to
fit in the tiny space between the headboard and the wall,
where no one could see him. Therefore, he couldn't be
thrown away. And three, he belonged to no one but
Amanda, and she could do anything she wanted with him.
He did not have to be kept nice — he was not a decorator
dog.

Cethlenn liked Muggles, and since she had been left in

control of the body, she hid him carefully in the place Amanda-Anne had shown her. Then she slipped into the closet and listened to the sounds from Sharon's room next door. Sharon's television was on, and the chaos of Teenage Mutant Ninja Turtles reverberated off the walls — Saturday noise. *Saturn's Day. Proof that the gods-be-damned Romans won.* She frowned, briefly wondering at the events that had changed the world from the place she'd known to the place she now found, and wondering what she'd missed. Then she shrugged off her curiosity.

The last thing she remembered from her own life was taking a knife in the gut, and pain. The next moment, she woke in the body of a child a long, long way from home. Even though the devices and customs in this land were alien, it was better being an unhappy child than a woman with a knife in her. Better than being a woman in a world ruled by Romans.

So it was Saturday. Good. Then perhaps it *was* the next day, and she hadn't lost much this time. She dressed in the closet — clean white cotton underwear, blue jeans and a white tee-shirt, white socks and red Halston designer hightops. Dressing was one of the things that had improved greatly since her days with the Druids. Most everything else was worse — but houses were better, and so were clothes.

She debated the merits of going downstairs for breakfast versus staying hungry. She decided against breakfast — there was no telling where the Father might be, or what mood he might be in, and she would just as soon not remind him of Amanda's existence. Instead, she nibbled on cheese crackers bought from another schoolchild, purchased with scavenged and stolen change and carefully hidden.

Thinking of the Father brought back fleeting images from what she suspected had been the night before. She wondered how Amanda-Anne had fared in the barn — and was fearful for the child. She could feel bruises and raw spots that hadn't been there before, and dull aches that she knew the meaning of well enough. It was strange that she should wake up "alone" in the body — usually when she was awake, she was watching Amanda-Abbey or looking over Alice or Anne's shoulder, so to speak. She decided to see if she could find Amanda-Anne, just to check on her. Cethlenn peered cautiously into the walled-off space that Amanda-Anne kept for herself.

At first, what she found puzzled her. Over the wall, there were usually more walls, towering constructs of brick that enclosed and protected the child and kept everything away from her. But the scenery wasn't like that this time. It stretched away in all directions, vast nothingness, gray and empty without ground or sky, without markers — except for the single wall to Cethlenn's back.

It was, the witch realized, a part of the Unformed Plane, although how the child had reached into it and made it a part of herself, Cethlenn had no idea. Initially, she couldn't see the child anywhere. Gradually, however, faint movements off to her left convinced her that something was there.

Cethlenn blended herself with the mist. Her last confrontation with Amanda-Anne on her own territory was still fresh enough in her memory that she had no wish to repeat it. As part of the mist, she floated toward the place where the movement seemed to originate.

Sure enough, Amanda-Anne was there, as happy as that child ever got, contentedly humming some monotonous tune in a minor key. There was no sense of fear or anger — instead, the child gave the impression that she was extremely pleased about something.

Without doing anything that would alert the little girl to her presence, Cethlenn thinned herself out to a fine thread of pure consciousness and eased closer.

The child was working on something, a sort of a doll, perhaps —

Cethlenn focused on the details of the "doll" until she realized what she was looking at. What had seemed innocent child's play became sinister. The "doll" the child made was nothing of the sort. It was a creature formed of fury, molded out of all the darkness in Amanda-Anne's soul — Cethlenn felt the ancient magic like a fire in her chest, felt a horror from memories burned into her centuries before. It was something derived from the magic of the Sidhe — and it must be linked to the visitation by the elven warrior the other day.

The child had copied the elf's magic by watching him, Cethlenn realized. She had discovered how to use the energy of the Unformed Planes to create a thing of order out of the chaos — but what she formed was horrifying. The user of such energies had to take her will and her experience to form the energy into whatever she desired. Cethlenn knew the strength of will it took to do such a thing — and in Amanda-Anne's short life, she had experienced no joy, no love, no laughter — nothing but pain and humiliation and fear and hatred. The thing she molded between her fingers was a misshapen nightmare formed of those emotions, and only those emotions.

Cethlenn watched the child with growing unease, as she played with the stuff of the Unformed Plane as other children would play with dough. She had molded a round, lopsided, lumpy head, rolling it into a rough ball, poking in eyes and a nose and scratching a gash of a mouth with a fingernail. She had formed the body in the way children made dough snakes, and then jammed the head onto it. The arms and legs she created in the same fashion while Cethlenn hovered and watched. When the thing was finished to the child's satisfaction, the little girl stared at her homunculus, all of her concentration and focus centered on it. At first, nothing happened. Then Cethlenn saw that the seams where the arms and legs and head were joined to the body had become thinner and smoother. The arms and legs began to move with weak, spastic shudders, and embryonic digits grew out of the flattened pancakes that were hands and feet. With a sudden flash, the thing's eyes flew open, and glowed with white light. Red fangs sprang from the wide, grinning mouth; a wet, pink tongue darted between them along the lipless rim. Fingers and toes sprouted black, rapier-like claws, and hair sprouted from the round, neckless head as if it had been scribbled there with a pencil.

Amanda-Anne giggled, and the thing giggled back at her: a high, empty, chittering imitation of a little-girl laugh. The child stood her creation on its feet and sent it walking. As it walked, Amanda-Anne stared after it, muttering "Bigger — big-ger — big-ger," in her whining, nasal voice.

And it grew bigger, and stretched and filled out so fast that it seemed the creature, walking away, grew nearer with every step. First it was tall as a child, then as a small woman, and then as a large man.

The golem shambled off into the mist — and Cethlenn knew that the movement that had led her to Amanda-Anne had come from another of its kind, moving out. Once she knew what to look for, she realized there were more them moving around in the mist — impossible to mark and count because of their aimless drifting and the perpetual fog of the Unformed Planes, but still . . . many. Cethlenn repressed a moan as, cross-legged and happy, Amanda-Anne began to build yet another one.

Oh, gods, Cethlenn thought. *Oh, gods, I've got to get help.* She left the child sitting in the gloom making her monsters and singing her discordant songs and shot toward the wall that marked the boundary of Amanda-Anne's space.

Once free from the eerie gloom of the Unformed Planes, Cethlenn discovered she was still alone and in control of the body. She would have worried about the whereabouts of Amanda-Abbey and Amanda-Alice if she had more time, but she had to admit there were things she could accomplish more easily if she didn't have company. Setting up a spell that would summon the Seleighe elves was one of those things.

Cethlenn dug through the closet and found galoshes and a neon-pink raincoat in the back. There was a part of her that dreaded the raincoat as too bright, too much of a beacon for the Father, who might see her moving through the woods and follow her. There was another, more practical part of her that insisted that the Father would want no part of the pouring rain, but that she would surely regret whatever happened if she came back into the house soaked to the skin and dirty from the rain and the woods. She

decided on a compromise. She rolled the raincoat up in a
ball and stuffed it in her black nylon book-bag. Then she
gathered up her kit — cords of various colors, a white
candle, one of the Step-Mother's filched cigarette lighters,
a bright blue crayon, and a vivid green crayon. Last of all,
she looked around the room for a gift. The tales she
remembered of elvenfolk, and incidents from her own rare
dealings with them, all indicated that they were shifty and
tricksy, and a favor asked had to be a favor repaid. She
recalled tales from her childhood in the old world — tales
of the fey folk who appeared, offering the heart's desire,
and desiring in return the one thing a human had that an
elf didn't: a soul. She wanted to have something to offer
that wouldn't cost her *that*. Her own continuing existence
was proof enough to her that her soul might be a real
thing, after all, and worth hanging on to.

Gifting elves was a chancy business by all accounts.
Stories indicated that there was rarely anything one was
likely to have that the elf didn't already have, and of better
quality to boot.

She thought back on her mother's tales. Elves were supposed to be fond of silver and gold, fine fabrics, good
music, good drink and good food. She had, quite frankly,
nothing to offer in any of those categories — except, she
thought with sudden joy, for the giant chocolate bar
Amanda-Abbey had bought from one of the band students
who was selling them to raise money. The last time Cethlenn had been around, none of the Amandas had yet
gotten a chance to eat it. Perhaps it was still intact.

She rummaged through the school pack, and indeed, it
was still there. She pulled the blocky gold-wrapped bar out
of the pack. It was somewhat wrinkled and battered from
its trip home on the bus, and she could tell that it had
broken into several fragments, but it was good chocolate.
Chocolate, she decided, was a gift worthy of elves, being the
other thing about this era that was an improvement over the
days with the Druids. And since it was the best she had to
offer, she hoped any elves she might draw in would give
her credit for effort.

With her pack slung across her shoulders, she opened the window on the right side of her room and scooted out of it. Then she pulled the window closed, slid around until she dangled off the sill by her fingertips, and dropped the final six inches between her feet and the sun-room roof which ran out at right angles from her own room. She scurried like a lizard along the peak of the wet, slippery roof to the very end, then slid down the steeply pitched side and shinnied down the old pecan tree that had grown too close to the house.

From there, she kept under the cover of the evergreen azaleas and the rhododendrons, which took her straight into the woods. The Father hadn't found her escape route yet. She hoped he never would.

Once in the woods, she put on the loud pink raincoat. Her tee-shirt wasn't too dirty, she decided. The Step-Mother wouldn't like it, but she wouldn't fuss terribly, either.

Cethlenn beelined for her tree, not following the usual devious route. She didn't have time. Amanda-Anne was still sitting in the Unformed Planes making golems as far as *she* knew, and that had to be stopped. At least the creatures were still *there*, but for how long?

Inside the safe barrier of the holly tree's limbs, Cethlenn took out her prizes. She wondered if the spell she'd learned for summoning the Faerie folk was any good anymore — or if it ever had been. After two thousand years or more, maybe the elvenkind wouldn't pay attention to cords and candles. Maybe they preferred the new technologies — the answering machines and car phones of this strange age. That would be unfortunate, the witch thought — because she didn't have access to car phones or answering machines. She just barely had access to cords and candles.

She spread out the cords — one green, one red, one black and one white. From the hollow of the tree, she removed Abbey's forbidden comic books. She placed the candy bar and the candle inside the hollow, wedging the candle in so that it stayed upright. She put the cigarette lighter beside it. She lay the blue and green crayons at the base of the tree.

Preparations made, she offered up a quick, sincere prayer to her Lord and Lady, then took the green cord in hand, and took a slow, deep breath to steady her nerves.

While her fingers worked the cord into the patterns of a Celtic knot, she sang in the Old Tongue:

"Fair folk who have danced in the wood, on the green —
I would call, I would beg, to your king, to your queen,
To you who listen, all unseen,
I bind your ears with my knot of green."

She lay the elaborate knot at the periphery of the tree and pressed it firmly into the dirt with her foot.

Next she took up the black cord, walked one quarter of the way around the tree, and while working the cord into her second pattern, chanted:

"Faerie folk with the strength I lack,
I dare not run, nor dare attack,
But I summon you still, and call you back —
I bind your eyes with my knot of black."

She took up the red cord, walked to the far side of the tree, and with her fingers weaving, sang:

"Fey folk drawn from board and bed,
Gifts I offer to quick and dead,
Think of me kindly whom I have led;
I bind your oath with my cord of red."

At the fourth quarter of the tree, she took up the white cord, and knotted it, and said:

"Old ones come from the long twilight,
Brought to the world of day and night,
I ask your aid to make wrong right;
I bind your power with my cord of white."

When the last knot was in place at the periphery of the tree, she moved back to the candle and lit it.

"Now you who are drawn from your Faerie mound,
And led by my beacon to this ground —
To my circle shall you be bound
Until my knots are all unwound."

She melted the tip of the blue crayon in the flame and drew a protective rune on the palm of her left hand. With the melted tip of the green crayon, she copied the same device on the palm of her right hand. Then she picked up the chocolate bar, huddled on the ground in the incongruous pink raincoat, and began her vigil.

Gwaryon, one of the original settlers of Elfhame Outremer, sat beside Felouen at the side of the Oracular Pool and stared with her at the ominous changes in the curtain of the Unformed that rippled in front of them. He was going through an Egyptian phase, and was at the moment dressed as an ancient pharaoh — from the massive amber scarab pendant around his neck to the draping see-through robes which Felouen found annoyingly pretentious, though she had to admit they showed his body off to good effect. His gold bracelets jangled with a flat heavy sound as he rested his arm around Felouen's shoulders.

She sighed. The effect was so completely — *Gwaryon*.

"I am grateful," Felouen told him, and rested her head against his shoulder. "Your presence here is a comfort to me — the visions from the Pool these last few days have left me feeling very much alone."

Gwaryon smiled, happily. "You are never alone, dear one. You know I would be with you always if you would say the word."

Felouen sighed and studied the lean, sinuous elf with deep sadness. "I know. And I cannot give you reason to hope in vain for that day to come — it will not. You are dear to me, but you are not the one I desire the most."

Gwaryon laughed and sprawled on his back in the deep, soft grass that grew beside the Pool. "Och, dearest lady, I know that well enough — but still I hope. You cannot extinguish hope, while we both breathe. And even if you don't want me forever, surely a moment's dalliance would relieve your mind of the weight of your duties." His grin broadened, and he arched his eyebrows suggestively.

She tried a smile, but it didn't feel convincing. "Ah, Gwaryon, you are ever considerate of the weight of my burdens," she told him with heavy irony, and absently stroked the hilt of her jeweled dagger. She ceased that,

point made, and rested her chin in her cupped hands.
Gwaryon's offer of pleasure didn't fit well with her mood.
Her worry was even stronger and more pressing than it
had been. The red glittering of the Unformed had
deepened and seemed angrier, somehow. And at rare
intervals, she was almost sure that she could see shapes
moving through that fog-shrouded realm of nothing,
where no living things should be. Not even the Unseleighe
creatures wandered at will through the Unformed — it was
more a state of mind than a place, and it welcomed only
madness with open arms.

Something was going to happen — she was sure of it.
And soon.

"Ho!" Gwaryon whispered. "Feel that?"

Felouen stiffened. "A pull . . . "

He nodded emphatically. "Human magic. I haven't felt
its kind since long before you were born."

"I want to go toward it." She glanced at Gwaryon, and
her eyes filled with worry.

He nodded. "Once it would have been very dangerous
to do so, but now — " He sat up and shook his head. "The
knowledge is there, but not the strength. We aren't being
summoned by some great mage, nor anyone whose power
will overwhelm us. And sometimes these things were calls
for help from those who had no other recourse."

Calls for help? "Should we arm ourselves for battle?"

Gwaryon laughed. "I would guess that the human who
dug that ancient spell out of an old tome doesn't even suspect
that it is real — much less that we exist. Such a human won't
be a threat to us. Let's just go and take a look."

A stirring in the forces she had woven into her net of
hopes roused her from her trance of concentration. Cethlenn turned from her spell-making to find herself staring
into the faces of two of the Old Folk, who were studying her
with mixed bemusement and disbelief.

Well, she thought, mouth agape, *At least I know it still
works.*

*   *   *

Lianne McCormick was keeping a wary eye on her companions, when both of them suddenly started, as if they had heard something she couldn't. D.D., perched on Rhellen's sumptuous back seat, cocked her head to one side, birdlike. "Oh, my," she whispered. "Maclyn, my love, my darlin' boy, do you feel that?"

Maclyn ground his teeth audibly. "All over, Mother. It's coming from out where we're heading, more or less."

She looked grim. "And a good thing, too. I think otherwise we wouldn't be able to go there — it would pull us to wherever it was."

"What are you two talking about?" Lianne asked.

D.D. rubbed both temples with her knuckles, as if she had a headache. "Mac feels something tugging at him, but he isn't old enough to recognize what it is — *I* haven't felt this particular sensation in so many years, I would have thought I'd forgotten what it was. And I've *never* felt it on this side of the ocean. I thought such summonings were left behind in the Old Country."

"Summonings?" Lianne asked, startled.

D.D. nodded. "Oh, aye. Someone has cast a spell to draw and bind the elvenkind. Such binding spells were known to a few priestesses and witches in the Old Country long ago, and to even fewer mages — but those who were willing to demand our presence were rare. We grew weary of being drawn into the world of Cold Iron against our wills, and we began to attack first and ask questions later. It took only a few toasted humans before that spell fell out of favor."

Lianne rested her head against Rhellen's door. She stared at the neat subdivisions they drove past, and at the stands of tall pines and the orderly young rows of cotton and soybeans that grew in the square, predictable fields. "Witches," she muttered, speaking to no one but herself. "And spells. Elves and telekinesis. Magic. Did I mention that I never cared about magic when I was growing up? Did I ever say that *I* was the kid who didn't give a damn about unicorns? I like science: nuclear physics, math, chemistry. I always liked the world when it was rational. Didn't I make that clear?"

D.D. looked at her son with concern.

Maclyn shrugged. "She's had several difficult days. She'll snap out of it."

"I *thought* I was dating a human," Lianne said, as Maclyn turned the Chevy down the dirt road that paralleled the Kendrick's property. "I thought this was a guy I might potentially take home to meet my folks."

"This is bothering you, isn't it, babe?" Mac asked, flippantly.

Lianne quit talking to the four winds and centered her attention on Mac. She glowered at him with disbelieving eyes. "No-o-o-o-o!" she drawled. "Having elves screw with my brain is just my favorite thing ever. Having my worldview and all of science refuted in two days' time has done *wonders* for my morale. You ought to try it sometime."

"You're welcome to keep thinking that the world is a nice, logical, rational, safe place," Maclyn said with a helpful smile. "You'll be wrong, but that hasn't stopped anyone else who thinks the same way."

Lianne growled something profoundly obscene, and Maclyn and Dierdre both laughed.

"If it makes you feel better, Lianne, magic works by laws, too. Think of it as another kind of science you don't know yet."

Lianne fumed.

Maclyn drove Rhellen up to the very edge of the woods, out of sight of the road or any houses. Behind them was a fallow field, standing tall with weeds. Maclyn got out of the car, and Lianne slid out after him.

"She would be safer here with Rhellen," D.D. said, as if Lianne wasn't there. Lianne hated being talked around.

"I probably would be," Lianne agreed, studying the woman who would probably not end up as her mother-in-law. "But I don't intend to stay here with the car — with Rhellen."

"Only until we see who has summoned us," D.D. said, placatingly. "Then you can join us and help us find the wee child's home."

"No thanks. I'd like to see that myself." Lianne pulled

her gray mackintosh tight, noticing that the rain fell all around her but not on her. The cold and the damp still blew straight through her, and the low keening of the wind gnawed at her nerves. *Great day for this sort of thing,* she decided. *Make a believer out of even the staunchest pragmatist. Wind sounds like a banshee, and I think I could see ghosts in broad daylight on a day like this.*

She had to remind herself that this was an attempt to find information that would rescue an abused kid — not a midday ghost hunt. *Amanda needs help,* she reminded herself. But it made her nervous that Mac and D.D. were being drawn against their will toward something that called from the same direction as Amanda's home. Could that bastard of a father be summoning them?

Bad thought, Li. Very bad thought.

Lianne watched the two of them walk, faces grim and tense, ducking around the dripping greenery — scrub oak and sassafras and willow; blackberry bramble, grapevine and kudzu — that made up this part of the woods. She walked a step behind them, staying quiet. They did magic, and this was something that frightened them. She was out of her element, way out of her area of experience, much less expertise. It was as if there was something out there that didn't *want* them to help Amanda and was trying to prevent them from interfering. That made her profoundly nervous.

Cethlenn stood with her back pressed against the trunk of the tree, the chocolate bar in her outstretched hand. Though it still rained all around her, no rain fell on her, nor did any fall on her — guests. She stared at the two elves, the woman in clothing similar to that which elves had worn in her earlier life — the man in a foreign-looking gown of some gorgeous filmy material she would have killed for once upon a time, and covered with gem-crusted gold jewelry.

"Child," the male elf said, "the last time I heard that bit of doggerel was a good two thousand years before you were born. And it had become uncommon then."

The female elf shook her head. "I didn't realize anyone could summon us."

Cethlenn shivered. She would have preferred to have been less of a novelty. She held out the chocolate bar and waggled it a bit. "I gift thee, lord and lady."

The female — one with the look of a warrior about her — studied the profferred bar, and shuddered. "Oooh, chocolate. Loaded with caffeine, and you wouldn't believe the empty calories in that thing."

"Summoning price has gone down a bit since the old days, Felouen," the male muttered with dry amusement. "It used to be that they greeted us with baskets of gold and jewels and fine silks and rare spices. But then we needed a bit more placating back then — too many calls for no good reason. No, child," the elven male added. "We won't take your candy. There is another gift we will require instead, for having come when you called us forth."

Och, and there goes my soul, Cethlenn thought with dismay.

Her face evidently mirrored her fear, for the female elf said, "We won't hurt you. We don't hurt children."

The strangely dressed male looked into Cethlenn's eyes and said, "That isn't what she's afraid of — oh, this is rich. Just rich. They used to think we stole souls, and that's what she is afraid of. It *is!* Look at her — that's exactly what she was expecting." He grinned at the witch in the child's body, and said, "Kid, if you had a really hot 486 with a VGA monitor, a solid keyboard, and a ton of software, I'd steal that in a heartbeat. But you can keep your soul. I *would* like to know where you found that old string-and-knot song and dance."

Cethlenn could hardly believe her ears — or her luck. "That's all?"

The elf nodded. "That's my trade. Information for our arrival."

Cethlenn smiled, confidently. "I learned it from the MacLurrie's first witch, when I earned my place as one of his advisors."

The elves stared at each other, and the female elf mouthed the name "MacLurrie?"

"An old warrior and rake who was a bit before your time, child," the male elf said, and nodded to his female companion. "He was a bit before *her* time. I remember the young boaster well enough, but I can't imagine how you could."

Cethlenn drew herself up as tall as she could stand — which was not very — and said, proudly, "I am Cethlenn, daughter of Martis and witch at MacLurrie's circle. I was not always this child, though how I came to be here, I know not."

The male's brow creased with thought, and he absently played with a great beetle of amber that hung about his neck. "Cethlenn . . . hmm. I vaguely recall a charming, dark-eyed creature named Cethlenn from around the time of the battles of the Gauls and the Gaels — as a matter of fact, now that I think of it, she was sharing her favors between MacLurrie's bastard son and one of our folk. Bryothan, was it? Or Prydwyn?

"Eodain was my other suitor," Cethlenn corrected. "Eodain. But he wasn't elven."

"Eodain . . . Eodain . . . It's been so long, I've forgotten." He stared off into space, while his long, graceful fingers twined in the many layers of his gold jewelry. "By Oberon's steed, girl, I believe you're right. It . . . was . . . " His eyes narrowed and fixed on Cethlenn, and he glared at her from beneath lowered brows. "Eodain. Who was one of our folk, although you certainly couldn't expect him to tell a mortal like yourself that. No tales of his little tryst were barded about — it was mere court gossip, which means —"

"That she either made an extraordinarily lucky guess, or she is what she says." The one called Felouen frowned.

The male gave his companion a somber look. "Then the price is met and our oath is bound."

"No!" Felouen snapped. "If this is not a child but a witch of the Old Country, then she has not called us in idle sport. She would have known the dangers. No matter how unlikely, and no matter how innocent she seems, she is a danger to us. You stay, I'm leaving."

The elven woman shimmered, but stayed solidly within

the child's hiding place. She made another obvious attempt to leave, and when that, too, failed, she turned on her companion with a snarl. "We're trapped here, Gwaryon!"

The male elf shrugged. "She means us no harm."

But there was veiled panic in the female's expression. "I don't care! I want out of here!"

Gwaryon looked at Cethlenn, and his face grew stern. "I also dislike this spell that holds us here."

There was no point in acting contrite. Not with those — things — out there, shambling around in the Unformed Planes. "I've met your price. Besides, 'twas the only way I knew of callin' the Fair Folk," Cethlenn said. "I need help. I am not the only one in this child, you see. . . ."

Cethlenn's voice faltered in mid-sentence, and a furious presence pushed her back and usurped her control of the body. *:No!:* Amanda-Anne screeched to the ancient witch. *:You . . . c-c-c- can't . . . tell . . . them about . . . us!:*

:They could help,: Cethlenn said, soothingly. *:They could take you away from the Father.:*

But Amanda-Anne was not about to be soothed. *:No-o-o-o! Stopping . . . is . . . not helping! They . . . w-w-w-would . . . only call us . . . bad girl. Make us . . . weak again. They would take . . . our m-m-m-magic.:*

:No, Anne,: Cethlenn told the child, her thoughts pleading. *:Let them help you. They can take you away from him, make the bad things go away — they can hide you someplace safe.:*

Amanda-Anne had quit listening. She looked at the elves who were held — trapped — in the circle, and her voice rose in a shrill sing-song. "I m-m-m-made me . . . gletchells and . . . sl-sl-slinketts . . . and m-m-m-morrow-w-waries . . . and . . . f-fulges. F-f-friends of me . . . friends . . . of me. And . . . *you* . . . w-w-want to hurt my . . . f-f-friends," she wailed on a rising note.

The elves stared at each other, amazement and confusion written clearly on their faces. *Oh, Lord,* Cethlenn thought. *What have I done?*

Amanda-Anne knelt in the dirt, and rubbed her fingers across Mommy's green bead on its new gold bracelet.

Without words, she summoned her "friends" and brought them through the bead and out into the charmed circle that was Amanda-Abbey's safe place.

The homunculi spewed into the haven under the holly tree in a cloud of black smoke, giggling as they took solid form. Their wide, grinning mouths split open, and their fangs gleamed red. They shambled and staggered on uneven legs, ducking gracelessly under the sheltering boughs of the holly. Their scimitar fingers grasped toward the elves.

Amanda-Anne waited until five of her pets were through the bead-gate. Then, laughing, she slipped out of the tree-shelter, and darted home.

To Felouen, her arrival in the child's spelled circle had been discomfiting. The spell was carefully wrought, so that her eyes saw nothing but the world inside of the magical boundaries, and her ears heard nothing but the sounds of the child's voice and the few creakings that the old holly tree made. Its branches blew in a wind she knew to be present, but neither felt nor heard. Her world narrowed to the tree itself, which soared upward, its dark, leathery leaves contrasted with the brilliant light green of new spring growth, and with the startling reds of the few remaining berries not yet picked away by the birds. And in the center of the circle, the child: frail, blond, brown-eyed, with skinny arms and legs covered by wet clothes, who stared at her with awe — but not surprise. All else was hidden in the obscuring darkness of the spell. Her senses and her magic were bound — she could not leave. She was trapped — by a child who, in all sincerity, said that she was a witch from the Old Country.

And then the witch in the child's body changed — no, *change* was not the precise word. The witch, Cethlenn, disappeared, or was abducted, and was replaced by someone — terrible. Felouen felt the newcomer, the child — for *this* one was a child — arrive, full of rage and fear and confusion. This green-eyed human, who was terrified of the elves without knowing fully what they were, knew only that

she wanted to hurt them. Wanted to hurt everything.
Felouen felt her slashing, unfocused rage like a blow to the
face, sensed her hatred and wondered, in the brief instant
before the child brought forth her monsters, what could
have twisted the youngling in such horrible and deadly
ways.

After that, she didn't have time to wonder about anything.

It was not the vision from the Oracular Pool — Felouen
wasn't defending the Elfhame Outremer grove. She and
Gwaryon fought to save their own lives. There were no
armies of elvenkin at her sides; but neither were there
armies of the great shambling things.

Her own situation, however, was no less grave than the
vision of the Pool.

The Pool had made a true showing of the monsters.
They were just as malformed and frighteningly senseless as
they had appeared in the glassy surface of the water — and
the ratio by which they outnumbered the elves was as bad.

Felouen regretted Gwaryon's casual response to the
summons and her own willingness to follow along. Now,
between the two of them and the child's nightmares-made-
real were only two little silver elven-blades, knives pitifully
small when compared to the claws of their opponents.
Felouen and Gwaryon scrambled up the trunk of the tree
into its upper limbs, hoping at best to escape the monsters'
talons completely, and at very worst for a defensible place
in which to make their stand.

Unfortunately, the things could climb — and they did.
Their glowing, pupilless white eyes gleamed in the pouring rain, and their high-pitched and horribly childlike
giggles carried over the pounding rain and the low moans
of the wind. They were slow climbers and clumsy, but
deliberate, and they seemed to stick to the tree as they
moved upward.

The leading monster reached a point just under
Felouen's ankles. It screeched with sudden wild intensity
and slashed out at her legs. Its talons ripped through the
sturdy leather of her boots as if it was silk, and dragged into

her flesh. Felouen cried out once at the sharp stab of pain and pulled her feet higher. Gwaryon threw his knife, and Felouen saw the little blade bury itself in the pallid thing's eye.

The monster grabbed for the knife with both hands, lost its balance, and fell. Even falling, it giggled, until the noise was cut short by the *thud* as it hit the ground.

Felouen slashed at the next golem within reach. The blade cut deeply and lopped off three of its fingers, but the wound didn't bleed and the creature showed no signs of pain. It kept climbing, and she was forced to climb still higher, onto a weak, green branch that bent alarmingly under her weight. The golem stopped and looked up at her, and its giggling became shriller. It grasped the branch to which she clung and began rocking it back and forth.

"Stop it!" she screamed. "Damn you!"

Beneath her and to one side, Gwaryon was fighting his own battle. He had wedged himself tightly into a crotch of a sturdy branch and was kicking the monsters in the head as soon as they were within reach. His legs were bloody ribbons, and his sandal-clad feet were unrecognizable as feet. His skin, at least that which wasn't bloody, was gray. Felouen saw the beads of pain-sweat standing out on his forehead — but his face never lost its determination. She watched one golem fall to the ground as Gwaryon kicked it loose from its perch. It hit heavily, lay still for a moment — then rose, and begin its climb back up the tree. It had already been replaced by the next monster.

Felouen realized with horror it was the one that had taken Gwaryon's knife in its eye. *They're unkillable,* she thought with sudden, overwhelming despair, and clung tighter to her branch. The monster beneath her kept rocking it, swinging it in faster and further arcs. Its hysterical laughter never stopped.

"Stop it! Damn you!" someone screamed from ahead of them, and the sounds of a desperate struggle and a blood-curdling chittering made the forest sound like something out of a horror story. In front of her, Maclyn apparently heard it, too. He started to run, "Weapons and armor," he told his mother. Silver swords materialized in their hands, and chased and enameled armor appeared around them.

God, I wish I could do that, Lianne thought, breaking into a run behind them.

They were faster than she was. They ran effortlessly, appearing to do no more than jog — yet they pulled away from her at an impossible rate. She ran flat out, putting everything she had into the effort, yet she fell further and further behind. The two elves darted through a thicket without slowing, and she stopped completely to disentangle herself from the inch-long thorns that held her clothes in fast embrace.

By the time she was out of the thicket, the elves had disappeared from sight, but she still heard the fighting, and the — other noises. The sounds came from the other side of the small hill she was climbing. She slowed to a trot, by necessity picking her route more carefully than the elves had. She wondered now what in hell she was doing out here. What good was she, an unarmed human, in a fight where at least two of the combatants were well-armed and armored elves? She suspected she would be more of a liability — someone who would end up needing to be rescued. By the time she'd reached the crest of the hill, she had decided to find a safe spot in which to wait out the fight.

Close up, it sounded even worse. Unfortunately, she couldn't see much. The holly's leaves blocked most of her view, but a steady green glow from the tree's center backlit shadowy forms; the fight was more terrible than she could have anticipated. In the cramped space under a holly tree's branches, Maclyn and Dierdre battled misshapen horrors that looked from the brief glimpses she got like the most awful nightmares the folks from Industrial Light and Magic could have concocted. She saw two elves she didn't recognize, stranded in the thin upper branches of the tree, fighting more of the things. She saw one of the white-eyed monsters then, and squeezed her eyes shut until she realized she couldn't wish the nightmare away. The elves in the tree were wounded and bloody — the monsters they fought appeared unscathed.

Lianne saw Maclyn bring his sword straight down on top of one monster's head in a two-handed blow that should have split the thing in half, but the monster never fell.

A scream of pure anguish drew her attention back to the treetop. One of the monsters had overcome the male elf and had severed one of his arms. It dropped like some macabre fruit to land against the tree roots. The elf screamed once more as the horror gnawed through his remaining forearm. Lianne shoved her fist against her mouth to silence her own screams; one last slash of the thing's claws and the elf's severed head hung from its grip.

The body tumbled from the tree, with unreal slowness. The golem threw the head in a lazy overhand toss that sent it soaring in a slow, graceful arc toward Lianne. As it passed beyond the spread of the holly tree, it winked out of existence as if it had never been.

Lianne stared at the spot where it disappeared and shuddered.

It was only the steady repetition of someone calling her name that brought her out of her stunned reverie.

"Lianne? Lianne? Can you hear me?" Dierdre shouted. Lianne could make out her shadowy form, back pressed against Maclyn's, keeping the monsters at bay with a steady barrage of swordstrokes.

"Maybe she ran off," Maclyn yelled. He parried a talon-strike aimed at his face and landed a stop-thrust that did no apparent damage to its victim.

"Maybe we just can't hear her because of this damned spell. I hope that's the case."

"I'm right here!" Lianne yelled from her hiding place.

None of the combatants paid her any attention.

Certain that she was exposing herself to attack by the monsters, Lianne did the bravest thing she had ever done. She stood up and ran toward the fight, again yelling, "I'm right here."

It was if she didn't exist to those battling under the tree. And that was as horrible as all the rest combined.

"Lianne," Dierdre yelled between swordstrokes, "if you're there, listen — a spell traps us in here. Look for knotted cords around this tree — probably four or five. If you —"

One monster got inside her defense, and the sound of talons raking across armor screeched through the woods.

"If you find the knots, untie them!" Dierdre yelled. "And hurry!"

Lianne heard the elves parrying claws and Maclyn's voice asking, between panted breaths, "What if she's not out there?"

She heard Diedre answer, "Then we die."

Lianne stared at the headless, armless torso that lay under the tree, and then through the branches, at Dierdre and Mac. Then she looked up at the bleeding, exhausted elf stranded in the upper branches. The one tireless monster who was trying to dislodge her had shifted tactics and was scraping across the branch with his claws. Bits of wood flew away with every stroke. It wouldn't be long until the branch broke.

Cords? she wondered. *Made into knots that I should untie?*

She could not imagine what good untying knots would do — but she was willing to concede that this was not an ordinary situation, and that the rules she knew didn't apply. She ran to the periphery of the tree and scouted around the branches.

In a moment, she had located one knot. It was tied in a heavy, glossy black cord, and it wove in and out around itself half a dozen different ways. It took her a bit of fumbling even to discover where the ends had been tucked, and once she had found them, even longer to return the cord to its unknotted state.

As soon as the knot was unraveled, however, Lianne heard Maclyn yell, "There she is!" One of the monsters suddenly noticed her, too, and charged toward her. Mere inches away, it broke through the branches and was brought up short by an invisible barrier. It shrieked in frustration, and charged again.

She backed away frightened.

"Get the rest of the knots," Dierdre shouted.

"What will happen when they are untied?" Lianne asked.

Dierdre looked puzzled, then shouted, "I can't hear you."

Lianne shrugged and hurried around the periphery of the tree. A flash of red caught her eye, and she stopped. The monster that charged at her as she pulled the red cord out from under the branches sent her heart leaping into her throat, and the other creatures' incessant chittering giggles made it almost impossible to concentrate — but with trembling fingers, she managed to untangle the second knot.

"If we survive this," Dierdre suddenly remarked, "I'm going to severely damage the person responsible."

"I know how you feel," Maclyn agreed.

There was a creak, and the branch that supported the third elf sagged. "Felouen!" Maclyn yelled, "Hang on!"

"I'd figured that out already, thanks," Felouen shouted back.

Giggles grated along her nerves. *Third cord*, she thought, and refused to let herself consider what would happen when all the cords were unwound.

It took a bit of digging in the spot where she thought it might be, but she did locate the third cord. It was white.

She ignored the crash that indicated the branch had broken through, ignored the scream of fear and pain and the heavy thud that followed. Lianne fumbled with the complex knot and worked it loose.

"Magic works again," Dierdre muttered, and that terse statement was followed by a flash of brilliant blue light and a loud sizzling sound.

Lianne ran to the fourth quarter of the imaginary circle the unknown magician had laid out, and within seconds had discovered a twisted length of green cord. Familiar now with the permutations the knots had taken, she quickly pulled it apart.

There was a low rumble, and the air around her shimmered like air over pavement on a hot day. For an instant, the situation under the tree continued unchanged. The monsters slashed at the elves, the one who had broken the hapless Felouen loose from her tree clambered down after her, chuckling evilly. The monster that had been charging at Lianne broke free of its circle and came straight for her, and Dierdre and Maclyn fought their way toward the body of their fallen comrade.

Then, with a resounding "crack," the monsters and the dismembered remains of the dead elf vanished.

Dierdre looked around as if she couldn't believe it was over, then sagged against the tree trunk. Maclyn charged to Felouen's side.

Lianne crawled through the holly's low-hanging branches with some difficulty and joined him.

Felouen was badly hurt. She lay, unresponsive, on the woodland floor, her breathing ragged and irregular. Dark blood seeped into the fabric of her shirt, and through a tear in the cloth, Lianne could see the white gleam of ribs and the dark bubbling of a large, open wound.

"Mother!" Maclyn's voice was hoarse. He knelt beside the downed woman, probing for hidden injuries. "Hurry!"

"Do you need me to get an ambulance?" Lianne asked. She felt foolish asking that question when, looking at the woman, the answer seemed so obvious — but she wasn't dealing with humans, she reminded herself. Elves might have other ways of dealing with emergencies.

"D.D. will take care of her," Maclyn said.

Lianne watched D.D. moving around the tree toward them. Her armor flickered once, then vanished, replaced by clothes that looked like the ones the other woman wore.

D.D. bit her lip and knelt beside her son. "How bad?"

Mac's voice was without expression. "We may lose her."

The elven woman nodded and rested her hand on Felouen's shoulder. "I'm taking her back. You and Lianne find out what you need to about your child. I'll meet you in the Grove when you're done."

Maclyn did — something. He sketched a kind of arch with his fingers, anchored on one side to the holly tree. Lianne watched the air around the two elven women shift and darken.

Something about that arch made her feel queasy.

But beyond that arch were hints of unearthly beauty. Was that the elven world?

The images of wet forest and misty, enchanted grove blurred over each other and shifted disconcertingly until the teacher had a hard time looking at the Gate. D.D. pulled Felouen through, and both of them took on the same hazy, half-there appearance of the world beyond. Then Mac spoke a few quiet syllables, and they were gone.

"Come," he said, turning to Lianne. "We still have to find out about Amanda."

• Chapter Nine

Belinda concealed herself and the entirely too fancy T-Bird along a riding path just out of sight of the Chevy and her targets. There was no way she was going to get out of her vehicle around that hexed Chevy again. There was no telling what might happen to her. She remembered the incongruous picture of a horse trotting through the night behind her first rental car, after the damned race-driver stole it — and the way the Chevy was mysteriously missing when she went back to try stealing it. She recalled the odd behavior of the '57's doors the time she ended up as Mac's captive. Certain pieces of her last few days began to form a picture — one she didn't like at all.

In a sudden burst of curiosity, and with some trepidation, she took the little black meter out of her pocketbook and flashed it at the car. The needle quivered and moved steadily across the scale, wavering slightly as it hit 3.71 P and came to a halt. Goosebumps rose on her arms, and the hair on the back of her neck stood on end. *A car sitting in a field doing not a goddamned thing rates higher on the psi scale than any people I've ever checked — except that bastard Mac Lynn and his blond bimbo mechanic.*

It figures, she thought. She panned the psi-meter in a semi-circle that encompassed the general direction in which Mac and company had been heading, and left room over for error. Sure enough, she picked up one narrow burst of activity at about 8 P's of intensity — mid-scale, and another of about the same reading. That would be the two of them, she thought — Mac and the mechanic. She scanned beyond them from force of habit, letting the meter play across the field at the dreary mix of scrub-oaks and long-leaf pines —

About fifteen degrees west of her two identified targets, the needle dove all the way across into the red zone, hitting

30 P, then kept moving until it vanished into the out of range sector. It stayed there.

Belinda leaned her head against the headrest and stared at the little ventilation dots in the car's headliner until her eyes unfocused and the dots blurred and appeared to move toward her. *What the hell have I gotten myself into?* she wondered. *The car, the driver, the mechanic — and something huge out there in the woods. Either this place is a hotbed of psi activity — or something is wrong with my meter.*

Now, *that* was a genuinely comforting thought. She knew she didn't even raise a .01 P blip on Mel's scale — she shuddered to think what might have happened to her if she had — so maybe her meter was screwed or picking up something else. Something cars and normal people and whatever radiated.

She pointed the psi-meter at herself and pushed the button.

The needle didn't budge. *Zip. Nada. Nothing.* Her eyes narrowed, and she pointed at her own car. She obtained the same results. To her left, coming from the same general direction as all the psi activity, a kid in a pink raincoat shot through the woods at high speed. She was heading straight for the fancy house with all the horses and pastures. *Testing, testing,* Belinda thought, and aimed the meter at her.

"Shit. Shit-shit-shit-shit-double shit!" Belinda snarled. The needle had again shot all the way across the meter and buried itself in the out of range zone. She flung the black box across the seat, and stared at the galloping kid. *What are the odds?* she wondered. *Just what are the fucking odds of running into that many TK's in one place?*

She bit her lip. *The odds are probably better than running into them one at a time and spread all over,* she decided after long contemplation, *if their being here was no coincidence. Do psychics attract psychics?* And another thought, straight out of a Spielberg movie: *Do adult psychics track down kids?*

Her head throbbed, and the thinking she was forced to do was making it worse, but the pain pills would make her fall asleep if she took any. *Live with the pain,* she told herself. *You may be about done with it anyway, champ. 'Cause kids are little*

*and weak and naive — and they don't drive haunted '57 Chevys.
And I'm betting you can heist a little kid way out here in the sticks
without anyone being the wiser.*

A thought occurred to her. *There were kids all over the
racetrack the day I did my little set-up. Wouldn't it just be a bitch if
the kid was the one I was looking for after all?* She started her
engine and pulled carefully out onto the road that led past
the kid's house.

"Kendrick," the mailbox said. And the flowing script on
the sandblasted wooden shingle read, "KENDRICK'S BAL-A-
SAR STABLES — FINE ARABIANS."

*Horses, huh? I can fake it with the horsey set. Oh, yeah, kid . . . I
can find you with no trouble at all. A new haircut, and a pair of
jodhpurs and riding boots, and I'll be back.*

Mel Tanbridge drove through Fayetteville accompanied
by his constant companion, distaste. Military towns
annoyed him. The entertainment wasn't classy enough, the
architecture was just plain drab, and the people themselves
— well, he decided, the less thought about them the better.
Rude, crude, and obnoxious were the kindest adjectives he
could come up with for these peons.

Take the maids at the hotel Stevens had been staying at,
for instance. Stevens' room was paid through the end of the
week, and they knew he'd been staying there, but they
refused to tell him anything about the man — whether
he'd left in a hurry, who he'd been with — anything.
They'd told him hotel visitors were confidential guests (the
way they pronounced "confidential" positively made Mel's
skin crawl), and even when he'd flashed a couple of twenties in their direction, they'd blinked their stupid cow eyes
at him and said they didn't know anything. He was ready to
believe them — the bitches. He'd gone on to break into
Stevens' hotel room and had scoured it with a thorough-
ness that would have left the simple-minded maids
chartreuse with envy. He came out with more questions
than he took in.

The room was beyond nondescript. That fit well enough
with Stevens' character. The thing that puzzled him was

that most of Stevens' belongings were still in it. The money was not to be found, of course — except for a bit of change on the dresser that made his stomach twitch in uncomfortable ways. Nobody *left* change if they weren't intending to come back — and pretty promptly, too, in cheap hotels. His bags were present, his clothes still balled up in the drawers. The bed was made, and the maids had placed the pile of dirty clothes neatly on the room's single chair next to the ubiquitous round hotel table under the equally ever-present hanging hotel lamp.

He left carefully, feeling that he had missed something important, but having absolutely no idea what that something might have been.

On his way to his next stop, Peterkin's hotel, he puzzled over the scene and came up completely empty. The room was a blank — there was nothing incriminating, nothing that gave him a clue to what might have happened to his employee.

He hoped for better luck at Peterkin's place.

His hopes fell with his first sight of the place. Stevens' hotel had been bland — but Peterkin's was positively tacky. It was one of those "adult" motels with twenty-four-hour hot and cold running movies and beds that wiggled for a quarter — no doubt so the rented rubber dummy would feel like it had a bit of life to it, Mel thought with disgust. While he might have more luck bribing the help, he doubted that he would find anything useful in a dump like the one in front of him. *Then again,* he thought, *I doubt they ever sweep under the beds here. I might find something useful.*

He obtained the room number from the blowsy, rumpled tub of a woman who sat at the front desk. He went back to his car and watched until no one was on the breezeway. Then he slipped up the steps and, ignoring the "Do Not Disturb" sign hung on the door, used one of the little tricks he'd learned from the burglar he kept on staff. He broke in without so much as a sound.

He closed the door quietly behind himself and waited for his eyes to adjust to the darkness. When they did, he wished they hadn't.

"Christ!" he yelped. Peterkin and Stevens were in the middle of something he would never have credited them with having the imagination for — or rather, he noted, as their silence and stillness caught his attention, they *had* been.

The moment that he took a deep breath, he knew that they were dead. What had caused their deaths seemed pretty evident, too. Drug paraphernalia was laid out on the dresser, and they didn't have any visible wounds —

He walked through the room, careful not to touch anything until he'd taken a towel from the bathroom. He used that to open drawers and look over the IDs lying on the dresser. They were false ones, he noted, but not the same false ones Stevens and Peterkin had left California with. Interesting, he thought. *Those are the ones Belinda had on hand for emergencies.*

There were only a few low-denomination bills and some change in the room, and Mel left all of the money. It wouldn't do to make this look like they'd been robbed. He left the false ID's, too. They were very good and very solid — he even had a couple of "widows" who would be only to happy to collect the insurance on their late "husbands." Best of all, they wouldn't be traced back to him.

Mel backed out of the room and closed the door behind him. He heard the lock click into place. Immediately, he began beating on the door and yelling, "I know you're in there, Kraft! I want my money, dammit! Open the door! You owe me eight hundred bucks, you flake! Pay up!"

Hotel management, in the form of the overweight woman, appeared at the foot of the stairs. "Sheddup or ah'll call the cops," she yelled. "Don' you go raisin' hell aroun' my place."

Mel took on a menacing air. "Lady, that S.O.B. owes my company eight hundred bucks — and he skipped town to keep from paying it. I'm the collector — I tracked him down here, and now I want my money. You see these papers?" He waved several sheets of paper at her from his safe spot at the top of the steps; papers that were actually contracts with his brochure printer back in California.

"These say I have a right to collect that money, and if I don't get it, I'm going to call the cops and have them raid this dive."

The woman studied him from the foot of the stairs, her bright black eyes nearly hidden in the rolls of fat. She grimaced and mumbled, "Aw, shee-it. Ah don' need that again." She waddled back toward the office, muttering over her massive shoulder-pads, "Jes' wait a dam' minute while ah git my keys."

After she returned and moved her vast bulk up the narrow cement staircase, Mel took his expectant place half a step behind her.

He waited, feigning impatience while she pounded on the door, then fumbled with the keys when she got no answer. He pretended not to watch her closely as she opened the door and flipped on the light. He noted, however, her absolute lack of shock as her eyes took in the room, its inhabitants, and the attendant sex toys and drugs.

"Oh, my," she whispered, her eyes gleaming with vicarious pleasure. "Oh my, oh my! Will you jes' look at that! Imagine them doin' that in mah nice clean *mo*-tel!"

"Dammit," Mel said, making sure she heard him. "There goes my eight hundred dollars."

Mel slipped back to his car and drove off before the police could arrive. He returned the Lincoln, took the shuttle to the Fayetteville airport, then another to a second car rental agency, where he used an alternate alias to pick up a car as different from the previous one as he could find — a bright blue Geo Metro. He didn't want to be bothered with the police in a town that had the two strikes against it of being military — and Southern.

Then he drove out toward Belinda's last reported address. The situation so far was not at all what he had anticipated. He didn't think for a minute that Stevens and Peterkin had died in the way they appeared to have. He felt the touch of his favorite redhead stamped all over their dead bodies. But there might be extenuating circumstances. It might be that he wouldn't have to terminate her from his payroll — he chuckled at that euphemism — as soon as he'd anticipated. But he would be careful. After all, she was dangerous — part of her charm — and one never knew.

Mac was as weary as he had ever been. The rain died down to a cold, sullen drizzle, punctuated by cloudburst exclamation points that showered the woods around them. Lianne and Mac trudged through the ugly weather, untouched.

"That was Amanda's hideout," Mac noted abruptly, breaking a silence that had carried them from the tree to the edge of the woods behind the child's house.

"Really?" Lianne said, sounding surprised. "How did you — oh."

Mac did not ask her what the "oh" meant. Perhaps she remembered catching sight of bits of bright junk that had hung on strings from the branches, decorating the tree like treasures in a magpie's nest. Perhaps she simply deduced — correctly — that he had been here before.

Lianne shuddered. "You don't suppose she was anywhere around those — things — do you?"

I would bet she had something to do with getting them here, Mac thought, but he didn't say it. There were so many things about the kid that didn't fit. She knew he was an elf, then she didn't. She did magic but didn't believe in it. She walked out of Elfhame Outremer on her own — a pure impossibility. To Lianne, he only said, "I hope not." That at least was the truth.

He covered the two of them with his "I'm not here" shield, and they moved out of the woods and across the yard.

"God — the police are here!" Lianne froze, then started backing toward the woods.

Mac grabbed her arm. "They can't see us," he whispered.

"Are you really, really sure?"

He gave her a half-smile. "Well, don't run up and pinch them on the noses to test this — but yes, I'm sure. We still show up on film and video, still leave footprints, but someone looking right at us won't see us. Wonder what they're doing here —"

"Rummaging through that little barn. Obviously." Lianne started forward. "Come on — let's take a look."

Maclyn lingered back as Power, twisted and sick, hit him like a board to the front of the head. "Gods," he whispered, "what happened in there?"

Lianne looked up at him and arched her eyebrows in a silent question.

"Are you familiar with the human term 'bad ju-ju'?" he asked.

She shrugged. "I've heard it. Means — oh, black magic, or something."

Mac watched the police with wary eyes. "Or something, actually. Well, bad ju-ju is stamped all over that little barn in glowing letters ten feet high. Something happened here, but not what the police see."

She shook her head, obviously confused. "The monsters under the tree again?"

Mac closed his eyes and stood very still, his head tipped to one side. "Funny — " he started to say something, then fell silent. Finally, he shook himself and looked at Lianne again. "You are almost right about comparing this to the battle this morning," he told her. "The traces of magic in the barn have some of the same touches as those golems had — but this magic is tied in to someone else as well. It almost feels like some kind of a ritual — group magic, or something involving a group." He wrinkled his nose and walked toward the barn.

"Bad ju-ju," Lianne snarled behind him, and followed his lead.

Mac's nerves screamed with every step that drew him nearer to the barn. The little building reeked of power drawn from pain — but the signatures of the magic-wielders and the victims were so tangled that he couldn't get a clear picture. When he glanced inside, his stomach twisted like a knife-pinned snake, and he drew in a breath between clenched teeth. The contents of the structure had been shredded apart fiber by fiber — he had seen the results of a food processor on occasion and had no difficulty imagining that the inside of the barn had been through one. The taint of Unseleighe work reeked through the place. And where, in all of this, did *they* fit in? So far, his dark kindred hadn't shown so much as a hair.

Mac and Lianne stayed to the shadows and watched the policemen digging through the mess.

"You find anything?" one of the officers asked.

"Sawdust," the other answered. "Plenty of sawdust. And I'll tell you something, Sammy — if we rake through this shit till the end of forever, that's all we're going to find."

The first speaker straightened and groaned. "Yeah. I think you're right. This place gives me the creeps. Feels like something's watching all the damn time."

Lianne gave Maclyn a worried look. He grimaced and shrugged.

The cop continued. "Why don't we check outside — maybe we'll find tire marks or something."

"After all this rain?" the second policeman snorted. But then he grinned. "Hell, walkin' in the rain is a damnsight cozier than pokin' around in here. Let's go." Both policemen headed for the door.

Lianne heard one mumble as they stepped outside, "Wish to hell I knew what could do that."

Mac leaned over and whispered in Lianne's ear, "I know what did it — I just wish I knew who'd summoned one up."

Lianne shuddered under his hand. "So tell me, what *does* do more damage than Hell's Cuisinart?"

He almost wished he didn't know. "A banesidhe wind — deadly, borderline intelligent, called up from the lairs of what you might call the Dark Elves. They're pure destructive energy. Pain and hatred born of torture on this plane create them out of the raw stuff of the Unformed Plane — but to 'create' one here, to call it out from its Unseleighe hiding place, the magician has to know it, to know that fear, that hate, that pain. And there aren't many magicians strong enough to call one out who are willing to be tortured to make one."

Outside the barn, they heard Andrew Kendrick talking

with the policemen. He was not happy. "You mean to tell me you've spent all morning poking around in my kid's barn, and you still don't know who vandalized it?"

An unhappy voice answered. "Mister Kendrick — we can't even begin to figure out how they did it. Given a few hours, maybe somebody could wreck things that completely — but not in a few minutes."

"Dammit," Kendrick snapped. And after a pause, he added, in a voice thick with sarcasm, "I can tell my tax dollars have been well spent on you two."

It's Amanda's barn. It was Amanda's hideout tree. Her classroom. And the magic signatures in all of these places have been the same. They haven't been Amanda — but they have all been the same! Who is with her doing Unseleighe magic? And why?

A different man walked into the barn and was framed for an instant in the dreary outdoor light at the doorway. He was tall, with sandy hair and light eyes, broad shoulders and the very early signs of a potbelly to come. He would have been a handsome man, but his expression was ugly, his lips clamped firmly on a smoldering cigarette, his demeanor cold and calculating. The man scanned the interior of the barn, his eyes fixing on Mac and Lianne and flicking quickly past them. Mac felt Lianne jerk once beside him.

The feel of this man was in the barn, too. His was the second signature present — and Mac would have taken him for the magician and maybe the torturer — but while the man had strong magical potential, it was completely latent. Still, the man carried a store of repressed hatred so deep-burning and all-consuming that the elf felt it as a physical presence.

Father and daughter in league with the Unseleighe Court? Maybe — but somehow none of the pieces fit —

Kendrick walked to the back left corner of the gutted building and started digging through the drifts of debris.

Father and daughter — and torture . . . there has to have been some kind of torture to have conjured the banesidhe wind. Mac clenched his hands and glared at the man across the little barn from him. *It's sure that the child didn't torture her father —*

but there was torment wrought here, and it has his signature on it. But stress has brought out mage-powers in humans before. . . .

Latent mage torturing developing mage. That matched. He took a deep breath to calm himself and leaned back against the wall.

There's my proof of abuse.

Belinda walked into her hotel room, and reacted an instant too late as the cold, heavy barrel of a gun was pressed against her ribs, preventing her from backing out of the room. A leather-gloved hand clapped over her mouth.

"Don't move or you're dead," the voice in her left ear said in an equitable and utterly reasonable tone of voice.

"Mel?" The word sounded muffled through the heavy padding of the glove.

A delicate snort, and the gun-muzzle didn't move a hair, but the glove moved enough so that she could talk, at least. "In the flesh. That was quite a nice little tableau you left at the Peterkin's hotel. Very artistic. I always have liked your style."

"Why are you here, Mel?" Belinda couldn't feel, in her heart of hearts, any deep urge to be chatty.

"You haven't brought me my TK yet," he chided gently. "And then Stevens and Peterkin vanished off the face of the planet, and you hadn't called in days — I started feeling a little lonely. And I thought you might have reeled in the TK and then found a higher bidder." His hand tightened over her mouth, and the gun began moving in slow, gentle circles over her side, and the glove covered her mouth again. "You haven't found a higher bidder, have you, dear?"

Belinda tried to clear her mouth of the glove, and failed. "Foo-fif fiff-feff!" she spat.

"Beg pardon?" Mel chuckled softly in her ear and lessened the pressure on her mouth.

"You stupid shithead!" Belinda repeated. "Do I look like I've been rolling in somebody else's money and taking it easy at your expense?"

Mel said, "Stay still." He released her and moved to one

side of her. Now they were both reflected in the mirror across from her. Out of the corner of her eye, she could see that the gun was still pointed steadily at her midsection. She kept her hands away from her sides and stared straight into the mirror on the far wall. She could see him taking in the bruises, the bandages on her head, the dark circles under her eyes and the gaunt hollows in her cheeks that hadn't been there when she left California. "Now that you mention it, you look like you've been dancing with trucks. What's been going on?"

She snorted. "You didn't tell me how dangerous hunting down a telekinetic could be."

Mel's eyes narrowed. "I didn't know. The racecar driver did all that to you?"

She shrugged. "Yes he did, in a roundabout fashion I would rather not discuss. I've got you a better prospect. I've found a child who is a sure thing — an even stronger talent than the driver. I'll get her for you — she's bound to be less dangerous to rope in than Mac Lynn. I'm going to kill him after you have the girl." Belinda smiled and rubbed absently at the bandage on her head. "Unless I have the opportunity to do it beforehand."

"You've really found someone else?" Mel's voice sounded eager.

Belinda eased into the Naugahyde chair beside the bed. "Just today — a little girl. Lynn led me to her. Probably, oh, eight or ten years old. A kid would be very easy to work with, wouldn't she? I figure whatever you have planned, it would be less hassle to do with someone smaller."

In the mirror, Mel's eyes brightened. "Check her out. TK ability is supposed to show up right around the time puberty strikes, and is supposed to be more common in girls. This kid fits the profile."

Mel ran one hand along the line of his jaw and stared at a nonexistent point somewhere over Belinda's left shoulder. "A child would be good — very good. Little girls are pliable and agreeable; I could probably obtain her cooperation with a few grand in toys — whereas getting cooperation from an adult male for what I have in mind would require

. . . more complicated measures." His voice faded off into nothing, and he refocused on Belinda. "Why did you kill Stevens and Peterkin?"

She yawned. "They double-crossed me. I don't take that from anyone, especially not from the hired muscle."

Mel sat on the long dresser that also acted as the motel room's writing desk. He crossed his arms and let the muzzle of the gun dip toward the floor. "The word 'double-cross' is open to a wide range of interpretations. Be more specific."

She spread her hands wide and gave him her most innocent expression — hard to do with all the bruises. "I should have had him on his way to you in a bag yesterday. They withheld a drug that would have knocked Mac Lynn out, then lied to me about it. I can't figure out what they hoped to gain by that maneuver, but there is no doubt that they lied to me. I tested the remainder of the drug on the two of them, just to make sure it wasn't faulty — you found the results, apparently."

Belinda went into greater detail, stopping only when Mel asked questions. She went over each point until she was sick of talking about it — and finally Mel seemed satisfied.

Mel lay the gun on the dresser top. "You aren't lying about this. I can always tell." He pulled one knee up to his chin and rested with his arms wrapped around his leg. He looked genuinely bewildered. "Why the hell would they turn traitor on me? They knew what I would do to them if they tried — God knows, they carried out my sentence on a couple of their colleagues."

Belinda leaned her head back and tried to relax enough to get it to stop throbbing. "I have no idea. I searched their rooms, their possessions, their car, their pockets — everything I could think of. I couldn't find anything incriminating." She sighed. "Whoever bought them kept the whole deal very well hidden — and they must have been offering a fortune. I just can't figure out why anyone would pay so much for such a ridiculous thing as a TK." She glanced at Mel through half-lidded eyes. "No offense intended."

Mel's face twitched into a slimy smile. "None taken. *I* know why someone would offer a fortune — you haven't seen the private offers that come across the desk of anyone who might have access to, ah, commodities like Mac Lynn. Believe me, dear, he's worth more to you on the hoof than in the bag."

"Pardon me for not giving a flying fuck." Belinda laughed. "I guarantee you he's worth more to me spread-eagled on a rock somewhere with a white-hot poker in his ass."

"Tch-tch," Mel said, shaking his finger reprovingly at her. "Language like that is not becoming a lady."

Belinda made a full-forearm gesture at him and ignored her boss' raised eyebrows. "I'll get you a TK. But I've gone through hell you wouldn't believe" — *quite literally couldn't believe,* she thought — "trying to get this one. You'll get the kid. And I'm going to take that creep out all by myself."

Mel patted the gun that lay beside him. "We really must talk sometime about this habit you have of killing people who annoy you, Belinda dear."

Belinda's laugh was short and harsh. "You should bloody talk."

He chuckled. "Not at all. I would never think of killing someone just because he — or she — has annoyed me. For example, Belinda, you annoy me, but you are useful. I only kill those people who are dangerous to me or who are of no further use to me alive." He smiled gently. "I thought you had passed that line, dear. I truly did."

A cold knot formed in Belinda's belly, and she repressed the shudder she didn't want Mel to see. "Friends again?" she asked with false cheerfulness.

His smile was just as false. "Of course — now that I know you're still playing on my team. I make it a point to stay friends with the people on my team. Get me my kid tomorrow or the next day, and we'll even be best buddies."

Belinda nodded, and winced as her hair moved with the nod. There were a lot of bruises under that hair. "I'll go out tomorrow. I already know how I'm going to get close. First, though, I've got to get some sleep, and then I'm going to the beauty parlor. I'm not going to be able to get anywhere near her looking like this. I'll have your kid for you in a day or two."

"Fine." Mel's eyebrows furrowed, and he looked down at his shoes for a long, silent moment. "I think I might like to go along to pick her up," he said when he finally looked up. "I want to have a good look at my merchandise."

Belinda sighed. "Hey, it's your party. Just so long as you still intend to pay me the full price, you are welcome to come along."

Mel chuckled. "You mean you aren't inclined to give me a discount if I come along and help out?"

She gave him a look of disdain. "You came along too late to earn a discount. Hell, I deserve a bonus just for pain and suffering incurred."

"We'll see." Mel stood, and they watched each other warily. Then Mel slipped the gun into the holster hidden beneath his windbreaker, and keeping his eyes fixed on Belinda, he eased out of the room. "I'll be in touch. Or if you need me, call me at the Prince Charles. I'm listed as Mel Tenner," he said just before the door closed.

Oooh, that's creative, Belinda thought. *Nobody would ever connect Mel Tanbridge with Mel Tenner. Idiot.* She listened to the click of the latch and held her breath until she heard Mel's measured tread moving away from her door. "Shit," she whispered.

The room would be bugged, of course — Mel would have kept his options open, even if he had fully intended to kill her. *"Do nothing irrevocable until the last possible moment,"* he'd told her more times than she cared to think about. *"And always leave yourself an out — two, if you can."* So he would have the room bugged, and he would now have someone keeping track of her movements.

What else? Threatening her family? Maybe — and if he tried it, he would find out how little that meant. Her lush of a mother wouldn't even notice a bullet between the eyes, her bastard stepfather deserved one, and if Mel's goons could locate her real father, who had skipped before she was even born, she hoped they'd make his life exciting.

Threatening her, then? If she screwed up, she was dead. But she already knew that. She was dangerous to Mel — she just had to make sure she kept herself useful. Well, as long as she was the only one who knew who — and where — the little girl TK-wonder was, she was useful. And after that, she'd get out of his reach. Fast.

In the meantime, she hadn't seen the inside of her eyeballs in far too long. She double-locked the door, then stripped and eased herself between the cold sheets.

Life was giving her real cause to consider another line of work.

Andrew Kendrick sat in the kitchen, staring out the window at the policemen who wandered around his property accomplishing precious little. He was satisfied that they wouldn't find anything incriminating in the barn. There *was* nothing — absolutely nothing — left. How that could be, he didn't know, but the fact that it seemed impossible didn't in the least change the fact that it was true. And with the worry of discovery of his questionable activities behind him, he could relax a bit. And since they hadn't found the person responsible for destroying his barn, he wished the police would just get the hell off his property.

He would have to rebuild the barn. Rebuild the little windowless locking room, he thought. For the time being, the other barn would serve — but not as well. It had its private places, and its private times, but they were less frequent, and less convenient. Convenience had become important to him.

He could see Amanda and Sharon playing Barbie dolls in the den, doing something that was not meant for adult eyes and whispering with their heads leaned close together. He watched them without making it obvious that he was doing so — something had just occurred to him as he sat there. Amanda was growing up.

He sniffed with sudden distaste. Amanda had once been an enchanting child. She had been innocent and vulnerable and tractable. Now, as she sat next to the delicate and fragile Sharon, whose hair still tumbled loose in a five-year-old's baby ringlets, whose face was sweet and round and whose eyes were gentle and uncomprehending, Amanda was a gangling and ugly colt. She looked plain and scrawny, Andrew thought — and she looked hard. She had lost the childish innocence of Sharon. She seemed somehow adult, as she sat there making sly little comments while the two girls changed their dolls' clothes.

His attention was suddenly riveted by something his older daughter did. Amanda's face and mood had changed, and her eyes glittered green in the dim light. She tied the Barbie doll's wrists behind her back and placed the Ken doll behind her in a pose suggestive of—

Andrew's fingers tangled around the tablecloth in unconscious rage. He knew what Amanda was telling the little girl — he knew what she was showing her. Sharon was watching her older sister, fascinated, hanging intently on every word. Andrew couldn't hear the words hidden in the hushed whispers, but he knew anyway that she was exposing his secret — exposing *him*. And in the same burst of insight, he knew something else.

He knew that he was going to have to get rid of Amanda.

What she told to her little sister was of no real importance. Sharon wasn't old enough that any rational adult would take her seriously if she repeated what her sister said. Assuming she even understood half of what Amanda was telling her, or that she considered it anything other than a scary story. But Amanda could talk to adults as easily as she talked to the little girl. She could walk out the door and tell the police in his side yard what he had been doing — and what would come of that? Where would his law practice, with his high-powered corporate clients, be? Merryl would leave him, and worse, she would take Sharon with her — sweet, beautiful, obedient Sharon.

It would only be a matter of time until Amanda let something slip — he saw it coming with terrible clarity. He could see it in the crafty, loathsome eyes of the homely creature in the other room. He would have to get rid of her as soon as possible, in some way that would leave him completely above suspicion.

With the police department's newfound interest in his home, that was going to be damned difficult.

Dierdre felt the Gate pull in behind her, felt it drain her of some of her energy as she bore the brunt of the snap for both herself and Felouen. Felouen was near death. She hovered there, suspended over the chasm of nonexistence by the finest of gossamer threads.

Dierdre stood in the sacred grove of Elfhame Outremer, and felt the magic flow into her — magic she had cut herself off from voluntarily for a very long time. The great trees seemed to bend over her, welcoming her home, and their acceptance changed her subtly. She dropped her lighthearted human persona, her years of human acclimatization. She seemed to stretch, becoming something both more beautiful and more terrible than the human-seeming creature she had hidden herself in for all those many years. Her human colleagues, who had never seen the ancient elven noblewoman she truly was, would not have recognized her — and would have felt the strong compulsion to kneel and beg mercy in her presence for ever treating her with anything less than deepest respect.

She knelt next to her wounded comrade and gently rested her hands on the torn and broken body. A soft, golden glow gathered around her; a faint sheen that grew in glittering bands until she became the pale, lovely center of a brilliant light warmer than any homecoming. Her lips trembled just a little as she sang, over and over:

"Gathwaloïr muelléiralra elearai ao;

Elearai, pallaiebaroa, ailoaüié houe.

Tué, atué escobeieada —

Tué, atué,

Tué, atué — tué."

The song was ancient, one of the oldest magics of the elvenkind — so old that its language was far removed from that spoken by the Seleighe Court. To a people whose lives stretched thousands of years, and whose language had not changed in tens of thousands of years, this made it a tongue of unimaginable age and power. Singing it, she gifted her strength and her health to Felouen. And as she sang, pain spread through her body, and Felouen's wounds healed under her fingers.

She kept singing until the pain blinded her and her voice faltered. She had no more strength to give — she could only take some of the damage to herself. Too much, and she would die in Felouen's place.

As her voice fell silent, though, another voice picked up the song, and other hands rested on Felouen's body. The Grove had felt her need and had summoned help. She fell back and lay in the soft velvet grass, and the Grove fed her and comforted her and promised her renewal.

She listened, unable to move, as the voices over Felouen changed; strong voices becoming weak, then being replaced by other strong voices, over and over. She felt like a child in her cradle again, rocked and safe, with others singing the old songs and whispering in the language of her childhood, the sounds familiar but the meaning of the words just out of the reach of her tired comprehension.

Homesickness, long foreign to her, overwhelmed her as she lay in the eternal twilight in the hallowed place between the worlds. The elven-tongue, so beautiful and long neglected by her, sang through her veins like hot brandy. Dierdre felt tears welling in her eyes, felt the uprush of repressed longing for a place and a way of life she had voluntarily forgone.

Homecoming — in such a way, with the death of one of her folk and the near-death of another riding her shoulders like a close-fitting cape — was bittersweet. The bitterness was only in the pain she brought with her from the low and dirty world of the humans, the unbearable sweetness in the touch of friends too long neglected, too long put aside.

Felouen would live. Her people had come to the call of the Grove, and her wounds had been shared by them.

And over Dierdre as well the elves began to sing, dispersing among themselves the agony that she had taken on alone when there was no one else to help her.

At last she was able to sit again, to hold her head upright, to look around her. She saw Felouen moving restlessly in the grass, her head tossing and her arms jolting out at intervals to stop the fall her mind would not release from present memory. Around her moved the beautiful folk in their flowing robes, their pale faces grave.

"Welcome home," said a rich, deep voice from behind her. "Too many years have you been apart from us, fair lady. Your home weeps in your absence."

Dierdre looked up and to one side. The elven lord had once been a friend and a comrade, had fought at her side under Dwylleth's leadership — and had been, with other friends, sadly neglected of late because of her other interests. "Yes," she said sadly. "I've been away a while."

She glanced around the Grove, and back up at her old friend, and touched his iridescent green robe. "But I'm home now."

• Chapter Ten

Amanda-Abbey "woke" to find herself playing Barbie dolls in the den with Sharon. Daddy was in the other room — she could just barely see him in the kitchen corner with his long legs stretched out under the table, while he sat and watched her. She had no memory of where she had been, or of how she came to be playing with Sharon — and the dolls in her hands were doing something that made her stomach twist, although she didn't know why. It looked naughty and *felt* naughty. She moved the dolls apart and stared at her hands with dismay.

What happens, she wondered, *when I'm not here? Why doesn't Sharon notice that I just woke up? What,* she thought with a shudder, *has my body been doing without me?*

She busily started putting clothes on her dolls, so that Sharon wouldn't interrupt her while she was thinking. She thought about Stranger.

Stranger had always seemed to be just a funny voice in her head, one that talked oddly and used a lot of words she didn't recognize, but Amanda-Abbey had always assumed Stranger was part of her imagination — like the elf had been. She had to wonder about the elf, however. Amanda-Abbey looked at the gold bracelet on her wrist and at her real mother's glass bead, and she wondered —

Maybe the elf was real. And if the elf was real, maybe Stranger was real, too.

Amanda-Abbey put down her dolls and dug her fingers into the cool, deep carpet. She stared at her hands, her odd, unpredictable hands, now pulling little bits of fiber out of the rug and rolling them into pills. *Suppose — just suppose — Stranger is real. Then the place where she took me, the place where that awful girl with the flying knives and whips and stuff was hiding behind her walls, was real, too.*

Stranger is inside of me. Is the awful girl? Is that what happens to me when I'm not here? The awful girl comes out?

"Don't pick at the carpet," her Step-Mother said, walking into the room. "That's destructive."

Amanda-Abbey stopped and began to put her dolls away. She needed to get away, to think. There were things going on that she didn't understand, but she wanted to find Stranger and talk to her if she could. She wanted to be alone when she started looking for her. For some reason, it seemed important to be alone for that.

"You said you'd play with me," Sharon whined.

"I already did play with you," Amanda-Abbey said, hoping this was true.

Now the whine was joined by a pout. "Not long enough."

Amanda-Abbey decided that it was time to be firm. "Yes, long enough. I have stuff to do." When the pout continued, she tried coaxing instead of ordering. "Why don't you watch Turtles, now? I bet they're on."

The pout turned scornful. "I already watched Turtles — they were on this mornin', dummy butthead. They're not on in the afternoon."

Amanda-Abbey shrugged and finished shoving her dolls and doll clothes back into their storage case. "Watch something else. I gotta go clean my room." She got up and started for the stairs.

"I want someone to play with me," Sharon wailed.

From the kitchen, Daddy leaned around the corner and looked past Amanda-Abbey to Sharon. He said, "I'll play with you, honey. Just give me a minute to finish my coffee."

Something about Daddy wanting to play with Sharon all of a sudden worried Amanda-Abbey, but she didn't know what it was. Her stomach twisted, as it had when she saw what she was doing with the Barbie dolls. Confused, she walked to the stairs and up them, trailing her doll case. The stairs, too, made her feel a little funny. It seemed that today everything in the house made her feel a little funny. Amanda-Abbey decided that she was probably getting the flu like Bobby Smithers in her art class, and next she'd have a fever and be puking on everybody.

She'd worry about that when it happened. Right now, she wanted to find Stranger if she could. She wanted to see if Stranger was real.

In her room, she stretched out on her bed and looked out her windows. The clouds outside were low and dark, and for a moment she expected to see rain — but there was none. She didn't know why, but this surprised her.

She lay very still. If she were someone else hiding in her body, where would she hide? She watched the clouds scudding by and wiggled her fingers tentatively. *:Stranger?:* she asked.

There was no answer.

:Stranger?: She closed her eyes and tried to hear the voice with its funny accent. *:Stranger? Are you there?:*

:Aye, lass, I'm here. What are ye' huntin', then?:

:I was looking for you — : Her thought faltered. It occurred to Amanda-Abbey that it was probably rude to ask someone to prove that they were real. Still, if she didn't ask, she wouldn't know. *:Are you just my imagination, Stranger?:* she asked.

:Nay, I'm not that. I'm as real as you are — how real that is, *I've no more way of knowin' than you.:*

With her eyes still tightly closed, Amanda-Abbey tried to see where the voice was coming from. She got impressions of a shadow, the outline of a woman —

:If you're wantin' to see me, I'll give you a light, child. Before this, you nay wanted to look at me.:

Amanda-Abbey considered that. It was, she realized, quite true. She never had wanted to see the face that went with the odd voice — not even the time she had seen that horrifying other girl, the frightening child behind all those walls. She had not looked into Stranger's eyes even when they had escaped, not even when the woman's arms had been around her, comforting her.

White fire cascaded in waves from the darkness, until she saw Stranger clearly. Amanda-Abbey stared at her, devoured the woman's features with her eyes — and suddenly knew why she had been afraid to see her.

Somewhere, in the back of her mind, she had been afraid that Stranger would look just like her, and that this would prove what she had suspected when she first started hearing the voice — it would prove that she was crazy. Amanda-Abbey knew stories of people who heard voices and were locked up.

Like my real mama. That's what Father said.

But there had been another fear, equally deep, equally bad. She had also been afraid that, even though the voice belonged to a stranger, the face would belong to her mother — her real mother, who was dead — and that this would mean she was seeing ghosts. She wanted her real mother back, but did not want her back as a ghost.

Stranger looked like no one she had ever seen. The woman was short and extraordinarily pale, with a long dark braid and a pointed, pixie-like face; her clothes were funny, too, like they were made out of kitchen towels or horse blankets pinned together. She smiled, and Amanda-Abbey nervously smiled back.

:*Hi. I'm Abbey.*:

The woman nodded politely. :*I know you. Merry meet,*: she added. :*I am named Cethlenn.*:

Cethlenn. Not Stranger, Amanda-Abbey thought. She rolled the name on her tongue a few times. The woman looked real enough standing there in that short cape that was nothing more than a horsehide with round pins holding it on, with her boots looking like something she'd made herself. Yes, she did look real enough, Amanda-Abbey thought, *At least while my eyes are closed.* Experimentally, she opened her eyes. The woman vanished. She closed her eyes. Cethlenn still stood there.

:*Prove you're real,*: Amanda-Abbey demanded. Inside, what she was hoping was that Cethlenn would prove she was not crazy.

The woman nodded. :*Fair enough. Get up and walk to your mirror. Look at yoursel' in't, an' say what ye see.*:

Amanda-Abbey followed these directions — and found herself staring at her reflection. :*I see me, of course.*:

From over her shoulder, it seemed, Cethlenn said, :*Quite

right. Now, close your eyes and imagine that ye stand behind my shoulder, and let me look in the mirror.:

Amanda-Abbey found this difficult to accomplish. Several times, right when she was sure she had it right, she opened her eyes just at the wrong moment and found that nothing had changed. When finally she got it right, she didn't even know it until Cethlenn said, *:There. See?:*

She opened her eyes and discovered, to her surprise, that *the* eyes had opened already. She had the feeling that she was standing behind Cethlenn. When she moved her arms, they felt just fine, but *the* arms, the ones attached to the body which she could see quite plainly in the mirror, did nothing.

:Oh!:, she cried out, and no sound came out of *the* mouth. The face that was and was not hers said, "See? I'm real."

She looked on in fascination as the arms moved without her will, as the lips smiled, as the eyes — *brown* eyes — blinked in a rhythm different from her own. The face in the mirror looked unaccountably fierce, and though the hair was still blond, and the skin still had a little of last summer's tan to it, she could see that the person inside was Cethlenn.

:Oh, Cethlenn, you are real!: she said, with a rush of joyous relief. And, suddenly bewildered, she asked, *:But why are you here?:*

The face in the mirror looked back at her, and the uncertainty reflected there matched her own. "Och, child," Cethlenn whispered, "I have na' the faintest idea to that. I dinna even remember how I got here. I only wish I knew what I was supposed to do now that I'm here."

The trip back to Lianne's apartment was mostly silent. Maclyn stared at the road that unfolded ahead of them — Lianne leaned back on Rhellen's soft gold upholstery with her eyes closed and pretended to sleep. Maclyn didn't expose her pretense for what it was — he didn't particularly want to talk anyway.

Old Gwaryon was dead — weird old Gwaryon, with his fascination for ancient human cultures and his reputedly bizarre personal habits — who had been a part of Maclyn's life since his birth. Dierdre had liked Gwaryon, had seen some value in his tedious memorization of long-dead human languages and his eccentric love of human books and his freakish emulation of long-outdated human fashions. She'd thought the old elf bright and funny and clever, and so Maclyn had grown up surrounded by his elvish imitations of human worlds that — Mac suspected — bore only a faint resemblance to the long-gone realities. Dierdre had lent these suspicions some truth when, to young Maclyn's unending questions, she would admit nothing but that Gwaryon preferred to see only the good in every human culture and work.

Old Gwaryon had, in his way, been a friend. He had died bravely — but not well. In Maclyn's estimation, there was no way to die well. Dead was dead, and the longer one put that state off, the better.

And that brought him to Felouen. What of Felouen?

The image of his mother dragging Felouen's unmoving body through the temporary Gate he'd made into the Grove of Elfhame Outremer left a queasy hollow in his stomach and made every breath painful. What of Felouen? He felt she was still alive — he thought that surely her death would have left a bigger ache in him than the one he carried right then. She had said that she had been waiting for the one she loved for hundreds of years and had implied that she loved him. He glanced anxiously over at Lianne, whose eyes were still closed — and he allowed himself to acknowledge the deep and painful yearning for Felouen he intentionally ignored, the one that came roaring back to life every time he saw her.

It was a yearning, he had to admit, that invariably and promptly got quenched by Felouen's stiff-necked, hard-headed, do-it-or-die approach to every damn thing. Witness her insistence on dumping him with a Ring.

Unconsciously, his fingers made their own way into his jeans' pocket and pulled out the scrap of silk in which the Ring resided. Felouen was wounded, maybe dying — he didn't know if she would survive. She had wanted him to wear the Ring, had wanted him to be her knight.

He started feeling a little guilty. It hadn't been that much to ask of him — just that he accept the role of one sworn to uphold the Seleighe Court's edicts. It wasn't as if he had to start walking perimeter on guard duty if he wore the damn thing. It would, he thought, have made her happy if he had worn the Ring. Hell, Korindel, over in Misthold — California — wore *his* Knight's Ring openly and constantly, and *he* spent most of his time in the human world.

Against his better judgment, he slipped the carved gold band on.

Nothing happened. *There*, he thought, *that wasn't so bloody difficult, was it? Show a bit of respect for your own folk, show a bit of backbone, stand up against the Unseleighe things — you'll still survive it. Plenty have before you — that's how they earned their high places in the Council.*

It isn't driving racecars — but then, what is? It's probably less *dangerous to be one of the Ring-wearers than it is to drive racecars.*

The dull gleam of the gold ring on his right index finger mocked that last assertion.

Rhellen pulled into the apartment parking lot.

"Wake up, baby," Mac said, in deference to her act.

She barely stirred. "Mmmph."

He shook her, gently. "We're home. Time to get moving."

One slit eye glowered at him. "I'll wake up in a minute."

"Okay." He pause, on the brink of delicate negotiations. "Lianne, I know you have some classwork you need to finish. And we didn't find out anything that we can use to get Amanda out of that house a minute sooner — but maybe Felouen did. She was out there at Amanda's tree before we got there, and somehow all of this feels tied together. While you grade papers or whatever it is you have to do, I'm going home to check on Mother and Felouen. If I find out anything useful, I'll stop by later and let you know."

Instead of looking disappointed, Lianne looked relieved. "That sounds fine, Mac. Tell you what — unless you find out something earth-shattering, why don't you just stop by tomorrow morning. I feel like making an early night of it."

Perversely, Maclyn's feelings were hurt. "I'll be happy to spend the night — " he started.

She waved him off with one slender hand. "Actually, Mac, the idea of having the bed to myself for a night sounds appealing. I want peace and absolute quiet. I want to think for a while — and I also want to scrounge around the house and not have to worry about how I look or how I act or what I do. I'm a bit too tired to be social."

"Well," he pouted, ignoring for the moment the fact that the outcome was exactly what he had hoped to accomplish, "if that's really what you want . . . "

She nodded. "Yeah, I think so. Gimme a kiss and I'll see you tomorrow."

When Maclyn drove off, he noticed that she hadn't even stayed outside long enough to wave goodbye — something she almost always did. *Maybe,* he thought, *she's mad at me for something.* He pondered that notion while he and Rhellen drove toward the permanent Gate the elves had hidden in the center of the Grove on 15-401, out back of the Beauty Spot Missionary Baptist Church.

Maybe, he decided at last, *she's pissed off at me because I didn't thank her for saving my ass out there in the woods today — and neither did Mother.* That, he thought, was a good possibility. He would have been pissed if the situations had been reversed and no one had thanked him.

It was just that elves didn't often have occasion to think of frail human women in the role of rescuer. Ah, well — he supposed in this case, he'd better show up with an apology offering first thing in the morning.

The Grove spread in front of him. Rhellen drove off-road, carefully picking his way. As soon as the car was well into the trees, Rhellen shifted, and the two of them charged through the Gate into Elfhame Outremer.

Even though the on-again-off-again rain might be annoying if one had to be out there in it, it made ideal sleeping weather, Belinda decided. Too much of a good thing, though, would get her in trouble. She rolled over and stared at her clock.

It was a bit past two in the afternoon, and she had just finished a well-earned nap that had left her feeling better than she had anticipated, by a long shot. Her head still ached, but less than it had when she went to sleep. Still, she was going to have to get all her hair chopped off, which was damned depressing.

And Mel wasn't happy with her, which depressed her more. An unhappy Mel was a dangerous Mel. She couldn't spend a great deal of time worrying about him, however. She had her afternoon plans mapped out. Worry wasn't on her list.

Screw Mel, she finally decided. Then she laughed. *It would probably solve a few of my problems if I did. I'll bet the little bastard is kinky as hell, though; that's one of those personal details about my employer I'd rather not discover firsthand.* Belinda's personal sexual preference was abstention — a fact that would have surprised any number of people. Including, no doubt, her employer.

Ah, well. She stretched, then lay under the covers a few minutes longer, lazing. She had to spend some time with her modem and laptop computer. She needed to access files on the Kendricks and see what bounced. Then she needed to get herself looking good again. There was a salon out by the mall that was open nearly all the time. She could go there without an appointment and get her hair clipped and styled in some fashion that hid her new bald spot. Then she could get the kind of clothes that would make her look like a well-heeled member of the horsey set, and she could visit the Kendrick stables — get a close-up look at her target and the obstacles she would be facing.

Let's see: to do this right, you gotta walk the walk and talk the talk. Belinda had spent some time on a job pretending to be a rich woman who wanted to be part of California's moneyed crew, and that meant an interest in horses. And not just any horses, either. She rehearsed vocabulary. *Breeding terms: broodmare, stallion. Buying terms, colt, filly, yearling. Good on those. How about words for things to look for when buying. Ah, good legs . . . hmm. Yeah, that includes fetlocks and hocks, pasterns, withers — no, the withers is that hump on the back up near the neck. Riding things: good gaits* — brisk *walk*, comfortable *trot*, springy *gallop*, and . . . easy *canter. Performing things* — uh — *dressage training, jumper, cross-country* —

She carried on mentally in that mode for several more minutes, then called up an online encyclopedia from her laptop computer. She searched by keywords — horse, Arabian, Andalusian, stud, all things she'd need with an Arabian breeder — and scrutinized the entries until she was sure she could pass herself off in that unused persona again.

Then she stretched and crawled out of bed.

Out of habit, she scanned the room, and her attention fixed on the door. It bothered her that Mel had broken in with so little difficulty, had caught her off guard so easily. While she showered, she wondered if she was losing her skills. God knew, she hadn't managed to pull in the racecar driver, whose IQ had to be on a par with that of a Boston fern or cold mashed potatoes. She didn't give herself any breaks because of the extenuating circumstances. There were *always* extenuating circumstances.

While she dried herself off, she entertained herself with the television. A news teaser caught her attention with the "bizarre drug-related death" of "two gay men" whose bodies had been found in a roadside motel — details at six. She cheered up again. After all, she decided, for every one wrong thing she did, she also accomplished a multitude of right ones.

Once she was dry and dressed, she hacked around the Fayetteville school system's computer setup, running one up and one down from the long list of phone numbers, until she got in. Security was weak, and very forgiving of errors — for that, she grinned. It was so much easier to break into schools than into, oh, police departments, say, or restricted installations.

Once she was into the system, she ran a search for any Kendrick files, cross-reffing with the Bal-A-Shar Stables address. In a moment, she had a match.

Kendrick, Amanda, was the name of the kid she'd seen. She was on the verge of adolescence; her records indicated plenty of personality disturbances, some of them pretty odd, her grades and teachers' comments marked her with all the stigmata of the erratic genius. And she was part of a "blended family" — a term Belinda considered a euphemistic hype.

Blended family. *Right. Mom has one, Dad has one, and now we are four. Sure we are.* More stress, which, according to Mel, made for psi-powers popping out.

Plus you made my little black box happy, kid.

The information she had turned up was good enough for Belinda. She disconnected her modem and reconnected the hotel room's phone, then picked up the Fayetteville phone directory and located "Kendrick's Bal-A-Shar Stables" in the Yellow Pages. "By Appointment Only," the ad announced clearly. Belinda called.

A clipped, feminine voice answered on the other end after the third ring. "Bal-A-Shar Arabians, Merryl Kendrick speaking."

Belinda affected her persona from the old California job. "Mrs. Kendrick, this is Alessandra Whitchurch-Snowdon," she said in the upper-class Brit accent that could only be obtained by speaking without moving the lips. "I've recently moved to the States, and I'm looking for a yearling filly, probably green-broken, with good conformation and potential as a dressage contender. Your stables were highly recommended to me, but I'd like to come have a look, informally, before I go any further. Even if you don't have fillies suitable now, if your establishment impresses me, I'm willing to wait to look at the new crop in the fall." Belinda grinned at the phone. *Come on, snob appeal,* she thought. The Brit accent had never failed to get her access among the wealthy yet — something, she suspected, to do with making the local upper-class feel like provincials who needed to prove themselves.

It didn't let her down this time, either. "Yes, certainly, Ms. — ah?"

"Alessandra Whitchurch-Snowdon. But it's *Lady* Rivers."

"I *see.*"

Belinda saw, too. She could see the dollar signs clicking merrily in the other woman's eyes, but more, she could see the other woman sampling the prestige factor possibly offered by her name. "Oh, yes, Lady Rivers rides Bal-A-Shar Arabians," she pictured Mrs. Kendrick imagining telling her other clients.

The woman came very close to concealing her eagerness — but not close enough for Belinda. "When would you like to see the horses?"

A little more pressure. "Have you an indoor theatre?" Implying that anyone who didn't wasn't worth visiting.

Eagerness became avarice at the hot prospect. "An indoor arena? Certainly."

"Splendid," Belinda replied. "Then would tonight be too much of a bother — say, nine?"

Avarice became anticipation. "That would be fine."

Belinda allowed her voice to warm. "Lovely, then. I'll be off."

Anticipation swelled. "Ah, yes. I'll look for you at nine."

Belinda hung up the phone and laughed merrily. One every minute — and, boy, did she know how to jump 'em through the hoops. P.T. Barnum would have *loved* her.

She slipped into some dressy clothes — for shopping later in the "right" stores — and trotted off for the hairdresser's, happy as a blacksnake in a nest of baby rabbits. *We're back in business, now, babe,* she thought. *Oh, yeah.*

As soon as Mac was out of sight, Lianne darted out of the apartment and took off for the discount bookstore that was hidden away in one of the town's indoor malls. When she got there, she hunted down Jimmy, her favorite bookseller. She found him crouched down inside the cash wrap, sorting special orders.

"Lianne McCormick!" His eyes lit up when he saw her, and he gave her a warm smile. "Nice to see you again. Dare I hope that you have given up dating car jockeys?"

She flushed. "I'm still dating, uh, Mac Lynn."

He sighed. "So the answer to my question is 'no.' What a waste of a woman with brains." He stood and leaned against the counter, his expression mock-wistful. "You ought to give some of us bright guys a chance."

Lianne glared up at him. "I've seen those creatures you date. All big bleached hair and legs up to their ears — so don't you feed me that line about looking for 'women with brains.' Now, I want everything you have on child abuse."

"Change the subject, why don't you?" Jimmy stroked his goatee and stared off into space. "Well . . . child abuse? Ugh! That's a nasty subject." He propped his elbows on the cash wrap. "Not thinking of taking up another new hobby, are you?"

Her glare became truly vicious, and he backed down.

"Just a joke," he said, and tried a placating waggle of the eyebrows. "Really. I don't normally make jokes about that subject, but you looked so — ah — threatening."

"The books."

"Foot-in-mouth, huh? Sorry. I won't joke anymore." He headed back toward the psychology section. "I think we actually might have a few. They'll either be in Psychology, or True-Crime, or — um, Biography. I just remembered one that's pretty highly recommended."

He pulled a thick paperback off a shelf and handed it to Lianne.

"*When Rabbit Howls,*" she read aloud. "By the Troops for Truddi Chase?"

He made a "you've got me," gesture. "Abuse, a woman with multiple personalities — all kinds of stuff. I haven't read it, but several of my customers have. They told me I ought to, but I wasn't into getting depressed right then. It's apparently all true. And pretty awful."

Lianne nodded. "I'll take it. Anything else?"

He pursed his lips and thought. "We have a couple on adult children of abusive parents, one on alcohol and abuse — and a few novels have started dealing with the subject, even fantasy stuff from Baen." He pulled the books that the store stocked and handed them to her with a sigh. "There isn't a great deal on that subject available yet outside of special order or hardbound." He jammed his hands into his pants pockets and rocked back on his heels. "Why the sudden interest?"

She decided it was better not to let the cat out of the bag yet. Kendrick was a lawyer — and there was such a thing as "defamation of character." "There's a kid in one of my classes — I'm just suspicious, you know?"

He nodded. "I hope you find what you need."

"Thanks." She paid for her small stack of books and got ready to leave.

Books in hand, Lianne felt a sense of relief related to the feeling that she was beginning to accomplish something. She looked at the bookseller with her sense of humor renewed. "By the way, that pinstriped suit makes you look like a gangster," she remarked.

Jimmy grinned and bowed with mock-gallantry. "Wanna see my violin case?"

Lianne returned his grin and headed out the door.

Maclyn found Dierdre just behind the Gate of a Thousand Voices, sitting next to the singing water-flames and staring into their depths.

"How are you, Mother?" he asked, resting a hand on her shoulder.

She kept her eyes turned to the blazes that darted through the fountain in their ever-changing dance. "I'm better than I was, but feeling my age."

"You aren't looking it."

Maclyn was rewarded by the soft half-curve of her smile, seen in profile. "Ask what you're wantin' to ask, laddie, and spare me your silver-tongued flatteries."

He came straight to the point. "How's Felouen?"

Dierdre — he couldn't think of her as D.D., not when she looked like this — sighed. "In pain — more of the spirit than of the body now, I suspect — but pain hurts no less when it stabs the soul."

Maclyn recalled seeing Gwaryon with Felouen a time or two and remembered the infatuated expression the older elf had worn on those occasions. "She and Gwaryon were — ?" Maclyn couldn't bring himself to finish the question.

His mother understood him anyway. "No. Gwaryon loved her; she was his friend. But his death hurts her more than her own remaining wounds."

He rubbed his temple, wondering which would do the

most good — leaving her alone, or going to her. "Where could I find her?"

Dierdre nodded to her left. "She was still resting in the Grove when I left."

Maclyn swung onto Rhellen's back with a fluid motion. "I'll find you later, Mother. We need to talk — but I want to see Felouen before then."

He found her where Dierdre had said she would be. She was alone. She knelt with her forehead pressed against the base of the Grove's heart-tree, still dressed in the tattered remains of the clothes she'd worn earlier. He saw her shoulders heave and realized she was crying soundlessly. His chest tightened and he felt a lump in his throat. He wanted, at that moment, to put his arms around her and hold her.

The cynical voice at the back of his brain commented that this was most likely because this was the first time in his life that he had seen her looking like anything but the seamless and indomitable warrior-maiden.

He quelled his doubts and knelt beside her. Hesitantly, he rested a hand on the small of her back. Felouen froze. Maclyn had seen the same response in deer caught in Rhellen's headlights. "It's only me," he said.

She looked over at him quickly, not relaxing even slightly, and he saw that her eyes were red and swollen. "I — I — " she started, and her voice faltered. "G-g-gwaryon — " she choked out, and fresh tears streamed down her cheeks.

Aw, hell, Maclyn thought, and pulled her against his chest. "I know," he whispered, holding her and rocking her against him.

She cried against him like that for a long time. When finally the tears were all wrung out of her, she started to talk, still keeping herself pressed firmly against him.

"We felt the summons together," she said. "He was watching at the Pool with me." She gave him the details, what she and Gwaryon were talking about, the things Gwaryon had said. Maclyn let her ramble.

"This child called us," she said, and abruptly he found himself listening with complete interest again. "She looked like a child, but she wasn't really — she said she was Ceth-lenn, a witch who had lived back when the elves were still only on the other side of the sea, back when someone named McLurrie was a leader of the Celts."

"I don't know that I've heard of him," Maclyn waffled. History had never been one of his strengths.

A single faint flicker of a smile crossed Felouen's lips. "Don't feel too bad. I didn't remember hearing of him, either. He was, according to Gwaryon, a pompous, over-blown human warlord who died long before we were born — in the days when you could call yourself a king if you commanded more than a dozen men."

"Ah," Maclyn said. "That explains it." But her choice of words in describing Amanda puzzled him. "What about the child, though? You said she was . . . a witch?"

Felouen looked just as puzzled and confused. "Her body was a child's body, that was what was so strange. She was very young, even by human standards. Very thin and frail-looking, with pale hair and brown eyes. But she knew the old magics, and her speech was from the Old Country. She talked about people that Gwaryon recognized. I did not feel that she intended us any harm. Truly."

If Felouen hadn't sensed any intended harm, there hadn't *been* any. "Then what happened?"

"That was the strangest thing of all." Felouen pulled away and leaned against the heart-tree, gathering strength. "She started to tell us why she had called us — but something stopped her. There were two voices warring in her, and a sort of awful battle that I saw going on in her face. It was frightening. Her face seemed to change as I watched, so that one instant she was one person, the next, someone else entirely. The closest I can describe, is that it was as if we were watching a possession, a war for control between the witch and something else. And in the end, the witch lost the battle. When the child looked at us again, she looked like someone completely different — completely mad — and her eyes had become a green so pale they were almost white. *That* mad creature summoned the golems from a bead she wore around her wrist — from the Unformed."

"That *was* Amanda," Maclyn whispered, his uneasy feeling confirmed.

Felouen turned to stare at him. "You know her—or them?"

Maclyn pulled at a tuft of grass near his knee. "Them ... yes. *That* explains the day at the racetrack. *That* explains everything — " He hugged Felouen again, this time in relief. "There really is more than one person in that child's body. I've met several of them, but I don't know if they've met each other."

Felouen put a hand on his cheek, then hugged him back. "I'm glad you came here," she whispered.

"I was worried about you," Maclyn admitted, serious again. "I was afraid you were going to die."

She shuddered convulsively. "I almost did, Mac. I was standing with the Abyss in front of me, and I started to step onto the glowing bridge — but the singing called me back." She started crying again. "I wasn't going to come — but somehow, standing there, I remembered you. I suppose it wasn't time for me yet."

Mac found his voice suddenly hoarse. "Don't leave again. If you face the edge of the Abyss, walk away." He held her tighter.

She pressed her face into his chest, trembling. "I will, Maclyn. I promise."

Amanda-Abbey lay on her bed with her eyes closed and talked silently to Cethlenn. *:The other one, the crazy one — is she one of us, really?:*

:Aye,: came the grim reply. *:She's real enough.:*

Amanda-Abbey shuddered. *:She's so — bad.:*

:She is that, too. But she has been through things you canna' imagine, child — she has taken all the pain in your life so that you wouldna' have any. Fear and pain are all she knows, and if she has learned to fight, she's paid, and plenty, for the knowledge.:

Amanda-Abbey remembered the sick feelings she'd had earlier. *:I don't know what you mean,:* she said.

Cethlenn's expression darkened. *:There are times when you*

have bruises — when you hurt and don't know why — when things that you don't understand scare you — : the witch began slowly.

Amanda knew what the witch meant now. *:Like the Father.:*

Cethlenn nodded agreement. *:Exactly like the Father. You don't know how you got those bruises, or why you hurt, or why the Father scares you — but she knows. Her name is Anne, and she is very frightened, and very brave. And in her own confused way, she loves you.:*

Amanda-Abbey wrinkled her nose. *:I didn't like her. She scares me.:*

:You ought to be scared. She's very dangerous, and sometimes she doesn't know who is trying to hurt her and who is trying to help her. The only person she trusts is herself, because that is the only person she knows won't hurt her.: Cethlenn sat closer to Amanda-Abbey and whispered, *:She scares me, too.:*

Amanda-Abbey sighed. That was an uncomfortable revelation. *:Is she the only other one?:*

Cethlenn shook her head. *:No. There are others.:*

That was even more uncomfortable. *:Are they all like her?:*

:They are as different as you and I,: Cethlenn assured her.

Amanda-Abbey thought about that for a while. At last she said, *:Are there any I could meet?:*

Cethlenn considered the question. *:Those of you who I know are Anne, Alice, you — and Amanda. There may be others who are hiding. Anne hid from me for a long time, until she realized that she was stronger than I am.:* Cethlenn seemed to think of something, and she frowned abruptly. *:You can't meet Amanda, I'm afraid.:*

There was something ominous in Cethlenn's expression. She was afraid to ask, but she did anyway. *:Why not?:*

Cethlenn answered, after a reluctant pause. *:Amanda stays in a very cold place, and she never moves, and she never speaks — I'm not sure that she's really still alive. She is — or was — very young. Something terrible happened to her when she was three, and that was when she went away, and you and Anne were born.:*

Amanda-Abbey's body tensed. *:What about — um, Alice?:*

Cethlenn seemed relieved that she didn't ask anything else. *:Alice goes to church with Them on Sundays, and keeps your* *room all cleaned up, and makes sure you don't get your clothes very dirty. There are many things that she, too, has done to protect you. But I don't know that you will like her. Still, I think that you must meet her. If you can work together, I think we can beat Them.:*

A thought niggled at the back of Amanda-Abbey's mind, which grew larger and uglier and began to worry her deeply. *:Cethlenn,:* she whispered, *:if they have these things they do to protect me, what do I do for them?:*

Cethlenn smiled sadly. *:You're the one, child, who learns her school lessons, plays with her friends, and makes everyone outside of your family believe everything is all right. Anne decided that you couldna' tell what you didna' know, and protected you, so that you could protect them.:* A tear formed at the corner of the witch's eye, and she wiped it away with a preoccupied swipe. *:Alice protects you by believing things you might ask questions about, so that you don't get into trouble there — and by keeping your room and your things exactly the way the Step-Mother wants them so that there are fewer reasons to punish you. They have no life except for keeping you from the ugliness and the brutality and the pain that they know. You keep up the disguise tha' keeps them alive. Even so, they want to live.:*

Cethlenn's voice grew hoarse, and her expression grew far away. *:It's the only thing any of us wants, at the end.:*

The red-haired woman who stepped out of the late-model Thunderbird and strode across the gravel to the Bal-A-Shar barn bore little resemblance to the somewhat battered woman who had left a cheap hotel room for the beauty salon only a few hours earlier. "Alessandra Whitchurch-Snowdon, Lady Rivers," complete with expensive-looking business cards, wore her shoulder-length hair in a neat french braid, and affected riding boots, jodhpurs, a lean tweedy jacket with leather patches on the elbows, and a high-necked silk blouse. She carried herself with the effortless confidence that access to unlimited funds and a high social standing seem to confer. She managed to convey, in her cool, clipped accent, wry amusement at American cars which had their steering wheels on the wrong side, American roads which were positively rampant with insane drivers and impossible rules, and American restaurants, which didn't know how the hell to serve tea ("they serve it over *ice*, my dear, and sweet!"), or what went with it ("*everything* over here tastes like it's been bathed in sugar"). She saved her compliments for the horses.

Within ten minutes, Merryl and "Alessandra" were on a first nickname basis, ("Dear, I'm only Lady Rivers to the poor — my closest friends call me Bits,") and were comparing points on the three two-year-old fillies Merryl was offering. "Alessandra" narrowed the choices down to two, and then it became a matter of pedigree.

They returned the horses to their stalls, "Alessandra" making sure she watched gait and conformation even as they were led away, and then headed back to the house to flip through the pedigrees that Merryl kept up with on her computer.

After a thorough study of the pedigrees, for both of which the delighted "Lady Rivers" received laser-printed hard copies — "Want to see what both of the girls could offer to my breeding program before I settle on one, don't I?" — Merryl gave her a guided tour of the house.

"Cozier than the ancestral pile back home, don't you know?" the ersatz noblewoman offered about halfway through the tour. "You wouldn't believe the chilling effect suits of armor have on one if one happens to be wandering about the place in the wee hours. But nobody will let me change the bloody decorating scheme. National Trust, don't you know."

Prices for each of the two horses were discussed and agreed upon in between rooms — there was no dickering. This appeared to hearten the seller greatly.

The two women parted with "Bits" promising to make up her mind in the next day or so, and ring back with her decision. Both women were smiling as they went their separate ways.

Lianne skimmed the abuse texts first, and was surprised to find that they were more help than she'd anticipated.

They outlined signs and symptoms of abuse that went farther than just noting bruises with regular outlines, or a
high incidence of broken bones, E.R. visits, or days absent
from school. They also outlined personality traits — from
constant timidity, clinging behavior, or a desperate search
for anyone's approval, to erratic school performances.

One book focused almost exclusively on child sexual
abuse, and Lianne was surprised to find that sexual abuse
of children did not have to include intercourse. Inap-
propriate touching or kissing, verbal abuse with sexual
overtones, and some forms of humiliation were all forms of
sexual abuse. She was appalled to find that a shocking
number of children were sexually abused — statistics
varied slightly, but according to her books, by the time they
reached adulthood, roughly one out of every five girls and
one out of every nine boys would have encountered sexual
abuse. Most sexual abusers were also alcoholics, and almost
all of them were men.

Abuse of all kinds ran in families, with a high percentage of
abused children growing up to be abusers. It was agreed in all
of her sources that the biggest hope for eliminating child
abuse of any kind was to treat the children who had been
abused, *soon*, so that they in turn would not continue the cycle.

Lianne curled on the couch, lost in the horror of the raw
numbers. The odds were that Amanda was being sexually
abused — she fit many of the characteristics of abused kids,
though not all at the same time. Even worse, the odds were
incredibly high that Amanda not only wasn't the first
abused child Lianne had in her class, but that she wasn't the
only abused kid in her class right then.

I didn't know, Lianne thought. She felt sick. *Dammit, I just
didn't know.*

There had to be something she could do. *Maybe I could
lobby to have some sort of abuse-detection program added to our cur-
riculum. Let the kids who are being abused know that abuse is not
their fault — never their fault — and find some way to tell them that
they aren't alone.* The books had said that children felt — or
were told until they believed it — that they had somehow
caused the abuse. It also said kids thought such things had

never happened to anyone but them. And sometimes — this made her gorge rise — they thought it was normal. That things like this *did* happen to everyone else, and that there would be no reason why anyone would help them. They were often told no one would believe what the children said. Those were apparently the biggest reasons why kids didn't go to someone for help.

Another was that they were afraid that something bad would happen to their parents. They didn't realize that the abuse was as bad for their parents as it was for them — that their parents needed help, too.

They could come to me, Lianne thought. *And there are always a few teachers in any school that the kids know they can trust. Those are the people they should tell.*

Lianne stretched out on the couch, staring out the glass doors of her apartment at the quad and the faintly greening trees, and the few bits of dull gray sky that showed around the other apartment buildings. *Someone would listen — someone would believe them. And then they would get help.*

She felt emotionally depleted, but she picked up the Truddi Chase biography anyway, and was drawn into it almost immediately.

When she finally put it down, hours later, it was dark outside, and the wind had picked up again. She shuddered and drew the curtains across the glass doors.

That Truddi Chase had managed to survive her ordeal in any form whatsoever spoke for the strength of the human spirit. That she had gone on to make a life for herself left Lianne feeling very weak and insignificant in comparison. *I feel almost guilty that I had such an easy life.*

Lianne had a bad moment when she realized she could see similarities in things she read about Truddi Chase and things she saw in Amanda. Changes in personality, in abilities, in attitudes toward her and other teachers and the girl's classmates — she'd seen all of them.

Could Amanda be a multiple personality case? It seemed more than a little farfetched. But if she was, what sort of life could have fractured her into those multiples?

The door rang, and Lianne sighed with relief. *He's found*

something, then. Good. After reading *When Rabbit Howls,* she wasn't as eager to spend the night by herself as she had been.

She opened the door with a grateful smile on her face.

"Hi!" a masked stranger said, and wedged her riding boot into the door. "I saw your boyfriend wasn't here, so I thought I'd pay you a visit."

She shoved her way inside with her gun aimed at Lianne's midsection the whole time, and closed the door before Lianne had any time to react.

"Just us girls together," the intruder said cheerfully, and pulled back the hammer with an ominous *click.*

• Chapter Eleven

Feeling guilty is not the best way to start the day, Mac told him-self, driving slowly toward Lianne's. He worried about telling her how out of hand his comforting of Felouen had gotten, then rationalized that hang-ups about monogamy were a mostly human obsession. But then he reminded himself that he had known about that human quirk before he started dating a human —

Finally he made up his mind that he would just pretend nothing had happened unless Lianne accidentally found out otherwise.

Besides, he told himself in an attempt to soothe his aching conscience, *Felouen really needed me there last night. It made her so happy to see that I'd accepted the Ring's geas. She looked at me the way human women do when I've just won a race. And after Gwaryon's death, she needed comforting.*

And since when does "comforting" include jumping the bereaved's bones? his conscience snapped back.

So much for that approach. He dragged his feet as he walked away from Rhellen, heading as slowly as he could up the walk to the apartment. And he knew immediately that there was something very odd.

She's left the door standing open he thought when he stepped into the apartment entryway. The heavy gray door stood about an inch ajar. He could see that the chain lock wasn't on, either. *Considering the day she had yesterday, I'm surprised she doesn't have the whole apartment locked and barred. What did she do, just go collapse on the couch? Or maybe — maybe she left it open for me this morning. So I'd just come straight in.* He shook his head, puzzled, and knocked.

"Hey, Lianne!" There was no answer. He pushed the door all the way open, and looked inside.

Fear overwhelmed puzzlement.

He stared at the living room. It had been thoroughly and expertly trashed.

Oh, gods, he thought, *oh, shit!* With inhuman strength, he clamped down hard on the doorknob; it broke off in his hand. Before him, two living-room chairs lay on their sides with books scattered across them. The shattered television lay on the floor, one of the shoes he had last seen Lianne wearing resting in the debris. In the connecting kitchen, shards from broken glasses and dishes sparkled in the light of one errant sunbeam. A Rorschach blot of blood traced obscene patterns down one wall.

"Lianne! Lianne! Where are you?" he shouted. He ran from room to room. Beyond the livingroom and the kitchen, nothing had been disturbed. Lianne's jewelry was intact, her stereo and her computer were where they belonged, her clothes still hung neatly in the closet.

Only Lianne was gone.

In the sinister hush of the empty apartment, his sharp, irregular breaths and the tick of the kitchen clock were the only sounds. He stretched his psychic feelers — and came up empty. No magic had touched this room except his own. No demon creatures from the Unformed Plane had stolen Lianne away.

Scenes from a hundred TV cop shows played in his memory. Robbery wasn't the motive — and it wasn't magic, either Unseleighe or human. Rape? Kidnapping? Worse? Mac started looking for a message, a note, anything — going room to room and searching inch by inch.

When the phone rang right next to his ear, Mac jumped. "Gods, let it be her," he whispered. "Let this be some stupid mistake."

He picked up the handset and held it to his ear. "Lianne?" he asked.

"Not a chance, babe. It's Jewelene. I've got her." The voice on the other end of the line was muffled, the laughter in his ear was coarse and vicious. "You owe me. You owe me big time, baby — and you're going to pay. You know what?"

A dull ache gripped Mac's chest. "What?"

"You stole my car and slashed the tires. So I stole your

girl. You don't want to know what I've slashed." The voice was laughing again.

Belinda Ciucci.

"What do you want?" Mac whispered.

The voice was full of obscene gloating. "I'm going to kill her. And I'm going to enjoy every long second of it."

Think, fool! What can you bargain for her? "You don't want her."

Belinda made a *tsk*ing sound. "Sure I do, babe. You know what they say about a bird in the hand and all that."

Convince her. Somehow convince her. "You want me. Not her."

Deep breathing for a moment, as his heart raced and fear clogged his throat. "Yeah, but I've got her. Right now, pal, I just want to hurt somebody. She put up a fight — I've already hurt her a little. She's not as pretty as she used to be."

Gods, Lianne. What in hell have I done to you? Mac thought. *What did I get you into? How can I get you out again?* "You tell me what you want me to do, and I'll do it. Just let her go. Don't hurt her anymore."

"Damn shame you didn't have that attitude a day or two ago. Everybody would have been a lot happier." Maclyn twisted a butter knife lying on the counter into a knot. *Damn Belinda Ciucci,* he thought. *I should have wiped her memories instead of playing games with her.*

The woman cleared her throat. "First, don't call the police. I'll kill her at the first sign that you've involved them. For now, you get to wait. You're going to meet me somewhere, but I haven't decided where yet. Stay by the phone. I'll call you back when I make up my mind."

Mac clenched his hand on the handset. This woman was not sane. "When?"

Belinda laughed, and the note in her voice confirmed that she was not sane. "Who knows?"

"Let me talk to her," he pleaded.

"Nope." There was a click. The woman had hung up.

Mac refrained from smashing the handset to shreds. Instead, he set it gently back in the receiver. Then he put his fist through the wall. "Dammit! Dammit, I should have *been* here, dammit! I should have been *here*. Not with Felouen. Here. If I'd been here, none of this would have happened."

He stared at the phone, his only link with Lianne. He hadn't thought through the possible consequences of angering Belinda, then leaving her to her own devices. He could have taken care of her by himself earlier — that would have been the end of it. No one would have suffered. Now he needed help, and needed it badly.

And Dierdre and Felouen and all of his other potential sources of help were currently Underhill gearing up to wipe out golems. In fact, he should have been going straight from Lianne's place back to Elfhame Outremer. Instead, he was locked in place in the apartment.

He would have to construct a Gate in the apartment, he decided — one that he could leave up and use to shuttle back and forth between Underhill and Lianne's telephone. The energy drain would be bad, worse since his resources were already low. He was tired, he was needed by both his own people and a seriously disturbed child, he'd just lost a friend and had another seriously hurt — and now Lianne was a hostage somewhere. He was pulled in too many directions.

Which is exactly when people get careless and get themselves killed, he told himself. *Not that my state of readiness matters. There's no looking back.* He started pulling in the energy that would form the Gate.

Amanda-Anne sat like a spider in her web, centered in the Unformed Plane, singing loudly and off-key, making monsters.

She had started to vary them — somewhere along the line, she had gotten tired of the stick-men. She made a few two-headed stick-men, but even that was too boring. She made some things with four legs and long, spiky tails and huge teeth, and she rather liked those. She made a few more, similar but with wings. When the first of her winged monsters flew through the air, she laughed and clapped her hands — and began adding wings to everything she made from then on. Her monsters started getting bigger. One had dozens of legs and three heads on long, snake-like necks; it flew with less grace than a winged tank might have, but it did fly.

No one bothered her in the Unformed's nothingness. The Father couldn't find her. The nasty things that lived there were more afraid of her than she was of them. Nothing could touch her, nothing could hurt her. She had never had so much fun in her life. She had never had so many friends, either.

She rubbed the green bead strung on her wrist. "My m-m-magic door," she whispered. "J-j-j-just like the g-g-genie's lamp." She crowed with delight. To have been so weak, to be so strong — it was wonderful.

And the best thing was that her magic door could take her back into the elf's world. She thought about this as she worked on her current creation, an eight-legged nightmare with hundreds of eyes and a fanged mouth that ran the length of its belly. If it weren't for the goody-two-shoes elves, that place would have been perfect. The Father and the Step-Mother couldn't get there. In among all those trees, with all that magic, she would be safe. She could hide there forever — if it weren't for the stupid elves, who would make her go home.

She thought yearningly of how nice this place would be without bossy elves, about how much she would like to hide here forever.

She sang to herself and made another monster.

Lianne woke to a blaze of pain, with the tang of blood and a filthy rag in her mouth, bathed in the stench of car exhaust and gasoline. She felt as if she was lying on a bed of nails, with another one slowly descending on her. Her head throbbed, her eyes would not open, her face burned horribly and screamed with pain. Her ribs crunched ominously against hard cold metal and stinking carpet when she rolled off to the left. She felt the bones of her face shift relative to each other when she moved, and white-hot searing agony shot through her skull. She sobbed, and the movement of her rib cage stabbed fire along her nerves.

What have I done? she wondered. *Where am I?*

She fought to retrieve foggy memory.

She remembered elves fighting the monsters — or was that a true memory? She remembered magic, too — and Maclyn doing magic. And that was crazy. Absolutely crazy. Impossible. Everyone knew that magic couldn't exist.

Mac Lynn. Not Maclyn. He's a racecar driver. Not an elf. Something has happened to my mind — amnesia or something — to make me think of magic. However I got hurt like this — it's confused me.

But that wasn't so, was it? Maclyn, not Mac Lynn, wasn't human. She'd figured that out all by herself, using logic, using reason — and she'd caught him out. So the elves were real. That meant the monsters were real, too. The elves had won their fight with the monsters. Because of her. *I'm a hero — whoopee. Look where it got me.*

What happened next?

She remembered books. Child abuse books — she'd been reading, and she'd just figured out something about Amanda. Yes. It was coming back. She remembered the knock at her door, but it wasn't Mac waiting on the other side.

It had been a strange woman with a gun.

The woman had barged in — but Lianne hadn't reacted the way she'd expected. Lianne had grabbed a heavy ashtray and bashed the intruder in the face — *God knows where the courage for that trick came from, or how I managed it —* and blood had spurted down the inside of the pantyhose mask the bitch wore. A second bash, this time to the gunhand, and the gun had flown across the room.

I got first licks in — but she had obviously had training. Lots of it.

Lianne was starting to remember the other things, as well. Very unpleasant things. The woman was good at hand-to-hand combat — she'd probably used it on other people, given the way she acted. When she dove at Lianne, she took her down and flipped her on her stomach, slapped handcuffs on her — *what the hell was she doing with handcuffs?* — and then started kicking.

Lianne knew she had broken ribs. She remembered hearing them crack when the woman's riding boots struck, and she could feel them now, hurting more than she'd ever thought she could hurt, screaming with pain with every breath. Her nose was broken, too, and probably her jaw and her left cheekbone — those injuries had occurred after the woman retrieved her gun, when she started beating Lianne in the face with it.

Her eyes wouldn't open because they were swollen so badly. *I could go blind from this*, she realized with horror, then wondered if she was going to live through this to *be* blind. She couldn't move her arms — the handcuffs were still on. Her ankles were tied together.

The rag in her mouth tasted of blood, old and new.

Why I'm here doesn't matter. What matters is — how do I get out?

From her almost-fetal position — which she could not change without bumping solid obstacles or causing even more pain than she already endured — from the smells, and from faintly heard road noises, she figured she was in the trunk of a car. She did not remember how she got there. *She must have knocked me out, dragged me to the car — she was a hell of a lot stronger than I would have guessed.*

The car door slammed so hard right then that the shock wave jarred her head and rattled through her teeth. The driver's weight as she (or was it a he now?) bounced the vehicle around, confirming the fact that her cage was, indeed, the trunk of her captor's car. The engine started up, and Lianne was thrown from one side to the other as the driver accelerated and turned corners at high speed. The teacher debated making some noise to let the driver know she was awake — then decided against it. There was nothing in the woman's attitude last night that made Lianne think she would let her get a drink of water, or go to the bathroom — if the same woman was still the one who had her. Lianne figured if she made any noise, she was more likely to be beaten with a pistol again. A drink of water wasn't worth the pain.

Mac will know I'm gone today. No one else will miss me until tomorrow, but Mac will know. I hope he finds me soon — I think she's going to kill me if he doesn't.

Elves with mage-blades and gleaming gold armor sat on the grass next to elves in Kevlar who carried Steyr AUGs, shotguns, or high-tech graphite compound bows — and these sat next to elves whose only weapons were their expressions of scorn or amused disbelief. Felouen tried to contain her dismay at the meager attendance. Less than half of Elfhame Outremer's fighting force had seen fit to show up for her briefing. The few warriors present had listened in polite silence while Felouen described her ordeal. She began with the spell that had drawn her and Gwaryon in and ended with Deirdre's entrance. Deirdre took up the tale then, describing what they found, Gwaryon's death and the rescue by the human woman.

Felouen thought that she had done well — and Deirdre certainly sounded convincing enough — but it was obvious that the warriors were unimpressed.

One of the younger elves, who wore no weapons, sprawled in the grass, nonchalant. He'd listened with a bored expression on his face. When she finished speaking, he indicated that he had a question with an indolently raised finger.

"Yes?" Felouen asked him.

"I felt the spell you're talking about yesterday. I warded against it as soon as I noticed it, and it didn't bother me. If you hadn't been hanging around old weird Gwaryon, you would done the same thing, and then we wouldn't have been out here earlier using a lot of valuable energy saving your life." He shrugged and turned his palms up. "Not that I resent helping you out — but if you had taken a few reasonable precautions, it wouldn't have been necessary."

One of the older elves nodded. "You should never have answered a summons unarmed."

"How in all the hells would I know that?" Felouen snapped. "Humans stopped summoning elves long before I was born. And Gwaryon didn't mention it."

One of the others grunted. "He should have."

"Granted," Felouen snarled. "However, you are all missing the point. The witch-child who summoned us wasn't the threat. The other child and the Unseleighe things *she* called were the threat."

A mail-clad woman who sat near the front sighed. "I find it hard to believe that they are even a fraction of the threat you make them out to be, Felouen. The sort of weirdlings a child is strong enough to conjure would have to be pretty feeble. I know they killed Gwaryon, and I'm not discounting the injuries they did you — but neither of you was *armed*. Neither Dierdre nor Maclyn were harmed."

Felouen felt her frustration building. She hit her fists together, wishing each of them held one slow-brained elvish skull in it. "The only reason they were unhurt is that the human woman broke the containment spell and sent them back wherever they came from."

A shrug of indifference. "Yes. Precisely. We're talking about monsters that one *human* can banish."

"We're talkin' about five beasties that four elves couldna' kill — couldna' even scratch, Ymelthre." Dierdre, cross-legged to one side of the standing Felouen, leaned forward, her eyes glowing with contained rage. "With our enchanted blades, we couldna' even make them cry out. *And neither Gwaryon nor Felouen could break the binding spell that held them helpless.* A spell a 'mere human child' set. Felouen has seen these things in the Oracular Pool, and she says they are a threat to us. And I've fought them, and I say they are a threat to us. We need to stand a watch. We need to be ready."

Felouen watched them as the group broke into a debate over standing watch versus not standing watch. *I know what the problem is. Nothing really scares them anymore*, she thought. *They have been the fastest and the strongest and the best for so long, they believe they can't be hurt. Except by our Unseleighe kin, and this time they aren't involved.*

When the group announced its decision to post a bare-bones watch so thin that she knew it was merely a token thrown in her direction because she was the warriors' chieftain, she smiled bitterly. *Well, I hope they're right.*

After the main group had drifted off, several of the Ring-sworn, who had waited in silence, came up to stand in front of her. She recognized all of them from long-ago campaigns together, or from more recent social meetings. Of the group, considered by most of the elvenkind in Elfhame Outremer to be dreadfully conservative, Amallen was nominal leader. Amallen bent one knee slightly — Old World manners — and briefly bowed his head.

"Lady," he said in grave tones, "do not think too badly of them. They have not fought beside you — and they cannot imagine a human child who could bring forth anything that could endanger them. We," and with a nod of his head he indicated his companions, "have decided among ourselves to stand a separate watch. We will begin at once; we have already set our shifts. The others will realize that they were wrong later — and some may die learning their folly. We don't need to see the monsters to smell their taint. There is something sorely wrong here — and though we cannot fathom it, we cannot doubt it."

Felouen smiled gratefully, as relief so profound it made her knees weak washed over her. "Those who will later owe you their lives will thank you. I know that thanks is due now." She hugged each of the nine who had supported her for so long. "I wish this were idle worrying. As it is, I know you won't be standing your watches alone for long."

Belinda grinned at herself in the rearview mirror. *The worm turns — that's the phrase, I think. The worm turns.* She readjusted the mirror and stretched the stiff muscles in her shoulders.

The worm has certainly turned in my favor now. The light changed from red to green, and Belinda headed through the intersection and pointed the car out of town. She'd spent the night in the Thunderbird, unwilling to move her captive out of the security of the trunk, and equally unwilling to leave her in the trunk while she slept inside her motel room. No sense taking a chance on the teacher waking up and making enough noise to get herself rescued. And she couldn't think of anyplace to keep the woman — until she remembered the abandoned building out in the middle of nowhere that she'd hiked past the night Mac Lynn stole her car.

It would work well enough, Belinda thought. Tie the teacher up, steal her clothes so that she didn't get the urge to do any wandering even if she got loose, and leave her.

Of course, killing her immediately would be a lot less complicated. There was nothing to connect her with the woman; nothing left behind to incriminate Belinda. It would be just one more senseless abduction-murder — probably wind up on "Unsolved Mysteries." If she killed the teacher, there wouldn't be any witnesses who might cause trouble later, and Mac Lynn didn't need to know his little slut was dead — hell, the whole purpose of this business had been to get him by the balls. Belinda smiled. The tone of his voice over the phone told him she'd accomplished that. So Miss Teacher had served her purpose. He'd go where Belinda told him to go, hoping that his girlfriend would still be alive.

The abandoned house would *still* make a good destination. It could be weeks or even months before someone found the body — Belinda and the child and Mel Tanbridge would be well away from North Carolina by then.

She retraced her trip from that night carefully, stopping and backtracking on a couple of occasions as she missed a turn. It was a long drive, made longer by the fact that she felt obligated to drive the speed limit right then. It would be a stone bitch to get pulled with a well-beaten kidnap victim in her possession.

The sun rode higher and the day started getting hot — a nice enough change, Belinda thought, after the cold, wet crap of the day before. She drove past hundreds of little rural houses, all of them ordinary, all of them quiet — which suited her just fine. But none of them was the one she wanted.

Finally she spotted the place. Weeds had overgrown the drive, and kudzu, greening as the weather warmed, covered everything else. In another month, the house would be completely invisible under its kudzu blanket.

Perfect. I'll have to thank Mac Lynn for helping me find this dump.

Now, what to do with little miss schoolmarm?

Belinda considered only an instant, then decided. Hostages were risky, and too much trouble to take care of. Dead bodies, on the other hand, were very little trouble at all. She'd rather deal with corpses than captives any day.

So, she'd get the woman out of the trunk, march her into the place. Shoot her in the head, shove the body through some loose floorboards — there were bound to be some loose floorboards in there somewhere. Then she'd find a phone, call Mac Lynn, have him meet her — where?

Why not out here? Torture the bastard, dump him next to his girlfriend while he's still alive and can appreciate it — then kill him. That would be fair after what he's done to me.

First the girlfriend.

She pulled into the weed-choked drive, and the Thunderbird bumped along, weeds and sticks hissing and thumping against the glossy brown finish. She stopped the car when she was right behind the house. It was going to be hell to get back out again, she thought with displeasure.

The place was dilapidated, the wrap-around porch sagged to the ground in several places, and the only part of the structure that looked slightly solid were the boards nailed over the windows. There had been something nailed over the door, too, but that had been ripped away. The actual door hung on one rusted hinge, partway open. The place was a perfect haven for snakes and rats and God only knew what else. *At least that probably keeps the riff-raff out,* she mused. *More than that ludicrous little sign, anyway.*

The building was posted, "NO TRESPASS — G BY ORDER OF T — ." Rain and sun and wind had bleached the yellow sign to bone white on one side and obliterated much of its message. *Dump looks like the place where the universe goes to die.* It gave her the creeps worse in the daylight than it had at night. She realized that was because she could see it better in daylight.

Belinda pulled out her gun. It was a good, reliable

weapon. She didn't use it often — guns weren't subtle enough for her taste most of the time — but it had never let her down.

Still, she didn't much like the idea of killing the teacher — it would hurt the bastard race driver, but it was extra. She wasn't getting paid for it — and that made it dirtier, somehow, than killing for pay. Or for revenge.

Belinda looked out at the bleak ruin. *I'll be doing her a favor,* she decided. *It would be worse for her if I left her here alive.*

She slipped the gun into its holster and pulled the keys out of the ignition. It would be a long time before she made the mistake of leaving them in it again — no matter how little time she intended to be gone. She popped the latch on the trunk, got out, and walked around to the back, fighting her way through burrs and thorns and tenacious stickers.

She pulled her shoulders back and took a deep breath. The gap between the trunk and the hood looked odd for a moment. Peculiar. It gave her the shivers for just a moment, like someone had stepped on her grave.

She shook off the feeling.

Ah, well. Showtime, she thought.

She reached down to release the latch.

Cethlenn flew Abbey across the slick ice-barrier that Alice had created to protect her domain, then floated both of them down to stand in the long, white-on-white corridor.

Amanda-Abbey studied the high-arched ceiling and the unadorned walls that ran, unbroken, to the vanishing point. "She's in there?" she asked.

"Somewhere," Cethlenn agreed.

Abbey stared at the nothingness, puzzled. "How will we find her?"

Cethlenn didn't seem concerned. "We won't. She'll find us."

"We're just going to wait here?" Abbey asked, hoping that Cethlenn had some plan.

Cethlenn gave the girl a weary smile. "I wish it were so easy. No — we'll walk. Make lots of noise."

That made no sense at all. "Why?"

"You'll see," Cethlenn promised.

The two of them started down the corridor, stomping on the floor as hard as they could, sending the clamor of their footsteps ringing on ahead of them. Amanda-Abbey started hopping, and her heavy thumps increased the racket — until she noticed the noise becoming muffled, and the floor on which she jumped becoming springier.

She looked down at her feet. "Cethlenn," she whispered, "look! The floor is growing carpet!"

"Aye." Cethlenn did not seem surprised. "She always does that after a bit. Now we must sing. Know you a bothersome song that we can sing together?"

" 'One Hundred Bottles of Beer on the Wall,' " Abbey offered after a moment's thought.

Cethlenn shook her head. "Sing a bit of it for me."

Amanda-Abbey did, while the witch listened.

"Oh, for sure — " Cethlenn laughed. "That will drive her to distraction."

They resumed marching while they bellowed through nearly forty verses of the song. Again, Abbey noticed a change, as their singing echoed less and less, and seemed closer and smaller — though she knew she was making just as much noise as she had at the first.

Cethlenn looked up and pointed at the ceiling.

Amanda-Abbey's gaze followed the gesture. "She's lowered it."

"Now we bring her to us," Cethlenn whispered. "Here. Take this." The witch made a gesture, and a pail of bright yellow paint appeared in her hand. She offered it to Abbey, who took it and stared at it in confusion.

Cethlenn created blue and pink paints for herself, in the brightest tints imaginable. She took the pink pail, and slung it against one wall. Fluorescent streaks spread in gaudy profusion, and dripped messily down the surface of the corridor. The witch followed the same procedure with the blue.

Amanda-Abbey watched, appalled. "That's not very nice, Cethlenn," she said.

"It had to be done." The witch shrugged. "Now you do yours."

Abbey bit her lip, then tipped her can and dribbled just a bit of the yellow onto the floor.

"*Not on the carpet!*" a shrill soprano voice screeched, and a child raced out of hiding and yanked the can away from Abbey.

Abbey and Alice stared at each other. Abbey thought that the girl appeared to be about her own age — but that similarity was the only one Abbey could find. The other girl was as white as the walls around her — white hair, white face, white lips, white clothes — no hint of color touched any part of her except for her eyes. The girl's eyes were gray, but they were neither the bright and lively gray of kittens nor the safe gray of the bark of old maple trees, nor the firm and dependable gray of the stones in good fireplaces. They were the dismal gray of drizzly late afternoons when the sun hadn't been out all day. They were the flat gray of institutional paint, the kind Abbey saw used on garage floors and storage rooms, and the kind she suspected prisons would be painted in.

"I'm Abbey," she said, lost in the hopelessness of those gray, gray eyes. "I'm — I'm your sister."

The gray eyes narrowed. "*You made a mess!*" Alice fumed. "You tracked on my carpet, you were noisy, you were *singing* in my hall!" She glared at the two of them, then pointed her finger at Cethlenn. "*You* have come here before. I don't want you here."

"*Alice!*" Cethlenn took the authoritarian posture and voice of a demanding adult. "You are being rude to your guest. You have not properly introduced yourself to your sister."

Alice wasn't fooled for a second. "I'm not the one who went into peoples' houses and stomped and screamed and sang wicked songs and threw paint on the walls and tracked it into the carpet. That's evil. Evil! I don't have to be polite to evil people — the Bible says not to countenance wickedness."

Abbey raised an eyebrow and looked at the witch. :*This is my sister? She's awful. Why would anyone ever let her come out?*:

:*She's very good at cleaning up messes. That's something neither you nor Anne have managed yet. Adults think she is a very good child, she knows manners — and she is very organized and very patient. And she doesn't mind being alone.:* Cethlenn rested a hand on Abbey's shoulder. *:She also knows things you don't know. You need her.:*

:Then we shouldn't have dumped paint on her carpet.:

Cethlenn waved her hand at the paint that still marked walls and floor. It vanished, along with the paint cans that had contained it. *:Now she doesn't have as much to be upset about.:*

Cethlenn jammed her thumbs into the braided belt that wrapped around her narrow waist and leaned down until her eyes were on a level with Amanda-Alice's. "If you want to stop real wickedness, come with us," she told the pale girl. "You have yet another sister, who protects both of you. She thinks the way to protect you is by making monsters — and that is what she is doing now. She has to be stopped."

"Making — monsters?" Alice looked at Abbey. "You are going to stop her?"

Abbey shrugged helplessly. "Cethlenn says the two of us can't. We need more help."

Alice's eyes lit with a zealot's glee. "I'll help. When we've stopped her, I'll tell her about the Bible."

Amanda-Abbey, who had met Anne once before, had doubts about the wisdom of that, but she kept them to herself. She figured Alice would reconsider, too, once she'd met the other "sister." So she said nothing, just nodded.

Cethlenn said, "Excellent. I'm glad you're joining us, Alice. We can put your talents to good use."

Abbey tried not to be bothered by the fact that, where she had only had herself and the faceless voice of "Stranger" to rely on a few days ago, now she had the bossy presence of Cethlenn and the bizarre Alice. And Anne, who scared her badly, and whom she did not like at all, was yet to come.

Maclyn finished the Gate and sagged against the living-room wall, gray with exhaustion. *:Rhellen — stay put, and if the phone rings, come through and get me,:* he Mindspoke to his elvensteed — hoofprints in the living room were the least of the damage that had been done here. *:The Gate is in the kitchen — get me as fast as you can, and get me back here before it stops. I'll leave the side door open.:*

The elvensteed sent back affirmation, and Maclyn stepped toward the kitchen and through the Gate.

He stepped out at the periphery of the Grove and immediately looked toward its center. He had expected to see the fighting forces of Elfhame Outremer assembled, or at least to have been met by armed guards.

But there was no one. The Grove was devoid of warriors, devoid of elves of any walk of life. He listened and heard the gentle laughter and the music of normal days coming from Elfhame Outremer itself, and he frowned. Surely Felouen and Dierdre had brought their message to the city. Yet the sounds he heard were not the sounds of a people preparing for war.

"Ha, Thaerry, you almost had me," a light female voice called from the other side of the Grove.

Maclyn saw a red-clad beauty dart out from under the sheltering boughs of the trees, followed closely by her lean swain, elegantly robed in gold-shot blue.

"Droewyn, you minx — I'll have you yet," the would-be lover answered. He caught the girl and tripped her into the grass, and the two of them rolled together, laughing and fondling each other, oblivious to Maclyn's presence.

"Pardon," Mac said, stepping into the open arena of the Grove with them, "but have Felouen and Dierdre not been here?"

Droewyn straightened her bodice with some annoyance, and said, "Aye, they've been, Maclyn — gone, too, I hope. Old buzzards, prophesying their dismal tales of doom."

Thaerronal chuckled and nibbled on his companion's neck. He gave Maclyn a pointed stare and said, dryly, "They headed back toward the Oracular Pool, no doubt to bathe themselves in more of their gloomy worries. Why don't you follow them?"

Maclyn bit his lip and withheld the criticism he wanted so badly to give. Thaerry was about his own age — and one of the few Elves of the High Court even less inclined to involvement in Court affairs than he had been. Droewyn was Low Court, tied to the Grove — Maclyn wouldn't have expected any better of her.

So he nodded stiffly and ran in the direction they'd indicated.

The rich woodland scents, the soft whisper of his boots on the forest loam, the warm, moist breeze that brushed his skin, the twilight gleam of the eyes of the beasts that watched his progress along the path — all those things said "home" to him, reassured him —

:Halt, Maclyn, Ring-sworn Friend of the High Court of Elfhame Outremer.: The crisp Mindspoken command cut through the exhausted reverie into which he'd drifted. Maclyn skidded to a stop and watched the forest around him.

From behind a massive tree, an armed and armored elf stepped into view. The Uzi hung casually at her side; the Kevlar body armor fit her like a seamed skin. Her soft gold hair streamed like a river from the silver coronet that held it out of her eyes. She grinned at him. *:Nice to see you've finally joined us.:*

Maclyn smiled with relief. *:Hallara. Good to see someone standing watch.:*

The woman, one of his mother's contemporaries, laughed. *:Some of us know Felouen — and Dierdre. They have better things to do than chase imaginary bogans; if they say the Unseleighe — or anything else — are about to bite us, we won't wait until we feel the teeth. So. There are enough of us to cover the permanent Gates, with a few left over to raise the alarm throughout Elfhame Outremer. We may be caught short, but we won't be caught sleeping.:*

He nodded. *:Mother around?:*

:Checking the Oracle, I think. The omens were very bad, last time I got any news. Crisis impending, any second — of course, that's the Oracle. Damned imprecise. Makes you wish something would happen, just so you could get past the waiting.:

Maclyn's laugh was bitter. *:Don't you believe it. The waiting is a hell of a lot better. Things have broken loose on my side — someone kidnapped my girlfriend.:*

:The human? Is it related to all of this?:

:I don't think so. This crazy woman has been following me for about a week. I don't know what she wants, but she's not

Unseleighe, just mad, and evil. A bad combination, but there's none of the feel of magic to her.:

Hallara nodded, then whistled — a low run of rapid notes with a liquid trill at the end. The whistle was answered and repeated.

I really ought to keep up on the codes, Maclyn thought as he listened to the brief message making its way through Elfhame Outremer. *It would save a hell of a lot of footwork.*

In almost no time, Dierdre, astride her elvensteed, galloped into view.

"That red-headed bitch kidnapped Lianne," Maclyn told her without preamble. "I need help finding her — and some backup for her rescue."

"The timing on this couldn't have been worse. The Oracle is showing imminent disaster, Mac. None of us dare leave — it appears that an attack is going to be launched against us through one of the Gates within mere minutes. I'm afraid I'm going to have to leave you on your own where Lianne is concerned."

This was not only unexpected, it was disastrous. "Dammit!"

Dierdre shook her head, implacable. "I'm sorry. We're thin here as it is."

"I know — " he pleaded, "but I'm afraid for Lianne's life."

"And I'm afraid for all of ours." Never had he seen his mother look so drawn, so torn by conflicting duties. "I'm sorry, Maclyn. Go back, do what you can — I'll come and help you search if I survive this."

Mac stared at his feet, then looked into his mother's eyes, anguished. Conflicting loyalties and loves tore at him as well. "She's in trouble because of me. I can't stay and help you fight. I can't abandon her, Mother."

She nodded slowly. "Go. I understand. A single fighter more or less isn't going to make a difference. An army, now — but an army isn't going to have time to come to us. We've called on Fairgrove, but they're depleted and down after their last to-do. Nobody else is near enough."

Maclyn's shoulders sagged, and he turned and began the walk back toward his own Gate.

Amanda-Anne shivered. The cold mists of the Unformed Plane seeped through to her very bones, and the things she had made had grown restive. They looked at her with edgy calculation in their glowing eyes — circled around her along an ever-shrinking perimeter, snapped their toothy jaws and hissed at each other, slashed and growled. But always, they watched her.

And the closer they moved, the more she ached for a safe haven, and the more she yearned for safety, the more restless and dangerous her monsters became. Suddenly, making them didn't seem like such a good idea after all.

They grinned at her, the awful things, and they suddenly looked hungry. She didn't know what to feed them, but she suspected they would be only too happy to eat little girls. And now Amanda-Anne felt very much like a frightened little girl again. The Unformed Plane wasn't fun anymore. Making monsters wasn't fun. She wanted to be warm, she wanted to be protected, she wanted to be —

— in a safe place. Where the elves lived!

She "stretched" — reached out to take control of the body she shared with the others. It wasn't occupied — all the others were elsewhere, and the body itself was in Amanda's bedroom, curled on the bed. Amanda-Anne took control, opened her eyes, wrapped stubby fingers around Mommy's green bead. The first of the monsters appeared in her bedroom, following her.

Amanda-Anne shrieked and carved a road that drove straight into the heart of the elves' stronghold, and safety.

• Chapter Twelve

The trunk was so hot that riverlets of sweat ran down Lianne's face, back, and chest, stinging in her cuts. The metal handcuffs around her wrists slid up and down her forearms, and every time they did, it felt as if they added another set of bruises. Everything hurt. And what didn't hurt, she greatly feared might not be working anymore.

She squirmed a little, trying to find a more comfortable position. If only her hands were in front of her — wait a moment. Maybe this bitch wasn't used to kidnapping people Lianne's size. *Well,* she thought, *there are a few advantages to being both skinny and flexible.*

This might be something the bitch that caught her hadn't reckoned on.

She ignored the pain that movement caused her, and scooted her hands down over her hips, curling her back as she did. That hurt so bad she almost quit — but the promise of not being thrown forward on her face every time the car jolted was more than she could resist. She waited for the worst of the wave of agony to pass, then pulled her knees up to her chest and tucked her feet through the handcuffs as if she were jumping a very short rope.

A *very* short rope. The cuffs caught on her instep. *Better,* Lianne thought. *I always figured my twenty minutes of yoga at bedtime would come in useful for something. But I never thought it would be for dealing with a kidnapper.*

The pressure of her feet on the links of the handcuffs had pressed them halfway down Lianne's sweat-soaked hands. They hurt, but when Lianne experimentally shoved her thumb joint hard into the palm of her left hand, the cuff slipped down further.

The possibility that she might actually get the things *off* hadn't occurred to her until that moment. *I'll be damned! I think I can get out of these things!*

She pressed the bones of her left hand together as tightly as she could and pushed with all of her strength. The combination of her sweat, the looseness of the cuff, and her flexible joints worked a minor miracle. The cuff slipped off, scraping skin as it went.

She pulled the foul-tasting rag out of her mouth and reached down to fumble with the knots that tied her ankles. When they came loose, she got to work on the other side of the handcuffs. The right one proved to be more intractable than the left — her captor had shoved it tighter when she put it on.

It doesn't matter, the teacher thought. *I can move now. I'll bet that will surprise the hell out of her.*

In fact, Lianne realized, *it might surprise her enough to save me. That is, if I can get the rest of me to function. . . .* She tried to open her eyes again. Although they were badly puffed and swollen, she felt the lids of the left one move apart.

There was nothing but blackness.

Oh, God — I'm blind!

For a moment she felt panic clawing at her.

Then, hard on its heels, dry humor. *No, idiot. You're in the trunk of a car.*

Lianne considered her situation. She probably wasn't blind. She was within the confines of the trunk, but completely free. She hadn't made any noise that would carry over the road and engine sounds, so the driver wouldn't know this — wouldn't even know whether she was awake or not. She had a length of rope, the handcuffs, one of which was still attached — was there anything else in here she could use as a weapon? She felt around in the trunk and stopped when her fingers wrapped around the smooth metal length of a tire iron. In the darkness, Lianne grinned. Hot damn.

Those were her advantages.

She enumerated her disadvantages. She wasn't likely to have very long to make use of her element of surprise. Her captor, if she ever decided to open the trunk, could do so at any time. The only warning Lianne was likely to get was the click of the key in the lock. Also, she was hurt — the broken ribs were going to be the worst of it. She wouldn't be able to run away. Wouldn't be able to put up much of a fight — though, she thought with wry amusement, the tire iron had the potential to be a great equalizer. And finally, she didn't know where she would end up, while her captor would be on her own chosen ground — possibly with allies.

I've got a damned good chance of getting myself killed if I put up a fight. Lianne considered playing dead, or going along with whatever the woman wanted her to do, and hoping for a chance of escape later on, when she was alone. But her dad had spent a very short time as a P.O.W. in 'Nam — before he'd escaped. He had, in the course of years of later conversations, mentioned a fact about the art of escaping from a P.O.W. camp that Lianne considered applicable now.

"Baby," he'd said, with the air of one imparting the wisdom of the sages, "the sooner you attempt to escape after they've captured you, the less they'll be expecting it, and the better chance you'll have to succeed. When you're first caught, you're usually hurt, and damned confused — and you keep thinking someone is going to come from outside to rescue you. It isn't until later that you realize no one is coming, and you'll have to get out by yourself. So you take care of it while they're thinking you're still too messed up to take off." Then he'd winked at her and grinned his broad, easy grin. "Works in most any situation. You remember that, okay, baby?"

A kid in on her daddy's joke, she'd grinned back and had said, "Sure, Daddy. I'll remember."

Well — I remembered. Okay, Dad, she thought, *I'll go for it, first chance I get. Let's hope for baby's sake you knew what the hell you were talking about.*

The car bumped wildly, throwing her against the front with a vicious thump that sent every bruise and broken bone into fresh, screaming agonies. Lianne shoved her fist into her mouth to keep from howling. She heard grass and branches dragging on the sides and undercarriage. *Shit —*

we're out in the middle of nowhere, then, I'll bet. Not likely to be anybody friendly around. And no witnesses to see what happens next.

She planned her tactics with that in mind. Readied her weapons. Stilled her racing heart. Positioned herself as best she could in the cramped space.

Waited.

The Gate appeared with an unnatural shriek as time and space themselves were shredded. Winds raged out of the raw wound that opened in the middle of Elfhame Outremer, whipping the delicate silk hangings and bright pennants into a frenzy. Out of the pocket maelstrom raced a child, tiny, blond, green-eyed, with a fragile beauty obscured by the fear on her face, who ran like one pursued by all the devils of hell.

The elf who reached out and caught her, a patroness of the arts on her way to the premiere of Valyre's production of "Nine Lives of Woldas Toklas," could not imagine how the little human child had arrived nor what could have frightened her so. Her confusion cleared up an instant later, as the first of Amanda-Anne's monsters followed her through the Gate, to be followed by another, and another, and another.

The child wriggled free of the elf's suddenly nerveless grip and darted off among the trees.

The last thing the elven matron heard as the monsters leapt on her was the seldom-sounded attack-alarm, a clarion call that echoed from the top of first one tree, then many.

When the trunk lock released, Lianne tensed. *Wait for it, wait for it,* she chanted in a silent mantra. She gripped the tire iron like a sword.

She heard the door open, heard footsteps swishing through the grass.

Wait for it, wait for it.

Her eyes adjusted to the meager light that came through the tiny space between trunk-lid and body, and she discovered she really *could* see. She watched fingers sliding along the inside of the trunk, feeling for the catch.

Wait for it, wait for it.

"There it is," — a faint mutter, followed by the click of the latch, and light so bright it hurt.

Now!

Lianne stabbed with the poker and hit the woman in the throat, pumped full of adrenalin and with her attention focused someplace where the pain wasn't. The woman gagged, one hand flying to her throat as she staggered back a step, her expression one of shock.

If Lianne had a little more strength, it might have ended then and there. Instead, she only stunned the woman long enough to get the upper hand.

Lianne loosed a banshee scream, the accumulation of her rage and pain and fear tied into that savage howl, and tumbled out of the trunk. Her grip shifted slightly, and she backhanded the tire iron across the woman's face, then with both hands brought it down on the top of her head. The handcuff that dangled from her right wrist swung staccato accompaniment against the metal of the tire iron.

The woman threw her hands over her face and head to protect them, and Lianne staggered toward her, the tire iron held like a quarterstaff in front of her. Then she swung again, overbalanced, and fell forward, catching the woman across the chest with the tire iron. They tumbled to the ground together.

Lianne screamed with the pain of her broken ribs, but she forced herself to sit up, forced herself to hit the other woman until the bitch stopped struggling and her arms dropped to her sides and she lay still.

It was a pity, she reflected, as she sat on the ground and panted with pain, that she was so weak that it had been the weight of the tire iron that had done most of the damage. The woman lay like a lump in the weeds, a red welt rising on her cheek — but she was breathing, Lianne noted, with mingled disappointment and relief. She was still breathing just fine. Lianne poked her in the side once with the pointed end of the tire iron. She didn't move.

"I wish I was the kind of person who could do to you what you did to me. I'd beat *your* face in with your gun and kick *you* in the ribs." Lianne was so angry she shook, as conflicting emotions warred within her. *Damn, I wish I could do that!*

She looked down at the woman, lying unconscious and helpless. *Well, I can't.* She sighed, her adrenaline fading away. *Time to get out of here — wherever here is.*

Lianne went through the woman's pockets. She came up with the keys to the car, but none for the handcuffs. She toyed with the idea of taking the gun, then decided against it. At least she could take the clip out of the gun — leave her without bullets. That would work. When the police found the woman, Lianne wanted them to find plenty of evidence that would make it easy for them to throw her into a cell forever.

With the keys in hand, she pushed herself shakily to her feet and surveyed her escape route. She would have to retrace the other woman's path, which would mean backing the car down the long, overgrown drive to the road. She would have to twist around in the seat to back the car, which ought to hurt like hell, considering her broken ribs. She looked at the redhead, lying in the track broken down by the T-Bird, and sighed.

"I ought to just back over you, dammit. I really ought to."

But she didn't. She pulled the woman out of the middle of the drive, swearing with every step. An instant of weakness and the opportunity for revenge overcame her, though, and she dragged the woman over to the edge of a huge blackberry thicket, rolling her as far into it as she could, without getting caught in the vines herself. Limping over to the car, still suffering, Lianne wore the smile of the vindicated on her face.

She shoved the trunk down with difficulty, and leaned against the car itself to keep herself from falling as she stumbled over creepers and vines and fallen branches toward the driver's side door. She opened the door, leaned forward, wheezing; doubled over at the sudden stab of pain in her side, and fell onto the seat. Falling saved her life.

She heard the crack of the other woman's gun, a surprisingly unimpressive noise, at the same time that the driver's side window, in the precise spot where her head had been, flowered into an array of tiny concentric cracks.

Damn! Another clip? That's what I get for not killing you, isn't it! I should have taken the gun, she thought, pulling her legs in quickly, and closing the door as fast as she could.

Better yet, I should have left you where I could run over you. She shoved the keys in the ignition and curled low on the seat. The car started easily, and she slipped it into reverse and pushed lightly on the gas. She sprawled across the bench, as low as she could get and still reach the pedals, facing the rear of the car, her left hand clutching beneath the headrest of the passenger seat for balance, her right steering the car. *Thank God the thing's not a stick, anyway.*

She curved the car around the side of the house and aimed toward the road, praying like a gift-wrapped nun at the devil's birthday party. The car wallowed over a bump at the same instant that a bullet hole appeared in the front passenger window, and Lianne's foot slid farther down onto the gas pedal. The T-Bird accelerated wildly.

"Shit, shit, shit — oh, shit!" Lianne wailed, as various small trees and other obstacles loomed in the rear window, vanished at high speed and were replaced by others. She swerved and kept right on going. *I wish I could close my eyes,* she thought. *I doubt it would make much difference in my — oh, shit!* — she dodged another tree —*driving!*

She heard two sharp *pings* in the windshield behind her head. *Two more of the bitch's bullets. When is she gonna run out?* Lianne didn't dare look back. As long as she was still alive, anything else could wait.

The car bounced again, and a small tree splintered across the rear bumper. *Oh hell,* Lianne thought for some reason, *it's only a rental.* She didn't even remember the joke that punchline was from.

There was a crunch of metal and one massive heave — and Lianne felt the smoothness of pavement under the tires, heard the scrape of what must be the entire exhaust system under the car. A quick spin of the wheel, and she backed the rest of the way into the road. To her right were the dilapidated ruins of the house, and the red-haired woman, taking aim yet again. Lianne threw the car into drive and hit the gas. *What a persistent snake you are. I hope you enjoy your walk home.* She flipped the woman the bird and burned rubber in her acceleration. The rear window blossomed with its own bullet hole.

Well, Dad, she thought. *I owe you my life on this one, I think. And if I live long enough to get to a hospital, I'll have a story to tell that rivals even yours.*

When Maclyn heard the alarm through the trees, there was no question of going back to the apartment and waiting for the phone call. Rhellen would have to find him, Lianne would have to fend for herself — he armed himself as he ran toward the center of Elfhame Outremer, from whence the alarm came. Even as he ran, he kept thinking *What kind of fool would open a Gate in the heart of an Elfhame?*

Beside him, Dierdre on her elvensteed and Hallara on hers launched themselves toward the battle. *:This is it!:* Dierdre bellowed directly into his brain. *:Get Rhellen.:*

:I can't! Didn't bring him!:

Dierdre paused long enough to give him a withering look. *:Idiot.:* She pivoted her mount and leaned down to offer Maclyn an arm up. He took it and swung onto the steed behind Dierdre's saddle.

:I had to leave Rhellen to listen for the phone.:

:Brilliant, oh my son. Riding pillion is not the safest way to go to battle,: his mother said acidly, *:but you'd be dead in no time on foot. There's nothing to contain those monsters or slow them down here.:*

Dierdre wielded her sword left-handed, Maclyn held his in his right. They charged along the ground paths beneath the singing boughs of the gold-leaved home-trees, past the shimmering curtains of light in the flame-fountains, under the branch-braided arch of the Lover's Trees — and into the melee behind Hallara, who sprayed a broad blanket of machine-gun fire to try to clear them a path. From other sites on the perimeter, reinforcements arrived.

The vortex of a rogue Gate glistened hypnotically from beside the delicate blue-green filigreed sculptures in the Masters' Garden. Three elven mages engaged themselves in battling the Gate itself, trying to close it off. They threw containment spells and reversal spells over the maw that spewed the monsters into their midst — to no avail. Amanda-Anne's hastily-constructed Gate had ripped away part of the spell-formed reality of Elfhame Outremer itself. It fed on the energy of the destruction it caused, creating a direct road from the Unformed Planes to the center of the elves' safe haven. Amanda-Anne's nightmares advanced unchecked.

A horde of giggling, tittering stick-men and multi-legged screamers burst through and launched themselves against the scattered elven forces with bared fangs and razored claws. Initially, there was no strategy to the skirmishing. The elves hacked and slashed and shot, and the monsters failed to die. The grim things pressed forward into the elven ranks, pushed from behind by the larger monsters that moved through the Gate at their backs.

Hallara, Dierdre, and Maclyn joined forces with Felouen and a small phalanx of veteran warriors who were covering an elven spellcaster and one of Outremer's adopted human mages. The mages were mildly successful at individually spelling the nightmare things with the same containment spells that had proven useless on the Gate. But the effort required of them was enormous, while the number of horrors shoving through the Gate far exceeded those being contained.

Then Amanda-Anne's winged creatures arrived in force, lurching through the air like medieval stained glass demons and cathedral gargoyles. They dove on the defenders, howling like the damned, belching fire and dripping acid, diving down to pluck hapless elves from their elvensteeds and ascending far above the trees to fling them back to the ground below.

The defenders of Outremer were forced to retreat beneath the sheltering overhangs of the trees.

Then the trees began to burn.

The entire population of Elfhame Outremer — that part of it, at least, that had managed to survive the initial onslaught — fought back desperately. The few elven children lent their magical energy to parents who cast shielding around Outremer's untouched trees. A contingent of mages battled their way toward the Grove and dug in around the heart-tree. Weapons of every variety, human and magical, were leveled against the invaders. The Oracular Pool, the many fountains, and the Vale River that circled the whole of Elfhame Outremer were drained to feed a storm spell. Rain poured from the smoke-filled sky, and the conflagrations in the tree-homes and shelters of the elven haven began to die. And wet wood did not rekindle as easily.

Maclyn and Dierdre were part of the contingent who fought to protect the Grove. Their losses had been huge — more than half of the Grove's trees were charred stumps, with the bodies of their defenders scattered at their bases like fallen branches. Now, the largest of the monsters seemed to be concentrating on destroying the heart-tree itself. The death of the heart-tree would release the spells of thousands of years that had used it as the focus for maintaining Elfhame Outremer. Without the heart-tree, Elfhame Outremer would disappear back into the nothingness of the Unformed Planes. Mac had seen the movies — the battle to guard the heart-tree was a kind of Masada, an Alamo — there was no question of retreat. If the heart-tree went, there would be nothing to retreat to.

Maclyn had discovered that almost nothing slowed the monsters down, but if he cut off a golem's head, it stopped fighting until it could either locate the missing extremity or grow a new one. He'd passed this information on to the other elves, and the ground around them began to look like a croquet lawn designed by head-hunters.

The monsters became warier, and ground-fighting demons began to time their attacks with those of the airborne gargoyles.

Mac took a two-handed swipe at a winged demon that dove at him. He missed, and the demon sank its claws into a seam in his armor. Maclyn was ripped off of Dierdre's elvensteed, thigh muscles screaming in pain as he struggled vainly to stay horsed. The monster's screech rang in his ears, its breath blasted into his face, burning at his skin and making his eyes water. Then it dropped him. He lay, stunned, while the tides of the fray shifted.

When he was able to stand and wield his sword again, Dierdre was out of sight, and a new horror lurched at him with a grin on its foul face. He had no time to look for allies. His arms felt like lead, but he forced himself to slash again and again as the beast lunged at him. Three times the elven blade bit deep at the monster, yet it continued to giggle maniacally.

Around him, the elves were being herded into a few remaining pockets of resistance, and the toll of the dead mounted.

Amanda-Anne huddled in the hollow of a great silver elven-elm, shivering and miserable. *This* was the only safe place she had known of — this retreat far from the evil Father and the uncaring Step-Mother. This was the place she had thought to come and hide, where no one would hurt her, where nothing could frighten her. She had never thought that her own monsters would follow her —

And when they did, she had been *sure* that the elves would be able to get rid of them.

She had brought hell from her own world and from the Unformed Planes, and visited it here, in the only completely beautiful place she had ever seen. And she had destroyed it, all by herself; ruined it, made it worse than any place she had ever known, worse, even, than the pony barn. She stared out at the devastation that spread before her. Charred and smoking stumps were all that remained of most of the trees; the bodies of elves — so many beautiful, gentle elves — lay bloody and sprawled in the churned mud. The pretty green grass was gone, the sweet music was drowned in the screams of the dying, the bright pennants that had fluttered so briskly in the warm breeze hung in sodden tatters in the pouring rain.

Amanda-Anne, looking at the havoc she had wrought, felt something she had never felt before. She felt pain and guilt for those she had hurt. She felt regret for her actions. She felt responsibility.

She was as bad as the Father.

Maclyn shouldered aside a flailing arm as he cleaved another creature's fleshy skull. They came, still they came. One of the human mages had just been overcome by the monsters, his body clamped in the eight-armed thing's jaws as it laid into a second mage's defenses.

One of the Sidhe who had lived in the humans' world was doubled over near him, as if injured. Her lips moved as she concentrated on a Summoning-spell, and the air before her turned dark. Then a stack of wooden boxes materialized, and another, and finally a wooden rack of firearms with handwritten price tags on them. She stood straight again, pulling thick gauntlets on.

Maclyn hacked at his creature a few more times until he dismembered it, kicked its pieces far from each other, then turned to the female.

"Need help?"

"Could use it." She expertly undid the latch on a case and began loading a grenade launcher. "We need to buy some distance."

Maclyn winced at the amount of Cold Iron in the weapon, but decided that the time for desperate measures had come. "They'll be picking steel chips out of the Grove for years, but at least there *will* be a Grove."

Amanda-Anne huddled in her hidey-hole, and the first tears she had ever cried came to her eyes, scorching her cheeks, etching hot trails down her face.

"I am sorry," she whispered. "Oh, I am . . . so . . . s-s-sorry."

One of her monsters shuffled toward her hiding place, snuffling and casting its head from side to side, following the scent of the living. It looked down into the hollow where she hid, saw her, and chittered in soprano glee. Its bloodstained talons reached in after her.

"G-g-go *away*," Amanda-Anne whispered through her tears. "I d-d-don't want you here anymore!"

The monster vanished with a soft "pop."

:*Make them all go away, Anne,*: a quiet voice whispered in her head. Amanda-Anne closed her eyes and found her sisters, her other selves, facing her with angry or unhappy faces. Cethlenn stood before her, and Alice, and Abbey. Only the first-born, the real Amanda, was absent.

:*Make them go away,*: Cethlenn repeated. :*You are the only one who can. Only you have the power. Only you can work the magic — or unwork it.*:

:*Please,*: Abbey said, piteously, her own tears coursing down her cheeks. :*Oh, please. They're hurting, they're hurting so much!*:

:*You must,*: Alice added. "*You can't leave the people in this place to die.* You *did* it, *now* you *have* to undo it. It's all your fault.":

Amanda-Anne felt the hot tears streaking down her cheeks and choking away her breath. :*I know.*: She hugged her arms tighter around herself, and told the three who watched her, :*I'm sorry.*:

But "sorry" didn't fix things. She'd have to do that now, before they got worse. Amanda-Anne crawled out of her shelter and stood exposed to the sharp eyes of the monsters, the startled eyes of the elves. "Go away," she screamed, above the roars of explosions and gunfire, above the skin-crawling chittering laughter, above the howls and the prayers and the oaths and the crying. "Go *away!*" She concentrated on how much she didn't want her monsters, on how much she wished them to disappear. For a moment, there was nothing but silence.

Then the creatures of her imagination vanished, leaving behind only the dead, and the ruin they — *she* — had caused.

And then, miserable and afraid, fearing what the elves would do to her when they realized what she had done to them, and feeling that she would never deserve safety or beauty again, Amanda-Anne raced for the Gate she'd made. She threw herself through it, pulling it shut behind her.

* * *

In mid-flight, still spouting flames at the remaining treetops, the three-headed flier popped out of existence. The gothic demons flickered slightly and were gone. Maclyn, fighting a losing battle with a many-legged snake, found himself swinging a rifle-butt at an opponent that had suddenly ceased to exist.

All over Elfhame Outremer, cries of surprise became shouts of elation. The survivors fell together, hugging each other in disbelief and hysterical joy at the sheer miracle of it.

Those who were relatively unscathed soon enough began the grim task of sorting dead from dying, of dying from salvageable. They walked from charred body to mangled body, from one still form to the next, struggling to recognize in death some semblance of those they had known in life. Maclyn rid himself of his gloves and heavy armor with a thought and began that dark walk, too, looking into the faces of survivors, hoping to find his own loved ones, and seeing his own disappointment reflected over and over in each face that was not Dierdre, was not Felouen. He knew that for all of those who stared into his eyes and turned away in despair, his own grimed features represented one less chance that the ones they loved still lived.

He worked his way back to the point where he and Dierdre had become separated. All around him, the Mindshouted calls, the agonized cries for help, the screams of those who recognized the ones they had loved in the features of the dead, blotted out any hope of finding Dierdre or Felouen by Mindcall, or by simple shouting. He kept at his steady examination of each passing face, of each sad corpse, praying to all the gods he'd never believed in that he would recognize his loved ones in those who still stood, and not those who would never stand again.

Suddenly, across a muddied clearing, he recognized a familiar toss of the head, a quick brush of hand through hair.

"FELOUEN!" he roared, and was rewarded by a startled

jerk of the head in his direction, by a shriek of "Maclyn!" and by the woman's ungraceful two-legged gallop across the field of the dead.

Felouen threw herself into his arms, careless of her wounds or his, and wept. "By the gods, you're alive. When you fell, I knew I'd lost you, oh, gods I knew — "

She pressed a suddenly tear-streaked face to his, and Maclyn found to his surprise that his own eyes were not dry. He held her tightly, breathing in the scent of her hair and savoring the warmth of her, the hard-muscled strength of her lean body pressed tightly against his. "Thank all the gods you're alive," he whispered. Then he loosened his grip and looked in her eyes. "Dierdre?" he asked.

Felouen's face lost its animation. "She sent me to find you."

Maclyn, ignoring her bleak expression, smiled with relief. "Ha! Then she still lives! I knew she was too tough — "

"Barely," Felouen interrupted grimly. "She waits by the last of the beasts, the ones held in the containment spells. They didn't vanish with the rest of the monsters. She is summoning their thoughts to see where they came from — and why."

He sucked in a breath of dismay. "But if she's injured, using magic will only weaken her further."

She bit her lip, shrugged her helplessness. "Perhaps you can convince her to spare herself — I could not."

Felouen's elvensteed reached them, and Maclyn noted its burden for the first time. A body was slung across the saddle face-down. "Who — ?"

Felouen's face tightened. "Hallara. She died trying to put out a fire in the heart-tree. She'd run out of ammunition. The pike line around the mages broke, and one of the things took her when she tranced."

He closed his eyes and fought back despair. "Oh, gods."

"There will be time to count the dead later, Mac. Let's tend the living while we can." Felouen turned away from him and broke into a flat-out run, heading back toward the spot where the Gate had opened.

Maclyn followed.

They found Dierdre propped against one of the contained monsters, her body blood-drenched, her face white with impending shock. But her hands pressed against the thing's skull, and her expression was one of tight concentration.

"Mother!" Maclyn exclaimed as he saw what she was doing. "Lie down! Save your strength."

Dierdre opened pale eyes and quelled him with a single glance. "There is a man who must not be allowed to die," she said. Her voice was a hoarse croak, but her speech never faltered. And her expression was one of implacable hate. "These things were made by an aspect of the child, Amanda."

"What —" Mac was puzzled by her choice of words.

"The child was tormented until she shattered," Dierdre explained tersely, "like a fragile crystal, dropped by a careless hand. She is no longer one, but many. One of her number learned how to weave magic from you, all unwitting. To protect herself and her other selves, she wove these, monsters — fragments of her pain. They are constructs of her fear — her fear, Maclyn, fear so great they nearly leveled Elfhame Outremer and the magic of three thousand Sidhe with it. We did not win the battle, son of mine. Amanda released her fear, and when she did, our foes vanished."

He blinked, uncomprehending. "Mother —"

"Quiet." She pierced him with her eyes. "Do you know what she feared, Maclyn?"

How could he? "No," he replied carefully. Dierdre in this mood was not to be contradicted.

"She feared her father — and with reason. He has tortured her," Dierdre said, at last. "He has raped her — yes, you heard aright. For years, he has done unspeakable things to her — he has shattered her into a handful of strange, fragmented children that do not even communicate with each other. The aspect that created these monsters never knew love, or caring, or kindness. It knew only brutality and pain and hatred and fear — until it came here. This was where that aspect of the child thought it could hide and be safe from the horrors it had created — but because no one had ever been good to it, it feared us as well."

Felouen answered for all of them. "Not the child's fault. She had not the experience, could not have known what she did. Fragment or no, she was a child, and to a child, all adults are gods. She must have thought we could banish these creatures as easily as she. It is her father that has brought this upon us, not her — *he* is the cause that made her create them in the first place. For fear of her father, we have suffered and died."

"I'll kill her father," Maclyn said softly. "For what he has caused here, for what he has done to you —"

Dierdre shook her head. "No, Mac. For my revenge — for her revenge — I want something more." She let herself slip down to the frozen monster's feet. Her skin was the color of snow, waxy and translucent, her lips bloodless. Only her eyes looked alive. Mac stared at her rent armor, at the damage that could not be repaired by the greatest healer of the elves, and covered his face with his hands in grief.

"Listen," she told him.

He knelt and put his ear to her mouth, to hear his mother's dying wish.

Damn them, Belinda thought. *Damn all of them.*

She had never suffered so much or been hurt so badly in pursuit of a target. It seemed as if everything — her target, his feeble girlfriend, even his damned car, for crissakes — had conspired to destroy her. She had been foiled at every turn. She had been made to look like a fool.

Belinda had been through enough.

She leaned wearily against the phone booth's wall, searching the out-of-date phone book's battered pages.

There it is — the Prince Charles! She maneuvered a quarter into the slot and dialed.

A mechanical, but not electronic voice, answered. "Prince Charles, this is Sharon speaking. May I help you?"

"Connect me to Mel Tenner's room," she ordered thickly.

"May I ask who's calling, please?" the polite voice inquired.

Officious bitch. "This is Belinda, and it's an emergency."

The voice did not seem impressed. "Hold please, ma'am."

It was just like that miserable S.O.B. to have his calls screened, Belinda thought. *He'd better decide to take mine — I'll kill him if he doesn't. I don't need this s —*

Sharon returned. "I have Mr. Tenner on the line, ma'am."

"Fine," she said shortly, reining in her temper.

A few clicks, and a moment later Mel drawled, "What is it, Belinda?" He sounded supremely bored.

"Get a pen and some paper," she snarled. "I'm going to give you directions — I want you to come get me. Then we're going to pick up your girl. Bring your gun."

Mel laughed, as if she had made a joke. "I wouldn't leave home without one."

Belinda gave him the directions, tersely, keeping her eyes fixed on the phone.

He made an odd little grunt of surprise. "Belinda, darling, what are you doing at a convenience store out in the middle of nowhere? Slumming?"

"Working. For you," she replied, hoping he *might* feel a little responsibility. After all, she was still working for him, as he had so pointedly reminded her. "My car got stolen."

"Again?" The laughter in his voice was only too obvious, and he wanted her to hear it. Mel was not going to take on any belated responsibility. Not that she really expected him to. Mel believed that everything that happened to anyone was their own fault — including being caught in earthquakes, high-rise fires, and tornadoes.

She restrained the impulse to scream, and contented herself with shredding the pages of the phone book, one by one. "Sound a little less happy, Mel. I'm having a bad day."

"Why don't you just tell me where to go pick up my little TK," he suggested, with deceptive mildness, "and then you can get a taxi and go home to rest?"

And you can take off with the kid and skip paying me, scumball?

I don't think so. "Just come get me, Mel," she growled. "And bring your bankbook."

He sighed, as if with infinite patience. "Fine, sweetheart. If that's what you want. I'll be there in forty-five minutes."

Click.

Belinda slammed the receiver home and glared at a slip of paper. It was the schoolteacher's phone number. Belinda debated calling. Maybe the woman had gone straight back to her apartment, or maybe she had called first, on the chance that her boyfriend had shown up and found the place trashed. If she had, Belinda wouldn't be able to fool the race-driver — but if she hadn't . . .

Nothing ventured, nothing gained, as they say. She dialed, and the phone rang. Once.

Twice.

Three times.

"Come on, shithead," she muttered. "Pick up."

Four times.

Five times.

Maclyn was alone at the foot of Dierdre's grave beneath the remains of a giant white willow. The tree had protected his mother's Underhill home since she had come over from the Old Country — it was the part of Elfhame Outremer she had missed most when she was in the world of humans. It was now scarred and burned, and its loving inhabitant had come home forever.

I'm going to miss you, Mother, even more than you would have believed. Maclyn stood alone as the last smatterings of warm rain soaked into his clothes and ran down his face. Her death had destroyed a part of him. He felt suddenly old, watching the loose earth over the grave falling in on itself as the raindrops struck. He had never really given her cause to be proud of him. Unlike the rest of his colleagues on the racing team, he had not been motivated by any higher goals. The others, the elves and human mages of SERRA, had been raising money to finance shelters for teenage runaways, kid-rescue operations, any number of altruistic causes. He had been a member of SERRA only because he liked to drive fast cars, and because he liked to win. If the money he won went to "worthy causes," well, frankly, he hadn't wanted to have to hear about it.

In his own way, he was as much an escapist as any of the elves who lived Underhill permanently, as any of the dilettantes who idled away their days with music, dancing, gaming, loveplay.

Maclyn stiffened as he felt Rhellen's sudden presence in the Elfhame. The elvensteed called out in his blunt mind-images as he galloped, searching on the other side of the Gate for his cohort. He answered the elvensteed with a quick whistle, and the golden beast charged to his side. Rhellen saw the fresh dirt beneath the tree and gave a questioning whicker.

Maclyn shook his head. "Later," he said. "I'll tell you everything later." He sensed the elvensteed's horror at the devastation of Outremer, but there was no time to comfort him, and no time to explain.

Mac leapt to the elvensteed's back, and Rhellen charged back through the Gate. He skidded to a stop in the kitchen next to the phone, bumping against the sink top. Mac leapt off of Rhellen's back and answered the phone.

"Hello?" he said, thinking, *Please, no more bad news. Please.*

"I just about hung up, fella. You took a long time getting to the phone." The voice was the same one he'd talked to earlier — and, in spite of the muffling, he was certain it was Belinda Ciucci he was talking to.

"I was busy," he said. "In the bathroom. I got here as fast as I could."

She snorted. "I don't think calls of nature are as important as my call. Especially since I'm going to let you save your girlfriend's life now."

He spoke carefully, not loosing any of his anger. "What do you want me to do?"

"Meet me out in the woods on the right side of the Bal-A-Shar Stables," she said. "I know you know where. I followed you out there yesterday."

Well, now he had a rendezvous point. "Fine, Belinda. Let me talk to Lianne now."

"Not a chance, buddy—" Then, suddenly, silence.

There was a pause — Maclyn realized from the faint wash of emotions he caught over the phone that he had just tipped the woman to the fact that he knew her real name. Dammit, that was going to make things harder. "You're going to meet me in the woods at five p.m., and then I'll let — ah, Lianne — go," Belinda continued.

"What do you want me to bring?" he asked. "Money?"

There was a bitter, harsh laugh at the other end of the line. "Sure, why not? Write this down."

She paused, and Mac pulled out the pen Lianne kept on the clipboard with the notepad and got ready to write.

Belinda continued. "Bring me a hundred thousand dollars in small, used, non-sequentially marked bills. Pack it all in a little suitcase, drag that with you, and — oh, by the way, don't drive your car. I don't like it. You come in your girlfriend's car — the little yellow Volkswagen convertible. Big racecar stud like you oughta look cute in it. Park in the turn-around next to the dirt road that goes back to the cotton field. Get out of your car, walk along the road until you cross the culvert, and walk across the street and into the woods. I'll have a red ribbon tied around the tree you are to go to. Put the money down beside the tree — when you turn around, you'll see your girlfriend. As long as you follow directions and you're all by yourself, everything will work out fine."

For you or for me? Mac wondered, but he said, "Okay."

The line clicked, and Belinda was gone.

Felouen may come through this Gate, he thought, staring at the dark swirl of energy. *She knows about Lianne, and she knows we have to find Amanda — maybe she'll come through in time to help me. She needs to know what I need, and where to meet me.*

He took paper and pencil, and in flowing elvish script, wrote a note and drew a map to Bal-A-Shar Stables. Then he created a large, elegant leather case out of thin air and filled it full of very real-looking counterfeit bills. He would hand Belinda one-hundred thousand dollars in used-looking twenties, with only eight serial numbers between them. And as soon as she took the case, he decided, the faces on all

the bills would abruptly sport matching maniacal, toothy
grins. Maybe the motto would read, "Gotcha."

Cethlenn woke in Amanda's room, on Amanda's bed. The
child's clothes were soaked and filthy. Bits of the elven
domain's dirt and greenery still clung to her. In one hand,
she found a silver leaf — crumpled and tattered, it was both
beautiful and saddening. Inside her, the children huddled in
fear and stared out over her shoulders. Poor children —
they had been through so much, and a sixth sense told her
the worst was yet to come. Downstairs, she could hear Them
arguing.

"Don't you talk to me in that tone of voice! I've been out
working with the horses," the Step-Mother yelled. "I
haven't had time to watch where your weird kid got to —
she was in here with you the last I knew!"

"She isn't in here now! I've been all over the house looking for her." The Father sounded truly furious. "The little
liar said she was going up to her room. She isn't up there
now, let me tell you."

Fury filled the Step-Mother's voice. "I know where *my*
daughter is — and I want to know why the hell she came
running out to the barn in tears! What did you do to her,
you bastard?"

A pause, and then the Father countered, a hint of something Cethlenn couldn't read in his voice. "I didn't do
anything to her — don't change the subject on me!"

The Step-Mother snarled at him, "We agreed when we
got married that your kid would be your responsibility, and
my kid would be mine. You remember that? Huh? Well,
that means if you want *your* daughter, you find her! *My*
daughter and I are going shopping. And from now on, you
keep your hands off her!"

Cethlenn heard the Step-Mother's angry footsteps and
Sharon's short, light ones clipping across the floor. She
heard the door slam so hard the walls shook. She was alone
in the house with the Father.

She heard him storm from the front room back to the
den. There was a long, silent pause. *Mixin' himself a drink,*

Cethlenn thought. *Goin' to feed his anger with a wee drop of the uisge-beatha, no doubt. And then he'll go ragin' through the house until he finds us — and we're in trouble when he does, and sure.*

As if he'd heard her thoughts, the Father bellowed, "I know you're in here somewhere, Amanda! You can come down here right now and spare yourself a lot of trouble. Or I can come find you. I *will* find you. And when I do, I'll break your skinny, ugly little neck."

:You need to go, Cethlenn,: Alice urged. *:You have to do what he says. He's our father and we have to obey him.:*

Cethlenn shook her head. *:And if I do what he says, he'll break our neck without having to work to find us first.:*

Abbey said fearfully, *:Daddy wouldn't hurt us, not really. Would he?:*

Cethlenn cocked an eyebrow at Abbey. *:Why don't you ask Anne about that?:*

:I can't,: Abbey replied uncertainly. *:Anne's gone.:*

:Not back into the Unformed Planes, please all the gods!: Cethlenn felt her pulse race and her breath quicken in dismay at that thought.

Abbey answered slowly. *:I don't think so, Cethlenn. We could feel that she was there, before, even though we didn't let ourselves know about each other. But now there is nothing where she was but an empty place. I think after Alice yelled at her, she went away.:*

In the pit of Cethlenn's stomach, something twisted. *:Alice. What — did you say to her?:* the witch asked Alice. Now that she knew to feel for the emptiness, the place where Anne should have been nagged like a newly missing tooth.

Alice donned her most self-righteous expression and said, *:I told her the truth — that she was awful and evil and that we didn't need her or want her here.:*

And by all the gods, the child had the gall to look smug — as if she'd done something grand. *:Oh, no! Alice, Anne is a part of you! You can't just get rid of her! You can't!:*

Alice crossed her arms and glowered at Cethlenn. *:She did those — things — with our father. Nasty, wicked, sinful things. She was a bad, bad girl. Our father said so, and he is our father so he must be right.:*

Cethlenn reacted without thinking. *:Your father is a vicious* *brute who ought to be flayed and drawn and quartered and hung, then burned for good measure,:* she snapped.

Alice looked shocked. Her mouth opened and closed, but no sound came out. Her white cheeks flushed momentarily red, and angry tears filled her eyes. *:I'll — I'll — I'll tell on you!:* Alice finally sputtered. She flickered out of sight.

:Oh, dear,: Cethlenn told Abbey, with a twinge of guilt. *:I shouldn't have said that to her.:*

Abbey glared at her. *:You shouldn't have said it to me, either. I don't believe he's as bad as you and Anne say. Anne was crazy, and I'm glad she's gone.:*

Abbey followed her sister.

Cethlenn heard the Father coming up the stairs. No time left to find the children and retract her ill-thought statements. Apologies would have to take second place to survival. She hurriedly jumped off the bed, and noticed as she did that it was wet and dirty where she had lain on it. A beating would be the least she got if the Father caught her. She frowned and slipped out by her secret window escape. As soon as she pulled the window shut, she dropped to the roof below. Instead of running to the tree and climbing down to the ground this time, though, she stayed put, hugging the side of the house and listening to the Father as he rampaged through her room and then started searching for her through the rest of the house.

There was a drain spout that went right alongside one of the attic windows. Cethlenn was sure she could climb it. It had fastenings about every two feet that would serve as hand and footholds. It connected along the edge of the roof where she stood and soared to the attic window on the third story without going near any other windows.

The attic wasn't the safest place — the Father would certainly check there for her — but he probably wouldn't check more than once. If she climbed up after she heard him moving around in there, she should be able to buy some time. Perhaps the Step-Mother and Sharon would be home by then. He wouldn't do anything really brutal with them home, surely.

Cethlenn wasn't certain, but the attic plan seemed reasonable in theory. So she scooted down next to the spout and sat with her head pressed against the wood siding, listening for the sounds of the Father's footsteps ascending the stairs above her. Finally, she heard him crashing upward.

She stilled, waiting, and at last she was rewarded with his racket as he clattered back down the uncarpeted stairs. Cethlenn wiped her suddenly-damp palms on her shirt, eased her slender frame onto the gutter, and found the first tiny handhold. Almost afraid to breathe, she began the long ascent.

When Mel picked her up, Belinda flung herself into his car and said, without preamble, "Straight by my hotel — I have something special I need to pick up to finish this job. Then we'll go out and get your kid."

Mel gaped at his employee. Apparently he hadn't thought she'd have sustained any real damage. "You look awful. How did you get all those bruises on your face?"

"I walked into a door." She pulled down the passenger-side visor and looked in the mirror long enough to assess the most recent damage to her appearance, and bit her lip in dismay.

"Not really," he replied, as if he half believed her.

"No," she agreed. "Not really. But I don't want to talk about it." She glanced out at the passing scenery, then over at the speedometer. "Can't you drive any faster? God, you drive like the old coot who used to be my partner."

Mel frowned, disapprovingly. "I'm already going seventy, Belinda. I would just as soon not get pulled over right now. A cop might ask questions, once he gets a look at you, especially if he sees our guns. What are you in such a hurry for?"

She grimaced. "I have an appointment. Move it, okay? If I don't get to my appointment, you won't get your kid."

Neither of them said anything until they arrived at Belinda's hotel. As they pulled into the parking lot, Belinda swore. "Dammit, she took my keys and my fake I.D. I don't think I can get the clerk to give me another key without some identification."

Mel shrugged as if it didn't matter. "Have you done anything to the door or the lock since last night?"

Belinda rolled her eyes. "Oh, yeah, Mel. I installed a bomb so that the first person who opened the door would be blown away. The room is probably coated with Maid-Kibbles by now."

He sighed elaborately. "Hey, I was just asking. If you haven't done anything fancy to the locks, I can still get in."

She decided not to employ any more sarcasm on him; it was obviously wasted effort. "I haven't. Lead on, Macduff."

Mel did as promised. Once in the room, Belinda went to the dresser, crouched with her back to it, and lifted a corner of the heavy furniture a few inches off the floor. "Grab the case," she panted.

Mel, eyebrows well into his hairline, pulled the thinline briefcase out of the tiny space. "Nice hiding place. I haven't seen that one."

Belinda twitched her shoulders in dismissal, then nodded at the case. "That's an expensive toy. I didn't want it to walk off without me." She dropped the dresser, grabbed a bright red excuse for a skirt from a hanger, and with that in one hand and her little case in the other, headed for the door.

"May I ask —"

Belinda cut the question off. "It's a gun."

Mel looked puzzled. "To fit in that case, it couldn't be much of a gun."

Belinda climbed back into the passenger seat of the car. Mel slipped in. As they backed out of the parking space, she said, "You want specifics? Fine by me." She briefly opened the case to reveal a long, streamlined handgun and a loose scope packed in padded velvet. "It's an XP-100; a single-shot bolt-action handgun that comes tapped and drilled for scope mounting. I use a 12-power quick-mount scope on mine. It shoots a fifty-grain .221 Remington Fireball with a muzzle velocity of about 2650 feet per second. The velocity is still about 1150 feet per second at 300 yards. It delivers an impact over 400 pounds per square foot at a hundred yards, and 130 pounds per square foot at three hundred yards. It's machine polished, with a hand-carved conforming rosewood handgrip to make it pretty and easy to hold and not look so obvious on x-rays, and a bull-barrel to limit recoil. Best of all, at three-hundred yards, its point-of-aim is only thirteen inches above its target." She gave him a nasty little smile. "Feel better now?"

He only looked bored. "All of that babble means something to you?"

She snarled. "Yeah. It means this is a real nice gun if you want to kill somebody with one bullet from a long way off, but you don't want to drag a rifle around for everybody to see."

"Oh," Mel said, dismissively. "It's an assassination gun."

"It's an assassination gun," Belinda agreed. "An expensive one. I'm about to get my money's worth out of it."

• Chapter Thirteen

By the gods, I had no idea the ground was so far away. A mere strip of wooden ledge was all that separated Cethlenn from the plant beds and pine bark far below. *Och, I'd forgotten how I hated the heights. So, I end up here, in this wee bit of trouble, like a stranded chick and the snake comin'.*

And speaking o' which, I wonder what the bloody bastard's doin' now.

She heard the Father thundering around the lower floors, a bear deprived of his meal — a beast deprived of its prey.

She got eight inches of clearance before the attic window refused to budge further. Amanda was a thin child — Cethlenn could be grateful for that. She squeezed herself through the narrow space and into the cramped confines of the attic.

Boxes and other menacing shapes hulked in the gloom. Cethlenn felt among them, fingers probing for shelter. Her eyes refused to adjust — the darkness wrapped around her like a living cloak. Every breath sounded loud to her; every creak in the floor seemed to scream betrayal to the Father below. And always, it seemed that eyes watched from just over her shoulder.

She found a trunk, half empty, with old dresses and blankets in it. With a muttered prayer of thanks to the gods of her past, Cethlenn clambered in, pulled scratchy, dusty cloth over her head, and went to sleep.

Belinda snapped the sight onto the silver handgun and loaded the single cartridge into the chamber. There was a smooth click as the bolt slid home. She thumbed the safety, then laid the gun on her lap, pointed towards the passenger door.

"I want you to drive down to the other side of the horse stables you'll see on the left," she said to Mel as neutrally as possible. She didn't look at him. She began cutting narrow strips of cloth from her red skirt and tying them together. "Wait for me just down from the intersection. As soon as I'm done with this, I'll hike through the woods and take you to pick up your kid."

"Is she around here somewhere?" Mel asked, unable to conceal his avarice.

"General vicinity," Belinda told him. She knew what he wanted, and she tried to summon up the appropriate wariness — then the wariness melted into her overall exhaustion. *I'm getting paranoid. Mel's been waiting for this TK kid for a long time. It's only natural he should want to know where she is. He won't double-cross me — not after I've done so much for him. And not with all the dirt I have on him.* She smiled at her employer and said slowly, "Sorry I snapped at you. I'm edgy, Mel. I'll feel better when we get the girl and get the hell out of North Carolina. This place is driving me up the wall. I feel like every Billy-Bob G.I. jerk in this state is trying to get in the way of my job."

He nodded, his own smile, thin-lipped and unpleasant. "Don't worry about it, Belinda. I understand."

Belinda got out of the car and watched Mel drive off in the direction she'd indicated. Then she walked well into the woods, tied the red strips around a tree, and paced off two hundred and fifty yards to one side of that point, keeping a clear line of fire in mind. Belinda checked her watch — only fifteen minutes more until Mac Lynn would walk into her sights.

Lianne got out of the police car and breathed a sigh of relief. It was over. The cops had found the information in her kidnapper's purse very helpful — they'd traced the aliases back to Berkeley, California, and a woman named Belinda Ciucci, an ex-cop whose record ran to such interesting charges as grand-theft auto, kidnapping, and murder. They'd located her hotel room and staked it out; the woman was going to return to find company waiting.

The policemen would be by the apartment later for more information; until they arrived, Lianne had been instructed to take it easy.

Those were pretty much the same instructions the nurse in the E.R. had sent her home with. Her three broken ribs weren't misaligned — and how she'd lucked out there, she had no idea, what with all the twisting and turning and bumping around. The swelling in her face would have to go down before a doctor could tell how much work her nose and cheekbone fractures were going to require — if any. She didn't have any dangerous injuries, only ones that hurt. The folks in the E.R. had been sympathetic and encouraging. They'd given her scrips for an antibiotic and a painkiller, told her to put ice on all the swollen places, and to avoid any further excitement. She'd called her principal — and verified that, yes, she *was* in the emergency room and she wasn't faking all this and that, yes, the police *were* involved, and that she was the victim of something they could not specify. She could only imagine what stories would spread around the teachers' lounge in her absence — everything from rape by her racecar boyfriend to kidnapping by terrorists.

Certainly nice to know I have both medical and legal backing for taking a day or two off. I don't think I could face a class anytime soon. Soon as I let Mac know I'm all right, I'm going to lie down, take my pills, and sleep for the rest of the day.

Lianne felt around inside her mailbox for the spare key taped there, and walked across the quad.

When she put the key into the lock, she realized the door hadn't been locked in the first place. She walked in, ready to take off if anything seemed out of the ordinary. The place was a disaster — Lianne vaguely remembered how it got that way. It was dark inside. She moved quietly through the living room down to the hall and opened all three doors soundlessly. The rooms were undisturbed and nothing was missing. No one was hiding in any of the corners or under the bed. In spite of the mess in the living room, the apartment felt safe and peaceful again. Lianne breathed a sigh of relief. *Thank God for small blessings,* she thought, and headed to the kitchen to fix herself a cup of hot tea to go with her pills.

She noticed a piece of paper taped to the kitchen entryway. She pulled it down and stared at it. It was writing that looked vaguely Arabic or Hebraic or — Her brows knit in puzzlement. Not that — and not anything else she'd ever seen, either. There were lines that were clearly a map to somewhere, but the directions on it weren't anything she could decipher.

With the map in hand, she walked into the kitchen —

Or at least, she intended to. As she stepped across the threshold, her skin tingled and smoke and mist swirled around her. For an instant, she felt nothing under her feet at all. She screamed — and finished the step she had started into the kitchen.

Mac, you scum-sucking worm, what did you do?

She wasn't in the kitchen anymore. The smoke was even thicker here, blown by an intermittent breeze. She landed on her hands and knees in wet, tenacious mud, and caught her breath as her ribs reminded her of their injuries. She looked up at the soaring, sad remains of what had been an ancient forest. The massive ruins of burned trees towered over her, and a few unbelievably beautiful survivors in front of her made her heart ache for the lost glory. *I wish I could have seen this place before the fire,* she thought, surprising herself with the strength of that wish. *It must have been heavenly.*

She pulled the note she'd carried out of the mud, and looked at it gloomily. It was muddied and torn. She considered tossing it out, then decided against it. *Probably Mac's shopping list, written in elvish,* she thought. *But about the time I throw it out, it will be important.*

Lianne heard the quick, faint pounding of horse's hooves, steadily growing louder as she listened. After a moment, she saw a fair-haired man galloping toward her astride a huge chestnut horse. It was an elf — which meant this arrival of burned forest to the middle of her kitchen *was* Mac's doing.

I knew it. Lianne felt a bit smug at how calmly she was

taking all this. *I'm getting very rational about facing all these lit-tle episodes. Becoming quite the survivor.* She licked her dry lips and told her queasy stomach that this was just business as usual. At least, she thought it was business as usual. *Or else I've gone round the bend entirely, and I'll wake up in a charming little padded room wearing an I-love-me jacket.* She maintained her relaxed facade as the elf reined in his horse in front of her and rested one hand on the butt of a small machine gun, the kind she saw terrorists in news-shots toting.

Machine gun? Oh well, Mac races cars, so what's the difference?

"Hi," she said, wriggling her fingers feebly, in what was supposed to be a friendly, harmless wave. "I've got a note that I'm sure someone here could read." She waved the muddy paper up at him, and the elf took it suspiciously. He scanned it, muttered "Ah, bloody hell!" and reached down to pull Lianne onto the saddle behind him.

He was stronger than he looked. She sailed through the air, shrieking at the pain caused by the rough handling. "Hold on," the elf commanded, ignoring her cries, and launched the horse into a gallop that was closer to flight than any four-legged beast should have been able to manage. The horse's gait wasn't as rough as that of horses Lianne had ridden before, but with her renewed pain, she wasn't inclined towards favorable comparisons.

"I'd rather walk!" she yelled. "My ribs are killing me!"

The elf ignored her. Horse and rider danced through the trees, leaping dark, charred, human-looking forms that Lianne realized with sudden horror were bodies. The destruction wasn't limited to trees.

There had been a fight here — no, not a fight, a war. These were the survivors. No wonder this elf wasn't impressed by a couple of cracked ribs and a broken face.

She decided she didn't want to walk after all.

In quick glimpses through the wreathing smoke and mist, she caught sight of an open glade where rows of the dead were laid side by side, dreadful wounds visible on most; groups of the fair-haired elves digging beneath the roots of trees, burying their dead; shock and sorrow in pale faces, the grim set to mouths and eyes of people determined to survive and go on.

The destruction was recent; so recent that one or two fires still smoldered. *What's happened here?* she wondered. *What have I walked into — is Mac in this mess somewhere?*

"Felouen," the elf in front of her called. "A note for you from Maclyn. This human brought it."

Felouen, grime-streaked and weary-looking, put down her shovel and took the muddy paper. Lianne saw the paper glow blue, and suddenly it was clean and untorn. Felouen read, and with a puzzled expression, looked directly at Lianne.

She was incredibly beautiful — and vaguely familiar. "You are Lianne, the woman who saved my life yesterday, aren't you?" she asked.

The elf in front of her turned around and stared at his passenger with amazement. Lianne blushed. "Yes. I am."

"Then this letter doesn't make any sense. Maclyn says he's gone to a place near the Bal-A-Shar Stables to pay your ransom and rescue you from the woman who kidnapped you, and that once you're safe, he's going to pick up the little girl who caused all this damage and bring her back here. He wanted my help in rescuing you." She shook her head. "Unless he's already rescued you?"

Now Lianne was just as puzzled. "No. I got away by myself. She was going to kill me, but I clobbered her with a tire iron and stole her car. That was hours ago, uh, hours ago, back there, that is." She waved in the direction she thought her kitchen was. *God, this is like* The Lion, The Witch, and The Wardrobe. *I've got a tunnel to Narnia in my kitchen,* she thought crazily. *Why my kitchen? Was it more convenient than the closet, or is it just because I don't have a wardrobe?*

Felouen rubbed an incongruously dirty finger along the side of her nose. "I don't understand, then. When this abductor spoke to Mac, you must already have escaped her, for he could *not* have spoken to her before this. What can she hope to accomplish if you got away?"

Lianne frowned. "Maybe she thinks she can trick him

into giving her money — no!" The real answer hit her, and she groaned. "I was just bait to lure him to her. She hates him. The whole time she was beating up on me last night, she kept saying, 'This is for you, Mac Lynn. Next time it'll be you.' She's crazy. She'll kill him, I swear she will."

Felouen snarled, her face transformed into a mask of anger, no less beautiful but so frightening that Lianne shrank back from her. "No, she won't. I won't lose another of my folk today."

The elven woman whistled, and a black steed materialized out of the smoke-laden mist. "You'll ride with me," she told Lianne, as she leapt into the saddle.

"Oh, God," Lianne whispered, but only to herself. "I don't know if I can take any more of this." But they had plainly endured so much more, she was ashamed of her few piddly broken bones. She slid off the back of one elven-steed and cried out as her feet hit the ground.

"You're hurt," Felouen said in surprise, as Lianne's exclamation of pain penetrated her anger.

Lianne was a little blunter than she would have liked. "No lie. Three broken ribs, a broken nose, a bunch of abrasions, and pain that just won't quit."

Felouen reached for Lianne and muttered under her breath. In an instant, warmth spread through her broken bones, and the pain thinned and paled and sank without a trace. "I have dealt with the pain and strengthened the broken bones — everything else will have to heal naturally. I don't have enough power yet to do much more." The elvish woman sighed. "But I owe you my life — and you'd slow us both down hurt like that."

"Thanks," Lianne said, not quite certain how to react to the elven woman's words, but grateful for the relief. "This is the best I've felt in quite a while."

"Good. Let's get to Mac before that madwoman does." Felouen gave Lianne a hand up and clicked her tongue once. The magnificent black steed raced back to where the devastated splendor of the elven world met Lianne's kitchen.

*   *   *

Amanda-Alice woke with a start. She felt around herself — she was in a box, with cloth over her. It was pitch-dark, and the place where she was smelled musty. She was stiff and sore. She tried to stretch, but the box was too small. She pushed the cloth off of her, and things smelled better immediately. There was some light, too, but not much. Amanda-Alice sat up.

I'm in the attic. Yuck. It's always dusty in the attic. I'll bet I got dust on my clothes.

She climbed out of the box. Father was downstairs, thumping around. From time to time, he'd yell "Amanda! Amanda! Get down here right now!"

That Cethlenn is a bad person, for a grownup, Amanda-Alice thought. *She doesn't mind what she's told. I'm going to tell Father on her. If I don't, he might think I don't mind any better than she does.*

Amanda-Alice walked to the attic stairs and opened the door quietly. She walked out to the steps, and closed the door just as quietly behind her — *I never slam doors like some people do.* She walked down the stairs primly, like a lady, the way Father said to. It sounded like he was going through the bedrooms. Amanda-Alice followed the sound and spotted him in the guest bedroom, digging through the closets.

"Here I am, Father," Amanda-Alice said. "Cethlenn wouldn't let me come when you called."

She saw her father's back stiffen, and he turned. The fury on his face was something Amanda-Alice had never seen before; she backed up, frightened. "I'm sorry," she said. "Cethlenn made me. I couldn't help it. I'm sorry, I really am."

He growled, while his face got redder and redder. "You're sorry?" he breathed. "You're sorry? Not as sorry as you're going to be, you little bitch. Where the hell have you been hiding?"

Amanda-Alice gasped, confusion spreading through her at his tone as much as what he had just said. He had never, ever, spoken to her like that. She responded automatically, in shock, in the only way a good girl could when a grownup said anything so outrageous to her. "Those are bad words! You said never to say bad words."

He grabbed her thin shoulders with his big, thick hands and shook her. In a slow, deliberate voice, he said, "Never correct me." He slapped her across the face once, hard, and Amanda-Alice felt tears spring to her eyes. Why was he acting like this? Hadn't she come as soon as she heard him?

"I asked you where you were," he said slowly, his eyes full of fury.

She pointed timidly toward the attic. "Up there."

"I looked up there," he muttered, as if he didn't believe her.

Hoping to appease him, Amanda-Alice said, "Cethlenn made me climb up the drain spout after you went out. She was being very bad."

In the back of her mind, Amanda-Alice felt Cethlenn wake up and look through her eyes in horror. *Ah, child, what have ye' done? We're in his hands, are we? We're doomed.* She felt Cethlenn moving around in her mind, looking for Abbey and Anne. Suddenly she hoped that the witch would find Anne, the magic-maker, the only one of them with any power. This was not the father she knew. This was a stranger, an angry, unpredictable, frightening stranger. Could he — could Father have people inside him, too. . . . ?

And Cethlenn was afraid of him. That made her even more frightened. What did Cethlenn know that she didn't, that made her so afraid?

Father stared at her. "You're filthy," he whispered. "But it doesn't matter now, does it? You're too big and too ugly and too dirty and too bad — and you're calling attention to yourself. Sharon will have to do in your place. She's younger than you, anyway — and she's not a little slut."

Sharon? What did Sharon have to do with this? Amanda-Alice was even more frightened. She knew she was bad — she had to be, Father said so — but why did her call her a *bad word*?

He grabbed the back of Amanda-Alice's neck and propelled her out of the guest bedroom and down the hall toward the stairs. "I'm going to have to get rid of you," he told her coldly, all of his anger turned inside, but still there for all that it was hidden. "Before that frigid whore Merryl gets home."

Get rid of her? How? Why? What was he going to do?

She resisted a moment, and he shoved her forward, making her stumble. "Come on, you. Don't drag your feet." She looked back over her shoulder and shivered to see his smile. He wasn't talking to her — he was talking to himself. "Whatever it was that happened at the pony barn, it turned out to be good for me. Now the cops are going to look all over hell and gone for my mysterious enemy when they find you."

"F-f-find me?" she faltered. "F-f-father? Where are we going?"

He laughed, and something deep inside her went very small and very still. "We're going down to your step-mother's barn," he said, softly, "with all her precious horses. You're going to make me happy. And then there's going to be an awful accident."

Maclyn stroked Rhellen's dashboard. The elvensteed had been disgruntled to have to impersonate a battered yellow VW Bug. Then his mood had turned playful. He'd let Mac know in every possible way that such vehicles were far beneath his dignity, and he'd better not be asked to humble himself again in such a demeaning way. Mac hadn't had the heart to tell him about D.D.'s death, or about the massacre of the elves of Elfhame Outremer. Not yet. Instead, he took the teasing in silence because he knew the elvensteed was only trying to amuse him. Gradually, though, his mood communicated itself to the great beast, who withdrew into a state of watchful silence.

Mac and Rhellen raced in mounting uneasiness along the back roads to the spot Belinda had indicated. Maclyn thought it odd that she would pick a spot so near the place where he had intended to go next — but he told himself it was about time something worked to his advantage. Certainly the god of Luck had not been with him until now.

There was no sign of a car at the pull-off she'd indicated,

nor of a place to hide one. He parked where Belinda had
said, watching warily for a sign of long red hair. Then he
got out of Rhellen with his case in one hand. He patted the
VW on the fender with the other. *:Stay put,:* he said. *:See if
you can spot where she's hidden her get-away car.:*

Rhellen communicated anxiety.

He shared it. *:I know, old friend. This is a bad situation. I'll be
careful. But remember, this is your old buddy Belinda we're dealing
with, okay? She won't get away with anything, especially not sneaking up on me. She moves through the woods like an ox on skis.:*

Rhellen's soft mumbles subsided. Mac turned, counterfeit payoff in hand, and strode confidently across the road.
He slipped silently into the woods, eyes open for anything
that might be a clue to Lianne's prison, ears alert for the
faintest crunch of Belinda's footsteps. He spotted the red
marker easily and moved up to it, watching for traps.

Strangely, the woods appeared to be completely devoid
of Belinda or Lianne.

He wondered if he could be early. He glanced at his
watch, then turned slowly to scan the woods.

She didn't see him until he was in front of the tree. *How
the hell does he do that?* she wondered. But how he did it
didn't matter. Not really. He wouldn't be doing it anymore.

Belinda lined up the cross-hairs on her scope — a nice,
dependable chest shot. The gun had enough punch to kill
him from the distance she was at, without being close
enough for him to hear or see her, no matter how good his
eyes and ears were. Her finger tightened on the trigger.
She waited while he dropped the case. Then he turned,
slowly, scanning the woods, moving beautifully into a full-
face shot.

It was perfect.

At the instant that she pulled the trigger, he spotted her,
and through the scope, she could see that his face wore an
expression of terrible shock and dismay. And fear. It was
beautiful, it was wonderful, it was the sweet taste of
revenge.

In the next instant, a red blossom appeared on the white

of his shirt, high and to his left. The heart — she couldn't have hit it more perfectly if she had been a surgeon working on an operating table.

Belinda stood and smiled, and ran through the fringe of woods at the edge of the child's home, on her way to pick up Mel.

God, but revenge was sweet.

Rhellen heard a "crack" from the woods that Mac had walked into, and felt his partner suddenly overcome by pain and fear. He charged toward the sensations that were coming from Maclyn, shape-shifting out of his assumed form on the run. He crashed through the underbrush. To his right, running away, he saw the red-headed woman.

He felt fury, but he didn't dare follow her. He had to find Maclyn.

A clump of white showed up in the dimming light, along with red. Rhellen trotted toward it, smelling blood as he got closer. He tossed his head and snorted. Mac didn't answer, not by voice or in Mindspeech.

The white clump was Mac, all right. The elvensteed put his nose down and nudged the elf, whickering softly and radiating concern.

Mac's eyes didn't open. He didn't respond in any way.

Rhellen grew afraid. He knew he could take Maclyn back to help, though. Lianne's house had a Gate in it — he could go there.

He flattened himself in the middle and slipped under Maclyn like a knife shaving butter, then formed around Mac to prevent moving or jostling him in any way. Then he left the woods, rushing towards Lianne's house, ignoring the roads.

Amanda-Alice felt a jostling in her head, as she was suddenly joined by Amanda-Abbey and Cethlenn. They were tied at wrists and ankles, their mouths gagged, in the unused stall at the end of the stables. The Father stood bent over a little, a few feet away from them, spreading gasoline around the inside of the barn. He ranted under his breath,

"This will show Merryl. Let's see how she feels about all of her damned horses going up in smoke."

"Happy, you little whore?" he asked from time to time, looking into the stall where Cethlenn and the Amandas lay. "You won't ever disobey me again. Filthy slut."

Cethlenn struggled with the bonds, trying to work free. It was no use. The Father had too much practice with this — he knew how to tie up a child so that she couldn't slither free. Both girls were crying and shrieking. Alice was incoherent — she'd been the most sheltered from the Father's abuse — but Abbey was clear enough. :*We're going to die! Help us, Cethlenn! Help us!*:

Cethlenn wanted to weep; she was as helpless as they were. All of her magics required free hands and supplies, neither of which they had. :*If we had Anne, she could get us out of here. We have the bracelet on — she knows how to use the Gate. Can't you find her? Bring her back, tell her we need her.*:

The children cried, and Alice answered for both of them. :*She's gone. She isn't real anymore. I made her go away.*:

Cethlenn steeled herself. She'd passed through this once, already. Surely death could be no harder a second time? :*Och, my darlings, we're all going to cease to be real in a few minutes.*: She held her mental arms out for them, and they huddled inside. :*I cannot protect you, my little ones. Only Anne could do that. But I will be with you. I will not leave you alone.*:

The Father finished spreading the gasoline, and came in and squatted in the straw next to Amanda. He stroked her back in a manner that made Cethlenn's skin crawl and grinned down at them.

"We need to have one last party, little Amanda."

He stared down at her and frowned. "Shit. You look just like your mother, you know that? I killed her, too. Did you know that? I'll bet you didn't." He sat by the child. The smell of gasoline was sharp and overwhelming in the back of their throat. "She found out what I was doing with you — she didn't like it."

He laughed and stood up, and began pulling down his pants. "So I had her committed to a nuthouse, and I hired a woman to go in, pretend she was crazy, and get close to her.

That woman slit her wrists for her. Suicide — isn't that great? Everybody felt so sorry for me. And that left me with you."

Pants down, he knelt beside Amanda and smiled. "We've had lots of fun, too, haven't we? You've liked it, huh? Daddy's little girl. Filthy bitch. Oh, you liked it. You wanted it. You asked for it."

Cethlenn tried to call the bastard something crude, but the gag in her mouth changed her curses to a few weak grunts.

"Yeah," he said, "I'm going to have to take the gag out until we're done, Amanda. My little whore. Just like your mother now — " His eyes got a glazed look to them, and his face reddened. "I want to hear you tell me that you like it. Tell me that you want it."

He pulled Amanda's blue jeans down around her ankles, worked her panties down past her knees. Behind Cethlenn, Alice and Abbey screamed, frightened.

He was breathing hard and obviously very excited. *In my time, you pervert, we'd have cut your balls off and fed them to you raw,* Cethlenn thought.

The Father took the gag out of their mouth. "Tell me you want it," he said thickly. "One last time."

Mel and Belinda had seen the girl and her father go into the barn from their hiding place behind one of the horse troughs in the paddocks. Mel had grinned at her after checking the readings on his own black box. "Good job, Belinda. The kid's as hot as you said she was. I was starting to have some doubts about you."

Belinda felt cheerful and relaxed, now that it was almost over. Within a few hours she'd have her pay. Within twenty-four, she'd be on a beach somewhere. Bermuda, maybe. "I'm sorry about that, Mel. I just couldn't get the racecar driver. From now on, I'll know never to try collecting adults. The real TK's are too dangerous. We'll just have to get 'em while they're kids."

Mel nodded, as if she had just told him something profound. "I'll remember that. It's an important point."

He faced Belinda. "You think there will be any danger from this one?"

From a kid? How could there be? She rolled her eyes. "Christ, Mel — she's only ten years old. What the hell could a ten-year-old do?"

He shook his head, as if he hadn't intended to say that. "Yes. You're right, of course. Still, I have my gun with me."

Belinda watched the barn, and with a puzzled glance at Mel, started inching toward it, keeping behind available cover. "They're taking a long time in there," she whispered. "I'm not sure I like this. I think there's something wrong."

Mel followed, nodding, a look of concern on his face.

The lovely old post-and-beam wood barn had been moved from another part of the country and restored by real craftsmen, using the original wood wherever possible. The finished building had all the charm of the original, with a few modern amenities required by a modern horse-breeding operation. But the knotholes in the siding had remained. Belinda found one and looked in it.

"Horse's rear end," she whispered. "What a view."

She moved down the side, looking through whatever cracks or gaps came her way. At the far end of the old barn, she stopped and stared.

Jesus Christ. Jesus H. Christ. Her mind babbled obscenities, as her stomach churned. She turned away, the blood draining from her face, struggling to control her sickness.

Mel noticed her expression and pressed his eye to the hole. After a moment, he shrugged and turned to Lianne. "I'm surprised you're squeamish about *that*," he whispered. "Research seems to indicate that that's the sort of thing that brings out TK talents in some of these kids." He watched her, his expression suddenly fascinated. "My God, that really bothers you. I didn't think anything bothered you."

She swallowed. She tried to tell herself it didn't matter; in a few hours Mel would have the kid out of this stinking barn and into a sheltered, cozy environment. She knew that; she knew he'd treat his little prize like the pearl she was, like a precious gem. She'd never even have to think of this again. "I didn't realize we'd be doing her a favor taking her away from here," Belinda whispered. "All of a sudden I feel like a Goddamned hero."

Mel chuckled. "Don't let it go to your head," he told her as he climbed over the fence and headed around to the back door of the barn. He tried it and found it locked. He headed toward the front door. "If we have to rape the kid from time to time to keep her talents sharp, we will."

Suddenly, she didn't feel like such a hero. Suddenly, Mel's back was a very attractive target.

Mel disappeared into the barn.

Belinda's head swam, and the sharp burn of vomit hung in the back of her throat. There had been a fat old geezer in the upstairs apartment who'd groped her up when she was a kid. It sure as hell hadn't been her dad. She didn't remember much, and she hadn't ever been able to like men after the little bit she'd been through; now she wondered how this kid felt.

And Mel had nonchalantly said he'd see that the girl was tortured after they got her away from here if that kept her TK magic operating well.

Belinda gritted her teeth and stroked the holster that held her pistol under her jacket. There were financial considerations to be kept in mind, of course, but once she and Mel got the girl out to California, Mel might find that he wasn't going to do that, after all. He might find out it would be a good idea to treat the little girl like a goddamned princess.

Lianne gave directions to Felouen, who passed them on to her elvensteed, who had transformed into a jet-black Lamborghini. The three of them moved along the roads so fast the only scenery that wasn't blurred was that which was directly in front of them.

The topic of what had happened in Elfhame Outremer had been exhausted, and so had the subject of what had happened to Lianne.

The one thing they hadn't discussed was Mac. That subject hung heavily in the air.

Lianne broke the uncomfortable silence. She cleared her throat and said, "He'll be fine, I think." She was trying to offer reassurance to the elven woman, who was wired tighter than a banjo from tension, as best Lianne could tell. She also found that talking was better than silence. It helped keep her mind off of how fast they were going. She couldn't help but be bothered by the fact that Felouen's hands weren't on the steering wheel. "He knows so many tricks — how could a human hurt him?"

Felouen never took her eyes off the road. "My opinion of the damage a human can cause has gone way up," she said. "And Maclyn is an idiot. I love him," she muttered, "but all that proves is that I'm an idiot, too."

Lianne stared at Felouen. "You love him?"

The elven woman stared stonily out the window. "I have for several hundred years. It's been a most unrewarding occupation."

Lianne folded her hands on her lap and fixed her eyes on the road ahead of them. Her exhaustion must have just caught up with her, because she started speaking before her brain had a chance to clear the words. "I see. But you're beautiful, and you're intelligent, and you're an elf, too. Why — ?"

"Why doesn't he love me?" Felouen's lips quirked into a lopsided smile, finishing the question for her. "Why can't you hold the stars in your hands, and why can't you fly if you want to badly enough? The answer is — 'Because that is not the way the universe works.' Maclyn is destined to break his heart loving humans, I suppose, and I am destined to break my heart loving him. Just because we are near-immortal in your eyes, it does not follow that we cannot be killed — and just because we have the wisdom of the ages at our disposal, it does not follow that we are wise."

Lianne nodded, but remained silent.

The elven woman suddenly looked over at her. "I never thought I could envy a human," she said, "but I do envy you. I've had his sympathy, but you've had his love."

A familiar-looking golden Chevy roared past them, going in the opposite direction. Felouen's elvensteed bellowed like a foghorn and did a sudden controlled-spin turn that threw Felouen and Lianne around inside.

God, I'm glad this particular elvensteed belted us in, she thought. *A stunt like that in Rhellen would have turned us into tomato paste on the windshield.*

And indeed, Rhellen had slowed cautiously and made a careful turn that Lianne could have imagined her grandmother making. *That isn't how Mac usually drives,* she thought at the same moment that Felouen said, "Moortha just told me Rhellen says Maclyn is hurt."

Lianne shook her head. "No. He'll be fine. I know he will."

Felouen smiled at her, a slow, gentle smile that didn't even begin to hide the pain in her eyes. "You also love him," she said. "I'm glad for that, at least. The woman who broke his heart so long ago never really did." She patted Lianne's hand as the two cars pulled even with each other and came to a stop. "We're allies for now," she said.

The two women got out of the car and ran to the door Rhellen had opened for them. He'd rearranged his interior so that there was nothing inside but a firm, supporting mattress that contoured around the wounded passenger, holding him firmly in place.

"Gunshot," Felouen said, looking critically at the unconscious elf. She pressed her hands against his chest and his shirt faded out of being.

Oh God. Oh my God — Lianne had seen enough cop shows to know where the heart was. And she had seen enough bodies in the past few hours to know what death looked like. Waxy, pale — with a bullet hole in his upper chest that no longer bled. . . . Lianne bit her lip, and felt her eyes fill with tears. "Right through his heart," she whispered. "He must have died instantly."

Felouen turned around with a quizzical expression on her face. "Heart? Not at all. That's down here," she said, pressing her hand low on the center of his chest. "Lucky he wasn't human. That shot was very carefully placed." She suddenly grinned. "Lucky the woman was such a good shot. She hit a lung . . . some big blood vessels . . . we can fix this."

No, I can't believe it. It can't be true, she's just humoring me . . . .

"Really." Lianne tried to smile, but her lip quivered. Felouen gave her a long look — and took both her shoulders in her hard hands, shaking her like a stubborn child.

"Yes, you little fool! He'll be fine! I can fix him, I can do it *right now."* She punctuated each word with another shake, until Lianne finally had belief shaken into her.

Felouen let go of her shoulders, with a mutter of "damn fool mortals," and sighed. "Well, I can do a little for him, and there are others Underhill who can do more. Shit, I wish I had my strength back. And you don't even have much you can loan me."

Rhellen rumbled, and Felouen eyed him speculatively. "Well, there is always drawing from you, isn't there?" The car flashed his lights emphatically, and she smiled slightly, and nodded. "We'll do it. Thank you, Rhellen."

Felouen pressed one hand on Rhellen's doorframe, and one on Mac, and sang a soft, minor-key song in a beautiful language Lianne had never heard before. It was hard to believe mere words could be so beautiful, but the teacher felt a poignant sense of loss with each syllable — that this was a world that she could only know briefly from its periphery. The only other time she felt this way was when she watched a Space Shuttle fly. . . .

Lianne rested her hands on Mac's leg and willed him to get better. Felouen's head snapped around, startled, and then she gave the teacher a smile full of gratitude while she sang.

Under their hands, Maclyn groaned and shifted. Felouen kept singing, Lianne kept willing her strength into him—

And he sat up and spoke — dazed, but with only one thing on his mind, and that driving him past all sense or personal injury.

"We have to get to Amanda."

*   *   *

Amanda-Abbey and Amanda-Alice clung to each other and cried. :*I'm sorry, Anne,*: Alice sobbed. :*I didn't know! Please come back. Please help us!*: Gentle Abbey was too much in shock to do anything but weep.

Cethlenn pressed the two of them against her chest and cried helplessly herself, as all three of them shared the pain of the body they lived in. There was no protecting them this time. They were going to die, and before they did, they had to go through this. *Anne could have saved them — Anne would never have been caught by the bastard in the first place,* she thought grimly. *But if she hadn't protected them quite so well, they would have known not to trust him.* Cethlenn wiped viciously at her own tears. "*If only*" — *the most useless words in any language. Limit the damage as best you can,* she told herself.

Abbey, as frightened as her sister, and even more stunned, kept thinking, *Anne saved us from this. She let him hurt her like this so that we wouldn't be hurt. We never even knew.* She wrapped her arms tighter around her remaining "sister" and closed her eyes. *You loved us, and we didn't know enough to love you back. I'm sorry, Anne,* Abbey called. *Wherever you are, I'm sorry. I love you. Please, please come back. I really love you. We really love you. . . .*

Belinda followed Mel into the cavernous barn, stepping softly. She felt her trigger finger twitching. The idea of seeing the child's father with his brains spattered all over the barn wall became increasingly attractive to her with every passing moment. *Funny,* she thought. *I would have figured I had run out of noble motives for doing things a long time ago. It's interesting what you find out about yourself.*

The barn smelled — Belinda reflected that all barns smelled, but this one didn't smell right. The usual animal odors were there, but the place also smelled like — gasoline. Ugh! Just what her already-queasy stomach needed. Lucky she hadn't eaten since — God, sometime yesterday. She decided she was going to take better care of herself as soon as this mess was over.

In front of her, Mel pulled his gun out and shoved the stall door open with his foot.

"Good afternoon," he told the man, leveling his gun at him. "I regret having to interrupt your recreation, but we are in a bit of a hurry. So if you will just put the child down and step away from her, I won't have to shoot you."

The man stared stupidly at them. It took him a moment to see the gun, another few seconds for him to pull away from the child. He stood, pulling up his pants as he did, his face vacant and still.

"Very good. Bend down and pick up the girl while I cover him please, Belinda."

Belinda knelt and began untying the child and trying to rearrange her clothes, while the girl stared at her, disoriented and disbelieving.

"No, don't bother with that," Mel said. "Her father has conveniently packaged her for transport. Just pick her up and let's be going."

Belinda turned and snarled, "For godsakes, Mel, let me fix her clothes, at least."

"Do what I tell you," Mel said, coolly.

Without thinking, Belinda reached into her jacket toward her holster. Mel caught the movement, and his gun wavered for an instant between the man and her.

Lianne followed elves and elvensteeds across the yard toward the barn, running as fast as she could and falling behind again. Mac had paused just long enough to drop Lianne at the edge of the stable-area, then he and Felouen had headed straight for the barn. He'd probably intended for Lianne to stay out of this — but Amanda was her pupil, and she was, by God, going to be there. She'd expected for them to storm the house, but instead, Mac had shouted something about "bad magic at the barn," and the elves and their mounts headed that way.

She saw the elvensteeds hit the barn doors with their hooves. At the first blow, the doors flew open, and Mac, Rhellen, Felouen, and Moortha charged in.

Lianne was just inside the barn when the screaming began.

* * *

Andrew knew it was over the second the stranger kicked the door open. His mind raced, even as he feigned shock. He took his time, cultivated his face into a mask of stupidity, and did everything he could to make pulling up his pants seem the harmless actions of a stunned man.

His law career was over. This would get out, and he would find himself in prison. He knew what inmates did to men they found out were child-molesters.

His marriage was over — Merryl and her million-dollar dowry and her pliable, beautiful young daughter were as good as gone already.

He had nothing to lose but his life, and that had ceased to have any value. He decided then that he might as well die — but he wanted the people who had cost him everything to die with him. When the crash at the front of the barn drew everyone's attention away from him, his hand was into his pocket and out again before they could notice. His lighter was in his hand, and no one had seen. He clutched a wad of straw in the same hand.

The man with the gun swore and looked around frantically. "Grab the kid and c'mon," he told the woman.

Pounding hooves clattered at the front of the barn. Whoever was up there would be here in a moment. His daughter looked around at the three of them, a puzzled expression on her face. Andrew noticed that her eyes suddenly looked pale, pale green in the dim light. He'd seen the change before, but never before had he wondered at the cause. Now, though, he had a little time for puzzlement; now, when there were only a few more moments left of his life, and everything was incredibly sharp-edged and clear.

His daughter frowned — an oddly adult frown — and the ropes fell off of her wrists and ankles although no one had untied her. She stood, pulled up her pants, and brushed away the red-headed woman's hand as if no effort were involved.

"You h-h-hurt them," the child said to him, and Andrew felt the chill of unreasoning, senseless fear. "You hurt me — and — I d-d-didn't like it, but I didn't h-h-hurt you back because you left them alone. But now you hurt — them!"

The red-haired woman and the man with the gun both made a grab for her. Two tall blond — rock stars, Andrew thought, for lack of a better term — appeared in the stall and grabbed the man with the gun without pausing for a second.

They threw him. Picked him up, and *threw* him over the stall door.

Odd. The blond bimbo looked like a rock star and dressed like a rock star, but she had pointed ears.

Andrew tried to use the chance to escape, and found himself unable to move. So, apparently, did the battered red-haired woman. She writhed in place, but her feet seemed to be rooted to the ground.

The blond man, who also had those odd pointed ears, walked over and lifted him easily. Andrew found himself slung across the man's shoulders, completely helpless, unable to move at all against the man's unnatural strength. He didn't bother resisting after the initial attempt. It wouldn't change the outcome any.

Andrew thumbed the lighter, felt the straw ignite . . . and he opened his hand.

There was an instant when he wasn't certain it would work — but then the gasoline he'd poured around the inside of the barn caught, and with a satisfying *"whump,"* the inside of the building blossomed into flame.

Horses shrieked, the pale man and the pale woman started in dismay, and Andrew knew he'd won after all.

Chapter Fourteen

Fire licked within inches of them. The entire barn was in flames, there were strange people and guns and elves all over. None of it mattered — they were all together. Alice, Abbey, Cethlenn — and Anne. Alice and Abbey wiped tears from their eyes, and hugged her with illusory arms.

:Anne,: Alice said with real joy, *:you came back, you really came back! You* aren't *bad, you're good, you were right, I was wrong, you're good and you're strong, and — :*

Anne's lip quivered as she interrupted her sister. *:H-h-h-he killed . . . Mommy.:*

Abbey nodded solemnly and put her own arms around her sister, ignoring the flames that crept closer. *:He said so. He was glad about it. We* hate *him. Are you going to feed him to your monsters?:*

Anne shook her head slowly from side to side. *:N-n-no more m-m-m-monsters. That was bad. Th-th-they hurt lots of people, and nobody deserved it. I'm s-s-sorry about the monsters.:*

Alice crossed her snowy arms in front of her chest and pouted. *:But Father is very, very bad. Bad people deserve to be eaten by monsters.:*

Cethlenn rested her hand on Alice's shoulder. *:I don't think Anne wants to be the one to feed people to the monsters anymore. She hurts inside from all the pain the monsters caused.:*

Anne gave the witch a grateful look. *:Yes,:* she said simply.

The flames crackled and reached for the ceiling; horses screamed, including the strange elf-horses. That got their attention, and suddenly Abbey and Alice shrank against Cethlenn in fear. *:Are we all going to die in the fire?:* Abbey asked.

:No.: Anne looked at her sisters, and smiled. It was the first time any of them had seen her smile. *:I'm w-w-with you . . . now. We're g-g-going to g-g-g-get better.:*

*   *   *

Belinda backed away from the flames, but there was nowhere to escape. She was really trapped this time, with no place to run, no place to hide. She wasn't alone, but that was no comfort. Even with an escort to Valhalla like this one — Mac Lynn, Miss Teach Lianne, the little girl, her disgusting father, Mel-the-bastard, millions of dollars worth of horses — it was no comfort at all.

All of them trapped in a burning barn, and not one of them had a way out.

So much for noble intentions, Belinda thought, looking at the little girl; for some obscure reason, tears clouded her eyes. *I would have saved you if I could have, kid. But now we're all going to die — because of that shitcan father of yours.*

All of them — including the racecar driver. Nice to know, after all her hard work, that he was finally going to cross the Great Divide. Where the hell did he get the Spock ears, anyway? He looked like some Hollywood director's idea of an elf. *How is he still alive after I put that bullet in his heart? And how did he pick up Mel and throw him like a baseball?*

She was perversely glad that Mel Tanbridge was going to get what was coming to him. She just wished she didn't have to go with him.

The smoke thickened, wreathing around her and making her cough, and she knelt down, sucking for air. Maybe it would be easier to stand and inhale the thick, acrid smoke into her lungs. Get it over with quicker.

I just really don't want to die, she thought, as her eyes streamed tears and her skin started feeling as if she was getting a bad sunburn. Only this sunburn was going to be a real bitch. . . .

Mac stared helplessly at the sudden eruption of flames that penned them in. Lianne grabbed his arm and looked up at him, trusting him to do some wonderful trick to rescue them. But Maclyn had been too badly hurt — he didn't have enough energy left to work the simplest spell, much less create a Gate. When he'd been shot, the energy he'd been using to maintain the Gate in Lianne's apartment had snapped and drained off. That, as much as the bullet, had pushed him near death. Now he was fresh out of tricks.

Felouen, he knew, was no better off; she had drained herself to absolute exhaustion in order to heal the others, and had to borrow power from Rhellen to heal him. She told him with her eyes that she would be no help.

The old wood of the building burned like kindling.

Wait a moment —

There was a chance, Mac thought, looking frantically around, as his eyes lit on the terrified elvensteeds. The elvensteeds weren't immune to fire. But they might be able to transform, to take their riders out, shielded inside them. They probably wouldn't survive — but maybe humans and elves would. He grabbed Rhellen's mane and tried to communicate what he wanted to the terrified beast.

Amanda appeared at his side.

She put her hand on his, and he looked down at her, startled at the upwelling of power from the child. Her green eyes looked up into his. No more hate there, and no more fear. No insanity. He sensed that there were several people, still, inside her little head — but they were all together now, working as one.

"I know — the trick," she said. She pressed the green bead at her wrist between her fingers, her eyes closing in concentration —

In front of them, with a rush of energy, a Gate appeared.

The panicked elvensteeds dove into it. Lianne followed, with Felouen dragging Amanda's father, and Amanda holding back to maintain the Gate so that Maclyn and Belinda could escape as well. He reached for the child to pull her through.

Belinda suddenly shrieked "No!" and whirled to face them.

Mac froze. Belinda held a gun, leveled at him. "Let the kid go through, but you stay! You aren't getting away again," she shrieked, eyes glittering with madness. He opened his hands to reach for her; she was close enough — when a shape loomed out of the smoke and flames. It was the balding man they'd thrown, and *he* had a gun, too.

"Nobody move," he shouted. Mac and Belinda saw him
aim the weapon at the child. "She's mine," he screamed.
"You won't have her! Nobody gets her but me!"

Flames roared and circled them; Belinda's eyes flicked
from Mac to that son-of-a-bitch Mel. *Why isn't he dead?* she
wondered. He should have been. He was going to kill the
rest of them —
Including the kid.
The kid didn't deserve it. The kid deserved to go live in
fairyland after what had happened to her. Not to die in a
goddamn fire.
She bit her lip. Sweat streamed down her face, and she
squinted against the worsening smoke.
*Dammit. One bullet — why did I leave everything in the car
when I got ready to shoot Racer-Boy? One damned bullet —*
She could shoot Mac. Or she could save the kid. She
couldn't do both.
Belinda made her decision.
"Go!" she yelled to Mac, and the gun in her hands spit
fire and bucked — and Mel staggered back, as a crimson
dot appeared on his forehead.

:I couldn't hold the door anymore,: Anne said sadly, drooping
with weariness. *:I couldn't get the lady out. I tried, but I was too
tired.:*
Cethlenn looked around the charred remains of
Elfhame Outremer, and said softly, *:You did the best you could,
Anne. We all know that. I think you've made up for what happened
to the elves.:*
Abbey hugged her, then Alice, trying to reassure her.
:You're our sister,: Alice whispered. *:We aren't mad at you
anymore. You did the right things, and you tried to keep us safe. You
saved all of us!:*
:I'm really glad you came back,: Abbey added shyly. *:We need
you.:*
Anne smiled slowly, as if trying out the feeling for the
first time. *:I need you, too.:*

*   *   *

Maclyn shuddered and took in huge gasps of clean, cool air. Behind them, the crashes of falling timbers, the roar of flames, and the anguished screams of horses echoed, even after the Gate snapped shut.

He could hardly believe their narrow escape. And that all of it had been caused by — or for — one small girl . . . that was the least believable of all.

Belinda hadn't made it. Mac straightened and stood in the forest of Elfhame Outremer, his eyes fixed on the place where the Gate had been. On the other side of it, she was dying horribly. She had saved Amanda's life at the last minute, Mac realized after a moment, and spared his. He still had no idea why she'd wanted to kill him in the first place, and he certainly couldn't fathom why she had saved him in the end. Or had it really been Amanda she was saving? He wondered if it was the only selfless thing she'd ever done — or if once she had been someone who had been worth knowing.

He turned away, saddened by the waste of her life.

Andrew Kendrick figured that he was probably insane. He should have died — but a blond bimbo with special-effects ears and eyes had pulled him through a hole in the air. At first, he'd thought it was some kind of new firefighting technique, and then he'd thought it was an hallucination.

He blacked out, and came to surrounded by a crowd of strangers; he thought then that he might be able to get away — the only witnesses to what he'd done to Amanda were dead, except for Amanda herself, and who'd believe a kid? But all the strangers had those weird ears and eyes, and wherever he was, it wasn't North Carolina.

He was wrestled to his feet with no consideration for his injuries before he could say a thing and hustled off into captivity. Since then, he'd been kept in a tiny cell, given sparse food and brackish water at odd intervals, and otherwise ignored. He was in some bizarre tree-world, and his cell had been the inside of a tree. That was when he figured he had gone insane, and there was no point in worrying about things.

The tall blond people — Sidhe, elves, he'd been told, and he'd stared at the speaker with disbelief, then laughed at him — had avoided him entirely until several hours ago, when two of them came and told him he was to be tried. He'd laughed at that, too, at the absurdity of it. But they'd hauled him away, and gradually he had to admit that whether or not he was insane, someone had him in their power, and that same someone had plans for him that he probably wasn't going to like.

Now he sat in a high-arching hall whose ceiling had recently been blasted open to the elements. The walls were scarred and pitted and burned. He'd noted that with a sort of detached interest as he'd been led into the hall. He wondered why the place was such a dump. What could possibly have happened here? It looked like a war zone.

The audience wore pointed ears, the jury and judge wore pointed ears — in fact, everyone except his daughter and her damned teacher wore them. The sight of Lianne What's-Her-Name sitting there in the audience stunned him for a moment. Whatever in hell was happening here, she must have a hand in it. Was this the high school drama club's shindig, with the costumes and ears?

He began to think, coldly and with guile. The teacher had him stashed away somewhere. Eventually, he'd get away. Then he'd get her. . . .

As the trial ground on, he was told how this place the "elves" called Elfhame Outremer had come to be destroyed. He was told a litany of dead and injured that made him chuckle in disbelief. He also discovered that the elves maintained that sole responsibility for the damage and all the deaths fell to him.

Even given that these people were loonies, put up to this by Lianne Whatsis, Andrew Kendrick was having some difficulty with that. In the first place, he didn't believe that Amanda had done the things they said she had — if she had been able to make monsters out of thin air, and work "magic" like that, why hadn't she gone after him? Why hadn't she done something about their games?

The memory of what had happened to the pony barn

intruded at that moment, but he pushed it resolutely away. Whatever had happened there, Amanda couldn't have been responsible. She was only one little girl, one stupid, sluttish little girl. It must have some rational cause — and surely, surely some adult enemy had done it. Not the brat. Children were helpless, as they should be; property of those who fathered them.

Still, these "elves" insisted that was the truth. It only proved that they were loonies. He didn't know how Lianne Whatever had found them, but she sure fit right in with them.

Even *if* Amanda had been the cause for the "elves'" injuries, he didn't see how he could be legally held responsible for her insane outbreak. *He* hadn't conjured monsters or whatever the hell they were saying she'd done. He couldn't have if he tried — they even admitted that. But they were saying he *made* Amanda do it — and he'd never heard of any charge as crazy as that, not even in the kangaroo courts of Iran and Iraq.

Nuts. They were nutcases, one and all. Maybe Lianne had dragged him off to a nuthouse somehow?

But even nuts responded to some kind of logic, and before he could think about getting away, getting back to Fayetteville, he'd have to convince them that he was innocent. Since Amanda was admittedly as crazy as they were, she must be lying, and he was innocent of whatever they thought he had done. All right, they were trying him as some kind of an accomplice, perhaps. Why should he even have to take the rap for that? The "elves" didn't have any hard evidence. The testimony of a kid the "elves" frankly admitted had serious psychological problems wouldn't have held water for a second back in Fayetteville.

He summoned his best judicial manner and stood up to speak his piece. But when he'd tried his rebuttal, he'd been firmly silenced and told that in Elfhame Outremer, he had no rights. No speech of any kind on his part would be permitted.

At that point, he was just about ready to explode. He kept his mouth shut only by reminding himself that there

were other loonies on the "jury," and that even if they con-
victed him, he'd be able to get away at some point. And
then he'd bring the authorities down on all of them. After
silencing Amanda first, of course.

The "trial" took place over most of a day. At the end, he
sat, chin erect, eyes firm, expression noble and convincingly
innocent. He faced his accusers. Most of the people who had
been in the burning barn were there. The blond "elf," who
was also the local hero racecar driver Mac Lynn; his own
daughter, Amanda — who looked at him from time to time
and cried; Amanda's teacher, Miss McCormick; and the tall,
skinny "elf" bimbo who had dragged him out of the barn.
Felouen? What was that, Jamaican or something?

The kangaroo court prepared for the summing-up.

"Your actions were the direct cause of all of this," the
bimbo said. She looked at him as if he were a particularly
loathsome form of excrement she'd found on the bottom of
her shoe. "Because of your abuse of this child, almost half
of the people — innocent people — of Elfhame Outremer
are lost to us. The city itself is as you see it now because of
you — a ruin that will take hundreds of years to heal. Nothing will heal our many dead, nor the hearts of those who
loved them and buried them. There is no punishment that
we can give you which will mete out justice fully."

Andrew grinned at her. It was true. The worst they could
do was kill him, and he'd been ready to do that himself.
And if they didn't kill him, he'd get away, and then he'd
come back with the law on his side and ready to deal with
them all. Lunatics.

"However," the bimbo "Seleighe Court Lady" continued, "the one of our folk who discovered the true nature
of your crimes also declared a fitting sentence for you
before she died. In deference to her, and because her
demand on the course of your life comes as close as possible
to achieving justice, her sentence will be carried out."

Sentence? So they weren't going to kill him. Fine. He
was smart, he knew things — he'd learned a lot from some
of his less respectable clients. He doubted there was any
place they could put him that he couldn't get out of,

eventually. He discounted the fact that he hadn't been able to find a way out of the hollow tree they'd put him in at first. He just hadn't had time, that was all. He'd show them.

The bimbo kept right on with her pompous speech. God, how he hated women who got any authority at all, even granted by a pack of nutcases! They got so out of hand....

"We know that you were abused as a child. We discovered this from the Oracular Pool — and we regret that we were not there to intervene for you." A flicker of distant pity passed over her face, and he noted it with resentment. How dared she pity him? "However, your adult life was the result of a long series of choices you made of your own free will — and your decision to abuse your own child was one such choice. You never displayed regret and never sought help. Therefore, there are no mitigating circumstances to soften your punishment."

The bimbo Felouen waved one hand, and a pocket of blackness appeared to her side. The other "elves" watched it with calm interest. Only now did he feel a chill of fear. What the hell was going on?

She turned back to him, with a face as cold as marble. "You are to be banished to a pocket of the Unformed Plane that has been prepared especially for you. It is unlikely that you will ever die in there — it is also unlikely that you will ever be released. In order to be released, you must truly, deeply, and completely come to regret what you inflicted on your daughter, take responsibility for it, and to feel guilt for it. In this pocket of the Unformed, your punishment will fit your crime. We regret this, Andrew Kendrick. But this is the justice you have earned."

Andrew found strong hands clasped over each arm, and although he struggled, suddenly frightened of the dark pool that hung in the air in front of him, he was shoved forward with implacable strength and speed.

"It's not my fault," he screamed. "*She* did it, the little bitch! She made me do it! Little girls are whores, and she was *my daughter* to do with as I pleased, damn it! It's not my fault! It's not my fault!"

He was thrown into that spinning vortex of tenebrous

nothingness, and for a brief, disorienting moment, all detail and all sense of existence vanished.

Then he found himself on hands and knees, naked, in a room that glowed disconcertingly red. The room was hot, the light was dim, and a huge creature, as naked as he, stood at the far end. Beside the creature hung ropes, chains, horse tack and other implements that Andrew recognized. Only they were bigger, here, as if he were ten years old again. There was a narrow cot in one corner of the room. In fact, he recognized the room as a much larger version of the special "tack room" he'd kept for his use with Amanda.

The thing moved toward him, smiling. "Come here," it said in a voice so deep Andrew felt it before he heard it. "Come here. You want it. You know you do."

He looked at the monstrous thing's face. It shifted in the dim light, looking first like his father's face, then like Amanda's — and then his own.

"Come here, slut," it crooned. Then it seized him.

In the Oracular Pool, Andrew struggled in the bogan's grip; Amanda — Anne, Abbey, Alice, and Cethlenn together — shuddered and turned away, into Felouen's arms. The elven lady held her. Cethlenn felt Felouen rejoice that the child permitted herself to be held. Felouen banished the vision from the Pool, and led the little girl away, towards the tree-home of the driver Maclyn. He descended from his home to welcome them, with a smile for all of them. All four of them.

The moment that Cethlenn had sensed approaching came, although neither the elven lady nor the children knew it. They were about to become three, not four. It was time for Cethlenn to go.

:Children — : she said — and as usual, it was the sensitive Abbey who guessed what was about to happen.

:No!: the girl protested; the others understood in an instant and added their protests to hers.

:You c-c-can't leave,: Anne wailed. *:Who's g-g-gonna teach me the m-m-magic?:*

:*The elves are better teachers than ever I'd be, little Anne,*: she said, stroking Anne's hair. :*You're a fast learner, and Felouen will gladly teach you.*:

:*But who will — will tell us what to do?*: proper Alice asked, completely at a loss. :*You have to stay! We have to know what's right and what's wrong!*:

:*Look to Maclyn for that, my dear one,*: Cethlenn told her. :*He's learned in a bitter hard school, and he lives what he's learned. He is a most honorable man and a noble elven lord.*:

Abbey crept up beside her and nestled into her side. :*Who will love us?*: she asked piteously. :*You made us see each other, but who is going to make us all better if you go?*:

There her heart nearly broke, but the time was upon her, determined by a higher Power than she could fight. :*Every elf Underhill will love you, my darlings,*: she told them. :*And you will heal yourselves and make yourself whole.*:

They thought about that for a moment, and it was finally Alice who replied. :*You've never lied to us,*: she said. :*How? How are we going to be better?*:

The tugging on her soul became an insistent pull, and she had to fight against it to stay long enough to reply. :*Look for Amanda,*: she said at last, as the answer came to her from the same source as the tugging. :*Look for the littlest of you all, the most frightened, the one in hiding. And when you find her, show her you love her — and show her she is loved. Raise her up. Teach her that there is an end to fear and pain. Then you will find your way home.*:

The two elves with her sensed something going on. Cethlenn looked out of Amanda's eyes and into the eyes of Maclyn. He saw her there, and his lips formed a Word that he did not speak.

She nodded, gravely. "Blessings upon you, Fair One," she said in the most ancient Gaelic. "I give this one into your keeping. See that you deserve her."

Then, with a farewell caress to all three (and was there a hint of a fourth? A tiny, shy, frightened little child?) she spread her wings, and soared into the waiting Light.

Lianne and Maclyn stood in the kitchen beside the Gate

he'd opened one last time. She'd spent a week healing in Elfhame Outremer, and working with the elves to replant trees and reconsecrate the Grove. But Maclyn assured her that she was going back to the same evening she'd left, that no time would have passed in Fayetteville since she ran through the Gate and out of the burning barn.

He was so handsome, she thought, as if she viewed him from far away. She had spent most of her waking hours with him; she had watched him suffering over his mother's death, she'd worked beside him, had seen the first few smiles he'd managed. She'd seen him with Amanda, who was healing under the tender care of the elves. She knew him now, much better than she had ever known anyone before.

It would be so easy to ignore their differences, to accept the life he offered her straddled between the world of magic and her own mundane existence. Rather, she thought, it would be so easy for a while.

Then it would become impossible. Especially under the carefully uncritical eye of Felouen. Felouen, who loved Mac so desperately. Felouen, who needed him more than she would ever admit.

Then it would become impossible.

"What will I say about Amanda?" she asked, feeling the awkward silence as they looked at each other.

He shrugged. "Nothing. No one knows you were out there. They'll find simulacra in the embers of the barn — burned bodies that look just like hers and her father's. They won't need any more answers. My only regret is that they'll never know what he was doing to her."

Lianne nodded, thinking about the social worker who would never have to make that investigation. Would he be relieved? Or would he spend the rest of his life wondering if he had failed — wondering if he could have saved Amanda's life, if only — if only — "What about her sister, Sharon?" she asked. "*Her* mother is no prize."

Mac considered the question for a moment. "We'll watch the mother, I think. This might be the shock she needed to start taking care of her daughter better. If not — we'll intervene."

They continued to look at each other, and another awkward silence developed.

"Are you sure you won't stay in Elfhame Outremer with me?" Mac asked, softly; the very question she had been dreading.

Lianne looked at the floor, and rolled her foot back and forth across a pencil that lay there. "I can't, Mac. My family is here, my work is here, my past and my future are *here*. People need me in this world, Mac. And Felouen is waiting for you, and hoping the two of you will have a chance together."

He sighed — but was it with regret or relief? As well as she knew him, she still couldn't tell. "I know. I thought that was going to be your answer, but I still hoped —"

"There are some things that really aren't meant to be." Lianne made a stab at a brave smile, and gave it up as useless.

He licked his lips and stared deeply into her eyes. "I understand, or I think I do. You're sure?"

She nodded, not trusting herself to speech. The lump in her throat cut her breath short, and her nose was stuffy from the tears that were waiting to fall. One more word was all it would take.

He rested both hands on her shoulders. "One last kiss, then," he said.

His eyes looked — odd. She pushed him away, tensing with sudden suspicion. "No, Mac," she whispered.

"Just one," he asked.

"I saw *Superman*," she croaked.

That seemed to stump him. "So did I," he said at last.

She spoke with stiff lips. "I *hated* the ending. I always thought that Lois Lane got cheated at the end of the movie." She clenched her hands into fists, to keep from wiping away the tears that slid down her cheeks. "He kissed her and took away her memory of him, of who he was and what he was — and supposedly after that everything was back to normal. But she *earned* her pain. She would have lived without him — she could have kept on going even if she knew the truth."

Was she speaking about a two-dimensional movie character, or herself? Maybe both. "She would have known how special she was, though, if he'd left her alone. She would have known that she had been special enough to be loved by someone like him — and if it couldn't last forever, well . . . so few things do." Her voice turned fierce. "But he stole that from her, stole a part of her life that she couldn't ever replace — all because he thought she wasn't tough enough to handle it."

Maclyn blinked in surprise at her vehemence. "I sort of thought he'd made things easier on her."

She shook her head, angrily, to keep from crying. "Do you think she'd have chosen that if he'd asked her first?"

He hesitated. "Well . . . no. I guess not."

She lowered her voice. "Do you think he couldn't trust her to keep his secret?"

Mac whispered, "No. I think she would have kept his secret."

Lianne lifted her chin and glared at him. "Do you think you can't trust me?"

It was his turn to shake his head violently. "It wasn't that at all. It's just that you've had so much pain — and I thought I could save you some of it. . . . " Mac's eyes widened as he realized she'd caught him.

"That *was* what you were planning." Lianne glared at him with a kind of triumph. "I saw it in your face. You had that same stupid 'pity that poor girl' expression on your face that Christopher Reeve had on his." She kicked the pencil across the kitchen. "Don't do me any favors, Maclyn. I'm smart, and I'll get over you in my own time and in my own way. But I fought as hard for this day as you did — so don't you dare try to take it from me!"

Maclyn nodded and bit his lower lip. He moved toward the Gate, then looked back at her. She saw her own pain reflected in his eyes. "I'll miss you, Lianne McCormick."

"And I'll miss you. Tell Amanda I wish her luck," she added.

He bowed a little, courtly and solemn, offering her the acknowledgement of her own kind of royalty. "I will. She'll find safe haven and healing in Elfhame Outremer. And training for the incredible power she commands."

They gazed at each other from across the distance of the kitchen — from across an abyss than neither could breach — from across the centuries.

"I love you," Mac said into the silence.

Her heart contracted. "I know. I love you, too. It doesn't change anything."

"No. It doesn't." He licked his lips again, and asked, plaintively, "I can still come and see you sometimes, can't I?"

Lianne took a deep breath. "No, Mac. I have to get on with my life — and you have to get on with yours. We can't do that with each other around."

He nodded, as if he had expected that answer, too. "You're right. But maybe . . . sometime . . . you could come out to the track and cheer me on. I could use that . . . all the help I can get. . . . " He leaned over and gave her a gentle kiss on the cheek.

"Goodbye, fair one."

"Goodbye, Mac," she said for the last time, and left unsaid a million more things.

AFTERWORD

Children deserve to be loved, protected, and given guidance and careful discipline. They do not deserve to be starved, beaten, to have bones broken, spirits battered — or to be used for the sexual gratification of adults. Children are not the property of the parents, to be used or misused at the parents' whim.

No normal adult does this to children. No normal parent does this to children. People who do this to their children are sick, and need help; even more, so do the children who are being misused and abused.

If things in this book sound like things that are happening to you or someone you know, there is help. You don't need elves, you don't need magic, help is as close as the nearest pay-phone, and you don't even need a quarter.

Call the NATIONAL CHILD ABUSE HOTLINE: 1-800-422-4453. 800 numbers are free; follow the instructions on the phone, or dial 0 and ask for help from the operator. There are people on the other end who want to help you, who will know how to help you and will get you out of the situation you are in. If you can't call, go to a teacher you trust, or a nurse at the nearest hospital; don't stop trying until you find someone who will help you. Don't keep this a secret; hiding abuse only makes it possible for the adult to abuse someone else some day. Help yourself, now.

<table>
<tr><td><u>HIGH FLIGHT</u></td><td><u>BAEN BOOKS</u></td></tr>
<tr><td>Mercedes Lackey
Larry Dixon
Holly Lisle
Mark Shepherd</td><td>Jim Baen
Toni Weisskopf</td></tr>
</table>

MERCEDES LACKEY:
Hot! Hot! Hot!

Whether it's elves at the racetrack, bards battling evil mages or brainships fighting planet pirates, Mercedes Lackey is always compelling, always fun, always a great read. Complete your collection today!

Urban Fantasies

Knight of Ghost and Shadows (with Ellen Guon),
    69885-0, 352 pp., $4.99 ☐

Summoned to Tourney (with Ellen Guon), 72122-4,
    304 pp., $4.99 ☐

SERRAted Edge Series

Born to Run (with Larry Dixon), 72110-0, 336 pp., $4.99 ☐

Wheels of Fire (with Mark Shepherd), 72138-0,
    384 pp., $4.99 ☐

When the Bough Breaks (with Holly Lisle), 72156-9,
    320 pp., $4.99 ☐

High Fantasy

Bardic Voices: The Lark and the Wren, 72099-6,
    496 pp., $5.99 ☐

Other Fantasies by Mercedes Lackey

Reap the Whirlwind (with C.J. Cherryh), 69846-X,
    288 pp., $4.99 ☐
Part of the Sword of Knowledge series.

Castle of Deception (with Josepha Sherman), 72125-9,
    320 pp., $5.99 ☐
Based on the bestselling computer game, *The Bard's Tale.*℠

Science Fiction

The Ship Who Searched (with Anne McCaffrey), 72129-1,
    320 pp., $5.99 ☐
The Ship Who Sang is not alone!

Wing Commander: Freedom Flight (with Ellen Guon),
    72145-3, 304 pp., $4.99 ☐
Based on the bestselling computer game, *Wing Commander.*℠

Available at your local bookstore. If not, fill out this coupon and send a check or money order for the cover price to Baen Books, Dept. BA, P.O. Box 1403, Riverdale, NY 10471.

Name: _____

Address: _____

I have enclosed a check or money order in the amount of $_____